The Hanged Man

praise for the hex next door

"If The Ex-Hex and Practical Magic had a sapphic baby, it would be The Hex Next Door. A wickedly charming second chance HFN romance wrapped in a snarky, Cozy Witch package."
 - **Justin Arnold**, Author of *Wicked Little Things*

"Lou Wilham has created a vibrant, unique and queeralicious world. Where magic is part of the mundane, but the true story lies in the depth of the characters. They are fully fleshed out, relatable and diverse. From houses with personalities to the undead, the world painted by Wiham gives the reader the true feeling that magic is right next door and that life is painted in all the colors of the rainbow."
 - **G.D. Roman**, Author of *Bound Island*

"Once again, Wilham brings together a collection of unique characters who create a beautiful landscape of representation and individuality. The Hex Next Door is a lovely picture of family being more than just blood, and reminds us that those who truly love us, will always find a way to be there for us."
 - **Christis Christie**, Author of *Ephesus*

"An eloquently imaginative read with an intriguing plot line and creative setting. [The Hex Next Door] is a brilliantly magical start to a bright new series."

- **Nicole Northwood**, Author of *The Devil You Know*

Witches of Moondale: Book Two

The Ghost of Hexes Past

Lou Wilham

Midnight Tide
PUBLISHING

To the girl I was
I'm glad we figured it out eventually.

And to those still looking for themselves
sometimes it's less about a where and more about
giving yourself permission to be who you always were.

Chapter 1

IT HAD BEEN a month and a half.

Six long weeks of petitioning and politicking and ass kissing.

Forty-two days of Azure wracking her brain to get what they needed out of the Board of Magic. Of doing everything she'd always vowed she wouldn't, everything she hated, all for the woman she loved. Because Rus deserved to have a home for herself and for her girls. She deserved to be happy, and whole. And because this was the only way to keep Aihuan safe. Azure would be damned if she'd let a little thing like the fact that she hated talking to people ruin what Rus and her girls could have in Moondale.

So she'd swallowed down all of the bitchy things she wanted to say to the Board of Magic, pulled on a semi-neutral expression, and gotten things done.

The paperwork had been the easy part. Anyone could petition for the right to start their own coven in Moondale. Rus had joked about it once or twice when she'd been not more than ten. Laughing and saying that when she grew up, she was going to marry Azure and they would form their own coven with their own rules. Azure supposed not much had changed really. She was fool enough to want that—even then, even now.

The hard part came when the Board of Magic started to *consider* Rus's proposal. There hadn't been so much in-fighting among the elders, Aunt Carmine said, since before her own father had been the Jade Waters elder. Many wanted to dismiss the application out of hand, but Azure had shown up to every meeting—closed door or not—and made a nuisance of herself until they at least agreed to meet with Rus about it. It wasn't much, but she considered it a win. A tiny victory in a battle that might be otherwise full of defeats.

So that evening, Azure dressed appropriately for the meeting, a long pale pink skirt with a crisp white button down tucked into it, and a pointed felt hat perched firmly on her head. Then she'd gone off to the board building, fully expecting to meet Rus there.

A mistake, she realized some minutes later, when the meeting began and she was sitting in her seat, listening to Brant Ironwood drone on and *on* through the minutes from the last meeting, with an empty chair beside her. The only empty chair in the entire room, as it seemed rumor of Rus's petition had gotten around and the entirety of Moondale's magical community had come out to watch the drama ensue. A record number of folk in attendance, Brant had said when he called the meeting to order.

The watch on her right wrist ticked away, and a glance down at it told her Rus was quickly approaching the fifteen-minute mark of being late.

Fuck.

Rus was notorious for being tardy to *everything*. But this was important, and Azure had convinced herself Rus knew that, would respect that. Goddess, she was such an idiot. One would think she would know better by now. One would be wrong. Still, she wasn't going to let all her hard work go to waste. The girls needed the land of Moondale to protect them, and while simply joining a coven would be easier, Azure knew that was a non-option. For more reasons than one. So, if Rus wasn't there to state her case, Azure would simply have to do it for her.

"The board will now hear the case for the *Coven of the Forgotten*," Brant said in a nasally, knowing tone, his eyes almost gleaming beneath the yellowed fluorescents as he sneered around the name Rus chose for her coven. His gaze flicked down to the piece of paper in front of him, as if checking to make sure he was reading it correctly. An act that made Azure grind her teeth. "We call upon the petitioner, Icarus Ashthorne."

Everyone there could see Rus was not in attendance. Brant had likely planned this. Made sure it was the first thing on the agenda, so the woman who tended to be late for things would miss it. Maybe he—and the others against Rus—thought no one else would fight for her. One glance at Aunt Carmine, who looked thoroughly annoyed with Brant's antics, told Azure all she needed to know of that. If he weren't an elder, and Azure wasn't trying to get him to do what she wanted, she likely would have called him out on his rampant bias. But she needed the elders in a somewhat amiable mood, and getting into a shouting match with Brant Ironwood wouldn't ensure that.

"Icarus Ashthorne? Is Icarus Ashthorne in attendance?" Brant looked around, his dark eyes slightly lidded, a twitch of his lips betraying him, the absolute bastard. The crowd of Moondale folk collectively shifted in their creaking fold-up chairs, either uncomfortable with the obvious ploy, or looking for Rus. Azure wondered idly if she could get away with hexing Brant. Not a big one. Just a teeny tiny hex. One of inconvenience. Like he would forevermore forget about his freshly brewed coffee until it was lukewarm and thus disgusting to drink. *No sense in chancing it.*

Greer shifted beside Azure, his posture rigid. If Azure

didn't know any better, she'd say he looked like he wanted to stall for Rus. Rus would get a kick out of that. Her own nemesis trying to help her. Silliness, in Azure's mind, because Greer hadn't been able to hide from *her* how he adored Rus's daughters. How he took every excuse to stop by and make sure they were doing all right, how Aihuan had taken to calling him *Uncle Vander*. He was a softy when a person got right down to it, but Azure wasn't going to say as much out loud, lest it draw too much attention to it and make him change. Or, Goddess forbid, make Rus realize what an absolute nitwit she was half the time.

Azure wiped her sweating palms on her skirt and willed her heart to stop leaping into her throat. She needed to be calm when she did this. She needed to have a level head. She needed to not leap to her feet like an over-eager witchling.

"Well," Brant said, victory lining his tone, "since Icarus Ashthorne has not seen fit to join us, I suppose we can just—"

"I will speak for the Coven of the Forgotten." Azure leaped to her feet *exactly* like an over-eager witchling. Fucking damn it. Would Icarus Ashthorne ever cease to make her look like an idiot? Probably not. Anger simmered low under Azure's skin. She shouldn't have to do this for Rus. Rus knew how important this was, what was at stake here. Rus promised she would do everything she could to make this work. Rus should *be* here. Inhaling deeply, Azure willed the oxygen to slow the racing of her pulse, and hopefully keep her voice even. Brant would look for any weakness he could find, and Azure needed to offer none.

"You?" Brant asked. He leaned back in his chair, a king on his throne surveying a particularly lowly subject. Azure prayed to the Goddess that his familiar threw up a hairball in his shoes next time it had the chance. Maybe she'd have a chat with her own feline familiar, Lizzie, about how best to make that happen. That thought alone calmed her to a point. Made the heat recede from where it threatened to darken her cheeks in something that might be mistaken as shame. "As a member of the Elwood family, and the Circle of Jade Waters, I don't think that—"

"There is no rule that states a witch from a more established coven can't sponsor a fledgling clan or coven." Her heart pounded in her throat, threatening to choke off her words. She swallowed around it, sucking down another breath. *Slow and steady, Azure. You've got this.* Or at least she hoped so. She'd been practicing it enough. So much so that Indigo was quite sick of hearing this little speech. Not that he'd ever say as much—he was too good for that. But Azure had seen it on his face the last time she rehearsed; her baby brother was reaching his limit.

"In fact," she continued, licking her lips and resisting the urge to blanch at the feel of waxy lipstick coating them —this was the absolute last time she let Aunt Maureen help her get ready for a stressful day—"in the year 1789, a fledgling coven known as The Silver Flame was established under the sponsorship of one Irving Elwood of the Circle of Jade Waters."

Brant's eye twitched with annoyance, but he pursed his lips to hold back whatever words crossed his mind. Probably for the best. Azure's skin prickled under every gaze in the room. Greer cleared his throat behind her, and she wondered if it was to fill the sucking void of silence left behind while everyone waited for the other shoe to drop, or if he was simply hiding a laugh. She'd have to ask later.

"So, it would seem to me that an Elwood of the Circle of Jade Waters is the perfect person to sponsor an up-and-coming coven." Azure's fingers tapped at her sides, and she resisted the urge to tighten them into fists around the fabric of her skirt. All it would do was wrinkle it. Brant's gaze jerked down to the subtle movement, clocking it for the fidgeting that it was, but Azure lifted her chin, daring him to say anything. When another minute ticked away loudly on the clock on the wall, Azure realized he was going to save that weakness for later, and all she could hope was that her next words would be the nail in the coffin of his limited arguments. "After all, where would Elder Ironwood and his coven be if not for the sponsorship of the Elwoods?"

The twitching of Brant's eye increased in speed and strength to a satisfying degree that almost made Azure smirk. She thought she heard Greer choke back another chortle, but she couldn't rip her gaze away from Brant. It was like staring down a beast—if she looked away first, she'd be considered lesser, vulnerable. And Azure was neither.

"Very eloquently put," Cliantha Greer said, breaking the stalemate and drawing everyone's attention to her. A smile split her slightly wrinkled face, making her crows-feet more pronounced, but she didn't look happy about this. None of them would be. Just because Azure had leaped over this particular hurdle didn't mean the race was done. For appearance's sake, they would hold the hearing. They would let her and Rus state their case, dig their own graves. But Azure knew that until she thought of something to use as leverage, it would mostly be a farce. She was hopeful, not stupid. "As that is the case, you are welcome to act as sponsor and spokesperson for the Coven of the Forgotten once you have filled out the required paperwork. Until that time, I motion that we table this disc—"

"I have already submitted the paperwork. If you will turn to page five of the submission packet, you will see that under *sponsor*, I'm listed. My sponsorship was approved by my coven's elders." Was it wise to continue to cut off the elders? Probably not. But they couldn't wait another month for the process to officially begin. Another month and they would be in the depths of winter, approaching the solstice. They could do rituals, of course, to protect against the ever-shortening days and the thinning veil, but nothing would protect Rus and her girls quite like Moondale herself. Azure wasn't taking any chances. "As that is the case, I think we can move forward."

"I see." Cliantha practically huffed the words, annoyed by Azure's foresight. Good. Let them be annoyed. Let them realize they weren't going to get one over on Azure or Rus.

Azure ducked her head, hoping to hide the smug twitch of her lips. "Do I have your permission to continue, Elder Greer?"

"Please do." Cliantha flapped her wrist at Azure, dismissive and irritated. Let her be. All Azure had to convince them of today was that they couldn't cite any reason beyond their own biases to dismiss Rus's application out of hand. It sounded easy. It would be anything but.

"Thank you." Biting at the corner of her lip, Azure lifted her head again to look at the Board of Magic as a whole. They weren't all in attendance. The elder from the Grove of Elderwood was missing due to the druid hibernation season, but the remaining nine looked far from moved by Azure's position. They would not be easy to convince. The werewolf elder from the Chesapeake Pack looked particularly grumpy to be giving up her hunting time for this conversation. Azure couldn't do anything about that. "Icarus Ashthorne and I would like to petition for the right to start a new coven in Moondale. A place for the folk like herself, who find themselves outside of the usual clans, packs, and covens of Moondale."

"A place for necromancers, you mean." The elder from the Clan of the Emerald Forge, a slight man named Dhiren, leaned forward, his glowing eyes cutting into Azure like a knife. It had always been amazing to Rus, Azure knew, how ten beings so different in power and temperament could agree on one thing to the point of complete ignorance: necromancy was evil. Even a Djinni like Dhiren who had arguably done far worse before settling in Moondale couldn't think beyond his prejudices.

"That is not what I said." Her tone was impassive, but a growl grew in her chest. She cleared her throat to push it away, if just for the moment.

"But that is what you *meant*," Dhiren hissed, leaning farther forward onto the table, his fingers heating so much that Azure could hear the laminate of the table sizzling, leaving behind a permanent mark of his anger.

"No. It's not." Azure squared her shoulders. "If you review the packet again, you will see that the only necromancer listed under the coven roster is Icarus Ashthorne. Fernando Perez's specialty is kitchen magic, while the two children have not chosen their designations yet."

"We have not accepted a new clan or coven into the Moondale system since 1790, as you so kindly pointed out," an elven woman named Yaereene, the elder of the Clan of the Unseen Moon, pointed out, and Azure almost winced. She knew that would be a sticking point for them—it always was with the Board of Magic. They liked to say that this is how things had always been done, and thus they saw no reason to change things now. It was why Rus met so much pushback when she began experimenting with technology back in the late 90s. *Old goats, stuck in their ways.* "Why should we accept a new one now? It seems to me that ten clans are more than plenty for our little town."

It was an excellent point, one that Azure hadn't really come up with an argument against just yet, other than the fact that Rus didn't want to join one of the existing covens, *couldn't* join one of the existing covens. She didn't feel safe with them, knew that their old ways would limit her abilities and the growth of her girls who shared those abilities. Azure licked her lips again, her mouth suddenly dry. "Times have changed, Elder Yaereene. The traditional covens can be stifling in the way they see the world. Icarus brings a fresh perspective to magic and the way it interacts with technology, and other such advancements. Her insight will only benefit the magical community of Moondale."

The hall fell silent for a moment, all the elders processing the implications of this statement. Likely all thinking of how their particular clan could benefit from Rus's unique genius. Azure was counting on that. Their greed reared its head when Aihuan's power had been exposed. Why not use it against them now?

"That being the case," a thready voice said, and all eyes shifted to the elder of the Ladies of Nimue. She was the oldest being on the Board of Magic. Old enough that there was some rumor that maybe she had been one of the founding women of Moondale, but there was little proof of that. Nixie Virnan was a tiny woman of unknown origin. Some people thought she was a selkie, others a water sprite, but one thing was for sure: no one had done more to keep the delicate ecosystem of the bay from collapsing than Nixie Virnan. Azure had always respected her, wanted to be like her one day. Now, with those keen eyes boring into her, Azure felt her stomach fall out through her feet. Something was coming. Something bad. "If Miss Ashthorne is so very serious about starting her own coven, then where is she?"

Fuck.

Chapter 2

RUS HITCHED her bag farther up her shoulder and checked the address Sheriff Regan of Ironport sent her for the fifth time. The light of her phone burned her eyes in the dark of a dead streetlight. It had been on before she'd walked up the sidewalk to it but flickered off almost immediately when she'd stepped beneath it. Usually a bad sign when one approached a supposedly haunted building.

Huffing out a breath, Rus scrubbed at her face.

This was supposed to be a quick job. In and out. Rus had places to be. She'd only come because it was going to be easy, and because Sheriff Regan said the owner was going to show the place the following day. Why the fuck the owner had waited till the day before to call an exorcist, Rus had no idea. Either way . . .

Quick job. In and out.

The surly woman said nothing about an entire fucking *apartment building*. Rus's fingers twitched around the scuffed case of her phone, the urge to text Sheriff Regan that this was the last job she'd be doing for her so strong that Rus had to physically shove her phone into the bottom of her bag to keep from sending the message. It wasn't that she needed the money, although Aihuan went through clothes faster than a crow through bird seed—the perks of a growing child. Rus just didn't have it in her to let a spirit languish, and the spirits of Mirror Lake Park Apartments were definitely languishing. Sheriff Regan also made it sound like the owner was in a bind. Rus had a soft touch for people who wanted to do the right thing by the spirits in their space.

Spirits, plural.

Rus inhaled deeply, the cold November air getting caught in her lungs and threatening to send her into a coughing fit as she focused on the energy emanating from the building at the end of the sidewalk.

She guessed three at minimum.

Sheriff Regan said the building was haunted, but she hadn't done a headcount. Likely because she couldn't, not without a medium present or the use of some other apparatus to speak to spirits. And even those weren't always accurate since the spirits often tried to talk over each other and mucked up the works. Pinching the bridge of her nose, Rus nodded to herself and took the last few steps up to the front door without so much as a glance over her shoulder.

With one final prayer to the Goddess that none of the spirits inside would be combative, Rus turned the key in the lock and pushed through. The front door squealed on its hinges, letting anyone within a mile of the place know someone had entered. Not that it mattered—Rus wasn't exactly trying to hide. The spirits would know she was there whether she wanted them to or not. Trying to be sneaky would just waste time.

"If anyone is here," Rus called into the cavernous dark of the empty building, "show yourselves."

Her voice echoed back to her with no furniture or carpeting to muffle the sound in the main lobby. It wasn't a terribly large apartment building, only about ten units. But that didn't mean it would make for a quick clean up. Not if the spirits proved reluctant.

A chill ran up Rus's spine, and something small and

glowing shifted out of the corner of her eye. When she turned her head to look, it was gone.

"Of course, they wouldn't make it that easy." Rus huffed, tucking her chin down into her scarf to hide her neck from the cool air of the empty building. She wondered idly if they had turned the heat off or if it was the shades making the air so cool—she'd ask Sheriff Regan. The owner didn't need burst pipes on top of the ghosts.

Another quick glance around the empty lobby turned up nothing. Rus shook out her hands and pulled a jar of salt from her bag, then turned to crouch and sprinkle a thin line across the threshold of the front door. Not that she actually thought the spirits would try to leave the building, but it paid to be prepared. She didn't exactly have time to chase them all around the grounds, so if she could corner them in one room or apartment, that's what she'd do.

"I wish I'd brought Nando with me." Things would be easier if she had. He at least understood the process of all this, and having another set of hands to block off potential exits would definitely make things go faster. But someone needed to watch the kids, and everyone else was either working or planning to be at the board meeting later.

With that done, Rus put down her bag and dug around in it until she pulled a little pendant from one of the pockets. It shone bright in the security lights of the building, reflecting their yellow glare in a golden sheen. Rus weighed it in her hand for a moment, considering her options. Az would be absolutely livid if she found out Rus hadn't used it, especially after she put so much effort into designing it for Rus.

It was silver, forged in Phyre's workshop, and inscribed with the tidy characters of one of Az's protective talismans. There had been a small tiff over whether Rus needed it before Az had obstinately put it in with the rest of her exorcism kit, all while maintaining eye contact with Rus and not saying a single fucking word. Because that's the kind of bitch Az was. Goddess, she was hot when she had a mind to be. She was also hot when she didn't have a mind to be, but that was neither here nor there.

Focus. Rus huffed a breath.

Fuck it.

She didn't have time to jump through all the extra hoops that wearing the talisman would incur. She was already probably going to be late for the Board of Magic meeting, and that was unacceptable. Stuffing the pendant back down into the pocket, she rose to her feet, squared her shoulders, and did the one thing she knew Az didn't want her to do. She stepped through the veil for the first time since they'd saved Aihuan.

The world on the other side was colder and darker. All noise and color dull and muted by the barrier between the living and the dead. Like slipping under the surface of murky bay water and listening to the sounds of life from above. It took her eyes a moment to adjust, but once they had she could see the trails left behind by the spirits lingering in the space. Their lines thin and fading, a wake from a boat, but there just the same.

Her bag rattled against her side as she took the stairs two at a time, following the thin blue trail left by whatever Rus had seen out of the corner of her eye. If she had to guess, it was a relatively young spirit, both in length of time it had been attached to the property, and in age of the being before it passed—a thought that made her heart squeeze a little in her chest. Human, probably.

"Come out, come out, wherever you are," Rus whispered into the murky darkness as she pushed through the door into the corridor of the second floor. A name would make this whole thing much easier, but as Sheriff

Regan hadn't even known there were three spirits, and Rus hadn't had time to do her own research because she'd been so busy dealing with the Board of Magic . . . Well, she'd have to make do with other methods.

Bright green magic lingered around her wrists, whispering into the dark and lighting the way as she stepped into an apartment down the end of the hall. In the corner of the front room, she found the spirit from the lobby, a slight thing made smaller because they were curled around their knees, shaking like a leaf.

"Hey," Rus murmured, soft and soothing, holding up her hands to show she was unarmed.

The little spirit squeaked, jerking at the sound, and their trembling intensified. They peeked up at Rus from behind their knobby knees with wide glassy eyes. Rus crouched to set her bag down, the weight of it making no sound on the floor in the space beyond the veil. Then she pressed forward, her hands still held in front of her, palms out.

"It's all right. I'm not here to hurt you. You don't need to be scared of me." The tone of her words remained a calm rumble in her chest, the same one she used with Aihuan or Meiling when they got scared.

"You—you can see me?" Those words had a hopeful note as they floated through the air. Like the spirit was used to not being seen. Like maybe they had tried to make their presence known and been ignored. Poor kid.

"I can see you." Rus nodded slowly, taking another careful step toward the little spirit huddled on the floor. "My name's Rus. And I'm here to help you."

"Help me how?" The spirit cocked their head, bird-like and confused. Poor thing might not even know they were dead. They didn't sometimes. Sometimes that was the source of a haunting. It was sad, but also usually easy enough to correct and get them to leave. Oh, to have all hauntings be that simple.

"Help you move on, I suppose." Rus stopped just in front of the spirit and sat down, crossing her legs into a lotus pose in front of her. "You know you can't stay here, right?"

"Why not?"

"Because you don't belong here anymore." Rus had had this conversation enough times to know it could go a handful of ways. People never wanted to face the truth, especially when it didn't fit a person's internal narrative. And spirits, whether the living wanted to believe it or not, were just people. Lost. Distressed. Sad. Dead. But people, nonetheless. "Why don't you tell me what happened to you?"

"I don't remember." The spirit frowned but started to unfurl, their small hands no longer as tight around their forearms where they used them to hold their knees to their chest. Now that they had untucked their face, Rus could better gauge how old they were. Late teens, early twenties. Likely this had been their first time away from home, their first place all their own. They had so much life ahead of them—no wonder they clung to this place. She hoped they decided to reincarnate, for another go at it.

"All right." That would make things harder, but not impossible. "Can you tell me your name?"

The spirit opened their mouth, a black hole that looked like a scream and a swirling vortex of nothingness all rolled into one. Their eyes became the same nothingness, mirroring their mouth, and if Rus hadn't seen this a million times she might have screamed at the sight. A normal person probably would have. Good thing Rus wasn't normal, and she was used to the way spirits looked when they got lost inside themselves. A moment later, the spirit's face returned to looking like a scared human's, and they shook their head, pouting a little.

"That's okay too." Rus offered the spirit a soft smile and a wink. "What would you like to be called?"

"I always liked the name Holly." They grinned, their eyes glittering a little more in the softness of the security lights filtering in through the veil. "Like holly jolly Christmas."

"That's a pretty name," Rus murmured. "Do you know you're dead, Holly?"

"I—" Holly stopped, their cheeks puffing out in annoyance as they thought about Rus's words. They looked like they wanted to argue, tell her that she was wrong and to leave them alone. But then they deflated and nodded. "Yes, I do know that."

A relieved breath left Rus, her shoulders relaxing a little. "Good. That's good. Now, let's try again. Can you tell me what happened to you?"

"I can't. I don't remember. I just . . . I woke up like this."

Oof, that's the worst. Holly's legs fell to the sides, revealing more of them. They had a stain on their torso that might have been blood, or something else, but Rus didn't let her eyes linger on it. She didn't want to upset Holly any more than she had to.

"Let's try a different question." Brushing at the tip of her nose, Rus tilted her head to one side. "Do you know why you stayed?"

Holly blinked for a moment, their mouth going wide and hollow again, their face shifting into the terrifying rictus once more. Goddess, Rus wished they'd stop doing that. It wasn't scary so much as annoying as the seconds slipped away. Az would kill her for being late. And there were still two more spirits to contend with. She wondered how pissed Sheriff Regan would be if Rus told her she'd have to come back to finish the job in the morning. *Probably very pissed*. Rus didn't think she wanted to see that side of Sheriff Regan. Plus, she didn't know exactly what time the owner planned to show the place, and if the other spirits were worse than Holly . . .

Rus didn't want to leave them anywhere they could make contact with the living.

The minutes crawled by.

One.

Two.

Five whole minutes before Holly's face cleared again, and they shook their head. "No. I don't know why I stayed."

"Then don't you think maybe it's time you left?" Rus asked. She sent up a silent prayer to the Goddess that this would be enough to convince Holly. It wasn't usually that simple, but sometimes Rus got lucky. She held out her hand, her magic flittering around it in a soft, throbbing light.

"Will it hurt?" Holly stared down at the outstretched palm, their own hands fisting in their lap.

"No, sweetie, it won't hurt." Rus shook her head. She didn't know for sure, of course, because she'd never been on the receiving end, but she'd never had any complaints — spirits would return from time to time as a gesture of gratitude to help her when she needed it.

"What do I need to do?" Holly looked up at Rus again, their eyes wide and so achingly young. They lifted one of their own hands to their chest, clearly tempted to reach back.

"Just take my hand, and my magic will do the rest." Rus sucked in a breath, readying herself for the sensation of sending a spirit through to the other side. Holly still didn't look convinced. They held their hand close to their chest, their eyes flickering between wide and glassy to the deep pits of a spirit left to languish too long. "You can come back and visit, if you like," Rus said, trying to ease some of their worries. "Spirits do it all the time."

"How?" A frown pursed Holly's lips, and Rus resisted the urge to sigh.

Pinching the bridge of her nose, Rus shifted around on the cold hard floor. Her back started to ache from sitting there, but she wasn't about to move. Not until she'd gotten Holly to move on. Something passed them in the hall, a whisper of material and boots that told Rus the other spirit or spirits were close. She needed to get Holly out of there before the others scared them off.

"You just have to use my name," Rus explained, patient in spite of the rushed feeling nipping at her limbs. "Because I helped you move on, I can act as a direct line to come back whenever you'd like to check in. It's temporary, but many of the spirits I help come back every once in a while. Unless, of course, they choose to reincarnate."

"Rus." Holly repeated the name, and the wrinkle between their brow eased a fraction.

"Icarus Ashthorne." Rus held out her hand again, this time like she meant to shake Holly's.

Holly blinked at it another moment before lurching forward and grabbing Rus's hand to give it a hard shake. A shudder ran up Rus's arm, lifting every hair in its wake, and a bone-deep chill that ached on a cellular level followed. But she held firm, clasping onto the freezing, insubstantial palm clasped around her own. One second. Two. Then the light from her magic and from Holly faded, and Rus was left alone in the dark of the empty apartment.

Her breath was loud in her ears, her heart slamming

against her chest as if trying to make up for the fact that it had stuttered the second Rus helped Holly over to the After. A probably worrisome and unhealthy side effect of Rus's abilities that she didn't ever have time to contemplate. Especially not now as there was a soft *shush*ing sound, and she felt the cold breath of someone or some*thing* on her face.

The chill twisted around her throat as if it were trying to choke her, or maybe look for a pulse. Fuck. She really should have worn the damn talisman. And her bag was all the way by the door. There was no time to get to it and pull from it what she needed. She'd have to wing it.

"What I wouldn't give for names," Rus mumbled, lifting her lids enough to see the blurry shapes of two figures through her lashes. They drifted around each other, tangled together.

They cackled, the sound echoing and chilling. The grip around her throat tightened enough that Rus gasped for breath when they slammed her onto her back on the floor. Coughing, the breath knocked from her, Rus twisted, and her eyes flew open as she scrambled at the hand locked around her throat. A dark vine ran up it, thick and dense enough that it seemed to absorb what little light came in through the window from outside. It twisted around and around the first spirit's arm like a snake, ending at a face that peeked over its shoulder. The face—what Rus could see of it through its long dark hair—was sharp and angular, that of an older woman where the first spirit was a young man. And from what she could see of the older woman's spirit, there was no body. Just the vine . . . snake . . . thing that undulated around the man's arm, tightening until it looked painful.

"Creepy," Rus choked around the tightness at her throat, and the man's spirit snarled, breath misting her cheeks in ice before he lifted her head and slammed it into the floor again, causing her to see stars. The floor creaked with the impact. *Fuck, I hope that doesn't give out.* Pain lanced through her skull as he grabbed her by the hair, lifting her head in preparation for another hard slam against the floor that may very well render her unconscious.

Her phone rang right then, distracting the spirit with the bright tones of some K-pop song Az had chosen as her ringtone. Rus thanked the Goddess that her phone wasn't on vibrate, gathered her magic in the moment of respite, and slammed it into the spirit's chest.

He flailed back onto his ass, legs kicking out like an upturned turtle, giving Rus enough time to scramble to her bag and yank out the little spirit box she'd brought along. *Thunk*ing it hard against the old floor, she pressed the latch, and it popped open like a flower bud. A faint sucking noise followed—a vacuum cleaner with a sock stuck in it—then it ripped the spirits from where they were still trying to get their bearings. The box shut with a *click*, leaving Rus panting in the aftermath.

She sat for a moment, trying to get control over her upset magic again, the green light lashing out around her, leaving tiny burn marks in the floor. When her heart finally stopped pounding in her chest, she let herself slip back through the veil, pulled her hood up over her head, and reached for her phone at the bottom of her bag. A chill crawled up her spine, something lingering from beyond the veil that would probably slough off after she'd crossed the salt line. Still, she hated the way its eyes followed her, a feathery caress that made the hairs on the back of her neck stand on end.

A quick glance around showed no lingering spirits, but that didn't mean there wasn't something there. Rus shook herself, looked down at her too-bright phone screen to check her messages, and got a look at the time instead.

"Fuck me. I'm late," Rus hissed, clambering to her unsteady legs to haul ass back to Moondale. "Az is going to skin me alive!"

Chapter 3

A HEADACHE the likes of which Azure never had before throbbed behind her eyes. And she could already tell it would linger for days. No amount of peppermint extract, calming tea, blackout curtains, or complete silence was going to make it go away. Which was a real shame because by some Goddess-given miracle, she managed to convince the board to meet with them again the following evening.

Pulling the collar of her powder-blue peacoat up around her neck to ward off the nighttime chill, Azure sunk farther into the shadow of the Board of Magic building as a breeze whipped past, carrying with it the last of the season's leaves. She could wait for Rus in her car—it would be warmer— but waiting outside made a point. Was it petty? Of course it was, but that didn't make it any less valid. Besides, she wanted to be able to hear the members of the Board of Magic as they exited lest they decide to talk shit on their way to their cars.

Brant Ironwood was the first to leave, a plaid scarf hanging loose over his obnoxiously fancy-looking coat like it was a fashion statement more than a way to keep his throat warm. Maybe he'd catch a cold in the interim and be unable to attend the next meeting. Azure could only hope. His steps stuttered just under the streetlamp as he looked at her lingering in the doorway and frowned.

With her chin lifted, Azure met his gaze, daring him to say something, anything. She was in a mood to cut someone down verbally, her pulse pounding in her temples, and Brant looked like a likely target. It wasn't so much what he'd said during the meeting, it was just his face. She'd always thought that about him—he had a very punchable face. Not that Azure had ever punched anyone in her life, but if she was going to start, Brant Ironwood would be at the top of her list.

The door behind Azure banged open, letting out the warmth and light of the meeting hall. Air blew hot against Azure's back, making her front feel too cold by comparison. Brant looked over her shoulder, his lips twitching downward into a scowl before he ducked his head.

"Good night, Miss Elwood, Elder Virnan." A half beat of silence settled between them in which Brant Ironwood seemed to wait for a proper goodbye from the pair, but they simply blinked at him. He huffed and spun on his heel, his scarf fluttering out behind him like a flag of surrender as he stomped off.

Nixie waited until his slick red Tesla pulled out of the lot, well out of hearing range, before she stepped out into the brisk November breeze to address Azure. "Miss Elwood," she said, a knowing glint in her eyes as she leaned heavily against her cane, "a word?"

Azure thought to ask if she really had a choice, but decided against it. Brant Ironwood was already against her and Rus's petition, there was no sense in getting on another elder's bad side.

"Of course," Azure murmured softly, and followed Nixie around to the parking lot, making sure to stay a half step behind the other woman out of respect.

The parking lot was still relatively full as the other elders had decided to stay and mingle, enjoying the few stale cookies one of them brought to the meeting, and gossiping. Azure probably should have stuck around inside to make sure they weren't plotting new and increasingly difficult ways to hinder her and Rus's petition, but she was already running on empty as far as her social battery went. Plus, Aunt Carmine was still there; she'd tell Azure about any new threats. Hopefully.

Nixie sunk into the driver's seat of her car, throwing her cane across to the passenger side, and not bothering to offer Azure a seat. Which was just fine—if she got into the car with Nixie then the cold would no longer be a problem, and the conversation would go on for far longer than Azure wanted it to. Whatever Nixie had to tell her could be said quickly and from the position of her open car door.

Stuffing her hands into her pockets, Azure stood beside the car and waited for Nixie to speak. The heat blasted loudly against the quiet of the night, Nixie warming her hands in front of the vents before she turned to look up at Azure again, keen blue eyes assessing, judging. Azure fought the urge to stand up straighter, her spine tingling with the desire.

Nixie started with "It won't be enough," and Azure's jaw clenched, teeth grinding together. "Whatever you're thinking of doing, it won't be enough."

"Why not?" As much as Azure tried *not* to say the words through her teeth, she couldn't seem to unstick her jaw. Her nails dug into the meat of her palms where she clenched her fists in her pockets, magic running cool and almost wet along her skin.

"Because it won't be." Nixie shrugged her slight shoulders and turned back to look out the windshield, humming softly to herself as she thought, her fingers flexing in the warm air.

Pain pinched where Azure bit down hard on her tongue, and an ache started up in her sinuses from inhaling too much cold air too quickly. The ache combined with the ever-mounting headache. "Why are you telling me this?"

Nixie's lips curled into a smile, making the skin around her eyes wrinkle in a way that *almost* seemed friendly. If Azure wasn't so sure the woman was a siren who had likely drowned thousands of sailors in her time, she'd probably mistake Nixie for a sweet little granny. The kind of person she'd hold the door for at the grocery store or offer to help carry her purchases to the car from Elwood's. But Azure knew better. Everyone in the Moondale magical community did. Nixie Virnan was anything but sweet, and she was no one's granny. "I want to help you."

"Why?" Azure asked, her stomach dropping to her feet. No one wanted to hear those words from a folk of unknown magical origin. No one wanted to hear them from a folk of *known* magical origin. The offer of help always came with a cost attached, a price, and Azure was maybe just fool enough to get herself tied up in another deal even after she'd only just gotten herself out of one with Cagney.

"You were right," Nixie said, instead of really answering the question. "Back there. When you said that the covens have gone stagnant."

"I didn't—"

"You wanted to." Nixie turned the full force of her pointed grin on Azure, and Azure wanted nothing more than to shrink away from it. To hide. Nixie often wore a glamour, but during board meetings she tended to let it drop, and every tooth in her mouth was needle-sharp. Deadly to everyone and anyone who might cross her.

Azure swallowed against the fear that threatened to crawl up her throat and lifted her chin. She wouldn't cower. Elwoods didn't *cower*.

This seemed to please Nixie, for she tilted her head to the side, inspecting Azure anew with what seemed to be fresh appreciation. "As I said, you were right. We need fresh blood in Moondale. For too long the covens and clans have been stuck in the old ways, unable to move forward. I blame myself for that. I should have done something sooner, but you know how these things are."

She *didn't* know how these things were, and Azure didn't think she wanted to, either. "I assume there is a point to this conversation."

That earned her a soft scoff from the elder, and Nixie's eyes crinkled at the corners, real joy evident in her expression. Azure's chin tilted back a little further, pride licking at the corners of her lips, threatening to lift them into a smug smile. The approving dip of Nixie's head felt hard won, and Azure was going to treasure it for perhaps the rest of her life. It eased some of the irritation still lingering in her veins over Rus's failure to make the meeting.

"Yes, there is a point," Nixie said after a long moment, her smile widening to an almost alarming degree. "My point is, I want to help you and your wife—"

"She's not my—"

"But you want her to be." Sparkling dark eyes fixed on Azure's warming cheeks, knowing and sharp. Nixie hummed. "As I thought." She swiped a lock of graying red hair back behind one slightly pointed ear, then continued, "I'd be more than happy to help move things along for you, even give you my advice."

"For a price." Azure's brows pinched together, making the ache that had settled behind her eyes shift to encompass her brow as well. Goddess above and below, she was so fucking tired.

"Nothing in life is free." Nixie leaned back in her seat again, reaching over to turn down the heat and press a button that looked to turn on her heated seat instead. "And I can assure you, my insight is well worth the cost."

"They always say that," Azure mumbled to herself, her head ducking so she could scuff the toe of her boot against the pavement. It was true. Everyone thought they had information worth the price. But Azure was at her limits with the Board of Magic. She knew what was at stake here. She knew the struggles she would face. Aunt Carmine had not pulled any punches when telling her what kind of rampant bias ran through the Board of Magic. While Azure, Carmine, and Indigo were mostly able to change the minds of their own coven—and some of their friends tried to chip away at their clans—it was still an uphill slog. But if Azure could get Nixie on their side, the eldest of the elders? It wouldn't completely clear the way, but it would make things a little easier.

Nixie didn't respond to the muttered words, although Azure wasn't stupid enough to think she hadn't heard. She just sat, cozy and warm in her seat, awaiting Azure's acceptance of her terms.

"What will it cost me?" Nothing she wouldn't pay, Azure realized. She'd give anything to see Rus start her own coven. To see her settled. To know she and her girls were protected. And most of all, to know that Icarus Ashthorne wasn't going anywhere, and Azure would have another chance at something she thought she'd lost forever. There was probably something intrinsically wrong with that, but she couldn't seem to avoid adding it to the list anytime she thought about all the reasons this was important to her.

"Just a favor. A *small* one, I think, will be good enough, considering all the other good that Miss Ashthorne will do for Moondale."

"A small one." Anyone who knew anything about the

folk knew that *small* was relative and meant absolutely fuck all in reference to favors.

"Tiny, really," Nixie assured, but again, that meant nothing.

"I don't suppose you already know what this favor will be, do you?" Azure could only be so lucky. Fuck, she hated open-ended favors with folk. It was never *watch my cat while I'm out of town*, and always *on a full moon I need you to traipse into the swamp and pick this rare plant that smells like ass for a potion from the lair of a goblin king who eats nice girls like you for brunch.*

Nixie raised both of her graying brows.

Azure let out a long slow breath, hoping to ease the pounding in her ears. No good. "Of course not."

A car rumbled up behind them, the tires crunching against the cold hard ground, and Nixie's gaze flicked around the side of Azure's torso to see who was pulling in. "Best hurry it up, dear, before your wifey sees you making deals with devils."

Glancing over her shoulder, Azure saw a beat-up blue sedan heading toward her. Rus's car. She turned back to Nixie, who was looking up at her with another sharp, glittering smile, one brow raised as if to say *well?* Deals with devils indeed.

Azure bit out the word "Fine" and shook Nixie's extended hand, sealing their deal. The magic binding her to her word crawled up her skin like an itch, leaving behind the feeling of spider legs. She ground her teeth against the urge to rip her hand away before it was locked into place and hissed, "So what's your advice?"

Nixie pulled Azure down so her head was level with Nixie's and whispered into her ear the most cryptic bullshit anyone ever could at that exact fucking moment. "It's going to take a little more than a *sponsorship* from an Elwood to make that shit look legitimate."

The soft honk of a horn drew Azure's gaze back over her shoulder as Rus pulled up beside her. Nixie dropped her grip, gave Azure a firm shove, and shut the door, pulling away before Rus could even wind down the window of her car.

Rus leaned over the passenger seat to shout above the sound of her heater, "Az, I'm so s—"

"Where *were* you?!" Azure whipped around, her anger ripping through her again. She'd made a deal with an unknown water being. She'd talked herself hoarse. She was tired, and hungry, and she had a fucking headache. And Rus had the audacity to show up twenty minutes *after* the meeting had concluded? "Do you even care? Do you even *want* this to work?"

"I do. I was just—"

"I don't want to hear it." Stuffing her hands into her pockets hard enough to make the seams creak, Azure spun on her heel. "I'll see you tomorrow, Rus."

"Wait, what's tomorrow?" The noisy engine of Rus's car shut off, leaving them both in a too-loud silence as Rus scrambled over her center console to climb out the passenger side door nearest Azure. "Az, talk to me. What's going on tomorrow?"

"We have another board meeting." Her breath fogged in the aching cold, making her chest heave with each ragged inhale. Or maybe that was the anger she felt toward Rus. Azure didn't think she'd ever been so angry with Rus in her life. And that included when she'd left without a word. "I convinced them to hear us out. Don't be late."

Rus looked stricken, her eyes too wide in her pale face. Something was wrong, something had left her shaken. And a mark festered around her neck, dark and wispy, like a tattoo of smoke set into a collar on Rus's tanned skin. A lingering curse mark, but Azure didn't have it within herself to let that soften her. Not after the night she'd had. So she ignored it.

"I won't be," Rus promised, her throat bobbing with a hard swallow.

"Good." Azure needed to get away from her. Put distance between herself and the things Rus made her feel. Otherwise, she'd never be able to think over what Nixie said. It had been abstract, cryptic, but Azure thought she maybe knew what she meant. Rus didn't just need sponsorship from an Elwood, she needed a partner in an Elwood. Someone to share the burden of running the coven. Someone to give credence to it in more than just name. Could Azure do that? Could she . . . could she leave her own coven, her family, to make sure Rus's dream came true? She didn't know. "I'll see you tomorrow."

"Right." Rus's voice came out rough and croaking. "See you tomorrow."

And although she looked like she wanted to stop Azure, to pull her back, she let Azure go. And Azure wondered if that weren't answer enough.

RUS PULLED UP OUTSIDE OF 157 MOURNING MOORE approximately a half hour later. She had driven past the liquor store at least three times, debating if wine would make her feel better or worse about everything that happened. Her mind circled over and over to the way she always seemed to fuck up her relationships, a voice in the back of her head that sounded distinctly like her ex, Kaytee, telling her *that's what you're good at, Rus, darling.*

Fucking things up. Until Rus finally decided on worse, and opted not to go in. Cagney would be proud of her, if she knew, but Rus didn't think she'd ever tell her. Because she knew what *else* Cagney would say on the matter, and Rus didn't think she had it in her to listen to an I-told-you-so from Cagney now, or maybe ever again. Not with how things were going.

Someone had strung a short strand of twinkle lights across one of the rails on the front porch, likely Fernando at the request of the girls. They'd probably wanted to do the entire house—like Carmine and Maureen's place had been since just after Samhain—but hadn't had enough lights. Rus wondered if they asked 157 Mourning Moore if it would provide, but she shook away the thought. Now was not the time to worry about the annual Moondale Yule Lights Competition.

Darcy looked up from where he roosted on the porch as the front door creaked loudly to announce her presence, but he made no move to berate her as he normally might have. Good. She didn't have the energy for *that* either. She did catch him eyeing the curse mark around her neck when the light from inside shone on it though. Likely to bitch about later.

Since it was so late in the evening, the girls were already in bed. Which left Rus feeling oddly empty with the lack of being mauled at the front door. Even Meiling, for all she liked to act like a cool teenager, still came running for hugs when Rus got home after a job. A tiny blessing in a sea of fucked-upped-ness.

"How'd it go?" Fernando called from the couch. He'd paused whatever was on the TV—looked like *The Great British Baking Show*—so he could turn to watch Rus kick off her boots in the foyer. She braced herself heavily against the curved volute at the bottom of the stairs to maintain her balance, her hip playing up thanks to the wet and the cold outside. Oh, and the spirits, of course.

"How'd *what* go?" Rus shot back, already hating herself for the bite in her tone. But her neck ached, her feet throbbed, and all she wanted was to strip down to her skivvies and get into her bed, not even bothering to try washing away the curse mark. She did owe Fernando an explanation though, so she'd give him one. "The bit where I was so late to the board meeting that the elders were leaving as I got there, and Az was more pissed than I've ever seen her? Or the bit where Regan sent me to an apartment building with *three* spirits? Two of which decided it'd be fun to play Strangle the Medium."

"That bad, huh?" Fernando rose, his slippers scuffing on his way back to the kitchen, and Rus followed behind him, hanging her head.

"That bad." Her bag thunked hard against the kitchen table where she dropped it, and she reached for the steaming mug of tea Fernando had waiting for her. Her best friend, everyone! What a prince. "The nasty spirits were wrapped around each other, and I didn't have time to . . . *persuade* them to cross over."

"Ha. Persuade." Fernando snorted into his own mug. "I'll put them in the containment unit in your office. You can deal with them in the morning."

"Thanks, Nando, you're the best." Rus sighed, her weight sagging against the kitchen table. If she sat down, she'd never get back up, so she locked her knees and stayed standing. "If you've got a hot minute and the energy, could you maybe—"

"Yeah, I'll see what I can dig up about the past residents, and any accidents or deaths that might have lent themselves toward that much resentment." He turned to pull a plate from the oven that was also still steaming, and set it on the table in front of her. Fluffy white rice, creamy curry sauce, and chunks of vegetables that looked cooked to perfection made Rus's stomach gurgle with hunger. And she knew, without even having to taste it, that it would chase away the chill lingering in her bones and calm the riotous thoughts in her head. Kitchen witches, man, they knew their stuff. "Sounds like it was probably a murder, should be easy enough to find. You should eat. It'll help with the lingering effects."

"Ugh, what would I do without you?" Rus asked, moving over to him to press a quick kiss to his cheek on her way to the cabinets to pull out a fork. "I'm going to eat this in bed. Shout if they give you too much trouble."

"Will do." Fernando gave a little salute and pulled the ghost box from her bag. It was vibrating and whispering in outrage, but it would hold. She made that box herself—they weren't getting out until she was ready for them. "Get some sleep. You need it. And do something about that curse mark, it looks nasty."

Wincing, Rus rubbed at the black swirls of smoke that lingered on her skin like a tattoo, aching worse than freshly pierced skin. "You're right, you're right. I hate it when you're right." Rus scooped up her plate and mug and made for the back steps. "Oh, and I've got another board meeting tomorrow night. If you think of anything that might persuade a bunch of old buzzards to take in us poor crows . . ."

"I'll let you know." Fernando laughed, shaking his head, and Rus turned to head up the steps.

Chapter 4

A BUZZ in the air vibrated all the way down to Rus's gums, making them tingle in the most annoying way possible. And she hadn't even *opened* the fucking ghost box yet. It sat in the middle of the chalk circle, looking hilariously innocuous for having two aggressive shades inside.

Rus rocked back on her heels, her toes flexing on the hardwood floor of her bedroom as she pondered the best method for dispatching them. Fernando hadn't been able to find any names, but he *had* found some worrying articles about the rise of deaths in Ironport. If Rus were to hazard a guess—and she really, really, *really* hoped she was wrong—she'd say Ironport had a vampire problem. An infestation. Which meant only one thing for Rus, really: more nights like last night where she went in blind and pissed off spirits tried to drag her down to the depths with them. Because she was *not* fucking with feral vampires. She was reckless, not suicidal. The Huntsmen could handle that shit; that was their job, after all.

A chill settled into the base of her spine, like someone's hand lingering but without the warmth, and she pulled her faded black cardigan more tightly around herself to ward it off.

"Enough stalling," Rus muttered, slipping the hair tie from her wrist to pull her short hair up into a tiny tail at the crown of her head. With a snap of her fingers the box popped open, the flower petal–like lid spreading wide to release the shades trapped inside.

They came out hissing and spitting mad, a dark miasma of irritation crawling across the floor like fog. It stopped short when it reached the edge of the containment array she'd scribbled onto the floor in green sidewalk chalk, and Rus's shoulders drooped in relief. It was always a gamble with these kinds of things whether the array would be strong enough to keep the little shits trapped inside, and this wouldn't have been the first time she misjudged how much power she needed to pump into it. She had scars from the last time it happened. But this one had been overpowered—probably—to protect the home where her girls lived.

"Let me out!" the woman shrieked, her spirit twisting tighter around the man's arm, making it lift to bang against the barrier between them and Rus. The barrier shuddered but held. Good thing too—she was fucked if this thing got loose on her while no one was home. Fernando would be alerted, of course, but by the time he reached her it would probably be too late.

"No can do, sorry." Rus shrugged, dropping to the floor to squat just outside the barrier, her magic hissing softly against her skin, ready. Now that she was looking at them in the clear light of day, Rus noticed the things she'd missed the night before. The male spirit—the muscle of this particular duo—was blank-faced, devoid of anything that might have been considered *life*. A puppet for the woman to latch on to and use however she saw fit. That was going to be a problem. "Why don't you let this nice man go? Huh?"

Another hiss left the woman's lips, more snake than cat, her tongue flicking out to lick across teeth gone sharp with hunger. *Great, a soul eater.* "Make me."

Some of the tension that had bled away from Rus's

muscles returned, seizing them to near pain. She fucking hated soul eaters. Always more powerful than they had a right to be, and clinging to the world of the living like a tick tucked away someplace dark and moist. Sucking the life from almost anything and everything they could sink their teeth into. They were worse than demons, in Rus's experience. Demons had a clear motive, a clear idea of what they wanted, usually given to them by whatever idiot summoned them. More morally gray than evil, in Rus's mind. And demons, at least, had the excuse that they'd been born that way. Soul eaters didn't. Soul eaters had chosen this. Soul eaters were hunger personified.

"You know this is no way to live, don't you?" Rus asked, tone almost casual as she pressed to her feet and paced around the edge of the containment array. It was a shame, really, that this thing had wrapped itself around someone who might be innocent. Or, innocent-ish anyway; soul eaters couldn't feast on the pure, which might be why Holly lasted so long without this thing attaching itself to them.

It was also a shame that Rus was in Moondale. Out in the big wide world, no one would even blink at the idea of her using this thing to power something — a hex, or a spell, or a talisman. Energy was energy, after all. But if the Board of Magic found out she was using a soul like a battery? Evil or not, she could kiss her coven goodbye. So, it would have to go, end of story.

"And what would *you* know of living, little medium?" *Rude.* Rus hated it when they made this personal, but dark souls were often bitchy that way. Like they thought because they'd clung on for so long, outlasting the others who moved on, they were uniquely qualified to make catty comments about how others lived. "You're barely clinging to life yourself, aren't you? Almost not even worth the hassle of dealing with — Ah well, you get the point."

"Maybe I am. Maybe I'm not," Rus said, taking another slow, leisurely lap around the containment circle. The soul eater's eyes followed Rus, hungry. She'd loosened her grip on the man's spirit, his form flickering as if he were barely hanging on to this plane, her long neck stretching toward Rus to gnash her pointed teeth. A string of drool clung to the corner of her mouth, and Rus had to fight tooth and nail not to cower. She knew exactly what kind of meal she'd make for a soul eater. Her next words left her despite a throat made tight by instinctual terror. "Why don't you let go of him and come find out exactly *how* close to death I am?"

Another gamble. Rus sent up a silent prayer that Az would never find out she did this kind of thing on the regular. She'd probably never speak to Rus again if she did. Which was probably the least of Rus's worries at that moment, but Rus never had been good at prioritizing.

The soul eater considered Rus for a moment, her head tilted in interest, and Rus's lungs burned with a held breath, her muscles twitching where she'd forced them to stillness. If the soul eater took a moment to look at Rus as anything other than a meal, she might notice the way Rus's hand was fisted in her pocket, spell paper crinkling in between her sweat-damp fingers. Might smell the lingering traces of blood and ozone on the air where Rus's magic sat not dormant, but still. Might hear the whispers of other spirits waiting to rip her apart. That was Rus's bet—that this thing would be too hungry to see the signs of her own destruction.

Between one blink and the next, the soul eater released the other ghost, his form dissipating into nothingness, sucked dry by the thing that had wrapped itself around him. Guilt sat heavy in Rus's stomach, threatening to choke off the spell that hummed up her throat. She swallowed it down, diving for the floor to press bloodied palms and wrinkled paper into the chalk outline, the spell already crawling from her lips.

Putrid green flames caught on the chalk, spreading like wildfire across every mark until the whole array was on fire, the smell of burning flesh permeating the air. The soul eater screamed, voice pitched so high it made Rus's ears ache. Her hands twitched to cover them. A searing pain burned itself into the curse mark around her neck, threatening to never release her from its grasp. But she couldn't let go. Not until this thing was gone. Not until the magic had done its work.

It lasted for what felt like forever, her heart hammering in her ears so hard, she thought it might burst an eardrum.

Then, suddenly, the fire and the screaming stopped. Silence cut through it sharp as a blade, and Rus rolled onto her back, the hardwood pressing all the air from her lungs as she blinked away the afterimage of the spirit's face alight with flames. Pressing the heels of her palms into her eyes, she sucked in a hitching breath, the weight of guilt finally crushing her chest.

"Too late," she rasped from a throat raw with anger and pain. "I was too late for him."

Failure. You're a failure.

Maybe if she'd tried to exorcise the soul eater last night, maybe if she'd *realized* it was one at all, she could have saved the man it attached itself to. But now . . . now he was gone. He wouldn't even get the chance to reincarnate. No one, not even someone who had been terrible, deserved that kind of oblivion. She choked back another sob, letting her hands flop hard onto the floor at her sides.

"Hello?" a voice called from downstairs, the door creaking shut behind whoever it was. "Is anyone home?"

"I thought you locked the front door," Rus said, glaring

at the ceiling in accusation. The house didn't respond, and after a brief standoff with 157 Mourning Moore, Rus rolled onto her side and pushed herself up to sit. She couldn't stand quite yet, but it was better than being caught lying in the middle of the floor. "I'm up here!"

The stairs groaned under the person's weight, giving Rus time to consider the voice again now that her ears weren't straining to hear it past their ringing. Indigo Elwood popped his head in through the doorway to her attic room a moment after she'd placed his voice. "You okay up here? I saw a flash from across the street and got worried."

"Yeah, I'm good." She pushed her hair back from her face, frowning when her fingers carded through the sweat-matted strands without being hindered by a hair tie. Fuck. That had been her last one too. "You mind helping me down to the kitchen? I need some juice."

Indigo still stood in the threshold, his dark eyes jerking about the room to take in the pushed aside furniture, the whirlwind of papers littering the floor, and the char marks from her spell. 157 Mourning Moore would deal with that once she'd mopped up the chalk, but it probably wouldn't be happy about it. She foresaw a lot of missing socks in her future.

"Indie," Rus muttered, holding her still-bloody palms out to him. Between the burn marks and the cuts she used to generate the blood where she needed it—fuck if she didn't hate having to cut her hands for this—they stung like a bitch. Cagney was going to have a fucking field day when she stopped by later to help Rus get ready for the Board of Magic meeting.

"Huh?" Indigo looked back at her, then frowned. "Oh. Right. Sorry." He scuttled across the floor and grabbed her by her wrists to pull her to her feet before hooking one of her arms over his shoulder. With one arm looped around her waist, he helped her down the stairs. "So what was all that about?"

Rus bit down on the tip of her tongue, cutting her eyes to Indigo for a moment. "Promise not to tell your sister?"

"Yeah, no. I'm not promising that." But his lips had lifted at the edges, wry amusement lining them. "You know better."

"I do." Tilting her head from one side to the other to stretch out her neck, and almost losing her balance in the process, Rus sighed. "It was a soul eater."

"Oof, big yikes." They made it to the kitchen in time for Rus's knees to give out from under her as Indigo lowered her into one of the chairs. "Juice, you said?"

"Yeah. Orange juice will do. And if you don't mind, wet me a rag to clean the blood?" She arched over the back of the chair, her spine cracking from the movement, relieving some of the pressure that had built up there. Indigo slid a glass her way then headed to the sink.

"So," Rus said, breaking the quiet between them, "on a scale of one to ten, exactly how pissed is Az about last night?"

"Solid eight and a half, I'd say." He took her hand by the wrist, sitting across from her, and started to wipe away the blood that had caked around the slash across her palm, careful of the burns that surrounded it. "Worse than that time you stood her up at the Bay Festival."

"Eesh. That's bad," Rus hissed, sipping her juice with her free hand. Already the sugar eased away some of the jitteriness left over from an exorcism nearly gone wrong, but it'd be days before she felt truly normal again. She was just grateful it seemed like the curse mark had gone away with the soul eater. "Anything I can do to make it up to her?"

Indigo didn't answer right away. He took her other wrist, his hands gentle as he methodically cleared away the blood. So much like his sister in that way that it made Rus's heart squeeze in her chest. When he was done, he stood again to grab the first aid kit from the cabinet next to the stove. She'd question how he knew it was there, but he'd been over at the house enough in the last few weeks, he'd probably mapped out her entire kitchen. The Elwoods were like that. He sat across from her again, antiseptic already uncapped, and said, "Ask her out to dinner."

Rus blinked, the juice sitting in front of her forgotten. "I'm sorry. What?"

"An apology dinner," Indigo said, but he wouldn't meet her eyes, his focus solely on her injured palms where he pressed the skin back together with medical glue that Az had probably added to her measly first aid kit when Rus wasn't looking. He slathered aloe across the burns.

"Indie." Rus bit the inside of her cheek so hard, she was sure there would be a welt there tomorrow. "We aren't dating."

"I know that." His dark eyes lifted to meet hers finally, and he frowned. Inhaling through his nose, Indigo pressed on. "I just think making a little bit of time for her would go a long way, that's all."

"It wouldn't be a date."

"No. Of course not." But he smiled, his lips ticking up at the sides the way Meiling's did when she thought she was pulling one over on her aunt. He patted Rus's now-patched-up hands, guiding them back to her juice glass. "Just think about it, yeah?"

"Yeah. I'll think about it." She wouldn't be able to *not* think about it now. Even if she tried. Even though she had about fifty million *other* things to think about. Goddess, she was a mess.

"I'll go clean up upstairs," Indigo said, shuffling over to the pantry.

"Don't worry about that. Cags and I will get it when she comes over later. You should—"

His dark eyes met hers, and he stared at her as he pulled the mop and bucket from the back corner, one dark brow raised high. *Fucking Elwoods. Is there no escape from them and their meddling?*

"Shouldn't you be in school?" Rus drained her juice and rose from her chair on slightly steadier legs.

"Shouldn't you be at work?" Indigo countered, already on his way up the stairs, not even pausing to sass her. Fuck, Rus hated teenagers.

IT WAS HARD NOT TO THINK ABOUT WHAT INDIGO HAD suggested. Which only heightened the anxiety lingering under Rus's skin like too much caffeine and not enough water. Because *that's* what she needed—one more thing to be anxious about. The board wasn't enough. Raising her girls wasn't enough. Running a business wasn't enough. Add in Az, and all . . . *that*.

It wasn't that she didn't want to ask Az out, Rus reasoned as she gathered the little caddy from the pantry and filled it with everything she'd need to work out in the graveyard. In fact, it was the exact opposite. She wanted it a little too much. But Az was still so pissed about her missing the meeting last night. And there was all the shit with the board to think of. Maybe now wasn't the right time.

Wet soaked in through her jeans as she knelt to weed some of the graves. She threw herself into the action, digging up onions and scrub grass to make room for wildflowers—let it quiet her mind. She didn't even notice the girls until Aihuan squealed loud enough to wake the dead.

Rus turned to watch the two as they trekked from where they'd left their things on the porch out to the gravesite she was working on. "Good day at school?" she called, a smile tugging at her lips.

"The best!" Aihuan announced, skipping along with Meiling trailing behind with a glittering row of carrion beetles that Rus could just make out in the watery winter sunshine. Meiling tried not to step on them, likely on pain of being reprimanded by her little sister. "We did finger paints, and I drew our house!"

"Oh yeah? We'll have to hang that on the fridge when we get back inside."

Aihuan nodded, her chubby cheeks spread wide in a smile as she settled down beside the grave marker where Rus had been working. No shades lingered in this part of the cemetery, thanks to Rus's efforts to keep them appeased, but Aihuan offered the headstone a cheerful wave just the same, greeting the dead like an old friend. Her sister shifted from foot to foot off to the side, like she was unsure where to walk, not wanting to step on anyone.

"Didn't you have some decorations on this one?" Meiling asked, pulling the sleeves of her coat down over her fingers. She was right, there had been some things on this site last week. It was a newer grave, and someone in Moondale still cared enough to bring by small sculptures and banners to keep the place where Charlotte "Lottie" Miller rested looking loved.

"I didn't, but someone did." Rus blew out a long exhale with a frown.

"Did someone steal it?" Meiling's nose wrinkled.

"Probably. People like to do that. Especially if it's cute little kitschy stuff."

Meiling snorted. "Good way to get yourself haunted, if you ask me."

"Probably." Rus turned back to the grave, looking over the place she'd cleared. Whoever put the decorations there hadn't done any gardening, but that was all right. That's what Rus was there for. "Do you want to plant the seeds, little monster?"

"Me?" Aihuan asked, pointing at herself, her brown eyes huge in her face, cheeks rosy with joy.

"Yes, you. Do you remember the turn Auntie Cags taught you to sing to them so they'll grow even if it's winter?"

"Mm-hmm!" Aihuan took the packet of wildflower seeds like they were something precious, reassured, her voice soft as she hummed the growing spell Cagney taught them.

Meiling joined in, adding her magic to her sister's, filling the air with the warmth of their bond. Aihuan dumped the seeds, but before they could land in one large pile, Rus tilted her head, her own magic swirling around them, green and fluttering, smelling of ozone and rot, spreading the seeds over the dirt and helping them bury themselves underground where the frost wouldn't stunt them.

"Auntie Rus?" Aihuan asked, scooting closer, no doubt spreading grass stains on her leggings.

"Yes, little monster?"

"When will the flowers grow?"

"Not till spring, Huaner" Meiling grunted from where she was still standing off to the side, looking uncomfortable. "Can we head back in? I'm cold."

Rus nodded, rising to her feet. It would take time for Meiling to get comfortable with the dead again, but they had time for that. Time for her to adjust and learn the ways of being a medium. Time for her to find her feet. "Let's go. I'll make some cocoa for you two while you start on your homework."

"Yay! Cocoa!" Aihuan cheered and leapt to her feet. She was halfway back to the house by the time Rus gathered her things and followed them, laughing and whooping the whole way. Rus shook her head, smiling to herself.

Chapter 5

"YOU *CANNOT* BE SERIOUS," Violet said by way of greeting, the door to Elwood & Co. slamming behind her loudly enough to draw the attention of the customers lingering at the back of the store.

"Good afternoon to you too, Violet," Azure responded mildly, not looking up from the computer screen where she was currently trying to sort out their order for the winter holidays. She should have done this weeks ago, before Samhain really, and normally she would have. But with everything going on with Rus and the Board of Magic, some things had to fall to the wayside. Those things happened to be ordering, and stocking. Aunt Carmine wasn't pleased with it. She kept threatening to call in another Elwood to help, but Azure had decided to ignore her for her own sanity.

"You cannot be *serious*," Violet repeated, emphasizing a different word as if that would stress her point. Long fingers gripped the front of the counter as Violet leaned heavily on it, clearly trying to get herself as close to her sister as she could manage with the counter between them. Her long dark hair—usually pulled into a neat bun reminiscent of her ballerina days—was loose around her shoulders, static making it cling to her cheeks and the scarf around her neck, lending her a harried, disheveled look Azure didn't think she'd ever seen on her older sister. Lipstick stained her teeth.

"Yes, you said that." Azure wished Violet would get to whatever point she'd come to make so that she could get back to work. There was still too much to do before the board meeting tonight, and she had to spend most of her day behind the counter at Elwood's. Maybe she would take Aunt Carmine up on the threat of help after all. Surely one of the younger Elwoods could use a holiday job to keep them busy, and out of trouble, during the winter months. A little extra cash probably wouldn't hurt them either. Maybe Indigo knew of someone who would like the position. "But as I'm unclear what it is I cannot be serious *about*," Azure said, bored already with Violet's theatrics, "I don't know what you want me to say."

"You can't," Violet said, grabbing Azure's wrist and ripping her attention away from the screen at the invasion of her personal space, "leave Jade Waters."

Heart stuttering in her chest, Azure yanked her wrist out of Violet's vice-like grip. She hadn't told anyone she was considering that. Hadn't talked to anyone about what Nixie had said. Well, no one except— "Indigo needs to learn when to keep his mouth shut."

"He's worried about you. We all are." Lifting her chin, Violet pulled her shoulders back, her posture straight out of the Violet Elwood Big Sister Handbook.

This was exactly the pose she'd adopted when Azure first railed against her board-approved match, the phrasing almost down to the syllable, except then it had been Aunt Carmine and Aunt Maureen who were worried about her— not Indigo, who had been too young to give a flying fuck. Azure's breakfast soured in her stomach. Violet was pulling rank, like they were still children and she had any authority over Azure at all.

"Leaving Jade Waters would forever ruin your prospects. Not to mention the dangers that come with striking your name from a coven list. Azure, you could be set adrift! Moondale could reject you. You could—"

"What prospects?" Azure narrowed her eyes, puffing up her chest to mirror her sister's stance. She was a little shorter than Violet, always had been, and Violet liked to wear heels, which added to the feeling of her looking down her nose at Azure. But Azure had grown out of cowering and begging for her sister's approval years ago. Ironically, right around the time Rus left Moondale and Azure realized all the things that wanting her sister's respect had cost her. She was only now regaining some of what she'd lost all those years ago. She wasn't about to give that up.

Even as she asked the question, though, Azure thought she knew what Violet was talking about. How could she not? It was the same argument they'd had over and over again through the years, ever since she'd come of age. The one that had nearly severed their sisterhood entirely. The one that had gotten Sibling Bonding Night instituted. The one that Azure had come to understand she would never truly escape. So long as she stayed in Moondale, so long as she remained a member of Jade Waters, she would forever be stuck in this argument, this cycle, this *role*.

"You can't be the Jade Waters elder if you leave the coven," Violet said, confirming Azure's suspicions, and Azure had to resist the urge to grind her teeth. Her dentist was already going to give her a lecture at all the jaw clenching she'd been doing around the board members, and she didn't need to add to that with the aggravation of Violet Elwood.

"Believe it or not"—Azure took a step away from her sister, diverting her attention back to what she'd been doing in the hopes that maybe Violet would take it as a dismissal—"I am aware of that fact."

"And yet you're still planning to leave us in favor of this

—this—this—" Violet struggled for the words, or perhaps she struggled to not say something bitchy that would piss off Azure and make the next Elwood Sibling Bonding Night nothing but awkward silence.

"Nothing has been set in stone." It wasn't a lie; Azure hadn't made a choice yet. Which was likely what Indigo had said to Violet. But Violet had somehow missed the point entirely, only hearing what directly fit her narrative as she always did. And her narrative was that Rus was a stain on their family name, tearing them apart from the inside. Azure had to wonder sometimes, who other than Violet felt that way? Did Aunt Carmine secretly harbor a grudge about this whole thing? Only helping Azure and Rus on the surface while in the same breath going behind their backs to bad-mouth them to the Board of Magic?

No. Azure wouldn't let her paranoia get the best of her. She couldn't start seeing enemies around every corner. It would only make this harder.

"I'm just considering my options."

"But leaving the coven *is* on the table," Violet pressed, phrasing it like an accusation instead of a question.

"It is an option I'm considering. Along with several others." Her headache was back, pressing against the backs of her eyes, throbbing in time to her pulse. Azure pinched the bridge of her nose, trying to breathe through the worst of it, but it didn't seem to want to go anywhere. Leave it to Violet to make Azure wish she hadn't gotten out of bed that morning. "But as I've told you before, I have no desire to be the Jade Waters elder."

"Azure." Violet reached for her hand again, taking it in between her long fingers and squeezing almost painfully until Azure opened her eyes and met Violet's gaze. She did look worried, concern tightening her eyes around the edges, her brows drawn together. "An Elwood has always held the seat of Jade Waters elder."

"There are plenty of other Elwoods who could take the seat. There's you and Indie, and our cousins." The Moondale Elwoods may have grown smaller in number over the years as family members moved out of town or married into other families, but there were still plenty of them available. The elder seat didn't have to be foisted upon Azure and her siblings. And besides, *she* didn't want it, as she'd told Violet repeatedly. She didn't want to follow in her father's footsteps, in her aunt's. She wanted . . . Well, she didn't know *what* she wanted exactly. She just knew she didn't want to live in the shadow of her family for the rest of her life, and if she took the Elwood elder seat, she would.

"Not from our bloodline. From our bloodline, there's just you and I." Violet was pleading, her eyes gone wide and soft as they did whenever she asked Azure to do something Azure didn't want to. Azure had seen this manipulation many a time growing up and had yet to find a way to combat it. Because she knew that as much as it *was* a manipulation, Violet's heart was in the right place. Mostly. "Please, Azure, you know I can't do it. I'd have to give up my practice. And this is what Daddy wanted. Don't be selfish."

Selfish. The word stung needle-sharp in her sternum, burying itself deep, a thorn she'd never be able to pry out. Violet wasn't wrong; she would have to give up her practice to take the seat of elder. And Violet's practice was all she had. She'd given up everything else to do what the Board of Magic asked of her. Married a woman she didn't love. Tossed aside her own dreams of motherhood. Turned down offers to join organizations that would help the world over. All to stay in Moondale and do what the Board of Magic, and her wife, wanted. It wasn't fair, but it was the truth.

Now, all Violet asked of Azure was to one day take the seat of elder. It seemed a small price, by comparison. A price Azure had prepared herself to pay for years now. She didn't want the seat, but she'd been readying herself to take it. One more sacrifice for her family and her sister to add to the list she'd made throughout her life. All in the name of not being *selfish*.

Azure bit down hard on the edge of her tongue, thick metallic blood coating her teeth even as the pain brought her mind back to her sister's pleading gaze. She couldn't ask Violet to give up her practice too. Not after she'd lost everything else. Not if there was another option.

"It is a last resort. I promise." She squeezed Violet's hands in return, and the sting in her sternum eased as Violet visibly relaxed, a relieved smile pulling her lips upward around the edges.

With Violet placated, Azure turned back to her work, returning her focus to numbers and figures while Violet babbled on about a dinner party Taryn had hosted last week. The almost soothing murmur of her voice normally would have allowed Azure the time and space she needed to think about more important things, but something nagged at her. A question she didn't think she'd ever have the answer to. Because no clean and clear answer existed.

If she didn't leave Jade Waters to help Rus run the Coven of the Forgotten, then how could she lend her support in something other than name? How could she do what Nixie suggested?

"Azure," Violet said, drawing her attention back, "we're going to be at the board meeting tonight. To support you and Rus."

Warmth flooded Azure's bones, chasing away the lingering sting of the word *selfish*. "Thank you. That means a lot."

Violet hummed gently, her smile wide enough to make her eyes crinkle, then she reached over the counter to pull Azure into a bone-crushing hug before leaving her to her musings. Azure blinked for a moment, watching her sister's retreating form. The knowledge that Azure wasn't in this alone, that her family supported her, even if they might not technically agree with her, had her lips twitching into a smile. Maybe she and Rus could do this after all. So long as they didn't have to do it alone.

CAGNEY'S CAR PULLED UP OUTSIDE OF THE BOARD OF Magic building where Azure was waiting for them a full twenty minutes before the meeting was meant to start, pushing a relieved sigh from Azure's lips. She hadn't said as much out loud—hadn't even let her mind think the thought—but she'd worried Rus would be late again. That she'd get tied up in something and forget.

Not that Azure could really fault her for the previous night. Not after what Indigo told her about the soul eater and the spirits at the apartment building Sheriff Regan sent Rus to deal with. Then Cagney had been kind enough to say that Rus had been led to believe the job would be quick and easy. That Sheriff Regan had said there were minor disturbances. No indication of something that should have taken Rus more than a half hour to dispatch.

It wouldn't be fair of Azure to blame Rus for someone taking advantage of her kindness. She knew better than anyone how much it hurt Rus to know a spirit was languishing. Knew how that guilt could weigh on Rus. No. Azure couldn't blame Rus for selflessly putting the needs of the dead above her own. Not when someone rarely spoke for them.

Still, although Indigo tried to warn Azure about what Rus had been through since they'd last spoken, she wasn't prepared for the haggard look on Rus's face when she stepped out of the car. She limped, heavily favoring her right side. Her hands were bandaged so thoroughly, it almost looked like she was wearing mittens. And dark bags hung beneath her eyes. All indicative of a night spent with little rest, and a morning spent trying to force a soul eater from this plane.

"Indigo told me about the soul eater. Are you all right?" Azure asked, her palms itching to reach for Rus and pull her in close, ward off all that could or would hurt Rus with her own magic. Once upon a time, she'd have done it without question. Sketched a warding talisman into the back of Rus's too-thin tapestry-style kimono—something Indigo made for his midterms and gifted to Rus—and glared at anyone who tried to make Rus do anything before she completely recovered. But that was years ago now, and such attention would likely no longer be welcome.

"I've had worse," Rus said, shrugging off her concern as she perched her wide-brimmed hat on her head. She clenched her jaw in the shadow of it, eyes tense like she was readying for battle.

"A soul eater?" Cagney growled, her mouth twisting around the words. She had come around the car to stand next to Rus, her hands held out a little in front of her as if to catch Rus should she stumble. "You didn't say anything about a soul eater."

Pinching the bridge of her nose, Rus took a measured step toward the narrow cobble walk that led to the slightly crooked one-story resting in the shadow of Moondale town hall. The Board of Magic building, although integral to the existence of Moondale as a whole, looked like nothing more than a derelict old town hall to those of Moondale not in the know. Humans would walk right past it, thinking nothing of the building that had been left to decay when a new town hall was built. Perhaps they'd wonder why Moondale hadn't seen fit to demolish it in the wake of bigger and better things, but the diversion charm carved into its very bones would keep them from looking too closely.

"I handled it," Rus said over her shoulder in a tired voice when neither Azure nor Cagney moved to follow her. She turned back, her head tipping a little backward so she could eye them through eyes hazy with exhaustion. "Are you two coming or what? I want to get this over with and make it home in time to actually get some sleep tonight."

"Handled it," Cagney muttered, hurrying to fall in beside Rus anyway as Rus spun around to start back up the path. Azure took a minute to watch them, to catalog every change in Rus, before following.

Chapter 6

THE LIGHTS BURNED hot on the back of Rus's neck, making it feel like she was in an interrogation room. Again. Sweat trickled from her hairline down to the collar of the white dress shirt Cagney managed to wrangle her into underneath the well-worn band tee. Too many layers, she was *definitely* wearing too many layers. The thought had been to layer up to ward off the chill lingering in her bones that the soul eater and its curse mark left behind. Rus regretted every single clothing-related decision she'd made that day. But it was too late to strip them off now.

The heat wasn't the worst part though. Rus shifted in her chair—right at the front, dead center, so everyone in attendance knew why she was there and where to find her. The cutting glares of every board member threatened to eviscerate her, to shred her to ribbons till there wasn't anything left for her girls to bury. That was the worst part. She hadn't even taken the floor yet, damn it. And already nine pairs of eyes watched her like she was something disgusting they had stepped in.

Well. Not *all* nine sets. Carmine Elwood, at least, made an obvious effort not to stare the problem in the face. Rus couldn't decide if that was better or worse. And there was the elder of the Ladies of Nimue, Nixie Virnan, who looked kind of like she wished she had popcorn to better enjoy the approaching carnage. Again, Rus couldn't decide if that was better or worse. Probably worse.

Rus swallowed roughly around a knot of discomfort in her throat threatening to constrict her airways and deprive her lungs of much needed oxygen. She shifted again, her chair creaking a little under her weight, her thighs pressing first to Az on her right then to Cagney on her left. A reminder that she didn't have to go at this alone. That she had their support and strength should she need it. The thought eased the knot in her throat, unclogging it enough for her to suck down a shaky breath as the clock ticked away to the witching hour.

This close to the winter solstice, the shift in the air when the clock struck midnight was a physical thing, growing thinner, reminiscent of that time Rus scaled Mount Fuji with Aihuan and Meiling's parents. Rus felt more than heard every person in the room tense at the difference in the air, and she had to restrain the urge to roll her eyes. Even now, a decade later, they were all still so afraid of what lay beyond the veil that the witching hour in November and December made them want to run and hide behind their hearth.

Pathetic, the lot of them.

"Well," Nixie Virnan said, ignoring the tension that had spread through the room around her, "I think that's our cue to begin." She clapped her hands once, and magic snapped into place, sealing the Board of Magic building off from the rest of Moondale. Making it what had always been considered a safe place for the folk.

The wards scraped against Rus's senses like thorns on skin, reminding her that she didn't belong to the land of Moondale. Not yet. Threatening her that if she didn't behave within this hallowed place, she would be expelled from it.

Az reached down to take her hand, threading her long brown fingers in between Rus's own too-thin digits, pressing magic in through her palm that eased the feeling of wrongness humming under her skin. Released some of the pressure that might have made it impossible for Rus to rise to her feet.

She didn't know how she'd stood against it before. How she'd broken through the wards to enter the emergency meeting weeks ago, when all of this began. Maybe it was the strength of her conviction, the fear of what would happen to her girls. Or maybe it was her own stubbornness. But all of that abandoned her now, leaving Rus a mess of nerves and uncertainty.

Az rubbed her thumb across the back of Rus's battered and scarred knuckles, providing warmth and comfort where Rus likely didn't deserve it. Rus lifted her chin to meet Nixie Virnan's gaze and give the elder a small nod of assent.

Nixie's lips twitched away from too-sharp teeth before she said, "Would the petitioner Icarus Ashthorne please join us on the floor?"

With one brief squeeze from Az, Rus carefully detangled their fingers and stood. It took her two steps to close the space between her chair at the front and the place marked by a cracked tile that was the center of attention, but it felt like much farther. The cracked tile in question resided somewhere in the middle of the semicircle of peeling fold-up tables where the board elders sat. One chair was empty, left so for the elder of the druid clan, but having one less set of judgmental eyes on her did nothing to ease Rus's nerves.

"Esteemed Board of Magic," Rus said, dipping her head into a deep bow that she wouldn't have bothered with if she weren't asking the board for something. She needed them to like her, and she knew the quickest way to accomplish that was to appear humble, weak in comparison to them and their magics. They couldn't see her as a threat. She didn't lift her head, staring intently at the toes of her scuffed boots. "I ask for your permission to speak on the subject of my coven request."

The words were perhaps a little flat, recited over and over again in practice with Cagney and Az so Rus said exactly the right thing. Came off exactly the right way. Anything to keep the board from dismissing her request without at least starting the process or giving her a probationary period. That's what they were aiming for in all this—a probationary period. It wasn't much, but so far it was the best they could hope for.

A thought niggled at her that maybe they could go around the board, tie themselves to Moondale without the elders' permission. But Rus wasn't a fucking idiot. She knew how easily Moondale could reject her, and what would happen if it did. A rejection from the land itself was final. There were no appeals. No trying again. And it would be easy if Moondale rejected her coven for the board to simply throw her out, exile her beyond their wards, leave her children without the safety the nexus provided. It had happened before. Once. And no one had attempted it since.

"You have our permission," Nixie Virnan said, but Rus could hear a few grumbled protests. No doubt from Brant Ironwood, who stared at Rus with his lips pursed like he'd swallowed a particularly sour hex. Which was fine with Rus —she'd long ago given him up as a lost cause. She needed to convince the *other* elders.

"Thank you, Elder Virnan." When Rus lifted her gaze to meet Nixie Virnan's, the older woman was smiling at her, sharp and knowing. Rus tried not to squirm under the look, not to think about what it meant. Her tongue felt thick and heavy in her mouth, but she inhaled sharply through her nose and started the carefully constructed speech she'd spent countless hours going over with Az and Cagney. "As you are aware, my daughters and I moved to Moondale a couple months ago. Since then, Aihuan has been hunted for her precognitive abilities. We managed to scrape through that with the help of some of the Moondale folk, but I have little doubt that it's just a matter of time before someone else comes looking for her. Until she's grown enough in her magic to cloak herself from the searching eyes of the greedy, our safest route is for Moondale to do it for her."

"And yet you do not come asking for a place among one of the already established covens," Carmine Elwood said, her tone carefully neutral. This had been another thing they'd practiced. A way for Rus to get past any pestering questions without feeling like she was under attack. If the Goddess was on their side, the others would let Carmine take the lead in questioning Rus, and this could all be over in an hour. Rus wasn't banking on it.

"No. Because of my unique skill set, and the nature of Meiling's abilities"—*not to mention Aihuan's*—"I think it would be safest for myself and the existing covens if I were to start my own coven. That way no coven would be held responsible for my actions, and I personally would deal with any punishments dealt out by the board."

"That's all well and good," Cliantha Greer said, and Rus gnashed her teeth against the inside of her cheek. Cliantha Greer had the same air of superiority, the same nasally tone as her grandson, that left Rus fighting back every instinct to cut her down verbally. Goddess, this was so much harder than she'd bargained for. "But what benefit does another coven serve the Board of Magic? Why shouldn't we turn you and your lot out and be done with this whole thing?"

Fury burned through Rus like fire, lighting her veins with its heat and making the back of her neck flush. She bit down hard on the inside of her cheek to keep from saying something she knew she'd regret, and instead tucked her hands into the pockets of her kimono to hide the putrid green magic wrapping itself around her scarred arms. She said her next words through a clenched jaw. "Because my unique skillset would be valuable to all the folk of Moondale. I made numerous advancements before leaving a decade ago, and since returning, I've created—"

"Yes, yes. Your Witchling Tracker and the digital grimoire." Cliantha flapped her hand through the air, dismissing these accomplishments as if they hadn't cost Rus hours she could have spent with her girls—and sleep—to complete them. As if they weren't a marvel of mixing magic and technology. Rus had already implemented both these advancements, and the board knew that, so she didn't understand how they could belittle her inventions. But she didn't say as much. Cliantha didn't give her the chance.

"We know all about those. But they aren't widely useful, are they?" A snarl started up in the back of Rus's throat, threatening to loose itself into the air around them. The harried voices of the dead grew in volume enough that Rus was sure she wasn't the only one hearing them now, but Cliantha took no notice. "If you could create something useful to everyone, it would go a long way toward convincing us of your viability here as a contributing member of Moondale's community."

Clearly, she already had something in mind. "Is there something the Board of Magic would like me to try my hand at?" Rus asked, forcing a smile that did nothing to ease the churning of her stomach. *Whatever they want, it isn't going to be easy. In fact, it might be—*

"Something to track the fluctuations in negative energy and predict potential spikes in problem areas would be extremely helpful to the board, and the residents of Moondale."

—impossible.

"Something like this," Cliantha continued, her tone making it sound like this was somehow a *reasonable* request when it was anything but, "would go a long way toward making us seriously consider your petition."

"Pre-predict spikes in resentment?" Rus's voice broke over the question. The sweat that had been trickling down her neck the entire time she'd been in the board building turned clammy and cold against her skin, raising the hairs there. "That's impossible," she croaked. "That's almost as impossible as accurately predicting the weather . . ." *The weather. Fluctuations in barometric pressure. Weather balloons. Predictive algorithms. No. No. That could definitely work . . .*

"So you can't do it then?" Cliantha didn't frown, and no disappointment lined her tone. She looked victorious. "A pity. We were looking forward to your coven —"

"No!" Rus rushed forward without really thinking about it, her hands suddenly pressed into the peeling tabletop in front of Cliantha. Cliantha raised a brow, and Rus laughed nervously, pulling her hands away. "No." She cleared her throat, shaking her head, the challenge singing in her veins. "I can do it. I'll do it. You have a deal!"

Cliantha's smile crawled slow and syrupy across her face, her eyes sharper than they'd been, and Rus knew what she was thinking even without the ability to read minds. This was a win-win for the Board of Magic. Either she did what they'd asked of her, and they got a powerful tool that would dramatically change the way they handled resentful energy for the first time in centuries, making them able to plan rituals, to find problem areas, to keep the citizens safe and unpestered by vengeful spirits. Or she failed, and they booted her out of Moondale entirely.

"Wonderful." Cliantha clapped her hands, and Rus took a forced step back from the tables set up for the board members, her limbs oddly stiff. "Then I motion that we approve the introductory period for the Coven of the Forgotten. All in agreement, say aye."

It was unanimous, every board elder murmuring a soft "Aye."

"Motion passed." A softly glowing seal appeared on the paperwork in front of Cliantha Greer, shining red and ominous. "Icarus Ashthorne, the Coven of the Forgotten has until Yule, at which time we will revisit your introductory status."

"Yule?" Rus rasped, only managing to keep herself upright against wobbling knees by locking her muscles in place. "That's—that's six weeks. You want me to get it done in *six weeks*?"

"We will revisit this matter in six weeks," Nixie said, her voice soft, almost kind, before anyone else could speak up. "Please go home and get some rest, Miss Ashthorne. You have a trying time ahead of you."

"Thank you, Elder Virnan." Az was suddenly at Rus's side, her arm looped around Rus's waist, holding her up as best she could as they turned to head back to their seats. Rus leaned into her, letting Az guide her, and ignoring how her hands shook.

"Let's go home," Rus murmured, even though the meeting wasn't done and she hadn't been dismissed yet. Az didn't try to argue. She steered them toward the door, and distantly, Rus heard Cagney's heels clicking behind them. No one stopped them, and of that she could be thankful, she supposed.

Rus had been beautiful, otherworldly in the excitement that burned through her at the board meeting, and it stunned Azure. It shook her down to her very core. She'd seen the moment the idea had taken root in Rus's mind. Rus would need time to figure out exactly how all of it would work, but the seed was planted. The *what* of it, always so much more important than the *how* to Rus, would spread itself like vines through Rus's mind. Turning the cogs and slipping puzzle pieces into place. It was always fascinating to watch Rus's mind at work. Sexier than it had any right to be, really.

"Tell me what you need," Azure said, sliding a cup of steaming tea in front of Rus. She'd been disappointed when they pulled up to 157 Mourning Moore to find the house quiet and dark as everyone was asleep already. But that disappointment had melted away when Cagney waved at them from the driver's seat of her car before pulling away, leaving them entirely alone. Azure couldn't remember the last time they'd been entirely alone—maybe not since before Rus left Moondale. It felt strangely intimate.

Rus blinked up at her, her brows drawn together as her long fingers slipped around the black mug, confusion filtering across her gaze. The cold wind outside had left her cheeks red and chapped, and Azure wanted nothing more than to wrap Rus up in one of those ridiculously long scarves Indigo kept making, and never let her outside again.

"For your research," Azure clarified, although she didn't really mean just for Rus's research. She wanted to know what Rus needed, *period*. Anything at all, she just had to say the word and Azure would provide. She'd thought she'd made that clear when everything happened with Aihuan weeks ago, but maybe she hadn't.

Looking down at her tea, Rus opened her mouth, pressing the tip of her tongue to the point of one incisor in a gesture of thought Azure didn't think she'd ever seen on her before. But then, Azure was learning all sorts of new things about Rus. She treasured each new bit of information, let herself enjoy how Rus was an entirely different person but also somehow exactly the same. It was a strange sort of magic that left Azure aching everywhere, to touch, to taste, to kiss.

She shook herself, focusing again on Rus. Who seemed to have made her mind up about something, her hands tightening on the ceramic as if to brace herself. "I need you to go out with me," Rus said, her tone carefully measured, like she was testing out the words. "To dinner."

"For your research?" Azure's heart pounded against her rib cage, threatening to throw itself from her chest and onto the table, offering itself and all its ugly bits up for Rus to judge and find wanting.

"No." Rus laughed softly, looking up from her tea to fix Azure with one of those soft, sure smiles that Rus always seemed to keep tucked away for the people she loved. And if Azure thought her heart beat fast before, it was doing double time now. Sending her pulse skittering away into something nearly uncountable. "Like a date."

"Oh." *Oh?! Is that all you're going to say? Oh?!* Shaking herself, Azure unstuck her tongue from the roof of her mouth. "When?"

Rus hummed, her fingers tapping the side of her mug, that smile still tucked into the corners of her lips. "This weekend, I think. You're free this weekend, right?"

"I'm free."

"Perfect. Saturday. I'll pick you up at eight?" Rus practically beamed, taking a sip from her still steaming tea.

Azure nodded, all too eager to set the date. It didn't matter that she already had plans to work on stocking that night. She'd work overtime on Sunday. Or she'd have Indigo come in and help—he owed her anyway for the last time she had to cover for him with Aunt Maureen and Aunt Carmine. She'd think of something.

With a soft tap of her thumb against the handle again for a moment, Rus hummed happily, then added, "And any books you can find on meteorology and magical weather prediction."

Biting her lip, Azure frowned. "I don't know how much information we have on that. But I'll see what I can find. If all else fails, I'm putting in an order this weekend for our Yule stock."

"Thank you." Rus's smile spread wider, her hand reaching to cross the space between them and give Azure's fingers a gentle squeeze. Then she let out a long breath and craned her neck from one side to the other, making it crack subtly, before pulling away. "I should get up to bed. Meiling has school in the morning. Let me walk you out."

Pushing away from the table, Azure fought the urge to reach for Rus's hand again. Instead, she opted to follow her down the hall toward the front door. The limp Rus had when she first stepped out of Cagney's car had mostly disappeared now, Azure was relieved to note.

They stopped at the door, Azure slipping back into her shoes and Rus leaning against the banister in a way that might have been trying for artfully relaxed but really just spoke of exhaustion. "Get some rest, Rus."

"I will," Rus promised then shooed Azure out the door before she could make good on the urge to pull Rus into a hug so tight it might pop a lung.

Darcy grumbled at her from his roost on the porch, disapproving, as the door shut behind her.

"Be a bitch all you like," Azure told him, wrapping her scarf more tightly around her neck. "I've got a date."

Chapter 7

AZURE WAS the first to rise in the Elwood household the following morning. The excitement of her date shimmered through her veins like light and warmth, lending itself toward insomnia. Which was fine, she realized, maybe better even. It meant she'd have extra time to get over to Elwood's and get ahead on things for the Yule season. Maybe then she wouldn't have to enlist Indigo's help. Another thing that would probably be better as she knew how much bitching she'd have to endure if she asked him.

Sliding into her running shoes by the door, Azure stretched one arm across her chest, then the other, then opened the door to head out for her run. The toes of her shoes scuffed forward into the early morning chill and stopped when they bumped against something on the front mat that shouldn't have been there. *Didn't Aunt Maureen cancel the morning —*

There, lying motionless on the bristly doormat, a bit of pale blue ribbon tied around its neck — uncomfortably reminiscent of how Azure used to wear her hair when she was a girl — was a bluebird. Its neck had been broken, and its beak sat slightly agape like it had been in the middle of one final song when it succumbed to whoever decided to end its life.

With her hand wrapped in one of the scarves Indigo made for her — protective talismans crocheted into the very design of it, one could never be too careful—Azure reached down to scoop up the poor dead thing. It had gone stiff between when it was deposited on their porch and when Azure found it. Once she settled it on the kitchen table, nested cozily in her scarf, it looked like it could be napping —apart from the awkward spread of its wings.

There was no blood, no missing feathers, no other signs of struggle. Which, to Azure's mind, could only mean one thing. It had been killed by magic. The bluebird wasn't simply some unlucky creature who had flown into the glass on their front door and broken its neck, or been the victim of one of the many feral cats in Moondale. Not that she had thought it was, what with the ribbon tied so neatly around its neck like a present. But the more Azure examined it, the more she realized it was a message. A warning. The question was, from who? And what were they warning her against?

She had a few guesses, but Azure hated guesswork, and it'd be easier to have Indigo look at it. Even if that meant dealing with his crankiness this early in the morning.

Lizzie jumped onto the table, mrowing softly up at Azure, her tail flicking side to side in agitation.

"Yes, I know it's an ill omen, Lizzie. Thank you for that apt assessment." Azure huffed, tugging the gloves from her hands to stuff into the pockets of her now unzipped running jacket.

Tilting her head to one side, Lizzie reached out a fluffy white paw toward the bird. Azure quickly swatted her away.

"No. You can't *eat* it." Honestly, familiars—they'd put anything in their mouths. One would think cats wouldn't be as bad as say a crow, or a snake, but it just wasn't so. If anything, they were worse because cats liked to play with their food.

With a soft grumble and another irritated tail flick, Lizzie sat on the table, eyeing Azure dubiously, paw still half-extended.

Rubbing at the bridge of her nose where a headache was already beginning to form, Azure hissed, "Because it might be cursed or sick. You know better than that."

Lizzie growled back, but she settled more firmly on the table, licking her paw lazily.

"Right. I'm going to go ask Indie to look at it." Azure narrowed her eyes at her familiar, daring her to move, but Lizzie just laid down, her fluffy tail curling around her body. "You watch it. Make sure it doesn't do anything." Azure turned for the steps at the back of the kitchen that led to Indigo's room. "And don't *touch* it!"

Lizzie didn't dignify that with a response, not that Azure expected her to. She was like that sometimes—just as spiteful and vindictive as Darcy. Azure decided a long time ago not to look too closely at the similarities between her and Rus's familiars.

Indigo had his blackout curtains drawn to keep out the milky early morning light—like every other college student who didn't have classes until the evening. After having nearly twisted an ankle enough times, Azure learned that one did not walk across Indigo Elwood's room in the dark. Flexing her fingers against the door, Azure twitched her head at the curtains, and they jerked aside to let in the light from outside, revealing the mess of her brother's room. Fabric and clothes mixed in half-formed piles, and something glittered at the edge of one of them that might have been a very large sewing needle or a very small knitting needle. Either way, Azure didn't want to step on it.

"Indie," Azure hissed quietly, hoping she didn't wake the aunts. She didn't need them seeing the message that had been left for her. Not because they wouldn't find out eventually—familiars talked, and Lizzie was especially prone to gossip. But because she wanted to get ahead of it before they did. Hopefully in enough time to ward off whatever was coming for her before Aunt Carmine could freak out about it. "Indigo."

Indigo grunted and pulled the covers up over his head.

Fuck it. It took a few minutes of struggling for Azure to pick her way across the room so she could grab the corner of Indigo's comforter from the foot of his bed and rip it off him. Would it have been easier to tug the blanket away with magic? Yes. But then Azure wouldn't have gotten to see Indigo's face up close and personal as the chill of morning air on his tank-top-and-shorts-wearing-in-early-winter ass dragging him into the waking world. As an older sibling, it was her Goddess-given right to get a kick out of that, no matter how the younger sibling felt about it.

It took Indigo approximately twenty-three seconds of fumbling to grab for the blanket and miss before his brain fully registered what was going on. Cracking open heavy lids, he glared at Azure. "What do you *want*, Azzy-kins?"

"Don't call me that," Azure grumbled through gritted teeth.

"Don't wake me up at bumfuck-thirty in the morning when you know I don't have class till after one," Indigo bit back, sticking out his tongue at her. He was always such a grouchy bitch in the morning, which was why she hadn't wanted to wake him. But she didn't have much choice. No one else in Moondale had his ability, and even if they did, why would she bother them when she had Indigo right upstairs? "What. Do. You. Want. *Az*?"

Azure released a hard breath through her nose, dropping the comforter she still clutched between her fingers. "I received a . . ." She thought for a moment of the best word to use for what was waiting for them on the kitchen table, and eventually settled on ". . . message I need you to look at."

"All right, give me your phone." Indigo sighed, flopping over onto his back, one gangly hand held aloft to receive said phone.

"It's not on my phone." Maybe it would have been better if she told him what it was instead of wasting valuable time. And who knew how long Lizzie would wait before she decided to devour the poor bird anyway. But he wouldn't really get what it was until he saw it. Plus, he might shout or squawk, and they were much too close to Aunt Maureen and Aunt Carmine's room. "It's downstairs on the kitchen table."

That, finally, got Indigo's attention. He sat up, rubbing his left eye and looking at her with a frown. "On the kitchen table?"

"Yeah." With a twitch of Azure's head, the robe hanging on the back of his office chair flew across the room and smacked him in the face. "Come on."

Scrambling from his bed, Indigo followed her down the back steps to the kitchen table where the dead bluebird waited. When they reached it, he cocked his head and let out a soft whistle. "That's a message all right."

"That's what I said." A pressure had started up behind her right eye that had nothing at all to do with the fucking bird and everything to do with a lack of caffeine. Azure tried to ease it away with the heel of her hand. It did nothing except make her see spots.

"Who'd you piss off enough to have them sending death threats?"

"Is that what that is?" Even as she asked the question, she knew he was right. Azure had been so busy trying to figure out who it had come from, she hadn't really thought about what it *meant*. Goddess above, someone was really done with her shit, weren't they?

Indigo tilted his head at her, his lips pursed in what Azure could only describe as judgment at her lack of connecting the dots. "So you want me to what? Touch it and check its history for clues of who sent it?"

"I thought that would be obvious."

"Look." He pointed at her, his nose scrunched. "As much as I love it when you're bitchy at other people, I don't like it when you do it to *me*. Especially not when it's so damn early."

Rolling her eyes and scoffing was the only apology Azure felt up to giving him. She gestured to the bird with her head. "Get on with it."

"Did you check to make sure it wasn't cursed at the very least?" Whatever he saw on her face answered his question, and Indigo blanched. "Smart. Real smart, Az."

"I was in a hurry, all right? We'll do a cleansing ritual when you're done just to be sure you're clean, and we'll have Aunt Maureen check you over. But I need to know who sent this thing so I can get ahead of them before the aunts see it."

"They would have a shit fit over this, wouldn't they?" Sucking at his teeth, Indigo stepped closer to the table. "You owe me for this."

"Consider it your debt paid in full." A crying shame, if you asked Azure. She'd planned to milk all the favors she'd been doing for Indigo since he graduated for years to come. Still, there was plenty of time for him to accrue—

"And any future favors?" he pressed, like any true baby of the family might.

Sighing loudly, Azure let her shoulders sag. It wasn't cute that he hung this over her head, but she'd expect nothing less from her favorite sibling. After all, it's what she would have done. "Until you're twenty-one. And then you're on your own."

A sharp smile peeled back his lips, and he said, "Deal" before reaching out the last few inches to press his finger to the little bird's wing. Azure watched, breath held in burning lungs, waiting for an answer. But all she got was a furrowed brow and a frown.

"What is it? What do you see?" At some point, her knuckles had gone white where she gripped the back of one of the kitchen chairs hard enough to make her nails bend from the pressure, but she couldn't seem to let go. Was the threat from someone on the Board of Magic? Was it someone else? One of Rus's enemies from her travels, maybe? Someone new after Aihuan?

"Nothing."

The floor dropped out from under her, and Azure free floated in space, her voice small when she asked, "What do you mean *nothing*?"

"I mean it's been wiped, Az." Rolling his shoulders back, Indigo pulled his hand away, shaking out his wrist as if he'd been shocked. His lips pulled down in a grimace. "By someone powerful. There wasn't a trace of history left in it. Not even its birth."

"What—" Azure swallowed passed the tightness in her throat. "What should I do?"

"Your next best bet that's not the aunts?" Indigo tilted his head to look at her and waited for her to nod. "I'd take it to Rus and see if she can contact its soul. Maybe Darcy will be able to talk to it and get some answers."

Chaos reigned at 157 Mourning Moore that morning.

It wasn't terribly surprising—Rus learned pretty early on that living with a teenager and a toddler meant regular chaos. Especially at bedtime, and in the mornings, and at mealtimes, and . . . All right, it was *always* chaos. But it was a good chaos. A *happy* chaos. A chaos she wouldn't trade for anything in the world. Not peaceful nights on the couch watching something not toddler-friendly. Not sleeping in past noon. Not being able to walk through the house without having to worry about tripping over a book bag or stepping on a Lego. None of it was worth losing the happy chaos Aihuan and Meiling had brought to her life.

Thus, when she was sitting at the kitchen table, sipping her second cup of coffee for the morning and staring fixedly at the fifth chair 157 Mourning Moore had produced, she wasn't at all surprised to have her thoughts interrupted by an annoyed screech.

"Auntie Rus! She's doing it again!" Aihuan cried around her spoon full of congee. She'd made a mess of the table while adding enough goji berries to her bowl that it looked more berry than porridge at this point.

"I'm not doing anything to you, Huaner," Meiling grumbled back. But Rus could see where the hand not busy shoveling congee into her mouth was twirling under the table. When she glanced over at the cabinets, she found the dirty dishes from the sink dancing about in the air in front of the back window.

With a sigh, Rus set down her coffee mug and fixed Meiling with an annoyed expression. "A'ling, stop trying to scare your sister. Our house isn't haunted."

That wasn't technically true. 157 Mourning Moore was most definitely haunted. A building couldn't remain standing in Moondale as long as this one had, absorbing all the latent magic from the folk around it, and *not* be haunted at least a little. That was a law of nature. But whatever haunted 157 Mourning Moore stayed mostly out of sight and out of mind. Probably because the house suppressed it, more afraid of the house than it was of the necromancer living alongside it. But the girls didn't have to know that.

Not that having a ghost in the house really would have bothered Aihuan. She didn't mind spirits the way Meiling did. But early in the morning? Before breakfast was even finished? This little trick reminded Rus of the I'm Not Touching You game older siblings liked to play on their younger siblings to get them into trouble. Goddess, Rus thought Meiling had outgrown that shit.

Meiling grunted, her hand stilling beneath the table, and the dishes clattered back down into the sink. The narrow-eyed look she shot Rus was especially disgruntled, and Rus wondered—not for the first time in the last few weeks—if Meiling had finally hit those dreaded teen years that would stretch their relationship to the breaking point. She couldn't *wait* until the thirteen-year-old told her she wasn't her *real* mom. That was going to be an absolutely thrilling milestone.

The doorbell saved Rus from such dismal thoughts. Slanting a warning look at Meiling, she said, "I'm going to go get that. And you're going to stop teasing your sister. You've got about fifteen minutes to finish breakfast and get your butt out the door, or you'll be late for school."

"Yes, Auntie Rus," Meiling huffed, stuffing a too-big bite of congee into her mouth and nearly dripping it onto her sweatshirt. Rus would have chided her about that, but the doorbell rang again, and the air in the house had grown electric with tension. Something was wrong.

With one last threatening glance at Meiling, Rus pushed from the table, shuffling quickly down the hall to where she could see Az through the glass. "Open the door," she told the house, her pace quickening.

157 Mourning Moore complied, the hinges screeching loudly as the door creaked inward. It took Az one startled second before she stumbled over the threshold and into Rus's waiting arms.

"It's all right, I've got you," Rus murmured, her fingers fisting in Az's coat to keep her trembling form close to her chest. A quick glance down revealed that Az had something bundled up in a scarf. She held it away from herself and Rus, making Rus's embrace awkward. Az's fingers were white with tension around whatever was inside. "What's that?"

"A threat," Az said, her voice a hushed, strained sound that made Rus's throat burn, her magic already rolling from her skin in a mist, undulating and wrapping itself around them like it could hide them both from whatever was coming for them.

"A'Ling," Rus called. She waited for a grunted response before saying, "Why don't you and Huaner go up and brush your teeth, and pay your respects to your parents before you head out?"

There was a half beat where Rus thought maybe Meiling would fight her on it. Where she'd show how much of a teenager she was becoming. Then Meiling said, "Yeah. Okay." Rus heard the chairs dragging against the kitchen floor followed by the steps creaking under the kids' weight on the way up. Rus waited one breath, two, before pulling herself from Az and guiding her back down the hall to the kitchen.

"Let me see it," she said, sending a prayer to the Goddess that it wasn't Lizzie or one of the other Elwood familiars. Because Rus was intimately aware of what kind of threat Az had hidden in that scarf; she could feel the empty void where a life had once been like an undercurrent.

Az carefully unwrapped the dead animal to reveal a little broken bluebird. With a breath of relief, Rus reached forward to brush her finger gently against the soft down of its breast. Poor creature. It didn't deserve the agony clinging to it. An ache ran up every joint in Rus's finger to her wrist. "Can you bring it back?"

Stilling, Rus frowned. "What purpose would that serve?"

"I need to know who sent it." Az's hands tightened to fists against the edge of the table, her jaw ticking with tension. Fear made her pale and jittery, but anger and determination would make her deadly.

"I'll get my supplies." It was a struggle to draw herself away from Az, to put distance between them when Az so clearly needed her. "But . . ." Rus licked her lips, swallowing against a tongue rubbing rough as sandpaper against her teeth, "we can't do a resurrection here, and not until after I drop Huaner off at school." Chewing on the inside of her cheek, Rus grabbed a reusable grocery bag from under the sink. "Put it in here. Do you still have keys to the coven house?"

"You want to do necromancy in the heart of Jade Waters?" Az asked, voice flat, but her hands no longer shook as she carefully rewrapped the bird to protect it and them from the negative energies that might be clinging to it.

"I don't see where we have much of a choice. I can't bring a soul back from the After here. It'd draw too much attention from all the shades hanging out in the cemetery." Rus shook her head, fading pink hair falling into her eyes as she grabbed a second grocery bag from beneath the sink. "I'm not bringing that shit into this house, not with the girls here. Plus, I need an energy-neutral space. So do you have keys or not?"

"I have keys."

"Perfect." Rus kissed her cheek on her way to the pantry, only realizing what she'd done the moment the pantry door creaked behind her.

Good fucking job, Rus.

Chapter 8

"NO, you can't ride in the car," Rus grumbled to Darcy. He'd perched on her shoulder, his talons digging into her skin through her hoodie while she buckled in Aihuan.

Darcy cawed loudly enough, and close enough to her head, that her ear crackled from the noise. She scrubbed at the sensation while Aihuan giggled, little hands reaching to try to pull Darcy into a hug.

"Because you're a bird, that's why. You can fly there."

The crow let out a guttural sound, almost like he was about to hork up a half-digested mouse, and hopped off her shoulder—out of reach of Aihuan's seeking fingers.

Drama queen.

Between getting Aihuan loaded into the car, hustling Meiling out to the bus, and dealing with a familiar who was almost more ornery than usual, Rus had enough to handle that her slip was pushed to the back of her mind. Not for long. If she knew anything about herself, she knew that the moment she was alone, she'd overthink that little kiss—and how Az hadn't even really reacted to it—until her head spun. Thankfully, that inevitable freakout would have to wait till later because buckling Aihuan into her car seat came first.

"You warded your car" was the first thing Az said to her as she slid into the passenger seat of Rus's beat-up blue sedan, the reusable grocery bag containing the dead bird settled gently in her lap as she buckled.

Rus stopped where she'd been buckling her own seat belt and blinked at Az before laughing a little, nervous. "Of course I did!" She didn't know why she said that. Most witches—or folk for that matter—didn't ward their cars, but Rus wasn't most folk. "It always pays to have a safe space on the go. You can never be too careful. Not that anyone would get past Blue. She's a right B-I-T-C-H, even to me. Loves the kids, though. Don't you, Blue?"

In response, the music playing through the crackling speakers changed to some children's song that Rus regrettably knew all the words to. Aihuan hummed along, clapping her hands happily.

"See?" Rus glanced over at Az when they rolled up to a stop sign and found Az blinking down at the glovebox as if it held all the answers to life, the universe, and everything.

Turning to look at Rus with brows raised almost comically high, Az asked, "Blue?"

"The original owner." Rus shrugged, leaning forward to change the station when that stupid fox song that always got stuck in her head started.

"Auntie Ruuuus," Aihuan protested, and Blue switched the station back. Rus tried again, only for Blue to automatically switch it back.

The battle of wills with her own car lasted all of twenty seconds, with Rus turning the dial on the radio and Blue flicking the station back a total of sixteen times before Rus gave up with a grumbled, "Fine. Have it your way."

"You trapped the spirit of the previous owner in your car?" Az said, the words coming out strained, quietly scandalized, and maybe even a little impressed.

"What?" Rus's head whipped around to frown at Az, horror making her mouth hang open. Is that what Az thought of her? She *could* do something like that, of course —she knew how and she was strong enough, objectively.

But she never *would*. Not without the spirit's consent, anyway. "No! Blue was here when I bought the car. I just haven't figured out how to exorcise her yet." She shook her head, looking back to the road and clicking on her blinker to turn into Aihuan's school. "I've tried, but the old girl doesn't want to go. Do you, Blue?"

The car's horn honked once, a short sharp burst that made several of the other moms standing around gossiping during drop-off startle then turn to glare at Rus.

Rus hunched down in her seat, her smile going tight as she hissed a quiet, "We've talked about that, Blue."

But Blue didn't seem to give one single fuck. She never had because Aihuan was laughing, kicking her feet in joy, and that always seemed to be enough for the old car.

"All right, Huaner, what's the rule?" Rus asked, yanking up the parking break and twisting in her seat to look at Aihuan. Their preschool ritual didn't seem to annoy Aihuan as it might have Meiling, and Rus was grateful for that. Of the two of them, Aihuan was the one in real danger in Moondale.

"Necklace on. Eyes off," Aihuan sing-songed, tilting her head from side to side to her own little tune. She fished the chain hiding the talisman Rus had Phyre make her just before starting school out from under her sweater to show Rus. "All good."

"All good." Rus nodded, scrambling out of the car to unload the little girl and deposit her into the line of her waiting classmates.

Then she and Az were on their way again. Blue turned the radio to something less likely to get stuck in their heads and drive them up the wall, and Rus tried not to think about the awkward silence that settled between them on the drive.

Should they talk about the kiss? Should Rus apologize

for it? She had asked Az on a date, but that wasn't till this weekend, so technically they weren't even dating yet, were they? Or . . . *were* they? It had been so easy when they were teenagers. Rus had known Az liked her then, and she hadn't been so mired with uncertainty, with all the history that spanned between them now. But Az agreeing to the date had to mean *something*, right? Unless she was just being nice. No, Az never did something just to be nice. Well . . . she didn't *used* to. It had been eleven years. Things changed. People changed. Had Az changed?

Rus snuck a look at her from the corner of her eye and found Az staring out the opposite window, her fingers flexing around the bird in her lap. Should she ask her? No, that would be stupid. What would she even say? *Hey Az, you weren't just trying to get a free dinner out of me, were you?*

Just as Rus opened her mouth to put her foot in it, the Jade Waters coven house came into view, and she snapped her jaw closed with an audible click. It looked smaller than Rus remembered, but then so did a lot of Moondale. Like the town had shrunk in her absence. She knew better. She knew it was just her. That knowledge didn't change anything though. Didn't make her feel any less like she was wearing a too-tight turtleneck almost every day she was there.

And while its smallness should have made the building less intimidating — just as it should have made the Board of Magic *less* intimidating — it didn't. Jade Waters coven house was still as imposing, if not more because she no longer had teenage bravado on her side, as the last time she and Az had snuck into it. Back then, it had been to smoke pot and make out in one of the oversized beds reserved for coven guests.

The door opened on well-oiled hinges, silent and unassuming, light flooding into the huge foyer. A crystal chandelier hung in the center over well-polished wooden floors and dual staircases with long banisters that led all the way to the bottom.

Even as Rus stood there, the inside shadowed by drawn curtains, she could hear the faded giggles of a little girl who had been bright-eyed and so dangerously full of herself. The afterimage of a tiny Rus, only a few years older than Aihuan was now, sliding down the banister with an abandon that didn't just border on but truly *was* reckless, burned across her eyes as she stepped over the threshold. She glanced at Az in the hopes that maybe she wasn't the only one haunted by all they'd been, all she'd always dreamed they'd grow up to be, but Az's face was impassive, giving away nothing.

"Where should we do this?" Az asked, shutting the door behind them and flicking on the light switch beside the door, chasing away the ghost of them.

Clearing her throat, Rus stood up straighter. "The meeting room should work fine. You guys still have one of those, right?"

Az didn't answer. She turned on her heel to head down a long corridor off to the left, passing first a library, then a sitting room, then a bar, until finally coming to the large conference-style meeting room at the end of the hall. It had changed since the last time Rus was there, updated to resemble a modern boardroom with a projector and an interactive whiteboard instead of the chalkboard and old-school projector on a rickety wheely cart it had once sported.

"High-tech." Rus whistled, moving to pull the chairs away from the table. "Can you open a window? We need Darcy to be able to get in when we're ready."

Mumbling something under her breath that seemed to end in "pissy little blighter," Az set down her bag then went to do as instructed. The flap of wings let Rus know when

Darcy joined them, but she didn't lift her head to say anything to the crow, too focused on sketching out the protective circle in the middle of the table. She'd chosen orange sidewalk chalk today, and it looked garish against the slab of light-colored marble Jade Waters chose as a tabletop. They were rich and pretentious that way.

"What else do you need from me?" Az asked, and Rus clocked the motion of her shifting nervously from foot to foot out of the corner of her eye.

"Just sit tight, we're almost ready." Rus had never actually done necromancy in front of Az before—not *real* necromancy. She'd contacted spirits. She'd used their power and their anger to fight back when necessary. But Az had never seen Rus bring back a dead thing before. Maybe she should tell Az to leave now. Chase her off so she didn't have to know what it looked like, what it did to Rus. But with one quick glance from behind her unbrushed hair, Rus realized that wasn't really an option. For all that Az's body was a mess of nervous energy, her jaw was set and her eyes hard. She wasn't leaving, not until she'd gotten her answer. Rus's gut twisted, but she didn't stop the next words that came from her lips, half-hoping they might scare Az away. "It would be easier if we had a mouse or something to sacrifice. A life for a life, possibility for possibility, is usually the most direct path to bringing a spirit back."

Brows drawing together, Az worked over the words. "What will you use instead?"

Rus thought maybe Az knew the answer to that question, that she was just trying to work out her own nerves. Trying to understand everything from all angles. That had always been Az's MO. Well . . . except for when it had come to necromancy. When it had come to Rus's necromancy, Az hadn't *wanted* to understand. She'd just wanted it to *stop*. Had that really changed? Or was Az simply trying to distract herself?

"Blood." Rus sat her athame on the table, the blade making a soft *tink* against the marble. Fernando had recently polished it, saying she needed to take better care of her tools, and the black metal shone over-bright under the meeting room's fluorescent lights.

Darcy had come through the open window and hopped across the table, his talons making soft clicking noises as he went. He looked very much like he wanted to try eating the poor bluebird but was containing himself because he didn't want Rus to smack him.

"It won't be a lot. Just enough to draw out the essence of my magic, and then I can get in touch with the After," she said, almost conversationally, as she pulled a mortar and pestle from her bag to join the athame. Soft feathers tickled her fingers as Rus reached for the bird's outstretched wing with a soft "Sorry about this, little buddy" and plucked one to place in the mortar among a small selection of herbs. "Now for the final touches, the—"

Lightning quick, Az's fingers wrapped around Rus's wrist, staying the hand that held the glinting dagger to her exposed arm. "Let me."

"What? No, Az, you don't have to do that." But Az didn't let go of her, even as Rus wriggled her wrist to shake her off. Swallowing around a knot in her throat, Rus let out a long, steadying breath through her nose. "It's not comfortable. It—it hurts sometimes. I'm used to it. I'll do it."

Her fingers flexing around Rus's wrist, Az repeated, "Let me." She peeled Rus's fingers off the dagger with her free hand, Rus helpless to stop her. A warmth hummed under Rus's skin, running up her arm from where Az held her all the way to her shoulder. When Az let go and rolled up her own sleeve to cut into her arm, Rus felt strangely cold. "How much?"

"Just a couple of drops," Rus said, shaking out her hand and pulling the lighter from her bag. It took her a second to get it lit, and by the time she had, Az was already balancing a tiny flame on the tip of her finger like a child might catch a bubble or a butterfly. "Show off."

A smile twitched at the corner of Az's lips. "You like it."

Embarrassment and something much dirtier licked along Rus's nerves, making her skin tingle with heat. She did like it. She'd *always* liked it when Az showed off just how capable she was. As much as Violet liked to act like she was the alpha of the Elwood pack, her power would never hold a candle to Az. Az, who had always picked up things faster than anyone else in their classes. Az, who was quiet and diligent, and who never boasted. Except for when she did. And those times when she did? Goddess above and below, Rus wanted to sink her teeth into Az like an apple.

Rus cleared her throat. "As I was saying, this is probably going to pinch."

Taking Az by the wrist, she pressed the flame to the ingredients in the bowl where they caught, the flame bursting forth and burning white for a moment before fading to a putrid green that matched Rus's magic. A soft whimper caught her ears from Az, but she didn't let go until she was sure the spell would hold, and then it was only to rub her fingers into the muscle of Az's wrist to ease away the ache she knew would linger there for days. "I told you it would hurt."

"Now what?" Az flexed her fingers, her free hand rubbing feeling back into the tips where Rus knew numbness could settle—like carpal tunnel, only worse— after connecting to the After.

"Now"—Rus let go of Az to pull one of the chairs from

against the windows and hop into a lotus pose on it—"you and Darcy keep watch, and I try to contact our little blue friend." She wriggled a bit, the too-new leather squeaking under her jeans, as she waited for Az to protest. To tell her to stop this, that they'd find another way. Rus hadn't tried to contact the After in a while, and she wasn't exactly keen on it herself, not after the close call with the soul eater just days ago. She knew what could happen if she wasn't careful, how she could get lost there if she lingered too long. It wasn't a place meant for the living.

"How do I protect you from here?" Az had grabbed another of the chairs and sat across from her when Rus looked up to meet her deep brown eyes. "Should you be wearing the amulet I made for you?"

"No. It'll block the path to the After. That would only work in limbo. I just—" Heart beating double time, Rus held out her hands to Az and pulled their chairs closer until their knees touched, her fingers latching onto Az's wrist and Az's clutching her own in turn, almost painfully tight. "Pull me back, if I'm gone too long."

Az didn't ask how to do that. She didn't ask what *was* too long. She didn't bother with any of the questions people usually asked, and Rus thought maybe it was because Az knew her, perhaps better than Rus knew herself, and would be able to tell when the time came. Rus didn't sit with that thought too long; there wasn't time for it. The longer they waited to contact the bird's spirit, the farther it would get. So she wriggled one more time, straightening her spine against the chair back, and swallowed down her nerves.

With her eyes closed, the dark pressing in around her, Rus focused on the heat of the flame, the pull of it on her magic, and let it drag her under on a tide of mist and emptiness that had been known to leave a witch insane if they didn't know how to handle it.

The After, as Rus liked to call it, was the place beyond where she usually visited. Farther than the limbo she stepped into to free Holly. It had no direct contact with the world of the living, unless someone opened a pathway like Rus and Az had just done. Meaning nothing of that world slipped through—no sounds, no light, no buildings. To the dead, Rus knew this place looked like *something*, a forest maybe, a mansion, a library, whatever their happy place was, whatever they needed to feel at peace. But to someone who had created a pathway and entered as Rus just had? To someone who was technically still living? It wasn't anything more than a void. Empty, and echoing.

She wasn't dead, so why would the After bother to try to make her feel welcome? It wanted her *out*. Which was why she needed to tread lightly. Reaching into her pocket, Rus pulled out the feather she'd burned in the bowl in the land of the living, pressed her palms together, and muttered a soft spell against her thumbs. When she lowered her hands again, there was . . .

Nothing.

There was *nothing*.

Where there should have been a thin string of life, guiding her to the bird's spirit, there was just the void of the After.

"You've got to be here somewhere," she muttered, stuffing the feather back into her pocket and starting onward. It couldn't have gotten far.

# Chapter 9

IT WASN'T the *wrongness* of necromancy that had always bothered Azure about Rus's practices, although maybe that played more of a factor than she'd like to admit even to herself. It was the danger. Once something or someone was dead, it was meant to stay that way. To undo that, to upset the balance of the world, was dangerous for any folk that tried it, witch or otherwise. And while it was easier—Azure had been assured—for a medium to do it, that didn't mean there wouldn't be blowback.

But if Azure learned one thing since Rus had returned to Moondale, it was that she needed to trust Rus. She needed to believe Rus when Rus said she could do something, have faith where previously she might not have. Because it had likely been her lack of it that had driven Rus away all those years ago, and she wasn't doing that again.

So, fingers aching as much as an eighty-year-old woman's who'd been doing needlepoint all her life, Azure latched on to Rus's wrists and held on for dear life. She felt the moment Rus went under, her pulse slowing down to something that might usually have been associated with medication or meditation. Darcy had settled on Rus's shoulder, his head pressed in closer to her temple as if he could hear any changes in her heartbeat there.

Counting them in her head—one beat, two beats, three beats, four beats—Azure looked at the clock on the wall behind Rus. Rus hadn't told her what "too long" meant;

she'd have to trust her gut on it, which was foreign and unsettling to a person like Azure who had relied on rules and clear instructions for so much of her life.

Instead of the anxiety churning in her belly, Azure tried to focus on the power emanating off Rus. It was . . . *breathtaking*, the way her hands had worked while preparing the ritual, the confidence she'd shown in lifting her chin and diving right into the After. Coupled with the fact that she was doing this *for* Azure, Azure wasn't sure what to think of it. She couldn't really think past the need burning under her skin, a wildfire threatening to decimate everything else.

This place held so many memories. So many ghosts. That's why Azure had done her best to avoid Jade Waters coven house since Rus left. She'd only kept the key in case of an emergency.

Their voices echoed off every wall of the space. Laughter. Whispering. And in one heart-wrenching case, shouting. The night before the night Rus left, that final fight had taken place here. Maybe that was the real reason Azure had avoided it for so long. Because every time she stepped over the threshold, that final night and all she had lost because of it overshadowed all the good memories.

"What are you talking about? We're not breaking up," Azure said, breathless with a heartbreak that threatened to squeeze her lungs until they burst like balloons.

Rus wouldn't look at her, staring at the space just over her shoulder, to the left of her ear. As if meeting Azure's eyes was too hard, would test her resolve. Which proved Azure's point entirely—they shouldn't break up, this was stupid. Whatever absurd notion had struck Rus needed to be disregarded and buried along with all the other ridiculous things she'd said lately.

"Yes. We are." Rus's jaw ticked, but Azure wasn't sure if it was from irritation or upset. It was always hard to read Rus when she got like this. Her tone flat, her eyes distant. Like she was looking off

into a place Azure couldn't see, a place she couldn't hope to understand. Azure blamed the necromancy for that. It was a shroud between them, separating them from each other, and it grew thicker every time Rus used it.

Since Rus brought back Darcy, things had been . . . different between them. Azure constantly felt like Rus was just out of reach. And then the board decreed her match to Evander, and things had only gotten worse. Now, here they stood in the middle of Jade Waters coven house, the drip-drip-drip of the rainwater from their clothes splattering against the ancient hardwood floors, echoing off the magically enforced walls, ruining everything. The floors. Their clothes. Her memories. The lightning flashing outside provided Azure with brief flashes of Rus's face in the dark. Aunt Carmine would have an absolute conniption if she could see the mess they were making, but Azure had never given less of a fuck about her aunt in her life.

"I'm not what you need right now," Rus said, her hands tightening into fists at her sides. "I don't think I ever was."

"What does that mean?" Azure stepped toward Rus, needing to close the space, needing to feel Rus's warmth pressed against herself.

Rus stepped back, closer to the still-open door. "You need someone . . . better."

Azure could say a million things to that. She should have said a million things to that. But her mind stalled, focusing on the careful distance Rus kept between them—had been keeping between them for months now. This was it, wasn't it? This was the end. The thought struck her like a missed stair in the dark, making her stomach plummet and her heart race frantically against her ribs.

Rus didn't give her a chance to adjust to her crumbling world, to try to repair the damage. She took another step back, over the threshold, into the pouring rain, then spun on her heel and ran into the night without a backward glance.

Shaken from the memory by the feeling of Rus's nails digging into her wrists, Azure came back to the moment to find another heart-stopping sight before her. Rus had gone deathly pale, her lids fluttering, eyes jerking about beneath them, and her pulse had ratcheted up to near dangerous levels under Azure's fingertips.

Darcy squawked from where he was perched on the back of Rus's chair now, his talons digging into the leather enough to probably poke holes in it. That was a problem for later.

"Yes, I can see that. Help me pull her back." Wrapping her hands more tightly around Rus's wrists, Azure pressed her magic into where they were connected, searching for the tether that would drag Rus back from the After. It was there, a second heartbeat under Rus's pulse, strumming thready and nervous, the fragile beat of a hummingbird's wings. It had been pulled taught, near breaking, but Azure latched on to it with her magic, and pulled.

Sweat trickled along her hairline. Chills settled against her spine. And Darcy sank his talons into her shoulder, likely putting holes in her sweater, lending her his magic. His power was so similar in smell—all ozone and rotting leaves, the scents of fall—and feeling to Rus's, it made Azure ache all over, but Azure didn't let go, *couldn't* let go. Even as the tether cut into her magic, wire thin and sharp, threatening to leave behind wounds that would take months to heal over. The cut on Azure's arm had started to weep again, blood calling to blood, and Azure held her breath, hoping it would be enough. Praying to the Goddess that the winds of the After hadn't taken Rus too far, out of her reach.

Rus's pulse stalled for one heart-stopping second, and Azure felt her own trip along in her chest, threatening to skitter out of control. One tick of the second hand, one tock, and it started again. This time at a more sedate pace. Like a hard reset. Azure didn't release the breath still burning in her lungs until Rus's eyes blinked open, looking at her blearily. Her magic retreated under her skin, settling in with a new throbbing ache, drowning out the cold arthritis-like pain left behind by the blood magic she'd done to help Rus cross over.

Even as her magic pulled back, Azure held firm, her grip probably bruising Rus's thin skin, tears burning the backs of her eyes. She wouldn't cry, not until she was home again and could hide it in Lizzie's fluff, but oh how she wanted to wallow in the fact that she'd almost lost Rus, again. Clearing her throat, she asked, "What did you find?"

"Nothing." Rus sighed, slumping back into her chair, making Azure lean forward a little where their hands were still connected. But if Rus wasn't going to make her let go, Azure wasn't going to suggest it. She'd hold on to Rus until it felt like the danger had truly passed, which might be never.

"What do you mean *nothing*?" Finally tearing her eyes away from Rus, who was slowly regaining color in her cheeks, Azure looked over at the still unmoving bluebird on the table. On its back, cast in the green fire of the burning mortar, it looked more dead than it had this entire time. An eerie, cursed thing.

"I mean, its soul was gone." Rus turned her head to rub her face against her shoulder, seemingly as unwilling to let go of Azure as Azure was to let go of her. Which was small comfort in the wake of her words and the chill in her fingers.

"What do you mean it was gone? How's that possible?" If Rus could feel the way Azure's pulse hadn't yet settled, she didn't say anything, which provided some relief. Azure didn't think she was ready to talk about how close that had been—maybe not ever. What happened to Rus when she did this alone? What happened when she brought back something bigger than a bird? Had Rus almost died when she'd brought back Aihuan? Azure should have been there with her for that. Should have been able to offer her blood, her life force, and her support. But no. She'd been here. In Moondale. Halfway across the fucking globe, trying to play at being the perfect fucking—

"Soul eater, would be my guess," Rus said, her voice forced into a cracked lightness, as if she thought making it conversational would take away the fear those words brought, the sting of them. It didn't. They left Azure just as raw as if she had said them dead serious.

"We've never had a soul eater within the boundaries of Moondale." Azure pulled her hands away—regrettably—so she could wave one over top of the mortar, dousing the flames inside it, leaving the ingredients a sizzling, mushy mess. "Not in all of Moondale's history. Outside of the one you brought with you the other day."

"No," Rus corrected, running her fingers through her hair, catching them on knots with a wince. "There has never been a *documented* case of one in Moondale. That doesn't mean there have never been any here."

"But the wards." Azure swallowed around a tongue gone dry at the implications of that statement. It was true— history was written by the people who lived to tell the tale, by the victors. If any of the covens had once upon a time used soul eaters for whatever reason, it would be in their best interest to hide it. "How would one get past them? Not by itself."

"Either it hitched a ride on someone's soul, it grew here, or"—with a deep inhale, Rus licked her lips, stalling for time or maybe debating if she should say the next bit—"it was summoned here." She reached over to take the ribbon from the bluebird's neck, twining it around her fingers like she used to with the one Azure wore in her hair as a little girl. "Since this was targeted, a threat"—she cleared her throat, the ribbon cutting into her fingers—"my bet is on summoning."

Azure's stomach took another sickening swoop toward her feet. If whoever threatened her was willing and able to summon a soul eater, then . . . "How much power would it take to do that?"

"To summon a soul eater?" Rus asked, rubbing her nose with her knuckle. "Not as much as you might think, especially if it hasn't fed that much yet. It wouldn't take something super powerful to eat the soul of a bird. It could have even started out as another animal. A snake, maybe."

"But . . ." Azure pressed, hearing the leading tone in Rus's voice. There was more to it, something she wasn't saying. Something that maybe she was afraid to say because she knew it would scare them both. They couldn't have that. They both needed all the facts if they were going to protect themselves and the people they loved.

"But . . ." Rus stood, dropping the ribbon to the table and pacing around the room, her boots squeaking against the floor, thinking. "But to keep it contained? To keep it under control? To keep it *fed*? That'd take a lot. A soul eater's hunger is exponential. The more it eats, the *hungrier* it gets."

Azure crossed one leg over the other, wanting nothing more than to curl up into the chair, to make herself a smaller target. But she was no longer a child hiding behind her aunts; she couldn't do that here. Especially not when someone had painted a target on her back.

"We could be looking at any number of the senior coven and clan leaders in Moondale," Rus said, still pacing. She hadn't stopped muttering to herself, working herself up more and more. Hopefully she wouldn't spiral out. Azure needed Rus to keep her head on straight, to think this through. "Anyone on the board would be able to do this easy. Well, maybe not the werewolves, so I guess we can count them out, but that doesn't mean maybe they didn't hire someone. Fuck. This is bad. This is so bad, Az."

"Is there any way we can use the bird to track the soul eater to its nest?" Did soul eaters even have nests? Azure had only a rudimentary understanding of what they were from school. She'd never actually encountered one in the wild before. But from what she'd learned of Rus's travels thus far, it seemed Rus had run-ins with plenty of nasty things that she would have been protected from had she remained in Moondale. A thought Azure disregarded almost as soon as it struck her. If Rus hadn't left Moondale, there would be no Aihuan, no Meiling, and even if Azure would have preferred to keep Rus safe with her, she wouldn't sacrifice the happiness Rus found in being their mother for anything.

Rus lifted her head from where she'd been watching her feet, her tongue poking at one pointed incisor for a moment, and she shook her head. "No. Soul eaters don't leave a trail like that. They're a void. A black hole, if you will. But—" Snapping her fingers, Rus pointed at Azure as if she'd said something particularly insightful. "But that resentment radar the board wants me to make! That thing could definitely track a vortex like a soul eater."

"How close are you to creating something like that?"

"Not close at all." Rus laughed, but she'd already started scooping her supplies into the bag she'd brought, heedless of the mess she was making and the way the pestle clacked dangerously against some of the glass vials. "Which is why I need to get home, right now, and get started on it."

"Now?" The chair creaked as Azure pushed to her feet to stop Rus's mad scrambling. Was she running from something? Were their ghosts haunting her as much as they were Azure? Or was it something else? Was she hurt? "Rus, you just opened a pathway to the After. You need to sit down and rest before you try driving. At the very least, let me get you some water and crackers from the kitchen."

"No. No. I'm all right, promise." Even as Rus said it, her fingers trembled around the grocery bag strap on her shoulder. "I just need to get home and get to work, while it's still fresh." She tapped her temple twice, her lips quirking up at the edges, but she wouldn't meet Azure's eyes. And suddenly it was just like that night, all those years ago, all over again. "You know?"

"Rus, really," Azure said, taking a step toward her.

Rus side stepped and headed for the door. "You can get a ride home, right?" She didn't even wait for Azure to answer. "I'll call you later, Az. Let you know where I'm at with it! C'mon, Darcy, we've got work to do!"

And then she was gone. Azure heard Blue rumble out of the circled driveway before she could even make it to the front door to call out. Standing in the threshold, Azure listened to the gravel crunch beneath Blue's tires as Rus pulled onto the main road. She sighed before turning back to the house so she could clean up the mess Rus left behind. Again.

Chapter 10

RUS DIDN'T CALL. She said she would, but she didn't.

Now here Azure was, early Saturday morning, standing at her bedroom window, drinking a cup of room temperature coffee that Aunt Maureen pushed into her fingers before heading off to Elwood & Co. Someone decided—someone being Aunt Carmine after she learned about the bluebird from Indigo, the traitor—that it'd be better if Azure didn't go into the shop for a couple of days. If she stayed behind the wards of her childhood home for a little bit and focused on the growing pile of paperwork that came with starting a coven in Moondale. Most of which Rus should probably be filling out, but as Rus was busy meeting the Board of Magic's *other* demands, Azure didn't want to bother her with it.

Still, it was unusual for Rus not to call—or text at the very least—when she said she would. She had always been good at keeping the lines of communication open, even when she was neck deep in a project. Well. That wasn't technically true. Rus had always been good at keeping the lines of communication open with *Azure* when she was neck deep in a project—everyone else kind of fell to the wayside unless she needed their input or someone to bounce ideas off.

It stung a little more than perhaps it should have—it had been eleven fucking years, after all—to know that Azure was now being lumped in with everyone else. She supposed she could reach out first. Dial the number sitting in her contacts, and check in. But Rus said she'd call, and Rus had never *not* called before.

Light reflected off a car pulling into Azure's short driveway, drawing her attention away from 157 Mourning Moore to the sheriff's cruiser parking to the left of her own seldom-used hybrid. Pinching the bridge of her nose, Azure choked down what was left of her coffee and headed for the stairs to meet Greer at the door.

Before he even knocked, she pulled it open to eye him with a raised brow. "To what do I owe the pleasure of a visit from Moondale law enforcement?"

"You weren't at the shop," Greer said, shifting back onto his heels, his hands stuffed into the pockets of his navy-blue sheriff jacket.

"Aunt Carmine thought it'd be best if I stayed home for a bit. I've got a lot of paperwork to catch up on." Not that it should have mattered to Greer anyway. They weren't—wait. *Were* they friends?! When had *that* happened? Shaking herself, Azure stepped back to let him come through to the kitchen at the back of the house. Once there, she poured them both fresh mugs of coffee. "You heard about the threat, then."

"Cagney told me." Because that was a thing that happened now: Cagney and Greer talked. Azure shouldn't have been surprised. Greer had harbored feelings for Cagney for as long as she'd known him. He never said as much, of course. But it was always easy to see, even when they were younger. She liked to think *she* was a little more discreet in her affections, but that was a fucking lie, and she knew it. "She and Nesta are worried."

"She and Nesta?" Brows raised, Azure set down her mug on the island between them with a soft *thunk*. "Since when are you three—" Greer's eyes darted away, his cheeks taking on a soft pink hue. "Oh." There it was again. *Oh.* "Are you . . . ?"

"We've just been hanging out." Greer shrugged, but more heat crawled into his cheeks, and he wouldn't look up from his coffee mug for a long moment. Clearing his throat, he pressed through. "So what's going on with that? Do you need me to file a report? Open an investigation?"

Evander Greer—for all his faults—was a good friend. He cared about the people around him, even if he had a funny way of showing it. And for perhaps the first time in Azure's life, she was grateful to have him around. Grateful to know he was in her corner, no matter what.

"No." She shook her head, her fingers tapping against her mug. "Rus is handling it. She's working on that radar for the board, and she thinks it can be used to track whoever sent the threat."

"Did she try summoning the bird's spirit?" A frown wrinkled Greer's brow, making him look constipated, and maybe Azure would have told him so if his question didn't bring her up short. If he didn't know about what happened days ago at the coven house, then . . .

"Has Cagney not spoken to Rus?" That wasn't—that wasn't right. Rus might not have told Nesta. She might have kept things hidden from Phyre, who tended to mother hen every situation to death, being the person who looked out for Rus at the orphanage had that eeffect. But she'd never, not in the entire time Azure had known her, hidden something from Cagney.

Greer blinked for a moment, the constipated frown turning into a scowl, scrunching his face up further than it had any right to. "Cagney hasn't talked to Rus in days. Rus kind of . . . fell off the map."

"What?" Her grip on her mug tightened to the point where the hot coffee inside of it scalded her palms, but

Azure didn't let go. She needed something to hold, to keep her sitting. Or she'd run across the street and bang down the damn door to 157 Mourning Moore.

"Yeah, she's holed herself up in her workshop to work on that stupid fucking radar for the board. She's not even answering Cag's calls." Scrubbing at his face, Greer let out a tired sigh, like he already had this discussion with both Cagney and Nesta, trying to soothe their worries, and was ready to have it with Azure too. "You know how she gets when she's working on something like that. It's like the rest of the world disappears."

She did know. Hadn't she been thinking the same thing before Greer's arrival? Telling herself not to worry about the fact that Rus hadn't called when she'd said she would. But that was the thing . . . Rus hadn't called. She hadn't called, and now Azure learned that she hadn't been in contact with Cagney, her closest friend, either. Which just felt *off*, because if anyone in the whole of Moondale came anywhere close to the harebrained genius who was Icarus Ashthorne, it was Cagney Faraday. Before Rus had left Moondale, she'd spent a fair amount of time in Cagney's shed with her, fiddling with old cell phones and broken CD players, trying to find magical uses for them. Not much had come of it, but Azure always assumed that whenever Rus needed to bounce ideas off someone, she would go to Cagney.

"That's why Cags sent me over, actually," Greer hedged, turning his now-empty coffee mug in between his fingers. "She wanted to know if you'd heard from Rus."

It took Azure a moment to unstick her tongue from the roof of her dry mouth and say, "No. I haven't."

Greer grunted, as if he expected as much. He didn't seem unsettled at all by what that could possibly mean for Rus and her mental state. Maybe because he didn't actually like Rus, or maybe he hid it well. Either way, he rose from his seat, taking his coffee mug with him to the sink.

"We're supposed to have a date tonight," Azure added, although she wasn't sure why that bit was important. But it was.

"Okay." Goddess bless him, he didn't ask why she had to tack that on, he simply went with it. And Azure thought maybe she liked having him as a friend after all. "I'll let Cagney know."

"And if you find out anything?"

Tilting his head to the side, his dark hair falling across his creased forehead, Greer shot her a little smile. "I'll let you know what I hear."

"Thank you, Evander."

"You know," he said, eyes suddenly wide, "I think that's the first time since we were kids that I've heard you use my first name."

"Don't get used to it." She snorted, practically chasing him to the door.

"Wouldn't dream of it." He spun on the front mat to give her a lazy salute. "See you around, Elwood." Then he was gone, trudging back to his cruiser, his phone already out to dial Cagney.

"No. No," Rus murmured to herself, scratching at her nose and leaving behind a smear from the thick piece of neon green sidewalk chalk in her hand. "That configuration won't work either. Clear it."

The house groaned, like the pipes settling or the siding shifting in the wind. 157 Mourning Moore's own special way of letting her know it was unsure about something. Or maybe it was annoyed that she kept writing on the floorboards of her bedroom and expecting it to clean up behind her. There really was no way to tell this early on in their relationship.

Darcy picked up a piece of paper from the crumpled mess of discards and flapped it near her hand.

"I've already tried that one." She took it from him, spreading it across her thigh to smooth out the creases. "When *did* I try this one?" Eyes burning, Rus blinked down at the configuration on the paper, but the memory evaded her. Hours and formulas running together like watercolors into a blur. "Yesterday? Why didn't it work?"

Darcy squawked as he hopped into the air to perch on her shoulder, talons digging into the too-thin fabric of her T-shirt. She'd ditched her hoodie hours ago, the buzz from too much coffee making her feel sticky and gross under the thick fabric, but now as the buzz wore off, she felt the distinct chill in the air.

"You need a break," a voice said from the door, and when Rus looked over she found Cagney leaning against the frame. Tuning back into the world around her, she heard voices downstairs, mumbled enough that she couldn't make out the words, but she recognized them. Nesta and *Greer*.

"You know breaking and entering so you can ambush someone in their own home is technically illegal." Rus sucked on her teeth, which felt a little fuzzy from not having brushed them in . . . it didn't matter how long. "I'd have thought the girlfriend of a cop would know that."

"One, Evander isn't my boyfriend," Cagney shot back and crossed the floorboards with slow but deliberate steps. "Two, I didn't break in. The house opened the door for me."

"Traitor," Rus mumbled, glaring at the wall behind Cagney.

"And three, I'd hardly call this an ambush. More like"—Cagney hummed, as if considering what she'd term whatever she, Nesta, and Greer were there to do—"an intervention."

"I don't need an intervention. I'm right on the brink of something." The page crinkled under Rus's fingers, and she looked down to find that she'd balled her hand into a fist in her irritation at being interrupted. "I can feel it."

"Okay, and?" Cagney crouched in front of her, taking her wrist so she could carefully pry her fingers from the paper, halting its destruction. Probably for the best—it might not have worked, but that didn't mean it couldn't still be useful. Rus had learned she could always glean something from her mistakes. "This will still be here when you get back from your dinner with Az. Besides, you should really shower. It'll help get your brain going, and you stink."

"Dinner with Az," Rus said slowly, like a child sounding out the words for the first time. She was meant to be having dinner with—"Oh shit! Did I miss it?"

Cagney frowned and set aside the formula so she could grip Rus's shoulders and get a better look at her face. A hint of worry colored her tone when she said, "Did you forget about your date?"

"I didn't forget!" She really hadn't. She'd just . . . . lost track of what day it was, that's all. But if she said that out loud, she'd never ever live it down. Cagney would hang it over her head for the rest of their lives, forever threatening to tell Az to get Rus to do what she wanted. Who knew peaceful druids could be such manipulative bastards? Well, other than anyone who'd ever known a druid personally, that is. "I just got busy."

"Mm-hmm. Sure, you did." But Cagney didn't seem to believe her. Couple that with the fact that she had already started to pull Rus over to the bathroom, and Rus was a grumbling mess. Still, she let Cagney shove her into the shower without too much fuss and spent the next twenty minutes shouting ideas out through the curtain that she hoped Cagney wrote down like she said she was doing.

When Rus finished, her hair wrapped tightly in a towel, Cagney was waiting for her on the edge of her bed, along with Nesta.

"Don't you feel better?" Nesta asked, their smile stretched wide. "Now"—they clapped once, rising from their seat—"to pick out something to wear."

"Oh, come on, it's just Az. I don't need to—" But the words dried up in her throat at the look Nesta shot her on their way to the wardrobe.

"You most definitely *do*. I'm not having all my hard work go to waste." They threw things over their shoulder as they dug around for an outfit to make Rus look presentable. *Good fucking luck.*

"Your hard work? What hard work?" Rus asked, but Nesta ignored her and kept digging.

"Oh, before I forget." Cagney pulled something shiny from her pocket, grabbed Rus's wrist again, and pressed it into her palm. The key was cold against her skin, sharp from where it was freshly cut and unused.

"Thank you?" Rus lifted it to the light to get a better look at it. It wasn't labeled, and she didn't feel any magic humming inside to indicate its purpose. "What is it?"

"The key to my storage shed. Now that you've decided to stay, you can get all your shit out of there." Whatever her face was doing made Cagney huff an annoyed breath. "Don't tell me you forgot what was in there."

"It's not that." It was partially that. It had been over a decade, after all. "I'm not sure what good any of it would be now? I mean, all that tech was late 90s and early 2000s. It doesn't hold a candle to what we've got today."

"You don't want it?" Cagney scowled, her lips peeling back from her teeth in a distinctly threatening expression. "Give it back."

"No!" Rus yelped, tucking the key away in the pocket of her hoodie. "I'll see if I can salvage any of it. Maybe something in there will be useful for this project."

Cagney hummed her agreement, and they both returned their attention to the now near-frantic Nesta, who had emptied most of Rus's wardrobe onto the floor. Including the velvet dress she'd worn to the board meeting a few weeks back, as a statement. She wondered idly why that one was being discarded, but she thought better of asking.

"Find anything?" Rus called, trying to hide her smile.

Not well enough because Nesta ripped their head from inside the wardrobe to glare at her in a way that might have made her expire on the spot if there were any magic behind it. "I think you know perfectly well I did not. Honestly, Rus, what the fuck happened to you?"

Rus shrugged, leaning back onto her hands on the bed. "Function is way more important than style when you're out on the road. Didn't have much call for cocktail dresses and the like while hiking up mountains and spelunking in caves."

"You did *not* go spelunking. You hate enclosed spaces." Cagney laughed.

"Shut up," Rus grumbled, giving her a hard shove that almost sent her over the edge of the bed. "You don't know my life."

"Greer!" Nesta shouted from the door, ignoring the two women entirely.

"What?!" Greer shouted back, just as annoyed as any other time he opened his mouth. Honestly, how someone so grouchy could be . . . whatever he was doing with Nesta and Cagney, Rus didn't know. Surely between him and Cagney, there was too much grump to go around.

"I'm sending you to my place to grab some things." They'd already pulled their phone from their pocket.

Greer made a sound like an irritated grunt, but Nesta must have taken it as a question.

"Just some clothes and stuff. I'm sending you a list."

"Now?" If Rus didn't know better, she'd say he sounded whiney.

"Yes, now." With their tongue between their teeth, Nesta sent off their list then dropped onto the bed beside them. They all waited, listening, as Greer's heavy tread made its way across the house and out the front door. Nesta said, "In the meantime, we have *got* to do something with that hair."

"What's wrong with my hair?!" Rus lifted her hands to touch the towel as if she could hide it and the hair beneath it from Nesta.

Nesta didn't respond, just glanced over at Cagney, who nodded. They each grabbed one of her wrists and dragged her back to the bathroom to do whatever Nesta was thinking with her hair, whether she liked it or not.

Chapter 11

RUS HADN'T WORN high heels in the last five years, maybe longer. There was absolutely no call for them while traveling around the world, and she found—now that her feet were stuffed into a pair that were just this side of too small—she hadn't missed them at all. They were impractical at best, and uncomfortable at worst. Seriously, if she could just—

"Okay, but you look hot," Nesta said, taking a step back to admire their handy work. "Like, you're not my type *at all*, but I'd do you."

"Gross!" Greer shouted from the living room where he and the girls were parked on the couch watching princess movies. Maybe one of those songs would get stuck in his head just as they did in Rus's. That would be justice.

"Let me see! Let me see!" Aihuan jetted around the corner into the kitchen where Nesta and Cagney waited for Rus at the bottom of the stairs, glasses of wine in hand. Skidding to a halt, Aihuan let out a sharp gasp at seeing her Auntie Rus all cleaned up for the first time in . . . maybe ever. "Auntie Rus! You look beeeeeautiful!"

"You really think so?" Rus glanced down at the green satin dress Nesta chose for her. It was too short. There was no way she'd be hiking a mountain or scaling a fence in this thing—like she'd done so many times over the years. Not that she'd be able to in the four-inch heels Nesta practically shoved her feet into. The dress had a sweetheart neckline and no sleeves, and the heavy necklace Nesta added to "complete the look" did little to hide the scars lining Rus's sternum from a nasty bout with a poltergeist a few years back.

I hope Az doesn't notice them. They're ugly.

"Mm-hmm!" Aihuan bobbed, her smile bright. "You look like a princess."

"Not a princess," Meiling said from where she stood behind Aihuan, her smile all teeth. "A badass."

"A'ling, we don't say *ass*." Rus huffed, embarrassment heating the back of her neck. "But . . . really?"

"Really." High praise coming from a teenager who only a week ago had called Rus's favorite sweater a "frumpy mom sack." Which, Rus supposed, kind of fit—it was terribly baggy, and she'd cut holes for her thumbs into the sleeves. But she'd never really thought about how much her clothing choices changed since the girls came into her life.

"A badass princess!" Aihuan cheered, her little fists in the air as she ran toward Rus for a hug. Nesta snickered, and Rus cut them a warning glare.

Scooping her up, Rus pressed a kiss to her cheek, leaving behind a red lipstick print. "We don't say *ass*, Huaner."

"Okay." Although, Rus was sure this wouldn't be the last time she heard the word in the weeks to come. Aihuan had a tendency to pick things up that way, and when it was a word someone told her *not* to use? All bets were off. Rus and Fernando would have a pool before the beginning of the new week as to how long it would take Aihuan to use *ass* in front of someone she really shouldn't, and embarrass them all. Rus bet on seventy-two hours, but she'd been wrong before. "I love you, Auntie Rus."

"And I love you too, little monster. Are you two going to be good for Auntie Cags while I go on my date?" Rus asked, looking over at Meiling, who still stood in the doorway, her hands behind her back as she shifted from foot to foot. Whatever she was thinking, she'd either get around to voicing it, or she wouldn't, but Rus didn't have time to stand there and wait. "A'ling?"

Puffing out her cheeks for a moment, Meiling shook her head, stopped, then seemed to change her mind and nodded instead. After that, it was a couple of quick strides before she was pressing her face into Rus's shoulder, her arms wrapped tight around her middle. "I hope you have fun tonight, Aunt Rus."

Heart in her throat and blinking back the burn of tears that would surely ruin her makeup, Rus ruffled Meiling's hair. "Thanks, sweetie, that means a lot."

"You better go," Meiling mumbled against her leather-clad shoulder. "You're going to be late."

"All right." Sniffling, Rus set Aihuan on her feet. "All right." She gave both girls one final squeeze and headed to the front door to grab her purse.

The girls didn't follow her out, too busy with Nesta, who had asked them what kind of pizza they wanted. But Cagney was right behind her, the doorknob to 157 Mourning Moore in hand as Rus stepped over the threshold.

"I won't be late," Rus said, tugging the collar of her jacket up around her neck. Fuck, it was cold. Even the warming charm in her stockings wasn't warding off the chill. She missed her sweatpants already. "Don't let the girls stay up too late. I know it's a weekend, but I like to keep them on a schedule."

"I know." Cagney leaned against the door, amusement

crinkling her eyes. "You don't need me to come with you so I can give her a shovel talk, do you?"

Rus blew a breath out through her lips, laughing and rocking back, which only made her wobble on the too-high heels. Fuck, she missed her combat boots too. She was going to break her ankle in these damn things. "Nah, I think we're good on that."

Cagney nodded. "Try not to overthink it, yeah?" She shut the door in Rus's face, cutting her off from any hope that she could change her shoes without Nesta noticing.

"Right. Don't overthink it," she mumbled, turning toward the street and making her way down the front walk. "Easy."

THE DOOR CREAKED OPEN TO REVEAL AN ICARUS Ashthorne who was equal parts exactly as Azure remembered her, and totally different at the same time. A dichotomy that maybe should have made her head hurt, but instead made her throat go dry. Where Rus had *always* been achingly beautiful, there was an edge to it now that Azure wanted to cut herself on. Like she wasn't just burning the candle at both ends anymore but had actively thrown the candle into a bonfire and started making s'mores on it. And fuck, if it wasn't doing things to Azure.

"You ready to go?" Rus asked, breaking Azure out of her stupor.

Azure shook herself, forcing her eyes back to Rus's face when they had apparently been lingering on Rus's legs like she'd never seen a pair of legs before in her life. What the fuck was wrong with her? "Yeah, just let me grab my coat."

Her hands were *not* trembling as she struggled with the

buttons on the pale blue peacoat she'd shrugged on overtop of her black jeans and polka dot black-and-white button-up. She was underdressed. She was *so* underdressed. Did Rus think she didn't care about this date? People were going to look at them like this and think they didn't fit together. Not like they used to. She—

"I thought we'd go to a restaurant in Ironport." Rus led the way to where she'd parked Blue in front of Azure's house, her keys flipping around her finger over and over. "Just so, you know, we don't have to deal with . . ." The sentence drifted off, but Azure knew what she meant. Moondale's citizens hadn't exactly done much to hide that Rus was an anomaly in town. Still as much of an outcast as she'd been before she left.

"That sounds nice." Azure smiled, hoping to alleviate some of the tension making Rus's shoulders stiff under her black leather jacket. "I haven't been to many of the restaurants there."

Rus hummed, getting Blue into gear, then they were on the road. They listened to whatever music Blue decided she liked that evening and talked about the girls. It seemed Rus's default setting when she wasn't sure what else to talk about—chat about her girls—and Azure didn't mind. It was nice to hear how they were settling into Moondale. To learn that Meiling was doing well in school, and that Aihuan had even made a friend—who was not a spirit, Rus made sure to clarify, although Azure wasn't aware that was an issue. She made a mental note to ask more on that later as they pulled into the parking lot of one of Ironport's fancier Italian restaurants.

"I hope this is okay," Rus said, running a hand through her hair. It looked like it'd been freshly dyed and sprayed one too many times with a can of hairspray. Her fingers got stuck, and she huffed, "Fucking Nesta and their hair gunk." She shook her head. "Shall we?"

Azure climbed out, wrapping her coat more tightly around herself, and followed Rus up to the door. A smile ticked at the corners of her lips when Rus grabbed the handle. Of all the dates she'd been on, Azure didn't think anyone had ever held the door for her before. Not even when she'd gone out with men. Was she so intimidating that most people didn't think she'd want that common courtesy? Or did Rus just know her that well?

She didn't know when Rus had the time to make a reservation for them, but the hostess had Rus's name, and led them to a table without so much as a second glance. Maybe Cagney had done it for her, or Nesta. It didn't matter. None of it mattered. Because after days of radio silence, she was settled into a booth across from Rus, who looked just as nervous as Azure felt, her long-fingered hands fidgeting.

"It's weird, isn't it?" Rus asked, drumming her fingers on the table. "Us trying this again?"

"It's not." Azure shook her head, passing a menu across to Rus and fixing her with a smile she hoped would make the other woman relax. "Tell me about your radar project for the board. I think I've found some books that might help."

Which was the exact right thing to say, because Rus leaned forward, her hands gripping the edge of the menu. "I'm working on a configuration that could eventually be built into the Moondale wards to work like a weather balloon."

"A weather balloon," Azure repeated, excitement racing through her veins and lifting the hairs at the back of her neck at the spark this lit in Rus. Rus had always loved a project. Loved taking things apart and putting them back together. She was a tinkerer at heart, and Azure would wager she hadn't had a project this big since she'd left Moondale. It was hard to do magic on this scale when one didn't have a place to call home to protect them. "Out of curiosity, why meteorology?"

Clicking her tongue, as if that should have been obvious, Rus leaned back and lifted her menu to look it over. But Azure could tell she was only half paying attention to the words. If Azure knew anything about Rus, she'd pick something she didn't really want just for the sake of getting the wait staff to leave them alone for a few extra minutes. "Because weather prediction is all about understanding air pressure and patterns. And where does negative energy come from, primarily?"

"The dead?" Azure guessed, even though she knew it wasn't correct. She wanted to keep the enthusiasm in Rus's voice going a little longer. And watch as Rus's hands worked in swooping motions, making her jacket creak around her movements. Rus was a natural born teacher, and Azure wouldn't be the first to tell her so. Never so in her element as when she was teaching something to someone. *They'll never let someone who plays with the dead near children, Az,* Rus would say, her tone condescending when talking about something that Azure was beginning to think Rus ought to be proud of. Sure, necromancy was dangerous and could be used for evil, but Azure saw now that the kind of necromancy Rus did was different.

"Ehh," Rus said, lifting a hand to rock it back and forth in the air. "The dead affect it a little, but the primary source of negative energy is the living."

How many times had Rus given this lecture? Azure had personally received it at least twice when they were teenagers and someone complained about all the shades lingering in one place. It always sent Rus into a rage to hear people blame the dead for something that was essentially their own fault. Either Rus didn't remember those lectures, or she was too caught up in her own explanation to notice that Azure had asked a question she already knew the answer to. Azure didn't mind. It was good to see Rus so vibrant, so alive.

"The dead are drawn to certain kinds of energy. And the destructive ones, in particular, are drawn to negativity. So" —Rus grabbed the container of sugar packets from beside the wall and started laying them across the table in something that looked like a road map—"say you've got an intersection, right?" She tapped on the place that looked like an intersection, grabbing another packet to push around the table with her finger.

When did she start making cute little diagrams for explanations? Goddess, could she get any more adorable?

"And there's always accidents there." Another little sugar packet came speeding toward the intersection, not slowing, and crashing into the little Sweet'N Low packet. Rus made a noise that sounded like an explosion with her mouth. "Because there isn't a stop sign. Or because people always ignore the stop sign. Or whatever. What do all those crashes and angry people produce?"

"Negative energy," Azure said, following along with rapt attention.

"Right. Gold star!" Rus grinned, pointing at her with one finger before she went back to her diagram. "Now, say you're a bitter shade looking for a place to set up shop." She grabbed the saltshaker, waved it around, and made a couple *woo woo* noises like a ghost. "You aren't going to go someplace happy, are you? No. You're going to gravitate right toward all that negativity, already festering."

"A nexus."

"Exactly!" Their menus were completely forgotten

between them now, their sole focus the packets of sugar and the saltshaker Rus now waved in a lazy circle around her intersection. "And knowing that, you can use data from town records to predict where a nexus might form."

"Outside of a graveyard."

Rus clicked her tongue, dismissive. "You and I both know damn well graveyards aren't usually the problem. They're for the living to grieve. Why would the dead bother hanging around them? Especially the unmoored, unhappy dead? Nah, graveyard shades are nothing compared to the spirits who set up shop next to high-accident sites."

"So what about the air pressure?" Azure pressed, her mind working over all Rus said. It made sense, it made *so* much sense. So much that Azure was amazed someone hadn't thought of it yet. But then, it would take someone intimately familiar with the habits of the dead to make the connection. Someone who had seen enough of the big wide world and the spirits who haunted it to know what drew them. Someone who *wanted* to find a solution and had enough knowledge of technology and science to apply said solution.

"Oh, that's easy." Rus flapped her wrist, dismissing the question. "Most people wouldn't notice it, but someone who's sensitive does. Negative energy has a distinctly different density. It's why negative nexuses tend to be so cold—because the air pressure is lower."

"I've never noticed it." Amazement lingered in Azure's tone. How couldn't it? Rus *was* amazing. Always had been.

"You wouldn't. Most people don't. It takes someone who's spent years around these kinds of spirits to notice the difference. It's nearly imperceptible." She didn't sound like she was judging Azure for it, just stating facts. "But the tools meteorologists use? They're sensitive enough. And with some tweaking? They'd be perfect! I just need to get my hands on how to build—"

"Have you ladies decided what you'd like to order?" the waiter asked, his eyes flicking awkwardly between them and the mess Rus had made of their table.

"Oh." Rus laughed, looking down at her discarded menu. "Are you ready, Az?"

"Yes, I think so."

Chapter 12

"YOU KNOW," Rus said, pasta stuffed into one cheek like a chipmunk. A gesture that normally Azure might have found disgusting, but was somehow endearingly Rus. Like she couldn't wait to finish chewing before talking to Azure again. A compliment, in a weird way. "I've been going on and on about my work, and I don't think I've asked you, how are you?"

"How am I?" Azure blinked. She reached for her wine glass for something to do, hoping to hide the awkwardness that lingered in her joints at the question. How was she? What did that even *mean*? She hated it when people asked her open-ended questions like that. She never knew what they were looking for.

"Yeah. I mean, since I've been back we haven't really had time to sit and chat like this. So like . . . How are you, Az? How's your life? How's the store? What are you up to?" Rus set down her fork, giving Azure her full attention, those gray eyes sharp and searching. Azure wriggled; she'd forgotten how much she felt like a cell on a microscope when Rus looked at her like that. It had been so long, so *very* long. The rake of Rus's eyes over her face was enough to make Azure feel over-warm in her long-sleeved shirt, the wine sitting blazing hot in her belly. Goddess, she had missed that look. Even for how it was uncomfortable at times, being the person Rus focused on was exhilarating. "You know all about what I was up to while I was gone."

Which wasn't entirely true—she didn't. Rus hadn't told her everything, but Azure could guess at most of it. And the rest . . . Maybe it was better she not know. "So, I want to know what was up with you while I was gone."

"Nothing really," Azure mumbled, taking a gulp of wine that burned all the way down for the size of it. "Just running the shop."

"Just . . . running the shop?" Rus's face did something Azure had never seen it do before, twisting like she'd swallowed something foul. Disgust. That hurt but wasn't entirely surprising considering the circumstances. What *did* hurt and what *was* surprising was the disappointment that chased the disgust. There was fire under Azure's skin, shame racing through her. "You haven't been working on spellcrafting? Haven't played around with any of your talismans?"

Azure refused to lower her head, but she couldn't look at Rus anymore. She couldn't watch as every ounce of esteem Rus might have once held for her bled away. "Running Elwood's takes up most of my time."

"But your talisman work has always been—"

"A hobby." The word was bile in the back of her throat. No one had ever told her it was a hobby, not in so many words. But there had been teachers at Moondale U who had implied as much. Said there was no reason to pursue it. That it wouldn't go anywhere. That the power of talismans didn't hold a candle to things like potions and mastery of the oldest, most complex spells. So what was the point? They'd also implied there was no need for spellcraft in this day and age. That every spell of use had already been made. That she should turn her attention to more *important* things. So, even if Azure had found interest in spellcraft and talisman work, she'd set them aside to run Elwood & Co. as her aunts and her sister expected.

"Az," Rus said, her tone exasperated, hands tightened to fists on top of the table as if it took everything within herself not to reach out and shake Azure until her teeth rattled. Funny. Azure had the exact same notion only a few weeks ago when she watched Rus run herself ragged to protect her family without help. Maybe they were *both* idiots. "It was never *just* a hobby. You're too talented to—"

"Talented, but not creative. Not like you." Azure shook her head, ducking it to stare at her plate as she spoke the truth. For all she had the skill, built up over time, and dedication—hours of hard study. For all she'd always excelled to the point of being top of her class. For all she'd proven again and again how capable she was. She'd never had Rus's creative genius. Rus was a whirlwind of potential. In her hands, harebrained ideas turned into possibilities. Not *just* possibilities, but something of use. Something no one had thought of before but suddenly everyone needed. Like this negative forces radar. Azure had no such talent. "Nothing I made has ever—"

"Stop doing that!" The plates clattered, the table jolting under Rus's angry fists. When Azure looked up again, she found Rus's eyes blazing. Real fury embedded deep in the crease of her brow.

"Doing what?" Azure frowned, wanting to recoil from the rage burning too bright off Rus. She didn't think she ever had Rus's fury directed at her that way. Yes, they fought in the past. But those seemed petty squabbles compared to whatever this was. Azure didn't understand what she'd done wrong.

"Holding yourself back!" Rus bit out the words like every one of them was bitter on her tongue, her nose scrunching up at the smell of them. She'd leaned forward, so she could hiss her next words at Azure like they were the vilest thing she'd ever said before, and she ran her tongue along her teeth as if she were testing their bite. "You've spent your whole fucking *life* watering yourself down for the people around you. Making yourself less than what you are. And where has it gotten you?"

Azure hunched her shoulders, trying to make herself a smaller target for Rus's rage, but it didn't stop Rus, didn't stop the words and the truth of them landing like a knife blow against Azure's skin. Rus was right. Where *had* it gotten her? What had it *lost* her? Everything.

"A degree you didn't choose," Rus continued, dismissive—her voice unlike Azure had ever heard it before—not once stopping to notice how Azure's eyes burned with tears. Or maybe she noticed. Maybe she didn't care. That was more likely. It wasn't possible that Rus wouldn't notice. She'd never missed something like that before. "A store you don't want. A legacy that isn't *yours*." It landed like a slap across the face, stinging and violent. Rus was right. Azure had sold her legacy for what? For— "Stuffing yourself into a box of someone else's design won't make them love you."

Azure sat up straight, her eyes narrowing on Rus as her own anger simmered hot in her belly. She'd had just enough wine to make her reckless, stupid, defensive. To make the cut of Rus's words bleed like she'd hit an artery. And maybe it hurt more because Rus was right. She was fucking *right*, Goddess damn it.

"If that's what you think of me, maybe you're right. Maybe we shouldn't have bothered trying this again. You don't want to go out with a"—she hesitated, licking her lips, the word on her tongue gloopy and heavy—"a *loser*, like me."

"I didn't say—" Rus's brows lifted, confusion etching itself into her face, and Azure had to wonder if she meant to say any of what had just come from her lips. But it all felt so pointed. Rus had drawn so many of Azure's insecurities to light. There was no way Rus hadn't meant for those words to do the damage they'd done, because people didn't just say things like that. To wreak the havoc they'd wrought. And hadn't Azure heard them before? Or maybe not *heard* them, but wasn't that the implication—always—when it came to Violet? That Azure wasn't doing enough to live up to the Elwood name? That she would never be enough?

"You didn't have to." Azure shook her head, pulling cash from her wallet without much thought. "This should cover my half of the bill. I'll get an Uber back to Moondale."

"What? No. Az, don't be silly, I'll drive you home."

"No need." She shouldered on her coat and slipped from the booth. What little she'd eaten sat too heavy in her belly. She didn't wait for Rus to try to stop her again. Why would Rus bother when Azure had never reached for *her* to keep Rus from leaving? Just let her walk out the door. More proof that Azure wasn't, and never would be, good enough for Rus.

Even as Rus's muscles burned to push her to her feet and run after Az, she didn't move. Glued to the spot, staring after the pale blue peacoat as it wove through the restaurant and eventually disappeared out the door. She tried to open her mouth, to say something, to call after Az, but the words dried up on her tongue. Her body, heavy like lead, slumped further into the seat. Her mind was hazy as if she'd had too much wine.

You still have to pay the bill, her mind supplied helpfully, or unhelpfully, depending on how a person looked at it. *You can always apologize later.*

But could she really? What she said was inexcusable. And . . . And she didn't even know where it had *come* from! Yes, there was a part of Rus—a not-so-small part—that was frustrated with Az and how she seemed to have stagnated. Az could do better; she knew that from experience. And the fact that Az allowed people to make her think otherwise— let someone diminish her accomplishments—infuriated Rus to a point where even destruction might not be enough to quell her rage. But none of that had ever been directed *at* Az, nor should it be. She'd—she'd *fucked up*.

Don't you always?

"Good job, Rus." Her head bowed, resting in her hands as a headache started behind her eyes, pressure like she'd only ever known when dealing with aggressive spirits. Stress, she surmised, and wished she hadn't driven. Then she could get a glass of wine or two for herself. But that would likely only make her feel worse anyway, wouldn't it?

"Can I get you anything else?" The waiter had returned, doing his level best not to look at the spot Az had vacated. Which was kind of him, but it made him look more awkward than it might have otherwise.

"Just the check," she said, forcing the words out through a throat too tight with emotion.

"No dessert?"

"Just. The. Check." Rus raised her head to glare at the kid who made a soft *meep* before scurrying off to get her check. "Smooth. Real smooth, Rus." Because scaring teenage customer service workers was totally necessary, and a thing she should be doing. Fuck. She was a mess. She couldn't even go on a fucking date and act like a normal person for an hour.

With a soft click, the waiter set down the check and backed away quickly. Poor kid. She'd have to leave him a *big* tip. Her fingers trembled a little, aching in that strange way they did sometimes when it was going to rain or snow. Goddess above, she was getting old.

She paid the bill then headed out to her car. The sky had grown cloudy since she'd been inside, the air taking on that cold crispness that could only mean one thing. "Smells like snow."

By the time she reached 157 Mourning Moore, the flurries had started. They wouldn't stick—it had been too warm during the day—but that meant that there was some danger of ice in the morning. She'd have to be careful when she went out to grab the mail and check on Darcy.

Blue idled at the stop sign at the intersection of Mourning Moore and Grimwood Lane, right across the street from 154 Mourning Moore—the Elwoods' place. It was beautiful with the snow coming down, fluttering in fluffy white flakes, Maureen and Carmine's place lit up like some kind of sparkling gingerbread house straight out of a fairy tale. They always won the light competition, every Yule. And 157 Mourning Moore, just caddy-corner to their place, couldn't hold a candle to it with its one short strand of lights across the rail of the porch. There hadn't been time yet to decorate more, but the girls wanted to.

There were no cars coming, but Rus stayed there, idling at the four-way stop, looking up at 154 Mourning Moore. She could see Az's window from the street, the lights on inside, but that was the only indication that Az had made it home safe. No shadows danced across the gauzy curtains, no music broke the soft hush of snowfall.

How long could Rus stay there, idling, before it became weird? Just sitting, watching Az's window, hoping for some sign that she was all right. Hoping the girls would be asleep by the time she reached her own house.

Blue sputtered softly, irritable with the stillness, and Rus huffed. "Fine. We'll go home. You don't have to be a bitch about it." She released the break and took the turn down Mourning Moore toward 157, where only judgment awaited.

The stairs creaked under her, and Rus had just enough time to clock Cagney sitting on the porch so she didn't scare the living shit out of her before Cagney said, "You're home early."

Grinding her teeth together, Rus sucked in a breath of air that was too cold by half and seemed to freeze her lungs. "Yeah, well, I've got work to do. So."

Cagney hummed, and Rus heard the judgment in it. Great. Just what she fucking needed after the night she'd had. The pressure behind her eyes grew more insistent, like it might push her eyeballs from their sockets. Silence stretched for an uncomfortable amount of time before Cagney said, "I saw Az come home in an Uber."

Rus did not want to talk about this. She didn't think she'd *ever* want to talk about this. But she definitely didn't want to while standing out in the cold on her front porch, with Cagney looking down her nose at her. As if Cagney knew fuck all about Rus's relationship with Az. As if she knew fuck all about relationships *period*. What? Was she some kind of expert now that she was in one? Or two, rather? "I don't have time for this."

"All right," Cagney said, surprising Rus. She never backed down that way. But maybe she could see how the upset lingered in Rus's bones, making it almost impossible to keep herself upright. "The girls are still up. They wanted to welcome you home."

Nodding, Rus took another deep inhale and pulled herself upright, straightening her shoulders. She pasted on a smile that tasted like a lie and headed inside to greet her girls. Because what else was she supposed to do? Hide out on the porch with Cagney until they'd fallen asleep? Well . . . she could . . .

Coward.

The door to 157 Mourning Moore creaked open, hitting Rus with the warmth and light of the home she was building for her girls. It took all of seven seconds for them to notice her and come running, nearly bowling her over with hugs and questions. Helpless under the tide of their excitement, Rus did everything in her power to try to make it seem like she wasn't a complete failure.

But it's only just pretend, isn't it, Rus?

Yeah. It was.

Just another lie she'd tell the people around her to cover for her own inadequacies. What was one more?

Chapter 13

THROWING herself headfirst into her work seemed the only way to deal with the gaping hole Az left behind. Rus should have been used to that hole. It should have been an old, familiar ache in her chest. It had been there since the first time she left Moondale and lost Az.

Hadn't it been Rus's fault then? Wasn't it her fault now?

But this was more raw than that age-old ache.

Like her feelings for Az had shifted over the last few weeks since returning to Moondale. Morphed into something deeper. Which seemed impossible as she'd once upon a time thought she was as in love with Az as she could be with anyone. But this was . . . different.

Rus shook herself. Now wasn't the time to think on that. It had already been two weeks since the meeting with the board. She had less than a month to do the impossible. Less than a month to prove her worth to a group of people who would sooner chase her from Moondale with pitchforks than accept her among their ranks. And what did she have to show for it?

Nothing.

Because that's what you are. Nothing.

"Shut up," she grumbled to the voice in her head, the one that sounded like a strange echo of herself. She didn't have time for regret and second guessing. There was too much work to do. Much too much.

And besides, she'd already burned that bridge, hadn't

she? Fucked up whatever was left of her and Az's relationship and made it unsalvageable. Or . . . was it?

If it was salvageable, she would have called you. Texted. Checked in. She hasn't, has she?

"No. She hasn't." Rus scrubbed at her face, trying not to focus on how those words echoed, empty and hollow in her chest. There were more important things, anyway. She couldn't think about romance when she had her girls to think of and protect.

The little box of wires and circuits under her fingers sparked, shocking her. Rus jerked back with a yelp. Lifting one hand to her mouth to suck on her singed fingertips, Rus glared down at the box. It was meant to attach to a balloon that would drift through the air above Moondale. Not the most high-tech of options, all things considered, but Rus didn't plan to reinvent the wheel. She never had, even if people treated her like some kind of genius. Why create something entirely new when she could build on other people's inventions instead? Adapt them to be what she needed. And weather balloons worked, for all that people didn't know much about them.

A satellite or tying it directly into the wards would be better, but it would take longer. Maybe once she had time to tinker and better translate the data the balloon collected to a radar that any layperson could read, then she could work up to a satellite. There were global implications with this invention. It wouldn't just benefit Moondale and her Board of Magic—anyone could use it. If she released the method. It would—

"Icarus Ashthorne." Cagney bit out the name as if she'd repeated it at least three times and Rus hadn't heard.

"What, Cags? Can't you see I'm busy?" Rus didn't look away from the little box in front of her. If she could get the damn magic to meld with it how she wanted, it would save them all a lot of trouble. She could feed the readings through a predictive algorithm, and that predictive algorithm could create alerts that could be sent to a phone. Good. "They won't be happy with that," she muttered to herself. Not enough. No. What the board wanted was a map they could view in real time that would show them the fluctuations and predictions of the energy movements. And Rus would give them that, would prove she was worthy of the space she took up.

"When did you eat last?" Cagney sounded like she already knew the answer to that question, but Rus wasn't going to dignify Cagney's scolding tone with her attention.

"I had Chinese with the girls."

"That was two days ago, Icarus." Cagney huffed, exasperation in every word. She was beside Rus before Rus even heard her footsteps cross the attic.

"Okay, but I definitely had some of Huaner's carrot sticks when I made her lunch earlier."

"That's not—Rus. You need to eat something."

"I'm right on the verge of something big, Cags. I know it." It hummed in her bones, the certainty of it. She was on the edge of understanding, of making it work. She just needed to get the right combination of spellwork and characters. Something to hold the magic in the circuits, but not let it override the electronics. A tricky balance. One she had to find over and over for every device she worked with. The balance of magic was different on a phone than it was on a tablet than it was on a computer. Each one needed to be set together in a way that best fit the circuitry inside, even between brands and models. Which meant her work was never ending.

"Rus," Cagney tried again.

"Cags," Rus said, pulling her gaze away from the box of wires, which had thankfully stopped sparking now that Rus wasn't applying magic to it anymore. She wondered if a different model would receive the spell better. Or maybe she should try a different thickness of wires. Copper was always good, but some spells required heavier wires to better let the magic flow along them. Shaking herself, Rus forced her mind back to what she'd been about to say to Cagney. "I've almost got it. If I stop now, I'll lose all my progress. Just let me get the spellwork running through it, and then I'll take a break before I start on the app coding."

Cagney bit her lower lip, chewing it for a moment as she considered her options, then nodded. "I'll bring you up something. You can't survive on coffee alone."

"Can to!" Rus squawked, affronted at the insinuation. She'd sustained herself on caffeine before. But even as she thought that, her stomach gave an unhappy gurgle at all the acid churning away in its depths.

Cagney cut her an unimpressed look and turned on her heel to head back downstairs. The silence of her absence stretched on too long, making Rus's nerves jittery, jumping under her skin like grasshoppers or fleas. Then the box sparked again, nipping at her fingertips, and Rus turned her attention back to her work.

ACROSS TOWN, IN THE DEPTHS OF ELWOOD & CO.'S storeroom, Azure Elwood struggled to focus.

The urge to text Rus and at least check in, follow up, see if she'd cooled down, sat like a physical itch against Azure's skin. She *needed* to know. But Rus's words still stung. Her little diatribe about what a complete failure Azure was played on repeat in the back of her mind as she lugged boxes and reorganized books. Then there was the lingering threat. The body of that poor bluebird burned into her mind, although maybe not as much as the wild look on Rus's face as she ripped Azure down to her core insecurities.

Without the added stress of Rus and the mess of their bid for a new coven taking up her time, Azure had been able to get the holiday displays finished in plenty of time for the Black Friday rush that weekend. So maybe it was better they had fought. Better that Rus told her exactly how she felt about Azure before they got too deeply into whatever they were. Before Azure allowed herself to fall too much. Now that she knew, she could refocus herself and reassess her priorities. Maybe figure out how to tackle the sticky *stuck* feeling lingering in her bones.

Her phone buzzed for perhaps the seventh time in the last hour. Rolling her eyes, Azure dug in her pocket to pull it out and glare at the chain of notifications from Indigo, Greer, and even Nesta. Weird. Every one of them wanted to know what happened with Rus. If she'd talked to Rus since. If she knew what was going on with Rus's big project. Or *something* to do with Rus.

With a scoff, Azure put the phone back where it came from, debating putting it on sleep mode. She didn't have time to worry about what Rus was doing. She had responsibilities.

Get back to work, a voice that sounded vaguely like Violet's said in the back of her mind. It grated against Azure's nerves, but she couldn't say her sister was incorrect. Nor could she say she disagreed. Violet was right. If she was going to take the Jade Waters seat on the board, she needed to start acting like it, taking herself more seriously. None of that entailed chasing after a woman who clearly wanted nothing to do with her anymore.

"You're not answering your fucking *phone*," Indigo

snarked from the door to the storeroom, his dark hair artfully covering one eye. It did nothing to hide the irritation written across his face, lingering in the twitch of his tightened jaw. "I thought you were dead back here."

Dramatic. Azure scoffed. "Not dead. Just busy."

"Too busy to answer a text?" Indigo leaned against the doorframe, his arms crossing as he lifted a brow. He was composing himself into something careful and guarded. Whatever he'd come for, he was gearing for a fight. Fan-fucking-tastic.

"Yes," Azure said, succinctly, and returned to the box of tarot cards she'd been unpacking. They sold an unreasonable amount of them to tourists during this time of year, but she wasn't going to think too much about the lack of ethicality in allowing tourists to play with magics they didn't understand. Thankfully, there wasn't much someone without magic could summon with things like spirit boards and tarot cards. Minor inconveniences compared to what Rus could do with them.

There she is again, Azure chided herself, shaking her head.

"So I was walking by the marina today . . . ." Indigo sat on top of one of the boxes, not bothering to check what was inside and if it might be fragile. He probably already knew, thanks to his abilities. But that didn't make his disrespect toward their inventory any less irritating. "And I ran into Ms. Virnan."

Azure made a soft sound in the back of her throat that she hoped he didn't mistake as curiosity. Because she was *not* curious what Nixie would talk to Indigo about. For all Azure knew, Nixie kept to herself. Her bungalow on the water too small to even have guests. Not that Azure thought Nixie spent much time there when the bay stretched right outside her door.

Indigo, it seemed, didn't care if she was interested because he continued talking as if she hadn't reacted at all. "She wants to know why you haven't updated your application for the Coven of the Forgotten."

"Updated it how?" Like she didn't know. Like she wasn't intimately aware what Nixie thought she ought to do. She gripped the box in her hand hard enough that it dented under her fingers. Fuck. She'd have to discount that deck, or gift it. Did someone need a new deck for Yule? Not Indigo. Violet didn't play with tarot; she said she didn't want to know the future. Maybe one of the girls? Meiling was getting old enough to receive her first deck, if her parents hadn't handed one down to her yet.

"You know how." The flat quality to Indigo's voice leant itself to annoyance. Azure had heard that tone plenty of times. Usually directed at Violet when she was being particularly dense, or at Indigo's familiar, Emma, when she was being uncooperative. Azure didn't care much for that tone being directed her way, but there was nothing for it. She wasn't going to give in. She wasn't going to have this discussion, not right now. Not while the wound was still fresh.

"When did you run into Nixie?"

Pinching the bridge of his nose, Indigo let out a long annoyed groan. "You can be just as bad as Vi when you want to be. Do you know that?"

Azure shrugged and hooked her chin over a tall stack of tarot card boxes to take them out into the store. She kind of hoped Indigo wouldn't follow, would just sit and wait for her to return, but she knew him better than that. He was never the sit-and-wait type. That had always been Azure's modus operandi. And look where it had gotten her.

"Why are you still only sponsoring the Coven of the Forgotten?" Indigo pressed, refusing to let his perceived advantage lapse. Apparently, it didn't matter if Azure wanted to talk about this or not—they were talking about it. Thankfully, the store was closed, so there wouldn't be an audience for the fight that may very well ensue. Goddess, Azure was so fucking tired of fighting with everyone. With the board. With Rus. With Violet. With Indigo. It felt increasingly like everything she did went against the grain of the world around her, whatever path she chose.

As if you've ever made the right choice before. Why start now?

"I can't be in two covens at the same time. There are rules against it in the Moondale Code of Magic." She'd checked weeks ago, when this had first come up. Praying to the Goddess that there was some way around it. Some way to maintain her status in Jade Waters while also giving Rus what she needed. The Goddess had not answered her prayers, as she so frequently didn't. And Azure concluded that she had two choices: leave Jade Waters, or remain merely a sponsor for the Coven of the Forgotten. Her conversation with Violet had sealed that, the word *selfish* haunting her every step like a phantom.

"So?" Indigo asked, insolent as ever. Because he was the baby and he'd never had to think about things like reputation and responsibility. Because as the nephew of Aunt Maureen—who was an Elwood by marriage—he was an Elwood only in name, and he didn't understand the weight that name carried for her and Violet. Azure knew it wasn't right, wasn't fair, but she equal parts envied and loathed her little brother for that freedom.

"So, that means to do what Nixie thinks I ought to, I'd have to leave Jade Waters." It was as simple and complex as that, and the knowledge sat heavy in the pit of her stomach like a lead weight, threatening to drag her to the floor at any moment. She was failing everyone, *everyone*, in so many ways.

Indigo seemed to shrug off the enormity of that statement as he might have an ill-fitting piece of clothing. "Then leave Jade Waters."

"I can't do that." She couldn't. She'd already made up her mind. She'd considered it, but Violet was right—she couldn't. Jade Waters was her home. She'd been born into the coven. It ran through her veins. If she left, where would she be? Cast adrift. The Coven of the Forgotten would take her, gladly, but it would forever be an uphill climb with them, no matter what she did. And for what? For Rus to dismiss her at every turn? No thank you.

"Why can't you?" Indigo couldn't let things lie, as always. Azure should have known better, thinking she'd give him one-line answers and chase him away with her continued movement. He was persistent. A hound dog of a personality once he had the scent of something. And she had little doubt he could sense the turmoil roiling through his sister. It would be endearing if it wasn't so fucking *annoying*.

"Because I have a duty to Jade Waters, a responsibility. It'd be selfish of me to leave them behind just because of—" She pressed her lips together and bit down on them. She wasn't ready to expose that jagged, ugly part of herself. The part that said she'd done everything for a piece of tail. The voice that said she wasn't thinking with her head at all, but with some other part of her anatomy. That what she was doing for Rus didn't *mean* anything other than she needed to get laid. The voice, however loud, didn't sound like her own. But she was starting to wonder if it was right.

There was another voice. A quieter voice. A voice that sounded like her but much younger. She could hardly hear it over the other one, but it reminded her that maybe Rus had a point—she needed to stop making herself fit into a box for other people. Maybe Rus had a point that she should follow her passion. Maybe Rus and the new coven would finally set her free from the expectation of the Elwood name and allow her to chase her curiosity.

Narrowing his brown eyes, Indigo watched her closely, but he didn't ask her what she'd been about to say. Because he was good like that, sometimes. Instead, what he said next was so much worse. "Are those your words, or are they Vi's?"

"Mine." She wouldn't admit otherwise, not in front of Indigo. Because she knew exactly what he'd do with that information, and Azure was done with the fucking drama.

Indigo's stare was penetrating enough that Azure had to resist the urge to squirm beneath it. Aunt Maureen always said it was a byproduct of his ability. Being able to see the history of an object, to hold it and know it down to all its moving and unmoving parts, made a person see things differently than others. Just how Azure's ability sometimes made her see the world at a distance, like looking through a window. Or how Rus's had always made her more sensitive to the energies of those around her, even the living.

Either way, Azure didn't care for Indigo using his powers on her that way. Picking her apart into the pieces that made her up as if that would make him understand her better. It was invasive, and he had to know that. But he didn't stop.

"I don't believe you," Indigo said, after staring at Azure for too long as she moved around the display she'd been working on. The display still wasn't quite right, but her focus was split, so she couldn't perfect it until Indigo fucked off and let her get back to what she'd been doing.

"I didn't ask if you believed me." Irritation made the words sharp, her glare cutting Indigo from the corner of her eyes.

Silence beared down on them for a beat, and Indigo

frowned. *"Fine.* Be that way." He pushed to his feet and made his way to the door, shoulders pulled too taught beneath his coat. Azure didn't call him back. Just as she didn't call Rus back at the coven house weeks ago. Because that wasn't a thing Azure *did*, apparently.

Apparently, she let people walk away from her.

The door to Elwood & Co. swung shut, making the bell jingle over it merrily, and Azure was left with nothing but the rushing of cars passing on the street for company. That was fine. That was better. She had work to do anyway. Right?

Still, maybe she should check in with Rus and see how the radar was going . . .

Chapter 14

FUCK, it was cold. Was the heater off? Had Rus left a window open in her haze of work and too much coffee? She must not have made it to bed last night either. Her back ached from sleeping on the hard attic floor. Because *that's* what she needed right now — more aches.

Pushing herself up to a seat, Rus's fingers met the scratchiness of scraggly scrub grass and dirt. That wasn't right. Why would there be grass and dirt on the attic floor? Through her lashes — still glued mostly shut by sleep-gunk — Rus could barely make out what was around her, but she knew it was not her attic room of 157 Mourning Moore. It was not the heavy fourposter bed set in the corner of two charcoal-and-slate striped walls, blankets thrown haphazardly about. It was not her desk in the alcove where one window resided. It was not the dark stained hardwood floors. It was . . .

Outside. She was outside. The watery light of too-early morning hit her from all directions as cold and wet seeped into her bones through her thin pajama shorts. Shorts had been a stupid fucking idea, and a shiver wracked her spine painfully.

It took scrubbing at her eyes three times before she finally cleared the sleep from them enough to open her lids more than a crack, and when she did, she regretted even bothering.

"The graveyard," Rus groaned to herself, her head hanging forward. "That's a new one."

And she hadn't even been drunk last night. Although sleep deprivation and too much work could make a person act inebriated too—had made her act that way before. But that wasn't what this was. This was . . .

She smacked her lips, the flavor of sulfur clinging to her tongue.

"Fucking hell, I'm possessed. *Again*?" Scrapes on her palms stung as she braced herself on the ground to push to her feet, but she ignored them. Scrapes were the least of her worries. She'd have to check for more serious injuries once there was a locked bathroom door between herself and the rest of the house. There was also the matter of what this little fucker had done to her magic. Maybe that's why she couldn't get the spell to catch on the weather balloon.

"Three weeks to D-day and I'm fucking *possessed*," Rus muttered to herself bitterly, stumbling across the scraggly graves back to 157 Mourning Moore. She didn't have time for this shit. The Board of Magic wasn't exactly going to give her an extension because some shithead spirit had decided to hitch a ride the last time she'd stepped over the veil. They'd see this as an excuse for why they shouldn't let her run a coven. They couldn't trust her. Couldn't trust her methods. Necromancy, as they said before, a million times over, was evil. Had consequences. Was bad for the body and the soul.

Temples throbbing, Rus scuffed barefoot across the kitchen floor, hoping she didn't leave too much dirt behind, and tip-toed up the back steps. 157 Mourning Moore hid her tracks for her, muffling any creaking stairs or floorboards, and she had a door between herself and the rest of her family in a matter of minutes. The lock on the door in place, she frantically searched for her phone while the bath water ran.

She finally found it after searching under the bed, in the nightstand, in the covers, and on her desk. Strangely enough, it was hidden away in the wardrobe beneath a pile of dirty laundry. And it had a spiderweb crack right in the middle of the screen. At least one text notification flashed on it, but she couldn't tell who the text was from or what it said.

"Seriously? You *had* to break my phone?" She smacked her head against the wardrobe door, loosing a long exhale. There was nothing for it—she'd have to get a replacement. Sure, she could replace the screen herself, but who knew what damage the little bastard had done to the internals in its rage. The screen turned on, but that didn't mean anything. Goddess, she hoped she hadn't lost any of her pictures or videos.

"You better hope it was all backed up," she warned the spirit she just now noticed on the edge of her awareness. It clung, oily and slick, against her very essence. A piece of herself that most witches maybe weren't so in tune with, but when one cut a part of it out to give life to another, they became intimately aware of its existence and how it *should* feel. "Or I'm turning you into a battery. Fuck what the board thinks about it."

"Rus?" Fernando's voice came through the door, soft and tentative, his fingers rapping gently enough on the wood that Rus almost didn't hear the knock above the sound of the water in the tub.

The water! Fuck, it better not have overflowed.

"Are you all right in there?" Fernando pressed. He hadn't tried to open the door yet, and he wouldn't unless he thought she was in danger. He'd walked in on her doing more than one ritual that made his hair stand on end. Necromancy was a messy business.

"Yeah, but can you do me a favor?" She rushed to the bathroom to shut off the water. Another couple of minutes, and she'd have been giving the room below her a shower. 157 Mourning Moore would have been pissed about that. And she did not need a pissed off house on top of a possessed body, a broken phone, and a girlfriend—ex-girlfriend? Someone she was dating? What the fuck *was* Az to her now?—who wasn't speaking to her.

"Sure." Fernando was always ready to help. He was too good, in Rus's opinion, to have attached himself to a fucked-up mess like her. But she was grateful for him, every day of her life. Grateful that she'd reached out to him on that covenless forum and made friends. Grateful that she'd pulled him out of his shell, and he'd agreed to move to the States with her and the girls. Grateful that he never once blanched at the knowledge that they were running. Really, he was the best friend a girl like Rus could ask for.

"Text Cags and Phyre, and see when we can get them over here for a cleansing ritual." The spirit in her shifted, unsettled and unhappy at the implication of what she'd just said. If it could get control while she was awake, it probably would have tried. But that was the thing with these kinds of possessions—they usually couldn't get control of her while she was conscious. They could affect her mood, sure, which explained a lot about what happened on her date a couple weeks back, and her continued crankiness. But they couldn't seize control of her body while she was awake. Usually.

Fernando hummed, shifting just outside the door, likely pulling his phone from his pocket and doing as asked of him. "Picked something up?"

"Nothing high level. Three folk should do the trick." As

she closed her eyes, her magic poked at the slick black soul clinging to her. It gave a gurgle of annoyance but didn't otherwise fight back. It probably didn't have the energy to do much during the daytime. *Yeah, three folk will definitely do it.* "Probably caught it when I was in Ironport on that job for the sheriff."

"Probably. But just to be sure, I'm having Indigo take Huaner to school this morning." There was no room for argument in his tone, even if it was gentle and quiet, and Rus was struck all over again by how lucky she was to have him. "I'm not leaving you alone with this thing."

Slumping against the door, Rus let out a soft, breathless chuckle. "Thanks, Nando. You're the best."

"You bet your boots I am." It sounded like he was smiling. "Do you need anything for the bath?"

"No. I have supplies up here from the radar project that'll work. Just get the girls ready." Chewing on the inside of her cheek until she tasted blood, Rus pressed the heel of her hand against her suddenly throbbing forehead. Maybe the spirit would give her more of a fight than she thought. Or maybe her headache was from the lack of caffeine for the last few hours. Caffeine hangovers were the worst. "Don't tell them what's up with me. Yeah?"

A soft noise of irritation left the back of Fernando's throat. He didn't like lying to the girls, never had. Rus could understand that—she didn't care for it either. And they were both clever enough to see through any lie thrown at them. Which was a real pain in the ass about half the time.

"I don't like it either," Rus said, giving voice to what she was sure was going through his head. "But spirits still freak out A'ling. Imagine how afraid she'd be if she found out one could piggyback on her without her consent?" A hazard of being a medium, especially one with a low spiritual threshold, that Rus had grown accustomed to at an early age.

"They need to be prepared."

"They do. But not today, Nando. Not when everything is so uncertain. Let them feel safe for a little while longer. At least until I'm sure Moondale will protect them when needed." Goddess above and below, she was tired. So tired. Whatever the spirit had done with her body the night before had worn her the fuck out. But she couldn't fall asleep, not before she banished it. "Please, Nando, let them have this."

"Fine." Fernando sounded tired too, but his next words had a tone of determination. "But once the coven is settled, we're starting medium training."

"That was always the plan, Nando." It was. Already, she had worked with Meiling. That had been part of why Meiling's parents had chosen Rus to be her moonmother, neither of them were mediums. Meiling needed someone who could teach her about the world of the dead and how to protect herself from it. Meiling knew enough to keep herself safe in a general sense. But Rus hadn't felt comfortable taking her beyond the veil. Not yet. Rus's own first trip was traumatic. A guide would make all the difference, but Meiling wasn't ready. Not yet. Not after how her parents had passed—ripped apart by spirits. She might *never* be ready. Rus hoped that wasn't the case.

"Go take your bath." Fernando's phone dinged, and she heard him pull it from his pocket again to check the text. "Cagney and Phyre will be here in forty-five."

"Okay." Rus unlocked the door before he could tell her she needed to—because she wasn't an idiot—and turned back to gather what she'd need for the cleansing bath.

THE BATH DID NOTHING TO UNLATCH THE SPIRIT lingering on the edges of her awareness. It didn't even seem to loosen its hold, which was unusual but not wholly unheard of. Rus had been possessed enough over the years to see all different kinds of possessions, and some spirits—as weak as they were—could be persistent little shits. This seemed to be one of those.

"I told you not to go through the veil without your talisman." Phyre eyed Rus like she was a particularly errant child. Which Rus supposed was entirely fair. She did know better, and she had done something stupid and reckless in the name of expedience. And she'd have been pissed if anyone else had done the same thing. It just didn't seem to matter as much when it was Rus's life and soul on the line.

Rus shrugged, sheepish, rubbing at the back of her neck. "Lesson learned?"

"I call bullshit." Cagney stood beside Phyre, her arms crossed over her chest, her green eyes narrowed in fury. Where Phyre might have let Rus off with a light scolding, Cagney was not going to do any such thing. It consistently amazed Rus how although she had no family by blood—an orphan from infancy—she had these people. A brother. Sisters. Willing to put their lives on hold, take time off work, drive right over to help her with a cleansing ritual. She could put up with a little pissiness from Cagney in exchange for this. Besides, it came from a place of love. A place of wanting to protect her. And that made it beautiful in its way. "You didn't learn fuck all."

Scrubbing at her face, Rus tried again. "I won't do it again?"

"Also bullshit." Cagney's freckled face had gone red in

her anger, skin almost blending into her hair. "Go on. Tell me another one. I've got all day."

Irritation flared through Rus's veins, words flying to her lips that were not her own, not something she'd say to Cagney ever in her life. She swallowed them with some difficulty, like swallowing a chip she hadn't chewed all the way, cutting and aching all the way down, making her eyes water.

"That thing is an asshole, isn't it?" Fernando asked, features contorted in a frown.

"Lil bit." Rus shot him a self-deprecating smile. She thought for a moment to blame it for everything she'd said to Az. To try to excuse what a bitch she'd been. But she knew she couldn't, not really. She should have had more control than that, even with her lowered barriers. "So can we just move along and get this thing out of me? Please?"

Cagney huffed, like maybe she wanted to continue raking Rus over the coals for her poor life choices, but she didn't say anything else as she took Phyre's and Fernando's hands. The cleansing ritual was simple enough: a circle, a flame, some burning sage, and a number of witches—dictated by the strength of the clinging spirit—to recite the spell. It also didn't take any time at all.

The chanting blurred in Rus's hearing, her vision going blurry as the thing fought to hold its seat like a cowboy on a bucking bull. But Rus was stronger. Her friends were stronger. And after a minute or so of the chanting, something slimy crawled up her throat, and she coughed into the waiting bowl inside the circle. A precaution Rus used in case she was sick during the cleansing.

Some more hacking, the spirit sluggish in her esophagus as if trying to fight its way to keep hold, and it was out. Rus coughed phlegm into the bowl, but there was no trace of the spirit left—just the space where it had lingered, now empty of its residual bitterness.

"Are you all right?" Phyre asked, holding a bottle of water out to Rus. She took it with a murmured thank you before chugging half of it.

"Yeah. We got the little bugger. I'm all clean now." She swished some of the water in her mouth and spat it into the bowl to be sure nothing clung to the inside of her mouth. That had happened only once; a teeny tiny bit of spirit residue clung and made life unbearable for about a week before she noticed it. But it only took once for Rus to learn.

"You sure?" Cagney pressed, holding her hand out to keep Phyre from breaking the circle. She squinted at Rus as if she could see her aura and something lingering on it.

Rus sniffed, giving herself a careful internal once over and coming up with nothing amiss. "Positive."

"Right then." Cagney squatted to open the circle herself. "I think you should apologize to Az."

"Uuuugh." Rus groaned and fell onto her back in the middle of the circle, her arm thrown over her eyes. "You're right."

"She's right," Phyre agreed. She nudged Rus with the toe of her boot, and when Rus pulled her arm away to glare up at her, Phyre was holding out a chocolate chip cookie. "You'll thank us later."

Chapter 15

THE LITTLE BELL over the door to Elwood & Co. jingled merrily, the noise the only warning Azure received before she was ambushed with an aggressively large bouquet of flowers and a beaming Icarus Ashthorne. In her opposite hand, Rus carefully balanced a little cardboard tray with two drinks from Necromancer's, and a scone perched across the empty places for cups.

"I didn't have a white flag, but I found some white lilies at the shop down the street?" Rus's words sounded more like a question. She hadn't moved off the mat put in place for customers to dry their feet on yet, still standing there as if unsure she'd be invited in. Like a vampire.

Azure quirked a dark brow, her gaze lifting from the obnoxiously large bouquet to Rus's face. Her dark brows were pressed together, her gray gaze pleading. "Is that meant to be an apology?"

"No." Shoulder's relaxing, Rus scraped the bottoms of her boots across the rug then sidled over to the counter, sliding the bouquet toward Azure. The flowers were, objectively, beautiful. Not as lovely as something Aunt Maureen would grow in the greenhouse behind 154 Mourning Moore, but pretty nonetheless. Sucking in another breath, Rus said, "This is the apology." A soft *thud-thud* told Azure Rus had kicked the edge of the counter twice, clearing her throat. "I'm sorry for everything I said on our date. It was awful. I was being an absolute bitch. And I have zero excuse for my actions."

"I heard you were possessed." Azure's brow gave a little twitch as if it could possibly lift any higher, disappearing into her hairline. It couldn't. Phyre had texted the evening before to let Azure know what was going on. Probably because Rus's phone was broken by whatever pissy spirit had attached itself to her.

"I was, but that's no excuse." Rus shook her head, strands of pink hair falling into her face from where she'd pulled it back into a hurried ponytail. She looked tired, like the exorcism had taken a lot out of her. If what Phyre said was anything to go by, Azure guessed it had. "So. I'm sorry." She pulled on her most winning smile, the one that made Azure's stomach flutter with butterflies. "Forgiven?"

"Are those for me?" Azure nodded to the drinks and scone instead of answering.

"Only if I'm forgiven," Rus joked, tugging the tray away from Azure's reaching hands as if she might not hand them over.

Azure hummed thoughtfully. "The scone, is it . . . ?"

"Chocolate." Rus scoffed. "I know what my girl likes."

Heart stuttering in her chest, Azure plucked the scone from the tray with a murmured "Forgiven" before stuffing half of it into her mouth, hoping Rus wouldn't notice the heat lingering in her cheeks with Elwood's low lighting.

"Right. Cool." Rus grabbed her own cup and took a hasty sip, hissing when she burned her tongue. Embarrassment flared hotter in Azure's cheeks, her eyes darting away from the charming self-deprecating smile that split Rus's face. Azure was in so much trouble. So much. "So," Rus said, clearing her throat once more, "I want to try again."

"Try again?" *That can mean anything, Azure. Don't get your hopes up.*

"Yeah, another date." Azure's heart galloped along in her chest, threatening to leap up her throat. "Well, sorta." Rus's fingers flexed around the cup she held, nerves making her fidget. "The girls and I are going to put up the Yule decorations this weekend, and we could use a hand. And I figured"—she shrugged—"who better than an Elwood?"

"So not a date," Azure said slowly, sounding the words out like a child. Because she needed to be sure. She needed a label on this thing, whatever they were. With their history, she couldn't languish in the middle ground of "are we just friends?" To face losing Rus again because she hadn't been clear would be unbearable.

"It's not . . . *not* a date," Rus hedged, letting out a nervous chuckle at Azure's pursed lips and narrowed eyes. "Look. I don't know if it is or not, okay? Like, do people have their kids around on dates? When I was dating before, I didn't have kids. So is that a thing people, like . . . do?"

Lifting the cup to her lips, Azure took a slow meditative sip. She'd never dated someone with kids before. And the only person she knew who had children, Phyre, didn't go on dates. As far as Azure knew, Phyre hadn't really dated at all since high school and seemed perfectly happy with that. She had her children and her work at the Ironwood smithy. What else was there? Azure could understand that.

Rus shifted, her hands tapping an unsettled rhythm against the counter as she waited. "So?"

"It's a date," Azure said after a long moment. Although, she'd likely have to discuss this with someone. Phyre maybe? Or Indigo? Maybe Violet? Someone would give her advice, whether they wanted to or not.

"Oh. Okay then." Standing up straighter, Rus fixed her with that sunny smile again, her eyes squinting to accommodate it. "So we'll see you after the shop closes up for the day on Saturday?"

"Friday. Tomorrow." Azure frowned. "Saturday is too busy. I don't know that I'll have the mental bandwidth to decorate after dealing with customers on a weekend. If"—Rus's gaze was too bright, too warm on her face—"if that's all right with you?"

"That's—yeah, that's all right with me." Rus blinked rapidly for a moment, her cheeks heating again. "It's a date."

"It's a date." Azure nodded, trying not to fidget under all that focus.

"So I'll uh—I'll see you tomorrow then?"

"See you tomorrow."

Rus spun, stumbling a little over her own boots as if to make a quick getaway before Azure could change her mind. Then she stopped and spun back to face Azure again. "Before I leave, I just wanted to check in on something."

Tilting her head to the side, Azure released a soft "Hm?" around the last of her scone. That combined with the chai Rus brought, and the knowledge that they had another date scheduled, sat warm in her belly, spreading out through her nerves to make her languid and lazy. She'd get fuck all done the rest of the day, and she didn't care a wit.

"You haven't received any more warnings, have you? No more dead bluebirds with ribbons left on your front stoop?" The cup in Rus's hand looked like it might give under her tightened hold at any moment, the cardboard denting a little. Azure wasn't sure if Rus was upset, nervous, angry, or some combination of the three, but she shifted under the intensity of Rus's stare. There was something there—a dare, maybe, or something else—like she was waiting for Azure to lie to her.

Which, maybe Azure might have if there was anything

to worry about. Because Rus did have her own worries, her own full plate. She shouldn't be wasting valuable time and energy on Azure's safety. "I haven't. It seems that whoever it was has either gotten busy or given up."

Shoulders relaxing, Rus leaned back on her heels. "Good. That's good. You'll tell me if anything else comes up? Right?"

"I will," Azure vowed, without really thinking. And now Azure would have to, because she'd made a promise, and Azure Elwood didn't break a promise. Especially not to Icarus Ashthorne.

"You'll have to come by the house, or text Fernando though, for the time being. That little fucker broke my phone before we got it out. Replacement should be in on Monday." She didn't sound mad about it, just shrugged it off as if it was the price she paid for being a medium. Then, "Anyway, I'll let you get back to work. Bye!" and she was out the door.

Azure stared after Rus, her lips pulled into a smile she hadn't noticed spreading until the moment she was left alone. The foil on the flowers crinkled under her elbow, reminding her that they existed when she'd been unable to really think of them with Rus in the room. Rus, whose brightness outshone lilies.

Laughing to herself, Azure shook her head. "When did you become a poet?" she muttered, lifting the flowers to give them a sniff.

The answer, she assumed, was when she'd fallen in love with Icarus Ashthorne.

So . . . age seven? Eight?

157 MOURNING MOORE WAS A RIOT OF MUSIC AND lights and laughter. Rus still had a lot to do, so much, but she set it aside—at least for the afternoon—so she could focus on helping the girls and Fernando decorate for Yule. Nothing was more important than her family, she reminded herself. Even the board's greed. Besides, she'd finally gotten a prototype together. She just needed to run some tests then set it loose on Greer for him to try it out. Because he was the least tech savvy person she knew; if Greer could use it, then she was set.

Rus stood over the stove, her finger twirling to stir the pot of chocolate on the burner. Meiling had demanded hot chocolate for their "decorating party," as they'd taken to calling it, and Rus could never deny her girls something like this. A small joy in a sea of uncertainty.

"So a date," Fernando teased from where he'd taken over threading popcorn onto a string. The girls had been helping, once upon a time, but whispers and giggles now came from the foyer, echoing down the hall to reach her where she stood. "With Az Elwood."

"Don't start this now, Nando. I'm nervous enough." Rus huffed a breath, the air ruffling the short pink hair that had escaped her ponytail and stuck to her neck from the steam.

"If not now, then when?"

"Never."

"Well, it's not going to be never." He snorted, and when Rus looked at his reflection in the window over the stove, she caught him watching her, his brows pinched together. "You know you don't have anything to worry about, right? You know you're great . . . right?"

The sincerity made her skin feel too tight, stretched taut across bone and sinew like she was a fucking decomposing corpse. Another giggle cut through the air, turning both their heads toward where the girls had disappeared some minutes ago.

"What are you two up to?" She leaned back on her heels, trying to get a look at where Meiling and Aihuan were huddled next to the front stairs, but she couldn't quite see around the kitchen doorframe.

"Nothing," the girls said in unison, which confirmed Rus's suspicions that they *were*, in fact, up to something. Something they thought was hilarious and that she maybe wouldn't notice. Nonsense.

"Nothing, huh?" Rus asked, giving one final twirl of her finger before she lowered the heat on the pot of chocolate and milk. It likely wouldn't curdle for a while so long as it stayed simmering. "Where is this nothing? Show me."

"Nooooo, Auntie Rus," Aihuan squealed, tucking something behind her back so quickly Rus almost missed the dark green in her chubby hands. Meiling stepped in front of her younger sister, shooing Aihuan behind her, likely trying to get Aihuan to run off with whatever it was.

"No, Auntie Rus? No what?" Hands braced on her hips, she came to a stop a few steps from the girls, unable to resist the little smirks they both had. Goddess, Meiling was rubbing off on Aihuan, wasn't she? That was going to be trouble. "You can show me. Ooooor—" She lunged for them, knocking Meiling gently out of the way and scooping up Aihuan to spin her around in a squealing circle of toddler and brightly colored pajamas.

"Give it here, Huaner!" Meiling called, snatching the bundle of greenery from her sister and taking off at a sprint down the hall toward the back door. Aihuan still thrown over her shoulder like a sack of potatoes, Rus skidded after her, going the long way round through the living room, the office, the playroom, in an attempt to cut Meiling off at the kitchen. She just missed Meiling as the back door slammed behind her. Aihuan was a mess of flannel, hair, and giggles in Rus's arms, squirming enough that keeping a hold on her was a struggle.

The doorbell rang, and Rus had to course correct. She spun, leaving Meiling to whatever mischief she was up to, Aihuan slung over her shoulder, and headed for the door.

Chapter 16

BEING short with people was kind of Azure's brand, always had been. She didn't have the bandwidth for nonsense or superfluous pleasantries. That didn't mean she was rude to customers, but it did mean she tried to get them in and out of Elwood & Co. as quickly as possible. Efficient, she liked to think of it. Curt, is what Violet always accused her of.

No matter what it was, Azure was likely even worse than normal on Friday. Which, unfortunately, didn't go unnoticed. She'd received more than one knowing glance. Because this was Moondale, and everyone knew everything about everyone else. Especially when it was something as scandalous as an Elwood fraternizing with a necromancer. *Gasp*.

Indigo probably told Violet, who'd told Taryn, who proceeded to tell *anyone* within hearing range that Azure had a date with Icarus Ashthorne. Because Taryn couldn't resist that level of shock and awe. Thus, the whole of Moondale was abuzz with what it could mean that Azure Elwood was going on a date with Icarus Ashthorne. As if it were any of their fucking business.

Combine that with Azure's anxiety and excitement, and her normally abrupt, short manner became downright brusque. Honestly, Azure was fine with that. She didn't care if people were annoyed with her manner. She never had. And she wasn't outright rude, so they really couldn't complain. She simply used her ability more than usual to see what they needed and hurried them out of the shop, meaning less pleasantries than usual.

By closing time, Azure nursed a serious magic hangover that did nothing to quiet the rush of her thoughts, which had thankfully drowned out any anxiety over the lingering threat. Small mercies. Not that her anxiety was that high to begin with—it'd been long enough. If whoever sent the threat was going to make a move, they would have already. Right?

Pressing her fingers into her eye to try to relieve some of the ache behind it, she looked down to find Lizzie winding between her legs, getting long bits of fluffy white fur all over her stockings.

"Cut that out," Azure hissed, pulling the door to Elwood & Co. shut behind her and locking it with a touch while she balanced a bag of gingerbread muffins on her arm. Said muffins had been the work of an early morning and a little stress-baking, but they were sprinkled in powdered sugar and topped with a tiny gingerbread person, so she didn't think anyone would mind if she brought them along. "I don't want to be a hairy mess for my date."

Lizzie mrowed softly, looking up at her, blue eyes wide and guileless, as if she was fooling anyone. Azure had cleaned up the strewn entrails of the last mouse Lizzie caught; she knew exactly what the cat was capable of.

"No. I don't need a chaperone for my date with Rus." A laughable suggestion. As if Azure and Rus were still teenagers who couldn't control their hormones at all. If anything, they controlled their hormones a little too well these days. She'd missed Rus—the way her touch could set Azure's nerves alight—and she was *still* missing her. For all Rus was right across the street—in not one but *two* instances, because the Goddess thought herself amusing, that bitch—she remained stubbornly out of reach. Azure had never known she could miss someone, body and soul, with that person right beside her. It was ironic, and cruel.

But she wasn't going to push it. Not yet, anyway. Aunt Carmine had been right weeks ago when she'd said Azure needed to take the time and try to find her place in Rus's life. That if there was meant to be space for her, it would open up. And it was. Slowly. Azure just had to be patient. She *could* be patient.

Lizzie trotted along beside her down the sidewalk toward Mourning Moore, wholly unbothered by the cold, probably borrowing some of Azure's magic to keep herself warm. With another soft murmur of a meow, Lizzie's tail twitched.

"Yes, her children will be there. That's precisely why we don't need a chaperone. Not because we're both over thirty and can control ourselves." Sarcasm dripped from every word, and Lizzie seemed unbothered by it, used to her witch's many moods. Goddess, Azure hated being so seen sometimes. Out of all the creatures on the planet, she had to pick a familiar who could see right down to her heart and was more than happy to judge her for all her missteps.

A growl left Lizzie as she leaped over a puddle.

Chatty today, aren't you? Honestly, Azure had to wonder, why? Why was Lizzie bothering? She hadn't taken any interest in Azure's love life before. Well . . . not since Rus left. Rus seemed to be the only one Lizzie was interested in commenting on. Was it because she—like the rest of Moondale and Rus herself—believed Rus wasn't good enough for Azure? Or was there another reason?

"No. You can't come along," Azure said, shaking her head. "I don't want you underfoot."

Lizzie hissed, the hair along her back lifting in warning.

"Go ahead and throw up in my shoe. I'll just lock you

out of my room and you'll have to sleep in the kitchen with Peaches and Elinor. You know Aunt Carmine and Maureen don't let their familiars sleep in their bed." A car rushed by, turning off Main Street toward one of the newer parts of Moondale, and snowflakes fluttered down from the sky, sticking to Azure's lashes. It was the perfect weather for decorating. Even better if she had a warm drink, and a warm body to —

She shook herself.

The silence that followed meant Lizzie had read Azure's thoughts — which was patently ridiculous; familiars did *not* have that ability, they just liked to pretend they did — or she'd been cowed by Azure's threat. Either way, they'd arrived at the intersection between Main Street and the far end of Mourning Moore before Azure realized something vital about this conversation.

"If you want to meet the girls . . ." she hedged, hoping not to set off Lizzie's temper. It was always a gamble poking at Lizzie's emotional state. She was a typical cat that way. One moment she could be as lovey and cuddly as a newborn, and the next she would swipe and hiss, going for the eyes. Maybe Azure should have chosen a dog familiar. She'd thought about it, but cats were Elwood tradition. And she'd already broken enough from it by choosing a *white* cat. "I'm sure they'd like that."

Swishing her tail, Lizzie let out a soft mrow that was all arrogance and broke off at a run toward 154 Mourning Moore, not once slowing to say anything else to her witch.

"Right, of course not." Azure huffed, rolling her eyes. It would have to happen eventually — Lizzie meeting Rus's girls. If Azure got her way, it would be sooner rather than later, and the image of Aihuan and Meiling curling up to watch movies with Lizzie draped across their laps was cozy enough to keep Azure toasty the rest of the way to 157 Mourning Moore.

A squeal rent the air as she approached, followed by laughter, and Azure had a moment to watch Rus spinning Aihuan around like a doll just before 157 Mourning Moore rang its own doorbell. Because of course the house wouldn't allow her a moment to treasure what she was seeing. It made the longing buried deep in her chest worse. Right there, on the other side of the door, through a bit of glass, was the life Azure wanted. So close. So out of reach.

Rus whirled around, the giggling toddler still thrown over her shoulder, and at the sight of Azure, her face lit up again. Maybe not so out of reach after all.

"Come in! Come in!" Rus called through the door, and it creaked open on its own to allow Azure entrance. "I'm just trying to figure out what my monsters have been up to."

"Nothing, Auntie Rus!" Aihuan shouted from over her shoulder, her socked feet giving a kick. "Put me dooooooown."

"No can do, Huaner. Not until you tell me what you and A'Ling were hiding." Rus tilted her head at Azure and winked as if they were both in on some big secret, her tongue poking out through her teeth. "If you don't tell me, I'm going to hand you off to Miss Az, and then you know what'll happen?"

"No." Aihuan stopped wriggling for a moment, lifting her head, trying to peer at Azure from over Rus's shoulder. "What?"

"She's going to tickle you! Miss Az is the most ruthless tickler in existence." Mirth shook Rus's form, and Aihuan gave another squeal, her struggling to escape increasing enough that Rus had to put her down before she fell. Once her feet hit the floor, Aihuan took off at a run, her laughter following all through the house toward the back door. "Welp . . . there goes that."

"They were hiding something?" Azure asked, finally, her slippers scuffing a little on the floor as she paced behind Rus into the kitchen. She offered a wave for Fernando, who nodded his greeting, his hands busy stringing popcorn.

"Yeah. Not sure what, but I got a glimpse of something green. Best guess?" Rus scrubbed at the back of her neck where a red flush had blossomed, but didn't finish whatever she'd been thinking, busying herself with a pot on the stove instead. "Can you grab some mugs for us?"

Azure was sure Rus hoped she wouldn't press for answers, and maybe once upon a time she wouldn't have. A decade ago, maybe she'd have left what was unsaid alone, thinking Rus would come around to telling her when she was ready. But she'd learned something from Rus leaving: Sometimes Rus didn't come around to it. Sometimes, she kept things to herself until they ate away at her and chased her clear out of town. So instead, Azure dropped the muffins on the table, reached for the mugs, and asked, "Best guess?"

"Huh?" Rus looked up from the pot, her brows high on her forehead, then let out a nervous laugh when she realized what Azure was referring to. She ducked her head again to hide whatever expression drifted across her face. "Mistletoe."

Fernando coughed into his elbow, his face hidden from Azure when she turned to ask if he was all right. Before she could open her mouth, he shook his head and went back to work.

"Where would they have gotten that from?" Azure had some ideas. Everyone and their mother in Azure's life was meddling in this—why wouldn't everyone in Rus's too? She wondered idly what that said about where they were headed. What it meant to not have everyone against them this time. She should be relieved, shouldn't she?

Rus shrugged. "Probably Cags. She does stuff like that sometimes."

"I see."

The door to the back porch swung open with a clatter and Meiling spilled in, her eyes widening when they fell on Azure. "Miss Az!" Meiling glanced at Rus then back, her lips twitched into something devious and knowing because *teenagers*.

"A'Ling," Azure said, responding to the look with a questioning eyebrow lift. Meiling let out a soft laugh, went to grab her now-full mug of cocoa, as well as a second—presumably for her sister—and disappeared into the living room without another word.

"Well, I guess that's our sign that we ought to go help them with the tree." Rus laughed a little, bumping Azure with her hip, and held out a full mug to her. "Is the popcorn done?"

"What's left." Fernando shrugged. "The girls ate half of it."

"Come on then, before they cover the tree in tinsel and there's no room for the decorations. Huaner loves the shiny stuff." She didn't wait for Azure to respond, just headed off after them, sipping from her mug, and Azure was helpless but to follow, with Fernando trailing behind.

"The star goes first," Meiling declared, the glittery decoration held aloft where Aihuan couldn't snatch it from her. It looked like it had been handmade by one of the girls, maybe both, and was held together by nothing more than the hopes and dreams of the two children.

"I want to put it up." Aihuan pouted, her eyes fixed on it, arms crossed. She was about two seconds from a tantrum—Azure had learned in the past few weeks that that's what the slight tremble in her lip meant. "You put it up last time."

"We didn't even have a tree last year." A huffed breath ruffled Meiling's long brown hair, but she appeared to have clocked the tremble of Aihuan's lip as well. "Why don't we let Miss Az do it?"

The family of four turned to Azure, pinning her to the spot where she stood in the door to the living room like one of the specimens in Aunt Carmine's butterfly collection. Azure flexed her fingers around her mug, trying hard not to fidget under their attention. Meiling and Aihuan weren't Rus's children biologically, their eyes brown instead of Rus's telltale gray, but they fixed her with an expression similar enough to Rus's that Azure had a moment of deja vú. Her mind flashed back to when Rus had been a teenager—had been a little girl—so quickly, it made her head spin. When her gaze flicked to Fernando's for help, an escape from the penetrating stare of Rus and the girls, he just gave her a helpless little smile. Like he knew exactly what she was thinking.

"Me?" She forced the word past a dry, tight throat.

"Yeah, you," Meiling said. "Right, Huaner? Shouldn't Miss Az do it?"

For a moment, Azure thought Aihuan would save her from the awkward heaviness of this request by demanding she be allowed to do it herself. Children were like that sometimes—not able to pick up on the subtleties of things. Not teenagers though. Meiling 100 percent knew what she was doing in offering this to Azure. But maybe Aihuan would miss it. Would miss the heaviness of Azure participating in this particular ritual. How it would tie her magic to this house, to this family, all season long. Maybe even into the next year, depending how much power she put into the star when helping to ward it. It was a commitment wrapped up in cardstock and glitter glue. It made her throat go dry.

"Yes! C'mon, Miss Az." Aihuan crossed the space in a blink, grabbed Azure's wrist with surprising strength for a four-year-old, and dragged her over toward the tree where Rus took her mug and Meiling handed her the star. "Please?"

"I—" Azure looked down at the star, sparkling in the lights. It wasn't an antique like the one Aunt Maureen and Aunt Carmine put on top of their tree. Passed down through generations of Elwoods, warded every winter by the family to protect them through the darkest nights of the year. But this star, cut crooked, made from poster board and what appeared to be a whole bottle of rainbow glitter, held its own kind of magic, its own kind of charm. A family heirloom of its own. Made with love. Biting the inside of her cheek, she nodded. "We have to ward it first. Do you two know how to do that?"

"Sure do." Rus smiled, setting their mugs on the coffee table, and the four of them moved into a circle, a soft hum starting in the air from their magic shimmering to the surface. Pale blue from Azure, chartreuse from Rus, honey yellow from Fernando, red from Meiling, and pastel green from Aihuan swirled together to create a riot of color, of happiness, that flowed into the star, reinforcing it, giving it power. That done, Azure lifted it as high as she could, and her magic did the rest, perching the star at the very top of the tree.

When she turned back, the girls had already started to dig through the box of ornaments, picking their favorites to line the coffee table, and Fernando had started hanging the popcorn in lopsided rows. But Rus was watching her, a little smile on her face that Azure didn't think she'd ever seen before. Her heart stuttered in her chest, and she had a moment to wonder what it meant before the girls dragged her back into the fray of decoration.

HOURS LATER, RUS AND AZURE SAT ON THE BACK PORCH of 157 Mourning Moore, a bottle of wine between them, watching the snow slowly pile up on the tombstones in the distance.

"I think we should talk about it," Rus said after a comfortable silence that had maybe stretched on too long.

"Talk about what?" Curling herself tighter under the pale pink blanket they'd stolen from the back of the couch only served to press Azure's arm closer to Rus's. Not that Azure minded—it felt almost like old times. The chatter of the girls and Fernando in the house provided background noise, and Azure recalled when she and Rus would escape from the coven house to be alone in their early twenties, tucked close together for no reason other than because they wanted to. Azure had to remind herself—constantly, when they were alone like this—that they weren't in their twenties anymore. That so much had changed, even if it seemed like nothing had sometimes.

Rus took a sip from her glass, seeming to need to fortify herself for what was coming. "About what I said the other night."

"You were possessed, you didn't mean—"

"I did." Rus shook her head, draining her glass before she set it down. "Maybe not in that way. Like I said, I was a bitch about it, and I shouldn't have been. But I've thought about it a lot, you know?"

"Thought about what?" Azure *didn't* know. She didn't pretend to know what went through Rus's head anymore.

She had a feeling she didn't want the answer, but she was going to get it anyway.

"About you, and how you kind of—" Pursing her lips, Rus worked over the words. After a moment she shook her head, dismissing whatever track she'd been on and starting again. "What you're capable of. What you could be doing with your life."

"You think about that?" Why? Why would she bother?

"Yeah." Rus turned to look at her, her eyes sparkling in the lights from the house. "You're so smart, Az. So strong. So capable. But you've never really given yourself leave to explore all that means for you."

She hadn't, it was true. She'd accepted her lot in life. Let the burden of the shop drape itself over her like a shroud. Let Violet cow her into preparing to take the board seat for the Elwoods. Swallowing around a lump, she asked, "And?"

"And I just . . . I believe in you, Az. I don't know if I ever told you that before, but I do. I believe you can do whatever you set your mind to. And—" She huffed, a chuckle leaving her lips, and tilted her head to one side. "I want you to be happy. Whatever you decide to do. I want you to be happy."

"I am happy." The response was automatic, scripted. Azure could feel it the moment it slipped from her tongue, like someone else had sat it there and left it ready and waiting for this very interaction.

Rus didn't look like she believed it, which was wonderful and terrifying in a whole *new* way. Because what a scary thing it was to be *seen*. "Well, even if you're not," Rus pressed, leaning in closer to Azure to nudge their shoulders together firmly enough that it almost hurt, and taking Azure's hand to thread their fingers in her lap, "I want you to know that I'm going to support you, whatever you decide to do."

"I—" For the second time in an evening, Azure found herself speechless because of a member of Rus's family. Their love. Their care. It overflowed warm and free from every one of them, filling up Azure, dragging her into their orbit. Would she ever be the same now that she'd been touched by it? Probably not. And she was struck all over again how similar the girls were to Rus. How much of herself Rus had given to them. Beautiful. It was beautiful. And it made Azure warm down to her toes. "Thank you, Rus. I think I needed to hear that from someone."

"Thought you might," Rus murmured with a small nod, as if she'd read Azure like a book. She probably had. She was the only one who could. The moment stretched, and Rus gave Azure's hand an encouraging squeeze before turning her head away, like she sensed Azure needed a moment with her own thoughts.

Azure was grateful for it—the distance from Rus's aching loveliness gave her the reminder she needed that they weren't in their twenties anymore. They couldn't pick right back up where they left off. This was new, in its way, and she had to be gentle with it, so as not to scare Rus off again. Like trying to trap a butterfly.

Rus's head *thunk*ed back into the door they both leaned against, then she said, "Oh."

"Oh?"

"Think I found the mistletoe." A high-pitched giggle choked her words, forced into a lightness Azure could tell Rus didn't really feel. When Azure followed her gaze, tilting her own head back, she found the bundle above them, only just-lit by the light from the windows into the kitchen. "Sneaky little buggers."

Sneaky little buggers, indeed.

"What were they—"

Azure didn't let Rus finish that thought. She took Rus's chin carefully between her fingers, tugging it down so their faces were close enough to share breath. A sharp inhale from Rus was all the confirmation she needed that Rus wanted this too, and Azure closed the gap, pressing her lips to Rus's.

It was the same, so very much the same, but also so very different. Rus still smelled and felt like Rus, but Azure found a tentativeness there that hadn't been present in their twenties when they'd been dating a while and knew the steps. Each of them holding back, unsure.

Rus released a long, slow breath, her teeth nipping Azure's lower lip, and Azure forgot the history that spanned between them. Forgot how they'd spent a decade apart. Forgot . . . *everything* that wasn't lips, and tongue, and heat, and *Rus*.

It was easy once that all fell away—simple—to pull Rus in closer. The blanket slid, cold kissing Azure's shoulders as she hauled Rus over to straddle her lap. But it didn't slow her down. Didn't stop her. Her hand slipped from Rus's jaw, and she trailed the backs of her fingers along the long column of Rus's throat.

Rus let out a soft whine, her hips grinding against Azure's, and she pulled her lips away to scrape teeth down Azure's chin, across her jaw, nibbling and murmuring. Worn black hoodie fabric gave way to soft warm skin as Azure rucked it up, her fingers tracing along Rus's back, eliciting a soft hiss that pulled Rus back almost entirely.

"Too cold." Rus laughed, panting, her forehead pressed to Azure's as she tried to catch her breath. "It's way too fucking cold out here for this."

"Yeah." Azure licked her lips, but she didn't move her

hand, her fingertips skimming slowly against the knobs of Rus's spine. "Too cold."

They stayed that way for a moment, exchanging hot breath, the noise of the world around them kept at bay by the sound of their heartbeats drumming in time to one another. And Azure saw it, saw the moment Rus decided it was too cold but not cold *enough*, just before she said, "Fuck it" and dove back in.

That was the only warning Azure got before Rus pressed against her lips again. Harder this time. Openmouthed and desperate. Her hands suddenly everywhere as they sought skin. Azure had the fleeting thought that she was going to be hopelessly mussed when they went back inside, but it was quickly dismissed by the feeling of Rus's chilled fingers against her soft stomach, drawing out a murmured sound of want.

While Rus's hands went to work, Azure lost track of her own, let them act on instinct to brush up beneath Rus's sports bra at the back, and then around to graze lightly over one hardened peak. Rus arched. Though whether she was trying to push in closer or pull away, Azure couldn't tell, nor did she have time to care because Rus's teeth were on that spot underneath her ear, worrying the skin like she did her lower lip when she was thinking. Azure's brain stopped functioning entirely.

Rus had just gotten her shirt untucked from the waistband of her skirt when a crash broke the stillness of the night, and they both froze.

"Sounds like they broke something," Rus mumbled against a spot on Azure's throat, the vibrations trailing up to fuzzy her mind further.

It took Azure a moment to process Rus's words, but when she did, she huffed a quiet sound that might have been a laugh or might have been frustration—even she wasn't sure. "We should get that."

"Yeah." Rus pulled back with a sigh of regret, extricating her hands from where they'd been about to slip beneath Azure's clothes. "Probably."

Rus pushed to her feet, the lights from inside shining on her face to show a wrinkled nose and a little frown, and Azure grabbed her wrist, halting her movements. With her thumb brushing slowly over the thin, scarred skin on the inside of Rus's arm, she forced Rus to look at her and said, "We've got time." She stood as well, pulling Rus in for another soft kiss, more a brush of lips than anything else, and repeated herself. "We've got time."

Rus nodded, a small secret smile ticking up at the corner of her reddened lips. "We do."

Chapter 17

THE KISS PLAYED over and over again in Azure's mind. Seared there by the heat of the moment, making it nearly impossible to sleep.

Lizzie had been waiting in her bed when she returned home. She didn't say anything, but her mere presence indicated that she wanted to hear all about Azure's date. Even if she didn't, Azure was going to tell her anyway. And when Azure had run out of things to say, Lizzie curled up in a ball on the opposite side of the bed and tried to sleep. Only Azure kept tossing and turning, her eyes constantly darting to the window where she could see the corner of 157 Mourning Moore through the dark, still lit by sloppily strung twinkle lights. After about a half hour of that, Lizzie hissed at her and left the pillow for the cat bed on the floor. Which was just as well.

Even with the lack of sleep, Azure rolled out of bed at the first sound of her alarm and prepared for her morning jog without any grumbling. What was there to grumble *about*, really? She'd had a wonderful date. A splendid good night kiss. And slowly but surely, she could see how Rus's family was making room for her, opening up. Just how Aunt Carmine said it would. It was all working out. She just had to be patient. Had to keep showing up for Rus and the girls. So really, there was nothing to be grumpy about. Life was good.

Tightening her ponytail, Azure stepped out into the chill

morning air. It was still dark, but with the streetlights she'd be fine jogging down Mourning Moore along the sidewalk —mostly cleared by the latent magic of Moondale looking to protect her citizens from slipping and hurting themselves. Magical towns came in handy, sometimes. When they weren't trying to have a say in their citizens' relationships.

She wondered if Moondale knew about her and Rus. If the town could feel the shift between them as surely as Azure herself could. Did Moondale approve? While the people of Moondale hadn't before, the town herself had never seemed to have a problem with Azure and Rus as a couple. Azure had known couples the town *didn't* approve of. Watched them suffer through bad luck and worse timing as Moondale tried to tell them they weren't meant to be.

Violet and Taryn were an excellent example. Azure still remembered the smell of petrichor on their wedding day, the thunder rolling so loud it almost drowned out the board member officiating the ceremony. Before that day, Azure hadn't known that Moondale's magic could affect the weather, but it made sense now, looking back. Violet and Taryn had been married anyway, and Azure had to wonder what that meant for the health of their relationship. What it meant for their chances of staying together. But she'd largely decided to stay out of it. It was none of her business, after all, and digging into Violet's love life was likely to turn into a fight. Not that Azure staying out of Violet's relationships meant that Violet was willing to return the favor. But that was a different discussion entirely.

The forest that led into the mountains of Moondale loomed at the end of Mourning Moore, trees barren of their leaves, soft-looking snow littered among the roots, shining in the slowly dawning light. A road went through it, of course, up into the mountains that bordered one side of Moondale, acting as a barrier for the town between them and the outside world. That's why Azure's ancestors had settled here to begin with. The bay on three sides, the mountains on the fourth. Safety.

Something moved in the dark of the forest, darting from behind one tree to the next, getting steadily closer to where Azure ran in that direction. She'd planned to turn around a few feet before the forest, not wanting to deal with the slush that piled up where the sidewalk ended. But there shouldn't be anything in the forest, not this late in the season. Most of the creatures that inhabited it would be hibernating. And those that weren't wouldn't come this close to the town. Unless it was rabid.

Water seeped in through her sneakers as Azure drew closer to the growing shape, her magic already simmering to the surface of her skin, reacting to a witch on high alert. Between one breath and the next, the shape became clear, its form catching the streetlights. A fox. Patches of its fur had fallen away, leaving behind skin red and seeping slowly in places. In other spots, the skin looked empty, like the flesh had been eaten away, leaving only a flash of bone behind. The fox tilted its head just so, revealing eyes clouded over enough that Azure couldn't even make out the pupils. But its milky eyes pinned her to the spot.

Dead.

It was dead.

Or undead, rather.

Azure backed up slowly, her hands raised in front of her to fend off the drooling beast, which up to that moment had been moving so erratically she wasn't sure it even had a destination in mind. But it caught her scent, and even without pupils, she could tell that it zeroed in on her.

"Shit," she hissed under her breath, turning to make a run for it. If she could get back to 154 Mourning Moore, the wards on the house would be enough to boost her defenses. They'd probably do all the work for her—she wouldn't even have to murmur a spell. She just had to *make* it there. Heart hammering in her chest, she took her eyes off the creature.

Her foot caught on a slick patch of sidewalk, and the fox lunged.

Some instinct made Azure twist as she went down, her tailbone hitting the sidewalk first, hard enough to jar her spine. But there was no time to focus on the pain, no time to even *think*, because the creature was on her.

Its claws—too sharp, too long for a fox—dug into her skin through her thin running jacket. Panic took over, making her magic erratic, unmanageable. *Fuck*.

"Consider this a warning, *hedge witch*," the creature hissed in a voice that seemed a strange cross between a fox and a person, garbled by the limitations of an animal's voice box. It slammed an unnaturally large paw against her throat, pushing the back of her head into the sidewalk, cutting her air supply short. It weighed a ton. How could it weigh so much? It was just a fox. It was just—

It wasn't just a fox, she could see that now. Could see the way it was stitched together. Made up of parts. Weighed down by malevolent energy. It was possessed. By what? A creature of darkness. It compressed her lungs, sucking what little oxygen she could wheeze down her throat out of the air like a bonfire.

A spell. A spell. She needed a spell. Something to throw this thing off. Something to exorcise it. If Rus were there, she'd have already dealt with it. It would be nothing but a pile of bones and fur on the ground. But Azure's mind was hazed over by a lack of sleep, the early morning, the bite of the slush seeping through her thin clothes, the pressure of the creature's claws on her throat where blood began to well.

"Sssstay," the fox hissed, its muzzle pressed in closer to Azure's tunneling vision. Goddess, she was going to pass out before she could even do anything, wasn't she? Panic had made her useless, vulnerable. She was no combat witch. No world-wizened magic user who knew how to handle an attack in an instant. She'd always lived in Moondale, barely even left the wards of her town. *Safe.* Her life had been so *safe*. And now she wasn't equipped for this kind of thing. Not without a plan. Not without backup. She'd gotten lucky when they'd gone after the witch hunters weeks back. She'd had people to help her, had the drive to help Rus and save Aihuan. None of that drive resided in her now.

Even as her hands scraped at the fox's leg, she couldn't gather the strength to shove it off. *Weak.* She was so fucking *weak*.

"Away." Drool dripped from the creature's mouth, the liquid foaming and hissing in an unnatural way. It burned where it hit her skin, sizzling on her cheeks.

Who had done this? Who had created this thing? Who had set this thing loose in Moondale? Sent it after her specifically?

"From the crow witch." Teeth gleamed needle-sharp and yellowed in the low light as the creature peeled back its lips to snarl these last words so close to her face, she could smell decay on its breath. It opened its maw like a snake unhinging its jaw, and went for her neck.

The dark magic that had been taking and taking, eating away at her senses, finally stole her consciousness.

The device under Rus's fingers let out a sharp whistle like a teapot, which wasn't ideal. She didn't need the damn thing chasing off the local wildlife once it was set loose on Moondale. She'd have to deal with that later.

It seemed to be reacting to something. An influx of negative energy from somewhere. Maybe? Or maybe the grumble she'd released after drinking her now-room-temperature coffee. How sensitive was this thing? She wouldn't know until she'd done more tests. It would take months of tinkering, even once it was completed as a proof of concept for the board, before it functioned fully. She hoped they realized that. But knowing them . . . well.

"What are you so grumpy about, hm?" she asked the box of wires and circuits. Its only response was to stay where it sat at the center of her cluttered workspace, looking completely innocuous. It wasn't innocuous. She knew that better than anyone. She'd singed her fingertips at least five times during this process already. The magic packed into the wires was still almost completely unstable, even with Rus's fiddling. Another thing that would take time to sort out—time she didn't *have*.

"Helpful." Her tongue between her teeth, Rus returned her attention to the app on her phone. Coding it hadn't been overly difficult, not when she'd found decent open-source code to use as a jumping-off point. But getting the magic to sync up proved tricky. Technology and magic weren't exactly compatible, especially the newer tech, all ones and zeroes. Magic didn't *do* binary. It was too fluid for all that. Too natural. Still, she'd managed to get it to play nice before. Why not now?

"Come on. Come on. Come on." Her fingers moved fast, maybe too fast, sketching characters into the drawing part of her notes app. They were clumsy, especially on the phone, but they should work. Drawing them out on paper then scanning them in might have been easier but not quicker, and Rus was in a hurry. Slipping across the glass, she finished the last character with a soft exhale.

Her fingertip was tingly, raw, from all the magic she'd had to exert just to do that. Goddess, she was tired. Working all night probably hadn't been her best idea, but she'd felt so energized after Az left. Pumped and ready to throw herself into her project. And now, she was so close, so very close, to being done. She just needed to sync everything up, and she'd be in the test stage. The finish line in sight.

A couple more taps, and the characters transferred to the app, a progress bar appearing on the screen. Flopping back into her chair, Rus covered her face with her arms, blocking out the light from the window and letting her mind rest for the moment. Because the next bit—the bit where she worked on the settings and the configuration—would be tedious. Not difficult, like the matter of getting the two devices to talk to each other and read energy signatures, just time consuming and fiddly.

She didn't look forward to it. Wondered if maybe she could find someone else to handle it for her. Maybe Fernando could. Or Cagney. Or—

A shrill scream echoed through Rus's mind, and she stood up like a shot, the chair toppling to the floor. Heart pounding against her chest, Rus flew across the room, her slippers skidding on the steps down to the second floor. Checking the girls' rooms was quick, but it did nothing to slow the swell of whispers just beyond hearing range. Fernando's room, too, was clear.

"Where is it coming from?"

The question didn't slow her down. Rus skidded down to the main floor and out into the cold morning air without a second thought, following another scream. The whispers grew louder, faster, heightened by what was going on, or by her own fear, she couldn't tell.

Darcy waited for her on the front banister, and when he saw her, he let out an urgent cry and flew off.

"Right." She spun, heedless of the slush seeping into her slippers, chilling her toes, the cold air burning her lungs, as she followed him. She didn't know how many houses she passed, how far she'd run from home, but the forest loomed ahead of her.

That's when she saw the creature.

A fox, too big to be natural, and the telltale sign of possession fluttering around it in black wispy smoke. That's what had the spirits of Mourning Moore so unsettled. What had drawn the scream from one of Rus's undead sentries. That's what had put Darcy on high alert. And beneath it, her head lolling to one side, lying too still as the creature panted over her, was Az.

Another scream rippled through the air, this one audible to any person within hearing range, ripped from Rus's throat hard enough to make it bleed. She coughed, once, into the back of her hand, something wet and thick hitting her skin. Tripping over her soiled slippers, Rus darted across the street, her magic flaring around her in anger, fear. She'd seen this before. Been in this situation before. Many times. *Too* many times.

"Get off her!" A wall of magic, targeted and nasty, slammed into the creature, making it stumble, its claws ripping at Az's clothes, her skin. But it didn't let go. It didn't get off. Its sole focus remained the witch lying still beneath it. That wasn't good.

Hand flying, Rus released another burst of magic, doing nothing more than make the creature snarl, its head swiveling so it could bare its teeth at her.

"A warning," it said, milky eyes narrowed on Rus, claws

pressed harder into Az's throat, drawing an involuntary whimper.

Rus wanted to ask from who. She wanted to interrogate it. But there wasn't time. Not with it pinning Az like that. It could do so much damage in the time it took for Rus to get the answers she needed. That wasn't a risk she could take.

Slamming her shoulder into the creature, she finally managed to get it off Az and give herself a moment to check the other woman's breathing. It was steady, if a little strained, Azure's eyes fluttering behind their lids. Blood spattered her neck, her chest. Scratches, not deep, that would heal within days if treated properly. Wouldn't even scar, like the ones Rus sported from the last time she'd dealt with this kind of possession.

"A warning," the fox repeated, righting itself, its fur standing on end. "If you know what's good for you, you'll stay away from the hedge witch."

"Yeah, well, I've got a warning too," Rus said, scraping her palms against the rough cement to draw blood from under her skin. It wasn't as good as using her athame, not as clean, and certainly more painful, but it would do in a pinch. The spirits that always lingered on the periphery of her awareness grew louder, stronger, answering the call of her blood. She invited them in, let them feed off her in the way they craved. "Tell your master," she hissed, "to stay the fuck away from my *family*!"

Slamming her palms together stung like a bitch, maybe more than anything else she'd done so far, but it released the energy of the spirits in a wave so strong, it sounded like a thunderclap. She was sure if anyone in Moondale was awake, they'd feel the aftershocks for miles. The fox, or what was left of it after being dead for so long, crumpled into a pile.

Rus reached for it, intent on getting answers even if

they were from the corpse. But a second later, whatever had been holding the creature together failed, and it disintegrated entirely, turning into a pile of ash. An errant winter breeze swept it up.

"Of course they had a fucking fail-safe. Bastards," Rus grumbled, turning her attention back to Az, who had blinked her eyes open blearily at some point and was watching Rus with her mouth agape.

"Is it—"

"It's gone." Which should have been a relief, but wasn't. They might have gotten some answers had Rus been able to keep it animated for a while. Or even if she'd been able to halt the fail-safe before the corpse was destroyed. Now there was nothing to lead them back to its master. No way to check for a signature. No tether. *Fuck.* "We should get you home."

Az nodded and let Rus help her to her feet, looping one arm around her waist. Rus tried not to think about what that meant, about how much Az might be hurting to let herself be weak like this in front of anyone, even Rus. *Especially* Rus. She also tried not to think about how weak her own legs felt. They wiggled like jelly as she supported Az's weight, threatening to crumple under both of them. And already Rus's ears rang, a warning that if she didn't sit down soon, she would fall down.

"Did it say anything to you?" Az asked, her head lolling to the side to lean against Rus's shoulder. She was a head shorter than Rus, making the whole thing feel so strangely natural. But Rus couldn't fully enjoy the closeness or the vulnerability because she was replaying the fox's words in her head. *A warning. If you know what's good for you. Stay away from the hedge witch.* When Rus didn't answer, Az made a soft questioning sound in the back of her throat.

"No. Nothing." Rus shook her head and hated the lie

even as it left her tongue. But she didn't want to worry Az. Not right now. Not if there was nothing to worry about. Besides, when had Rus ever been accused of knowing what was good for her? Arguably, never. Necromancy being a prime example. Az being another. "What about you?"

"Nothing," Az said, perhaps a little too quickly, but Rus decided to let it lie. There was no point in them getting into a fight over this, not when they had an enemy out there they needed to turn their attention on. "Any ideas where it came from?"

Rus shook her head. If only the radar had been working. If only she'd been faster creating it. She might have been able to pinpoint where the creature originated. But she hadn't, and now she didn't have time to beat herself up over this because she needed to finish the blasted thing before this happened again.

Getting Az up the front steps to the Elwood house was enough of a struggle that Rus gave up on the idea of making it to her bedroom. She shuffled them through the house toward the living room, not even having to ask Az for directions. Which was probably better because she seemed wholly out of it.

154 Mourning Moore hadn't changed much at all since she'd last been inside it. It didn't even look like they'd touched up the paint of the soft taupe walls. The living room still boasted an overstuffed sectional, two deep wingback chairs, and a large ottoman instead of a coffee table, all in a modest gray tone. The TV was perhaps the only thing that had changed. Where Rus remembered a wooden console TV sitting back before she left, a shiny new flat screen now resided.

"That's Indie's doing," Az mumbled when she caught Rus staring at it.

"Right." Rus snorted softly, lowering Az to the couch.

"Cause you wouldn't catch Carmine Elwood dead with a big TV like that."

A smirk settled into Az's features, her eyes meeting Rus's steadily, still hazy as they were. "It's perfect for her true crime shows."

"No!" Rus gasped. She lifted a hand to cover her mouth, hiding the gleeful smile that stretched her lips.

"Mm-hmm." Az nodded proudly, slapping the back of the couch in search of something. "Blanket."

"Hang tight. I'll get you one." A basket in the corner behind one of the armchairs housed all the blankets. Fluffy mink things, and heavy blankets hand crocheted probably by Indigo. Rus grabbed two—a soft one and a heavy one—knowing Az would want the weight. It would make her feel secure, but she also needed the soft cozy feeling. Rus stumbled a little, flopping them over Az's prone form, tucking her in like she might one of the girls. "Do you want me to make you tea?"

"No. You should get back. You have work to do." But Azure held on to Rus's hand so tightly that Rus didn't think she could pry her off.

So instead of leaving, Rus settled onto the edge of the couch beside Az's hip. "I'll stay until everyone wakes up to sit with you."

Az's face scrunched up for a moment as if she might argue, then she hummed, soft and tired, and let her eyes slip shut.

Chapter 18

"IT'S WORKING" was all Rus said to Greer when he picked up his phone a few days later. She hadn't discussed with him the fact that she intended for him to be the first tester outside of herself. She hadn't even told him she was going to let him see the damn thing. But Rus knew enough of Evander Greer—they'd grown up together, after all—to know that he'd show up at her door. If only to bitch about her calling him in the middle of the day on Wednesday and all but demanding his presence.

What she hadn't expected was for Cagney and Nesta to be right behind him. Didn't they have to work or some shit? Well, maybe not Cagney—winter was her off season. But Nesta surely had a house to show or stage or something, right? And even if they didn't, did the three of them spend all their time together now? Were they living together and hadn't told anyone? Not that it would surprise Rus; each of them was difficult and secretive individually. She couldn't imagine how bad they'd be as a unit.

"Do you know how rude it is to hang up on people?" Greer asked, his voice a snarl when Rus met him in the foyer of 157 Mourning Moore. The girls were in school, thankfully, so there was no reason for him to play at being soft and kind. They both knew what he was, *how* he was, and Rus preferred this. The new, softer version of Greer kind of freaked her out, if she was being completely honest.

"Really? I hadn't heard that," Rus said, her own temper

flaring violently to the surface. Living on the edge the last couple of days was catching up to her. She'd hardly been able to sleep for imagining Az trapped beneath that creature every time she shut her eyes. What if she'd been a couple of seconds late? What if the spirits hadn't alerted her? What if Darcy hadn't been there to guide her in the right direction? The creature had said it came to give them a warning, but that didn't mean it wouldn't have taken advantage of the opening a panicked Az had provided. The kind of spirits willing to possess something that decayed were hard to control, vicious, and Rus had little doubt whoever had conjured it didn't realize that. Didn't know the true danger they'd unleashed on Moondale. Or maybe they did . . .

Good thing Rus had been there to dispel it.

"Goddess above." Cagney's calloused fingers tugged Rus's face closer so she could examine her. Rus hadn't even noticed her and Nesta crowding in to get a good look at her, and shame warmed her cheeks at both her obliviousness and what they must see there. "You look like shit."

Rus grunted, swatting her hands away. Embarrassment grew hotter at the back of her neck when she noticed how Cagney's heat lingered on her skin, making it tingle. Goddess, she wasn't *that* touch starved, was she? What the fuck was wrong with her? "Did you come to make fun of me, or did you come to check out the Ghost Tracer?"

There was a moment—Rus caught it, tiny though it was—where the three shared a look. An entire conversation flowing between them in that short, sharp beat. It was nostalgic and painful to watch. Once upon a time, Rus and Az had been like that. Able to say a million things in a tiny glance. Like they spoke their own secret language. The missing it sat as an ache in Rus's bones, worse than when her joints acted up in the cold.

Goddess, you're a fucking mess. Who would want you like this?

"Is that what you're calling it?" Nesta asked, their brows raised, a smile twitching at the corner of their perfectly painted lips. It was a tactic to dispel the tension lingering in Rus's shoulders—she knew that, but she was so grateful for it, she let it slide.

"Yeah, I am." Tilting her chin back, Rus fixed Nesta with an arrogant grin of her own. A challenge. "Problem?"

Greer snorted, which served far more to rid Rus of any lingering traces of tension than anything else could. Rus could almost say that she was grateful for him and his being there. *Almost.* And never out loud. "I don't care what you call it. Just show it to me. I've got shit to do today."

"Aye, aye, Captain." Rus gave a snarky salute and spun on her heel. All their eyes lingered on her, assessing, trying to sort out how bad off she was, a steady weight on the back of her neck that raised the hair there and made her uneasy. But she wasn't going to say anything. They were worried about her. They were her friends, after all. Well, two of them were, anyway. She couldn't be mad at them for that. Just annoyed.

She led them back to her office, flipping on the light on her way to the desk. It was organized chaos there, although maybe not as much as her workspace upstairs where she'd done the majority of the magic. Once she'd been able to pair the weather balloon with the coded app, and it was just a matter of fiddling, she'd moved down to the office on the first floor. The project itself was no longer dangerous to the girls, and she was happier in the thick of their noise and mess, even though it could be distracting sometimes.

"Okay so, the Ghost Tracer," Rus said, standing behind her desk while Greer stood on the other side. Cagney and Nesta were in the kitchen, if the sound of clattering dishware was anything to go by. She wasn't sure what they thought they were up to in there, but it didn't matter. There was business to settle. "The weather balloon has already been sent off on its merry way."

"You got permission to do that from the board?" The twitching eyebrow and head tilt of skepticism was a nuisance, but Rus wasn't going to let it bring her down. Let Greer judge. She'd never been able to stop him before—why should she try now?

"Nixie gave me permission via phone to start testing. I can show you the text, if you'd like, for confirmation that I'm following the rules." *Go on, Greer, test me like the good, mindless soldier you are.* Rus shook herself, unsure where that thought had come from. Sure, she didn't like Greer, never had much. But she didn't hate him as much as she had when she thought he was taking Az away from her. She wasn't that girl anymore, that child, who got jealous and possessive. She knew better now. Knew Az was her own woman and could make her own choices. Knew Az would come back to her, if that's what Az wanted, and she should respect that decision. Still, the insecurities lingered, a bad taste in the back of her throat: bile and rot. She tried to swallow them down but found her mouth dry.

"You okay, Ashthorne?" Greer asked. He'd leaned in closer at some point, his weight resting heavily on the desk between them. Brown eyes narrowed in what could only be suspicion; Rus wasn't stupid enough to think it might be concern. They weren't *friends*, after all.

"Fine." The word left her through gritted teeth as she bit down on the notion to respond with something snide and cutting. It wouldn't help any of them for her to get into a fight with Greer. Not now. But that didn't stop the rage growing into an inferno with every word he spoke. She wasn't even sure why she was so angry with him. It seemed unreasonable, illogical. But even as her brain said that, the rest of her seemed to disagree. Hormones maybe? Was she getting close to her cycle? The app hadn't alerted her, but that thing had a tough time keeping track of her irregular cycles after—

After you broke yourself into a million pieces to save a child who wasn't even yours.

"You don't look—"

"I said I'm fine!" Why was she so upset? Why was she yelling? Why couldn't she make it *stop*? Were these aftereffects from the possession? Or was it the exhaustion? Probably the exhaustion. Fuck, she needed coffee.

Tightening her hold on the edge of the desk, Rus let the bite of it on her still-scraped-up palms bring her back to the moment and steady her mind. There was no reason to yell at Greer. No reason to get in his face. He wasn't even being his usual dick-ish self.

When she looked up, she found Greer holding his hands up in surrender, his brows creased together as if he were trying to sort through a complex spell configuration.

"I'm fine," Rus repeated, her shoulders sagging with a harsh exhale that did little to rid her of the buzzing of irritation along her nerves. Her mood wasn't rational. There was no reason for it. She needed to get control of herself.

"Okay." But he didn't sound terribly convinced, which wasn't great. Still, they had other things to do today, and she didn't have the energy to fight him on whether she was all right or not. Spoiler alert, she wasn't, not *really*. But Evander Greer didn't need to know that. "Show me this app so I can tell you how not user-friendly it is."

With an annoyed click of her tongue, Rus held her hand out for his phone and waited for him to deposit it in her palm. Once he'd unlocked it and handed it over, it was simply a matter of a few taps and swipes before she'd downloaded the Ghost Tracer. She put the phone on the desk between them to give him a quick tutorial. He was right—it wasn't super user-friendly, not yet at least, but she had time to work on that too. To run updates to the code and the interface, to find a way to present the information that would be so easy, even someone as ancient and dense as Brant Ironwood would be able to use it.

"Then there's the matter of the predictive algorithm." Rus tapped again, showing Greer a small section of the app set for latent energy predictions. It wasn't going to change a lot in a town like Moondale, but she figured it'd come in handy if someone was planning a ritual or something. "I need your help with that."

"My help?" Greer's fingers twitched against the table beside the phone, as if itching to get his hands on this fancy little bit of kit. Which was fair; it was going to be fun, not to mention useful. The practical applications for something like this extended far beyond what the board was thinking. They always thought too small. In the hands of someone like Greer, someone in law enforcement, it could protect the people of Moondale from their resident spirits, and themselves. In the hands of the university, it could be an epic magical tool. Coven heads could use it to schedule rituals for days where they would be the most potent. There was so much potential here, and Rus wondered if anyone would really appreciate it.

Probably not. You're killing yourself for them, and they won't even give a flying fuck. Why did you bother coming back here?

"Yeah, your help." Rus cleared her throat, hoping to blot out the voice in her head with the sound alone. "I need all the data you have of accidents, break-ins, crimes in general for the last, oh . . . decade should do it. Twenty years would be ideal—the longer the better, really—but let's start with a decade."

"And you expect me to hand this data over to *you*?" He waved a hand at Rus, a judgment that had her grinding her teeth. How fucking dare he. How *dare* he try to imply she couldn't be trusted. "You know I can't do that. You have to get permission from the board first."

The board. The board. The fucking board. Every time Rus turned around, they were in her way with restrictions and senseless rules. It stymied progress. It hindered everything she was trying to do here. And yet, they wanted her to work under such a stranglehold. Wanted her to produce when they weren't willing to give her everything she needed to do so. Fucking idiots.

"I'll get the forms filled out for you," Greer continued with a shrug, as if he couldn't see the rage simmering under Rus's skin, making her magic flicker around her fingers. Maybe he couldn't. He was blatantly unobservant when it best suited him. And still, the words were a bucket of cold water, a relief. Because Greer was going to help her, do his best to make this easier.

So many emotions in such a short span of time left her dizzy, short of breath. Fuck. She was out of shape, wasn't she? Or maybe this wasn't that. Maybe she was coming down with something. The lack of sleep, the constant work, the expending of her magic . . . all of it finally catching up with her, making the room spin. Rus stumbled back, aiming for the chair, and missed. Her head smacked against something hard.

Darkness washed over her.

SHE DIDN'T KNOW HOW LONG SHE WAS OUT, BUT GIVEN the fact that her girls weren't home yet, she'd wager not that long. "The fuck happened?"

"You passed out," Cagney said, her tone annoyed at

having to state the obvious. She held a glass of juice, condensation clinging to the outside. Nesta and Greer hovered over her shoulder, each face a new shade of worry that Rus didn't think she cared for.

As if they fucking care.

"You didn't eat this morning, did you?" Nesta tutted, and Cagney forced the glass into Rus's fingers. They stared at her, hard, until she took a tentative sip, and then relief washed over them all. "How many times do we have to go over this? If you're going to do big magic, you have to eat. Honestly, I thought you'd learned that by now."

They just don't want to stay with you any longer than they have to. They want to get back to their own lives. And who can blame them? You left them all behind, and for what? For what?

Rus shook herself, hoping the voice at the back of her mind would be quiet long enough for her to assuage their worries. "I did eat. Fernando made me toast."

"You mean the toast sitting on your desk?" Greer asked, clicking his tongue. "That toast?"

"Yes. *That* toast." What was he getting at?

"*That* toast," Cagney scowled, "didn't even have a bite taken out of it."

"I was busy." Rus took another sip from the glass, hoping it would clear her head. It didn't. But it did make her feel a little less weak. Her muscles stopped vibrating under her skin from the strain of holding it to her lips. So that had to be good news. "You know how I get."

"What for?" Greer pressed, a growl in his voice now. He looked furious all of the sudden, and that fury was reflected on all three of their faces. Anger. Unjustifiable anger, in Rus's opinion.

"What do you mean *what for*?" Rus pushed herself up to a seat on the couch and set the glass on the coffee table. The movement put distance between herself and the other three, battlelines clearly drawn.

"I mean what the fuck are you *killing* yourself for?" The growl turned into a snarl, Greer pressing forward so his face was almost too close to Rus's. "For the board? For their approval. What the fuck is *worth* all this? Or are you just a fucking martyr?"

And that—that was *enough*. "Get out."

"Excuse me?" As Greer drew back, his eyes widened as if he'd been smacked. Rus saw Cagney and Nesta still behind him, their shoulders going stiff as if preparing for a fight.

"I said, get the fuck out of my house. All three of you." Rus pushed to her feet, her magic wrapping itself around her wrists, settling into the still-open wounds on her palms, making them sting. "You got what you came for. Now fuck off."

"Rus," Cagney started, her brows drawn up, "we just—"

"I've got work to do, Cagney," Rus hissed, shoving Greer toward the door to the living room, the other two backing up behind him, their hands raised as if expecting an attack. They were afraid of her. *Good*. She wanted them to be afraid of her. Although a part of her, a rational part, said this was ridiculous. That she was overreacting. That part was drowned out by the rage and the burn at the backs of her eyes threatening tears of frustration.

"Now come along, Cagney. You know how she gets when she's tired," Nesta tutted softly. "It'll be just like the discman project all over again."

"As your boyfriend so kindly pointed out," Rus said, talking over whatever else Nesta was going to say, "I've got to get back to *killing myself* for the board's *approval*." She spat, the words bile on her tongue even as the door to 157 Mourning Moore opened behind them, their shoes kicked out onto the porch. "Not like the safety of my family rests on this or anything."

"Rus, I—"

But whatever Cagney wanted to say was cut off by the slamming door, and Rus didn't wait around to see if they stayed on the stoop or left right away. As she'd said, she had work to do.

Yeah, get right back to martyring yourself for a town that couldn't give less of a fuck about you.

A mirror hung over the bench in the foyer. She caught a glint in it, something in her expression that drew her closer. She stepped over the shoes piled up there and the rug that had been rolled over at the edge.

The woman staring back at Rus in the mirror looked like death warmed over. Dark circles hung beneath her eyes. Her cheeks were just this side of sunken, her skin pulled too tight across the bones.

Honestly amazing you haven't keeled over yet.

She looked just like she did the morning after Kaytee . . . left. The morning after Aihuan and Meiling's parents were killed. But it was the thought of Kaytee's departure that clung on. Rus's mind casted back, remembering the morning before the ritual gone wrong, with Kaytee standing behind her in the mirror.

"It's going to work," Kaytee said, a manic light in her bright blue eyes that never seemed to leave these days. Like she was burning from the inside out.

"I don't—"

"It better *work, Icarus," Kaytee corrected, her tone as sharp as the nails digging into Rus's hips. She was taller than Rus, her chin propped on the crown of Rus's head so she could peer at her in the mirror. Words went unsaid there. Words like* if this doesn't work, it'll be your fault. *Words like* if we fail this time, it's because of your stupidity, because you didn't read the

directions, because you should know better. *It was always Rus's fault.*

"It will. Of course it will." She forced a smile. The scab on the side of her hand tugged, threatening to seep blood, reopen the wound caused by her own anger at herself, at Kaytee. It'd been stupid to punch the wall. Stupid to not pay attention to anything in the way. Because she *was stupid. Because Kaytee was —*

Kaytee was there. In the mirror.

No. Not Kaytee. A spirit.

Something dark and angry, its mouth twisted in a vicious line, arms reaching through the mirror to wrap cold fingers around Rus's throat. She gasped, trying to suck down air as her vision darkened, tunneled down to a point.

"How did you get in here?" The words came out on a sharp exhale. Magic fluttered around Rus's hands as she brought them up to latch onto the spirit's wrists.

The spirit didn't answer, it just bared its teeth. Rus's fingers tightened around its wrists, almost going through them, but she managed to dislodge the grip and swallow enough air to keep her from blacking out.

"Ssss-sssst-ssstay away." The spirit struggled to stay corporeal long enough to get its message across.

"Who sent you?" Rus stepped back, out of the way of its clawed fingers. It didn't seem like it had enough power to come all the way through the mirror, which was a bit of a relief, but not much. She bent to dig through the shoes and bags at the front door. The fucking thing had to be attached to one of them. It had to have been brought in by them. There was no other way it could have gotten past the house wards.

She found it a moment later: a marking burned into a leaf tracked in on someone's shoes. Hers? The girls'? Fernando's? Someone else's? Maybe none of them. Maybe it had blown in when the door was open, taking the invitation given to someone else. That meant someone was watching the house. Someone was waiting for an opening.

Shit.

It would also explain . . . some things. Maybe not the added self-deprecation, but if this thing hung out in the mirrors and reflective surfaces, interrupting her sleep, maybe even whispering in her ear at night . . . fuck, anything was possible.

"Well?" Rus stood, green flames licking at her fingertips but not yet catching on the browning edges of the leaf. "They sent you to give me a message, right? What is it. Spit it out."

The spirit's mouth moved like a fish out of water, gasping for air before it finally got out an agonized moan. That seemed to clear the way for it to finish its message. "Stay away from the hedge witch."

"Yeah, yeah, yeah." Rus rolled her eyes. "I get it, stay away from Az. Well how about a return message?" She leaned closer, letting the spirit's fingers brush cold and biting against her neck. "Fuck you and the horse you rode in on."

The leaf went up so quickly, it didn't give the spirit time to realize what she was doing. The spirit screamed again, smoke billowing around it where it resided in the mirror for a long moment, and then it was gone.

Ringing ripped Rus away from the mirror, her phone vibrating hard in her back pocket. Pain zipped along her nerves from where she'd been clenching her fists at her sides so hard the knuckles ached, joints screaming for release. She let go, shaking them out, and pulled her phone from her pocket. The picture on the lit-up screen showed Fernando, his smile shy but bright.

"What is it?" she asked before the phone was even fully situated against her ear, spinning from the mirror.

"Do we need to talk about what happened with Cagney and her partners?" Fernando's voice was soft, coaxing, on the other end.

"What's there to talk about?" Rus balanced her phone between her ear and her shoulder and went in search of the broom in the kitchen pantry. She'd have to leave it by the door for a little while, just to be sure.

"Rus."

"Nando." Mouthing the words to a spell, she began sweeping the foyer, the bristles of the broom swishing softly against the dark stained hardwood to clear away anything else that had taken leave to enter her home without permission. If she only had fucking Moondale's magic to reinforce her wards, this would all be so much easier. But the lack of it, combined with the thinning veil? Fuck. This was a recipe for trouble.

"I need to know," he said, taking a breath as if gearing himself up for a lecture, "is this like a self-sabotage thing? Is this you freaking the fuck out about settling down here? And don't bullshit me. I know it's not just that your project is making you act like an asshole."

"I—" Rus frowned, scrubbing at her nose, the broom leaning against her shoulder. How did Nando know her so well? How had he learned her so quickly? It was a little scary, honestly. She had kept things from him so far—not told him about the bluebird, or the fox. Not told him that someone was threatening her and Az. But she supposed it was time to come clean with it. "I just had to sweep a spirit out of our house. It was attached to a leaf and has been fucking around in the mirrors, apparently."

"Okay . . . And that answers my question how?"

"I think someone is pissed off about the coven and is trying to scare me off. So they—" She moved to sit on the step, the broom leaned into the corner by the door where it would be easy to grab and do another sweep once everyone got home. With her shoulders slumped, her elbows braced on her knees, she told Fernando everything.

She explained the whole business, and when she was done all Fernando said was, "I'm going to stop by the store on my way home and grab some supplies." Then he hung up.

Chapter 19

"SHE APOLOGIZED," Azure said for perhaps the fifth time since Violet stormed into Elwood & Co. Why she'd felt that was necessary, Azure didn't know, but this had become a bit of a pattern, and Azure didn't like it. Honestly, if Violet could mind her own fucking business, they'd all be a lot happier. Maybe not Violet, personally, as she seemed to thrive on sticking her nose where it didn't belong. *She means well*, Azure reminded herself, but it did fuck all to steady the slowly mounting frustration burning in the pit of her stomach alongside the jitteriness from the close call with the fox.

Her body still ached—even days later—from where the creature had knocked her to the ground. Her magic still felt slow and fatigued from where the thing had drawn power from her. She didn't have the energy to fuck around with Violet and her fucking busy-body mentality. Not that Azure got a choice in the matter. *She means well.*

"So?" Violet pressed again, ruthless in her inability to understand anything outside of her own scope. Which was hilarious because it wasn't like Taryn was the ideal wife. And yet, Violet forgave her. Every. Single. Time.

"So"—Azure took a breath through her teeth—"she apologized." She wasn't sure how many times she had to repeat that before Violet got it through her thick skull. But she'd keep going if only because she wasn't going to listen to the alternative. The alternative being she took Violet's advice. Violet's advice being that Azure should break up with Rus. Fuck all the progress they'd made so far. Fuck the kisses, and the space opening for her in Rus's family. Fuck the warm feeling that had flooded her when she helped Rus and the girls infuse their magic into the star of their Yule tree.

Yeah. Azure wasn't doing that. Violet was out of her fucking gourd, as Indigo would say.

"Is that how it's going to be between you two?" Violet asked, vicious in her flaying of Azure's poor nerves. Honestly, Azure felt a little like Mrs. Bennet, but it didn't seem to change the fact that maybe Mrs. Bennet was onto something. Hell was other people and how they could affect one's nerves. "Any time she fucks up, she's just going to go *haha, I was possessed. Oopsies*," Violet pressed in a poor imitation of Rus's rasping voice. "She's using it as an excuse."

Violet's imitation of Rus was piss-poor at best and derogatory at worst. Rus did not sound that idiotic, ever. It made Azure want to come across the counter and smack Violet. Which said something since Azure was largely considered nonviolent. By other people, of course. Azure knew herself better than that. Knew that even if she seemed polite on the surface, she was anything but in her own head. And currently she was calculating how many hexes she could cast on her sister before Violet realized she was the culprit. Maybe more than Violet thought. Best not to test it. She didn't need Aunt Maureen on her ass for making Violet upset, again.

"She's not using it as an *excuse*," Azure said instead, because it was the truth — Rus wasn't. She'd even said there *was* no excuse. Her contrition had been clear. And while Azure knew there was some truth in what Violet said, it didn't change the fact that Rus *wasn't* trying to brush off her behavior simply because she was possessed. The trouble was, how to ensure it didn't happen again? How to protect Rus for not just her own sake, but for Azure's feelings. Azure hadn't figured that out yet, but she'd applied herself to the study of it for a few days now. Looking for answers in the limited books available on necromancers and mediums. Rus should really write a book on her experience with both. Or teach a class.

Shit. She'd gotten sidetracked, and Violet had noticed, if the knowing look she gave was anything to go by. No one needed that kind of judgment from their elder sister, least of all Azure. She shook herself. "She's not using it as an excuse."

"Yes, you said that." But Violet's tone was still skeptical. Like she thought Azure would forgive Rus anything and everything, and honestly, she likely wasn't far off base with that. Azure had always been unable to hold on to her anger when it came to Rus, even when she might have tried. She was just . . . *soft* for Icarus Ashthorne. That seemed all there was to it. Always had been, even as a child when all Azure had wanted was to follow the rules to the letter, to be the perfect little Elwood. "So what now, then?"

"What do you mean, what now?" Open-ended questions like that were the absolute bane of Azure's existence. Especially coming from Violet. From Violet, they always led to something else. To Violet giving her opinion on yet one more thing Azure didn't want to hear about. Goddess above, when was Violet going back to her office? Surely she had patients to see, didn't she? It was sniffles season.

Violet shrugged, seeming unaffected by the mistrust seeping off her sister in waves. "I just wonder, now that you've forgiven her, what happens next? Will she try to avoid being possessed again? Mend her naughty ways and stop dealing with the dead? Or is this going to become a recurring thing with her?" Violet tilted her head, a bit of hair falling from her bun in a way that could only be described as artful, and likely intentional. Because Violet Elwood was the image of perfection, always had been. It grated on Azure's nerves perhaps more than it should. After all, Violet didn't do it to hurt her. Violet was simply very . . . image focused. It frustrated Azure. "I just don't want to see you get hurt, Azure."

The *again* went unsaid, but Azure heard it anyway. And honestly, the Azure of a few years ago might have been touched by her sister's concern. She might have allowed her resolve to melt and done exactly as Violet said. But that Azure died the day Icarus Ashthorne got on a bus and left Moondale for what seemed like forever. Fate had different plans, but it didn't alter how that singular event changed Azure.

Azure wanted to say that Violet should mind her own damn business. That she should look at her own relationship and the turmoil within before trying to give advice to someone else. What she said instead was, "I have been dedicating some of my time to finding a solution to the problem of possession."

"I see," Violet said, standing up straighter, her lips pursing. She didn't approve, likely swallowing back some biting retort. Another thing she'd claim was for Azure's own good. But Azure was sick of people telling her what to do for her own good. She was in her fucking thirties. She could make those decisions for herself, thank you very much. "Does Aunt Carmine know about this?"

"I don't see where that's any of—"

"She should know if her niece is fooling around with necromancy like an idiot." The words hit Azure harder than if Violet had slapped her, and she wasn't sure why Violet thought it appropriate to say something like that. While

Azure reeled, Violet reached for her, her eyes full of apology. "I'm sorry. I didn't mean that. I'm just—I'm worried about you, Azure. You have to understand, I was there. I picked up the pieces after she left last time. I don't want to see that happen again."

"I—" She didn't know what to say. She didn't know how to react. She didn't— "I understand." The lie left Azure's tongue syrup thick and sticky. She didn't understand how Violet could say something so hurtful and then try to brush it off. Violet had never been that way before. Never been outright combative. Never mean. Maybe sometimes she was out of touch with the words that came from her lips. Maybe sometimes her views were a little stilted, a little narrow. But Azure had never felt lashed by her words before. She did now. "I—"

Thankfully, she never had to know where she was going with that because the bell above the door to Elwood & Co. rang, and both Elwood sisters turned to see Meiling standing in the door, her hair windblown, her expression wild. She looked—she looked worried.

"What's happened?" Azure asked, pulling her hands from Violet's and turning her attention entirely to Meiling, who still stood in the doorway as if unsure if she should enter.

"I need to talk to you." Meiling's brown eyes flicked to Violet mistrustfully, her nose curling a little. Violet hadn't made herself available to Rus's family the way the other Elwoods had. She had her own life, her own family to tend to, and she didn't live at 154 Mourning Moore anymore, so it made sense. But still, there was something in that wariness. Something in the way Meiling shifted under their combined stares, as if she weren't entirely sure she should even be there. "Alone, please."

Violet looked as if she might protest. Her mouth opened

to do just that, then she sighed, her teeth clicking together at the snap of her jaw. "I'll leave you to it. Just"—she turned back to her sister, giving Azure a soft pat on her hand—"think about what I've said. Please, Azure. For your sake."

Azure nodded, felt the lie behind it, and brushed it aside because there were more important matters. The bell rang again at Violet's exit, and Azure followed her to the door, locking it, and turned the little sign to "Be right back." At a second glance toward Meiling's distressed look, she grabbed a pack of Post-its from the front counter, drew up a couple of silencing charms, and stuck them to the door as well.

"Let's go make some tea," she said when she was done, motioning Meiling to the back room. Meiling turned to look over her shoulder at the street beyond for a moment before following.

Once Meiling sat, the chair creaked under her, her fidgeting making her stress even more evident. It could be anything, Azure tried to tell herself. It could be a bad grade she was nervous to tell her guardian about. She could have gotten into a fight at school. Maybe some of the other witches bullied her. It wouldn't be the first time something of that nature had happened. There was absolutely no reason for Azure to jump to the conclusion that something was wrong with Rus. No reason to think there was danger. Except, Azure had a sense for these things sometimes, and she knew better.

Sliding a mug of hot tea toward the girl, Azure sat across from her and waited. She could prompt Meiling, but some things took time, and Meiling would be able to articulate what was going on better if she was given time to calm down. Her thin fingers wrapped around the mug so tightly, her knuckles had almost turned white, but still

Meiling took a long inhale of the steam and let her shoulders drop a little. "Peppermint."

"It always helps me focus when things feel jumbled. The mint clarifies things." Azure didn't say Rus had taught her this trick when they were younger. Before Rus, Azure hated the very idea of peppermint tea. Tea was meant to be herbal, not minty, and honestly, she hadn't been much of a tea drinker at all pre-Rus. But they'd learned the magic of it together from Aunt Maureen, and it had stuck with Azure even years later. "Just take your time."

Meiling nodded and sipped her tea. The clock ticked overhead, silence and time stretching. Azure was patient, she really was, but she needed to know what was wrong, and soon. Before things inevitably got worse. She resisted the desire to fidget, clenching the mug in her hands more tightly instead of tapping her fingers. Her toes curled in her shoes. Uncurled. Curled again. An invisible sign of the tension racking her nerves that she hoped Meiling wouldn't catch on to.

Mug half-empty, Meiling set it down and lifted her gaze to meet Azure's again. "Auntie Rus is sick."

The harsh swoop of Azure's stomach nearly made her vomit up every bit of lunch she'd had an hour ago. She swallowed it down, forcing the next words out past a tongue that felt too thick in her mouth. "What do you mean, she's sick?"

Meiling shifted again, her fingers flexing around the mug, spinning it for a moment with a grating noise that was loud in the ensuing silence. Chewing on her cheek, Meiling took another deep breath as if to say something else, but then shook her head.

"A'Ling, if I'm going to help your Auntie Rus, I need to know what's going on." Terror gripped Azure's heart, making it pound against her chest, her fingers going cold even for how her pulse thrummed in overtime. "You can trust me."

"I know I can," Meiling said, her eyes wide, guileless. "That's why I came to you."

What had Rus told her girls to make them trust Azure so implicitly? Azure had a feeling she didn't want to know. Because whatever it was, Rus's approximation of her must be high. But while it grated to think that she'd never live up to the expectations of being an Elwood, made her shrink from it, Rus's expectations felt like a challenge. Like something she could maybe rise to. Shaking herself, Azure pressed on. "Then tell me what's wrong."

"I can't explain it." Meiling frowned, twisting the mug faster and faster so it wobbled, not seeming to notice when tea splattered over the lip and onto her fingers. "There's just something off about her. She's not being mean, not like she was before the exorcism. But she's not sleeping. She hardly eats. And . . ."

Azure didn't ask. Didn't press. She waited. Because whatever Meiling was going to say next, Azure knew it would sweep the rug out from under her, and she had to ready herself for it first.

"There's this whisper sometimes." Meiling had gone oddly still, a deer caught in headlights. "Just on the edge of hearing."

"That could be the spirits Rus uses. I hear them too when she's calling on her magic." At least, that's what Azure wanted it to be. She wanted Meiling to be wrong. To learn she was making something from nothing. But Meiling had spent much of her life with Rus, hadn't she? She'd seen Rus use her magic time and again. There was no reason why those whispers would worry Meiling. If anything, she should find comfort in them and the knowledge that they would protect her, and her Auntie Rus. So . . . this had to be something *else*.

"It's not when she's using her magic. And this voice . . . it's not like anything I've ever heard before." Meiling shook her head. Her leg jittered under the table, making their tea slosh in their mugs, but Azure hardly cared if it made her feel better.

"But they did an exorcism. So she can't still be possessed." Right? That sounded right. Azure didn't understand enough about spirits to know if that was right. If exorcisms always worked, or if sometimes they failed. Rus might have told her once upon a time. But it was murky, lost in the haze of memories and overlapped by other, happier lessons. Azure had never liked hearing about the dead when Rus spoke of them before. Now she wished she'd paid more attention. "And she hasn't been beyond the veil since."

Not that that meant anything, Rus would have said, and indeed Azure could hear her voice in the back of her mind. Chiding, exasperated for how little Azure knew of the true dangers of their world.

"It depends on how strong the spirit is." Meiling sounded scared now. Scared and tired. Azure could relate. "I saw the notes Auntie Rus made when they did that ritual. It was a catchall cleansing. Enough to slough off most pesky spirits. But something bigger, something more malevolent, could have clung on."

Goddess, she sounded just like Rus. Her tone level, even though the fear lingered. Like this was a teaching moment, and she was grateful to give this information to someone she cared about. Looking across the table at her, Azure saw the shadow of a thirteen-year-old Rus sitting in Meiling's place, giving Azure the rundown on her latest adventure beyond the veil. Except where there had been excitement in Rus's gray eyes, Meiling's only sported fear and worry. Poor kid.

"How long has this been going on?" She had to know. Had it been since the exorcism? Since before? How much time did she have until it was too late? Goddess, Azure really should have paid attention when Rus tried to teach her about being a medium all those years ago.

"A couple of days. Probably since before she kicked Aunt Cags, Nesta, and Evander out of the house." Meiling shifted uncomfortably at those words, as if remembering something particularly unpleasant.

Inhaling deeply through her nose, Azure decided not to wonder why none of them had brought this to her. Why they had maybe seen what Meiling had and neglected to mention it. Maybe they hadn't noticed the voices. Maybe only a medium could hear them. She'd give her friends the benefit of the doubt. Still.

"I'll go by and check on her," Azure promised before she'd even finished deciding to do it. "I'm not as good at reading auras as my aunt is, but I should be able to ferret out if there is something more to this than Rus running herself ragged."

Meiling's shoulders drooped in relief, and she graced Azure with a tiny smile. "Thanks, Miss Az. You really are as awesome as Auntie Rus always says you are." Then she flung herself at Azure to hug her tightly around the neck, and before Azure could catch her bearings again, Meiling had disappeared out the front door, the bell chiming merrily behind her. Her words replayed in Azure's mind.

You really are as awesome as Auntie Rus always says you are.

Huh. Rus thinks I'm awesome.

Chapter 20

GETTING through the rest of the day without closing up shop right after Meiling left was a test in self-control and willpower the likes of which Azure had never experienced before. All she wanted to do was run to 157 Mourning Moore and check on Rus. Forget her responsibilities at the shop. Forget how the store slowly filled up as the afternoon wore on, the weekenders filtering into Moondale and thus into the shops.

She almost didn't make it. More than once she looked at the clock, the time ticking by in a slow crawl, and thought about how easy it would be to kick everyone out of the store. It wouldn't be the first time she'd done it, nor likely the last. But then Azure would remember how the Yule season sales sometimes carried them through the slow months of January and February. Aunt Carmine would be livid if Azure squandered that just because Rus *might* be in trouble.

Might be. As if Azure weren't positive based on what Meiling said about Rus kicking Cagney, Greer, and Nesta out of the house. Her hand twitched for her phone—stored under the checkout counter in case of emergencies—but every time she reached for it, someone approached the counter with a pile of purchases. She couldn't catch a break. The Goddess was testing her.

The clock finally ticked to three minutes before closing

time, and right then a small gaggle of tourists came through the door, brushing water from their coats onto the rug.

"We're closing in five minutes," Azure called by way of greeting. Maybe not the politest thing to say, but they had to understand that Azure was not keen on them browsing for hours on end as some tourists were wont to do. "If you'd like to come back tomorrow for a longer look around, we'll be open again around ten."

"Oh, we won't be long," the head of the pack promised, a wide smile on her face that made Azure's eyebrow twitch. Forced sweetness. Faux kindness. Azure would bet her last dollar that woman's name was Karen. She probably thought she understood retail workers and the stress they were under during the holiday season. Probably thought she was being a good person by lying straight to Azure's face.

They didn't wait for Azure to say anything else, just continued into the store, their soft murmurs following them. Azure toyed with the idea of shutting off half the lights in the shop; then maybe they'd get the hint and fuck off, save their shopping for another day. People like that never did though. So she settled for locking the front door and turning the sign to "Closed." Then at least no one else could wander in.

An hour. It took them a fucking *hour* to get their shit and get out. Normally she would have bustled them out of there —she'd done it before. But they needed customers during the gift-giving season. Every sale counted toward getting them through the slow months when Moondale was barren of tourists.

Azure looked down at the handful of items they'd purchased and groaned internally; they weren't really enough to warrant staying open late. The markup wouldn't even cover the cost of the electricity for the lights and heat. A vindictive part of her hoped the planner supplies were haunted. They weren't. Planner supplies didn't get haunted. Well . . . not usually. But Azure could hope.

"Have a nice evening," she said, handing over their bags, but no smile accompanied the words, and the maybe-Karen looked a little put off by that. Well, good. Maybe they wouldn't come back then. That was just fine with Azure.

Azure switched off the computer before they even turned for the exit. She retrieved her purse and coat from under the counter—where she had stored them after Meiling left just in case—before the bell over the door tinkled. After a quick, pointed nod, the lights in the place shut off, and she followed the customers out onto the wet, miserable Moondale streets. The temperature had warmed slightly, melting any snow that might have lingered, and turning the flakes they'd been getting the last few days into rain so cold it turned her cheeks to ice.

Azure pulled her scarf up to cover the deep scratches on her neck that stung in the dry air, and she started on the walk back to Mourning Moore. Maybe she should have brought the car, especially after the events of Wednesday, but she wasn't going to be cowed into changing her routine. Wasn't going to let some faceless shithead scare her. She was an Elwood, for fuck's sake. Capable. Powerful. There was no reason a sloppily raised fox should frighten her, none at all.

Still, Azure found herself looking over her shoulder regularly, curling more tightly into the coat Indigo had sewn protective charms into. There were eyes on her, someone watching from a distance, and their attention set a buzz against her skin. Worrisome. Annoying. Frustrating. Terrifying.

Just a little ways farther. Mourning Moore was right at the end of the block. She could make it. Then she'd be within shouting distance of 157 and 154. At least close enough that if something happened, Darcy would hear it. Not that he would *want* to help her, but he would if he had to. Ornery as he was, he cared for the things his witch cared for.

A caw sounded overhead, and Azure's eyes were drawn up to the hovering form of a crow. Darcy. As if he'd been summoned by her thoughts alone, like some fucked-up version of Beetlejuice. Great.

He landed on her shoulder, his claws tightening to the point that they threatened to poke holes in the outer layer of her woolen coat. Bastard.

"What do you want?" she asked, annoyance layering every word, although she was grateful to have a second set of eyes. Maybe he couldn't use magic to protect her, and she couldn't draw on his magic like she'd be able to with Lizzie since they were bonded, but it was a relief to have someone else watching her back. Someone who could potentially fly away and sound the alarm if something happened. The buzz of being watched eased off her nerves, the hair at the back of her neck settling once more as her shoulders relaxed.

Darcy released a rather loud and undignified squawk that made Azure's ears prickle.

"What do you mean she didn't send you?" That didn't sound right. Darcy didn't do things of his own accord—not for other people, anyway. He'd do them for Rus, for her family. But for Azure? No, he'd never much bothered. She could die by way of curse magic for all he gave a flying fuck. Lizzie wasn't much better, honestly. If Rus were bleeding out on the sidewalk, she'd probably prance right by with her tail swishing merrily. They were both bitches. Bitches who were forever linked to two bleeding hearts— that's what Rus used to say. Azure wondered if she still felt that way.

Another annoyed caw drew Azure's mind back to her conversation with the pissy little crow. She was probably lucky he hadn't snapped at her yet. He seemed frustrated with her slow pace. Or maybe with the fact that he had to speak to her at all. There was never any way to tell with Darcy.

"She's holed herself up in her workshop," Azure repeated slowly, sounding the words out. It wouldn't be the first time Rus had done something like that. She regularly locked herself away to work on a project. Only—only she should have been slowing down now, right? She'd sent the prototype off with Greer, or so he'd said. That meant all that was left was tweaking. Surely that would give Rus a bit of down time. "You're worried about her."

Darcy hissed, as if this were an accusation instead of a statement of fact. Azure wasn't sure what was wrong with Darcy worrying about his witch—that was his job, after all. To worry, to guide, to lend his magic whenever she needed it. If not, why bother with familiars at all? It wasn't as if they could cast spells, make potions, or draw out arrays.

"I'm not judging you." Azure tilted her head back, looking up at 157 Mourning Moore as it drew closer. The first floor was lit up like a Yule tree, life teeming from every timber, but at the very top, in the small window Azure knew was Rus's, only a dim light shone. Barely enough to see by. If Rus was up there, she was probably straining her eyes like a beautiful idiot. Azure paused at the front gate to 157 Mourning Moore, feeling the energy of the place and how it had shifted since she'd been there last. The lingering spirits were upset about something, unsettled. And the house itself seemed to hold its breath, waiting for disaster. Her hand on the gate, fingers flexing against the bite of the wards, she said, "I'm worried too."

Darcy leaned closer, bumping her jaw with his feathered

head, rubbing the water that had melted against her skin. It was as close to affection as she'd ever gotten from him, and that was sign enough of his concern.

"Yeah, I'll do my best to get her to take a break," Azure promised and started up the walkway. Darcy left her shoulder with a sharp caw, returning to perch somewhere in the eaves of the house, probably near one of the windows into the attic so he could supervise his witch even though he was not allowed inside.

The door opened before she could knock, Meiling standing in the threshold, her hair thrown into a bun so loose that it wobbled with her head when she tilted it back to raise her chin. "Auntie Rus! Miss Az is here!"

"I've brought some paperwork we need to finalize for the coven," Azure said by way of explanation as she wiped her feet on the rug and kicked off her boots at the door. Meiling mouthed a soft *thank you*, and Azure nodded her understanding before the teen ducked back into the living room. The coffee table was littered with paper, pencils, and textbooks. Homework time, clearly.

"Hi, Miss Az!" Aihuan waved from her spot at the end of the little table where she was coloring in what Azure could only guess was a dinosaur from this angle.

"Hello, Huaner." Relief washed through Azure at the sight of them both. They were safe. They were cheerful. There wasn't much more she could ask for. And the clear indication that whatever affected Rus was localized to just Rus made Azure's shoulders fall from where they'd been bunched up around her ears most of the day. It didn't assuage Azure's concerns about Rus and her state of mind, but at least the girls were safe. For the time being.

"Az." Rus was out of breath by the time she got down the steps, her hair a greasy mess brushed into a ponytail that barely held any of it from her face. The black hoodie she wore—at least two sizes too big—looked like she'd been sleeping in it for days. Dark bags hung under her eyes, the skin on her cheeks gaunt. "What's up?"

"Paperwork." Azure reached into her purse, conjured the documents she'd need from her desk at home, and pulled the folder from her purse to wave it around. Holding the paper made it easier to restrain the desire to reach for Rus and pull her in close. She couldn't do that, but maybe she could do the next best thing. "I'll order us a pizza to snack on while we work."

Rus tilted her head, bird-like, as if she knew exactly what Azure was about, and maybe she did. That was just fine. Azure wasn't exactly trying to be sneaky. Rus licked her lips, stalling, as if maybe she was going to call Azure on her motives, but she nodded. "Girls, what kind of pizza should Miss Az order?"

"No peppers," Aihuan called, her footsteps preceding her arrival in the foyer with them.

"She wanted to know what you want on it, not what you *don't* want." Meiling huffed, her arms crossed over her chest, but a light of approval sparked in her gaze. She must have caught on to what Azure was up to as well. Azure ached under that knowledge, seeing again how Meiling was a younger version of Rus. A chance to make sure the Moondale Board of Magic didn't ruin another medium. "Just get Huaner cheese. She'll probably pick off all the toppings anyway."

"Will not." Aihuan stuck her tongue out, her hands perched on her hips.

"Will so." Meiling rolled her eyes. "I like vegetarian. Auntie Rus?"

"Vegetarian is fine with me and Nando. Right Nando?" Rus called into the living room where Fernando was presumably hiding. He poked his head over the back of the couch, and Azure realized he'd been crouched on the floor leaning against it, likely helping the girls with their projects.

"Works for me," Fernando said in a soft voice.

"Right then." Rus clapped her hands and snagged the folder from Azure's hands before spinning to head through the house to the kitchen. "I'll get started on this while you call it in."

BELLIES FULL, NANDO AND THE GIRLS EXCUSED themselves, leaving Rus and Azure room to spread out more on the kitchen table. They had started before the pizza was even ordered, but they were still only about halfway through the thick packet Aunt Carmine brought home from the Board of Magic the other day. Azure wondered how much of this paperwork was truly necessary.

Rus had hardly touched her pizza, the cheese taking on that rubbery consistency as it sat beside her with two bites from it.

"I don't understand why I need to do ten fu—fudging copies of this." Rus glared at the paper in front of her. "And why they *all* have to be handwritten."

"Likely has something to do with the magic of a person's handwriting. It's to seal you to your words." Or at least, that was Azure's best guess. Although every time she watched Rus shake out her cramping hand, she wondered if the board was just making them jump through hoops to dissuade them from applying. She wouldn't be surprised.

"You'd think"—Rus set down her pen so she could crack her knuckles—"that since there hasn't been a new coven in some hundred years or so, the process would be fairly straightforward."

Azure couldn't disagree. She doubted—heavily—that when the Ironwoods started Silver Flame, they had to jump through this many hoops. All in all, they may have had to fill out a singular packet and wait a probationary period. This seemed a bit much, even for someone who liked order and organization like Carmine Elwood. Which explained the expression of apology when she handed the packet over.

"We ought to be done soon." It didn't matter how quickly they were done. This was for show. The board had already made its decision. She just hoped it wasn't going to be a refusal. "You should finish your dinner."

"It's fine. I ate earlier." Rus grabbed her pen and ducked her head to start again, trying to cover the lie Azure heard in the words.

"How much earlier?" She didn't mean to nag—she didn't. But Meiling came to her because she was worried, and Azure promised she'd check up on Rus. This was her checking up. That was okay. Right?

Rus stilled, her shoulders going rigid, and Azure thought she heard a whisper on the air. Something cold and cutting that sent a shiver down her spine. Wholly unlike any of the others she heard follow Rus before. "Are you going to start in on me too?"

"No. I—" Azure swallowed, something sharp and aching clogging her throat. Meiling was right: something was *wrong* with Rus. Something she wasn't sure how to face, not yet. Maybe she never would. Something she couldn't put her finger on. Was Rus's depression rearing its ugly head, or something worse? "I'm just saying, the girls are worried about you."

"The girls?" Rus snarled. Her head lifted and when she looked at Azure, the bashful tiredness that had resided there earlier had vanished. Lifeless. Bitter. Pitying. "When did you talk to my girls?"

Cheese and bread soured in Azure's stomach. She'd misstepped. She'd spoken without thinking. She should have taken her time, moved more slowly. What would Rus do now? And how could Azure backtrack quick enough to stay? To maybe figure out what the issue was.

"Meiling stopped by the shop earlier today," Azure said, trying to make it sound offhanded, nonchalant. "She said you've been working a lot lately."

"So that's why you're here then." Rus gripped the pen hard enough that Azure half wondered if she'd break it, spilling ink everywhere. Goddess, of all the times for her to speak without thinking first. What the fuck happened to her filter? "To check up on me?"

"No, I—"

"Why don't you worry about *yourself*, Azure. That's what you're good at, isn't it?" The whispering grew louder, faster. Like it was feeding Rus what to say. But that didn't ease the sting of her words.

"Rus, that's not—" Sucking in, Azure forced herself to calm down, to ignore the racing of her heart. She didn't want to fight Rus. She knew the hurtful things Rus said weren't *her. But aren't they?* a voice that sounded like Violet asked. *Are you going to let her use possession as an excuse every time she hurts you?* "I'm just concerned for you. I care about you."

"*Care.*" Rus snorted, the word echoing strangely in the eerily silent kitchen. When had the sounds from the living room stopped filtering in? "When are you going to get it through your head?"

Azure's blood ran cold. There was a leading nature to those words. A storm brewing that stole her breath. Had her gripping the table so hard, splinters threatened at her fingertips. "Get what through my head?"

"I didn't *want* you," Rus hissed, the words a slap across Azure's raw nerves, even for how quiet they were. Tears pricked at the backs of her eyes. Sharp, too hot. "If I'd wanted you, why did I leave? Why didn't I take you with me?"

Azure wasn't sure what happened next. The following movements happened without any consent from the rest of her, but an indeterminate amount of time later she was on the front porch, the cold biting her cheeks and bare neck, her coat clutched in one hand. She breathed through the pain in her chest. Tried to get her bearings. And almost succeeded in forcing herself to return to the table, to *make* Rus explain herself, to make the thing hitching a ride on the woman she loved show itself. But then—

Is that how it's going to be between you two?

I didn't want you.

Chapter 21

THE DOOR SLAMMING FINALLY SNAPPED Rus out of whatever fugue state she'd gone into. She found her cheeks burning with tears. The pen she'd been using exploded, but she couldn't tell if it was because of magic, or because she squeezed it too tightly. Either way, ink was everywhere. Staining the paperwork Az worked so meticulously to gather and collate for her. To explain and mark up where she needed to fill in information. Az went above and beyond what she needed to do as a mere sponsor of the Coven of the Forgotten, and what had Rus done to repay her?

What you always do.

The voice in the back of her mind was traitorous, horrible. It had an edge to it that Rus never heard in her own voice. But it was her own. Wasn't it? It *sounded* like her. Just like the words that had come from her mouth when she spoke to Az. They had to be hers. Who else's could they be? She'd done an exorcism. She hadn't played with any spirits since then. There was no way they could belong to anyone else.

Goddess, she needed an *out*. She hadn't felt this itchy since she left Moondale all those years ago. Suffocated. Stifled. Skin too tight. The walls closing in.

"Nando," she called, knowing what she was going to do before she'd even completed the thought. Like the idea had sprung to life in her mind fully formed. She needed . . . she needed to not exist for a little while. To not be Rus. She needed to escape. This was the best way to do that.

"Yeah?" Fernando materialized in the doorway, like he'd been hovering nearby. Listening. A judgmental tilt to his mouth said he'd definitely overheard the conversation with Az, and he didn't approve. Well. He wasn't going to approve of what came next either. But fuck it. Rus didn't have the time or the patience for an explanation.

"I'm going out. Can you take the girls over to Cagney's for a sleepover?" The request caught at the back of her throat, hitching there in a breath that threatened to turn into a sob.

That's right, pawn your kids off on someone else because you can't handle it. Weak.

Shaking herself, Rus breathed through the tightness in her chest and hoped Fernando wouldn't ask any questions. She was already on the verge of tears. She didn't think she would survive an inquisition from her best friend. Not that she'd escape one once Cagney found out what happened. But maybe she could waylay that by fucking off to Ironport for a little bit. Get outside the tight wards of Moondale and let herself disappear. Just for a couple of hours. Just until she could get her head above water again.

Something must have shown on her face because instead of a lecture or an interrogation, Fernando said, "Okay. When should they be back?"

"Tomorrow is fine." Rus shrugged, even though she wasn't sure how true that was. Tomorrow might not be fine. Tomorrow might be worse. It depended on how much steam she could burn off between now and then. But she told herself one night out would be enough.

One evening to get a glimpse of the Rus she'd been before she was a single mother of two. Before she'd given up life and travel for the sake of her daughters. She didn't want to wind up resenting them, so this was necessary. She had needs too. That was understandable. After all, she hadn't chosen this as some women did. Hadn't prepared for it. Motherhood had been thrust upon her. Escaping for a bit made sense.

After a long moment of observation, Fernando said, "I'll call before I bring them back."

Goddess, Fernando was a fucking saint. Rus was blessed to have him. Blessed he had decided to tag along on her harebrained scheme to keep her children safe.

You're taking advantage of him and his goodness right now. Pitiful.

"Girls," Fernando called, not taking his eyes off Rus, "grab some jams and clothes for tomorrow. Auntie Cags wants us to sleep over with her."

"Sleep over?!" Aihuan squealed, her little feet pounding on the way up the stairs. She didn't question why this was happening so late in the evening.

"Yes, a sleepover." Fernando still watched Rus, his head tilted as if trying to make sense of something. But he couldn't seem to find purchase on whatever it was, so he shook himself. "You're going to be all right on your own for an evening?"

"Me? Yeah! I'll be super." Rus laughed, the sound forced and grating on her throat.

"I heard what you said to Az," Fernando started slowly, his words carefully measured. Weighed and fitted together beforehand to keep her from flying off the handle.

Guilt heated Rus's belly, settling in all the places that ached from the cold and the muck. Making her syrupy slow. Goddess, she hated herself more for making him sound like that. For making him think he needed to walk on eggshells around her. He was her best friend, for fuck's sake. More proof that she desperately needed this night out.

"If there's something going on that you're uncomfortable with, that's making you unhappy, you can tell me. Or if you need something. Anything. You know that, right?"

He really is too good for you. They all are. You don't deserve their kindness. Their love.

Rus shook herself and forced a smile. "I know. Of course, I know that." She did. She really did. Fernando had proven over and over again how much he cared about her, about her family. Been there for her through some of her worst days. Pulled her back out of her head after she lost Meiling and Aihuan's parents. Helped her build a coven for them from nothing, from broken pieces. He was one of the best things that had happened to her. "But it's not that. I promise. I just need to blow off steam."

He eyed her for a moment longer, considering, likely trying to determine whether this was one of those times where her mouth said one thing but she needed another. Spoiler alert: it was. But if he noticed, he seemed to decide that instead of pressing further he would trust her.

Big mistake.

"I'll go help the girls pack their things."

"Perfect. I need to go"—she lifted her hoodie to her nose and blanched—"at the bare minimum, shower. I smell like I haven't bothered in weeks."

"Not weeks," Fernando said, teasing, and headed up the steps. "Days, maybe."

"Hardy har har," she called after him, then turned back to the packet on the table. The papers were ruined. She'd have to let Carmine know she needed another set. Collecting the debris of her fuck-up and making her way to the recycling bin, she nearly jolted out of her skin at the sight of Meiling waiting for her there. "You should be upstairs packing."

Meiling stared at her, her eyes narrowed in concentration as if she were trying to focus on something that kept moving. Trying to understand what she was seeing. It was just over Rus's shoulder—whatever it was—and it scared the teenager.

"A'ling," Rus said, making the girl jump and feeling immediately guilty for it.

"Huh?"

"Sleepover. Auntie Cags. Shoo," Rus said with a shooing motion, the papers still flapping in her hands. Meiling twisted herself around and headed up the steps without any further strangeness. Rus turned around, looking for what Meiling might have seen. Did a spirit linger outside of the house? Was something off about the kitchen? No. Nothing that she could see. She shook her head and followed the others upstairs.

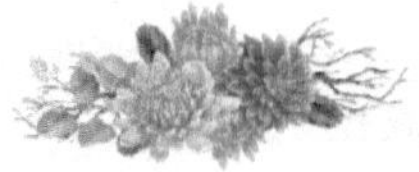

Mediums and substances didn't mix. Whether those substances had an addictive nature or not didn't seem to matter. Anything that lowered one's inhibitions was dangerous for a medium. Especially a medium with a lower-than-usual spiritual threshold. Objectively, Rus knew this. She'd been the first medium to actively speak out about such things online, adding it to the database for the covenless she found in the early 2000s after she had a few too many close calls herself.

If a medium—especially one like Rus—went out drinking and partying, she should wear something to ward off the spirits. A necklace with a talisman carved into it. An item of clothing with protective charms sewn into the lining. Something. Rus had those things, all of them. Because she wasn't an idiot, despite what people seemed to think of her. She knew what she was doing about 90 percent of the time. Maybe more on a good month.

Point being, she knew exactly what kind of trouble she was inviting in when she left behind the wards of not just 157 Mourning Moore but also Moondale without any of those things. Knew exactly what could follow. She just didn't fucking *care*. Consider it self-flagellation. Self-hatred. Whatever. She needed to get out of her own head for a couple of hours, and sometimes the easiest way to do that was to get drunk and let a spirit do the walking for a while.

Once the alcohol wore off, she'd have control again. There was no harm in letting a passenger take a ride for a bit. Checking out. Maybe if Rus had been in her right mind . . . Not plagued with guilt. Not dealing with the constant racing thoughts about what a failure she was as a person, a mother, a friend, a significant other. Not exhausted and burnt out from throwing the candle onto a fucking bonfire. Maybe then, she'd have realized how harmful this thought process was. Maybe she'd have checked the depressive episode before it got any further. But that was the thing about these kinds of episodes: a person didn't usually recognize them when they were on the inside. It took having a bird's eye view from outside to see it.

Well. I sure as shit have a bird's eye view now, don't I?

She hung by her ankles from the second floor of a large spacious foyer that she didn't recognize. The balustrades dug into her skin where her jeans had been rolled up to give whatever possessed her body in the time she'd been gone better leverage. The floor below loomed— hard, some type of stone. Marble maybe? Granite? Did they use granite on floors? It didn't fucking matter. Whatever it was looked like it'd crack Rus's skull open like an egg if she wiggled the wrong way and plummeted toward it.

"The fuck were you doing up here?"

The only answer—which wasn't from the spirit that had gotten her there—was the lurch of her belly, threatening to spill its meager contents on the posh-looking floor below. With a groan, she used what limited stomach muscles she had to lift her torso toward the railing, latching on to two spindles that both groaned under her weight. She unhooked her feet carefully.

Goddess, don't let me fall to my death here. I'd never live down the embarrassment.

Somehow—a miracle of divine intervention of some kind—she managed to scramble over the railing and onto the landing on the other side. Another wave of nausea hit, the world tilting more dangerously than it had when she'd been hanging upside down. What the fuck was that about?

"I'm too fucking old for a hangover." Rus's knees crackled as she pushed to her feet, but at least the floor stayed where it was supposed to be. She made it down the steps without falling on her ass. There were a couple of close calls, but all things considered, not too bad.

At the base of the stairs, a trail of something glistened in the dark. Rus pulled her phone from her pocket and flashed it with the light. Blood. And not a small amount either. Was it hers? She didn't feel any place where she'd been cut that deeply, but that meant exactly fuck all. Her nerves were shot after years of wounding herself for her magic, leaving behind an unpleasant numbness in most places. She could walk into the side of the coffee table and not feel a fucking thing, even the next morning when her shin was black and blue. Fun superpower, right?

Following the trail, Rus found deliberate lines drawn in blood. Tilting the phone light back, she got a better picture of what it was, although not what it was *for*. An array of some kind.

"Let's see." With more groaning joints, she crouched to get a better look at the characters around the edge of the circle, doing an awkward crab walk to look at them one at a time. Was it for protection? For travel? For communication? For—Fuck. It couldn't be a summoning array, could it? How the fuck would the spirit have learned to do that? And *what* was it trying to summon?

She was just about to put it all together, her mind running over the characters and filtering through her mental Rolodex of arrays—they looked terribly familiar—when she heard sirens outside. Because of fucking *course*. This night could *only* be improved by the introduction of law enforcement.

"Don't move," a familiar voice shouted as the door burst open and lights flashed in Rus's eyes, blinding her.

"Sheriff Regan, I promise this is a misunderstanding." Rus held up her hands, forcing a laugh and hoping Sheriff Regan would laugh with her. But Regan motioned with her stun gun for Rus to kneel, and honestly, Rus had been shot with a stun gun before. Fuck that. She was not getting shot with another one. So she knelt.

"Icarus Ashthorne," the sheriff said, and Rus was at least grateful she wasn't pretending she didn't know Rus. That might save her some trouble. "You're under arrest for breaking—"

"I don't see anything broken, though," Rus tried to come to her own defense. Why couldn't she shut the fuck up? Let Regan cuff her, then call to have someone come get her out once she was back at the station.

"Do you know whose residence this is?" Sheriff Regan asked, tone almost conversational as she yanked Rus to her feet by her cuffed hands.

Please say it's abandoned. Please say it's abandoned. Please say it's abandoned.

"Mayor Chadwick."

"You mean like—you mean like from the Council of—"

"That's the one."

"Fuck me." Rus groaned. Great. Now she was pissing off *other* magical councils in *other* towns.

"Yeah," Sheriff Regan said, sounding a little amused, "fuck you." She shoved Rus out the door toward her squad car.

Chapter 22

LIGHTS BURNED hot on the back of Rus's neck, giving her flashbacks to the last time she'd gone before the board. She remembered how it had felt like an interrogation room, too hot, stifling, purposefully uncomfortable to put the suspect off their game.

Suspect. She was a *suspect*.

It wasn't the first time. Rus had been in interrogation rooms a fair bit growing up. Being the only necromancer in Moondale meant that sometimes people blamed things on her, regardless of whether she was anywhere near the scene.

Ritual gone wonky? Must be Ashthorne and her necromancy.

Someone grave robbing? Let's call in the necromancer.

The usual suspects, the old sheriff liked to call them, and she was on the list. There were a couple dark fae who lived in the forest, the town drunk, and scrawny little Rus, the necromancer. She'd never actually done any of the things she'd been accused of, but that didn't mean the sheriff wouldn't try to pin them on her. Because it was easy. Because it would make the other folk in the town feel safe. Because he was a bastard.

She *had* done what she was being accused of this time. Well . . . her body had, anyway. But that distinction meant fuck all in the eye of the law. Rus's blood had been on the floor. Probably. Hopefully. Rus's hands had picked the lock. Rus had been caught at the scene.

In the past, Rus knew she'd be all right, no matter what *evidence* the sheriff had. Because Az would come and save her. She'd thrown the Elwood name around like a wrestler throwing their title around in the ring, and she'd always gotten Rus out in enough time that she wouldn't have to spend the night in jail. Which was *amazing* of her. Maybe *amazing* wasn't the word. Maybe *sexy* was the word. It didn't matter.

What *did* matter was that this time—*this time* Rus knew damn well she'd done what she was being accused of, at least in the physical sense. And because it was in Ironwood, she also knew damn well that even the Elwood name wouldn't get her out of this mess unscathed. Besides, why would Az come and save her after what she said the last time they'd been together? Az wouldn't want anything to do with Rus now. Who could blame her? Not Rus.

Pressing her forehead into the metal table, Rus tried to breathe through another spell of nausea. She needed water. But she wasn't about to piss off the officers standing right outside the room by bugging them. She was in enough trouble as it was. No sense in making enemies.

"They at least could have given me my phone call," Rus muttered. Although she didn't know who she'd call. She didn't have a lawyer. Cagney would yell at her and likely leave her in lockup, at least overnight. She didn't think she could handle the disappointment and guilt in Fernando's voice when he realized she'd had him take the kids so she could do exactly this. Phyre had her own family to worry about. Nesta would probably laugh, then *also* leave her in lockup overnight, which would serve her right. Az likely wouldn't even pick up the phone. And that was . . . it. Rus's tiny circle of people she knew and trusted in a circumstance like this were all present, accounted for, and disregarded. Fuck. She was in trouble.

You're reaping what you sow. You did this to yourself.

That didn't sound like her. Why didn't that sound like her?

"Yeah, thanks for the reminder." Goddess, she was a fucking mess.

"Talking to yourself again," a sharp voice called from the open door, and Rus looked up to find *Greer*—of all people—leaning against the frame, posture forced casual, like a cop in a police drama. And he called *her* ridiculous.

"Have you come to gloat?" Not that he didn't have a right to—he most definitely did. Rus had done enough over the years to piss off Evander Greer. Him showing up when she was at her lowest to poke fun at her seemed on par with their relationship.

Because you're pitiful.

Greer looked over his shoulder. At what? Rus couldn't see, and when he turned back, he'd raised a brow so high, it disappeared into his hairline. "Sheriff Regan called me. She said she caught you breaking and entering at the mayor's place."

"I can explain."

"I'm sure you can." Greer stepped into the room, shutting the door behind him. "And you're going to."

Rus's neck burned more. She wondered if the skin would blister and peel as it had that time after she'd buzzed her hair and forgotten sunscreen when she went to the beach. "The cameras?"

"Sheriff Regan has everything shut down. We don't have to worry about any normies overhearing." Greer pulled the other chair from beneath the table and dropped down into it. He was in civilian clothes: sweatpants and a hoodie. Like maybe he'd been dragged out of bed by her ridiculousness. Maybe he'd been over at Cagney's with the girls, or with Nesta. Maybe she'd interrupted a rare night off. She almost felt bad. *Almost.* "So, tell me, why the fuck were you summoning a demon?"

"I wasn't—" Rus broke off, sucking in a breath to calm the churning of her stomach. A demon. The spirit had been trying to summon a fucking *demon*? What for? What level demon? That had been a lot of blood. A *big* array. "I wasn't summoning a demon."

Greer's only response was a snort.

"Look." Scrubbing at her face, Rus tried to think of the best way to explain this that wouldn't make her sound off her broomstick. Nope. No good. Any way she sliced it, this would make her sound like she ought to be in a straitjacket. She could only hope Greer would understand, to some degree. That he wouldn't immediately call child services. Fuck, what if they took away the girls?

They'd be better off.

She shook herself. No. No, they wouldn't. She was a good mother. She had done everything for those girls. Given up everything. Made them her whole world.

And don't you resent them for it?

No! No, she didn't!

"Rus. The demon," Greer prompted, and Rus clenched her fists, her nails digging into the now-scabbed meat of her palms, forcing herself to focus.

"There are side effects," she said, her words carefully measured. She needed him to understand. "To what I do now. Before—before if I dealt with a restless spirit, let it in so I could use it and exorcise it, I was just fatigued afterward. Now . . . now I pick up some of their traits, their habits. Like a residue."

"Okay," Greer said slowly, more question than statement.

"So, sometimes—I don't do this a lot, and it's been a long time since I have, I need you to know that. This isn't something I make a habit of, it's just—it's just a way I've found of letting go for a couple of hours." She was rambling. Fuck. She was rambling, and that wasn't going to help her case. Not at all.

"Get to the point." Gruff. He was losing patience with her. And why shouldn't he?

"The other thing you need to know"—Rus licked her lips—"is that because of an . . . incident"—she couldn't tell him about Aihuan, not yet—"my threshold is particularly low. That means if I use any substances, sometimes things can sneak in. And I've found"—this was it; this was where she'd lose him—"that *sometimes* it's a great way to get out of my own head for a bit."

"Like tonight."

"Like tonight," Rus agreed a little too easily.

"So you're telling me"—Greer leaned forward, his brows pinched in the middle in agitation—"that you went out drinking with the intent of getting possessed?"

"Basically. Yeah." Goddess, it sounded so much worse when said out loud. What the fuck was *wrong* with her?

Do you want a list?

No. Shut up.

In alphabetical order, or by fucked-upped-ness?

I said shut. Up.

"And the spirit created the summoning array?" His tone said he was going along with this out of some twisted sort of amusement, but at least he was listening to her. That was more than Rus expected from him.

"Yes." But there was still something Rus had to know. An answer she needed. If the spirit was trying to summon a demon, she had to know how successful the little fucker had been. "Listen, the demon—"

"It didn't work," Greer said, and relief swept through Rus so forcefully she slumped down onto the table, letting out a long groan, a puppet cut from its strings. "You must have been really trashed. I've never seen your array work so sloppy."

Goddess above and below, she'd gotten lucky. *So* lucky.

Greer huffed, shaking his head. "Do me a favor, yeah?" Rus wrinkled her nose, but Greer didn't wait for a response before he continued. "Next time you need some *me* time, stay home, take a bath, and drink a bottle of wine like a *normal* person." He waved a finger at her, but he didn't look as angry as maybe he should have been. "Don't go out binge drinking, get possessed, and try to summon a demon at the mayor's house!"

"I can't make any promises?" Rus said, because humor was as good a way out as any, wasn't it? Seemed to work for her, usually.

Greer *tsk*ed and pushed from his seat. The door shut behind him with a click. He was going to leave her here to rot, she was sure of it. There was no reason for Greer to help her. No reason for him to throw his weight around as a sheriff and get her out of here.

That's what you deserve: to rot.

It was. Wasn't it? After what she'd done. After how she'd told Fernando to take the kids and go, knowing full well what she'd do once he had. Goddess, the girls were going to hate her for this. Especially Meiling. She was old enough to understand what a fucked-up mess Rus was. Aihuan would understand at some point—maybe not for a while, but some point. Rus was an awful mother. The worst. Maybe it'd be better if Greer *did* call Child Protective Services. Maybe they *would* be better off living with someone else. Someone more capable. A more powerful witch family. One who wouldn't encourage necromancy.

"You ready?" Greer asked, ripping her from her downward spiral for the second time in one evening.

"Ready?"

"Yeah, to get the fuck out of here. You should probably go home, and at the bare minimum take a shower before the girls get back." He stood at the door, holding it open for her, and waited for Rus to rise on unsteady legs.

They didn't speak again until they were in Greer's car headed back to Moondale, and Rus couldn't stand the silence anymore. Maybe clearing the air would help. "Okay, look, I made you go bald for a couple of months—"

"A year, Ashthorne," Greer responded, not once taking his eyes off the road. He didn't even sound angry about it anymore, just tired. Which was kind of nice, she supposed. "It was a fucking year."

"Fine." Rus flapped her wrist, brushing it off. A year, a couple of months. What was the difference, really? "But you were matched to the love of my life. I think that more than makes us square, don't you?"

Greer scowled, his face going hard and wrinkled as he seemed to consider her words and all the history between them. To be fair, it was quite a *lot* of history, almost more than Rus shared with Az. They'd been friends, once upon a time, she remembered. Before he'd realized what it meant to be a medium. Before someone had poisoned his young mind against the possibilities of speaking to the dead. Before the necromancy and the matchmaking, they'd been friends. Rus thought she might miss that sometimes, but it was so long ago now she didn't even remember the shape of it anymore. Not how she remembered the shape of her love for Az, of her sisterhood with Cagney and Phyre, of her friendship with Nesta. Greer was a faded childhood memory. Someone she'd played tag with, once or twice, before his parents caught wise to who he hung out with.

After a silence that stretched on for far too long, Greer gave one terse nod. "Fine. Forgiven. But—"

"Not forgotten," Rus finished for him, a smile twitching at the side of her face that he couldn't see from where he sat. Better he not realize how she'd delved down memory lane there for a minute. He'd hate her for that. "Right back at ya, buddy."

"Was there a point to that?"

"Yeah, I need you to do me a favor." She chewed on the inside of her cheek, a thought forming, a plan. It was indistinct and probably better that way. Because she'd realized something while they spoke—something that would change everything.

She had a passenger. A dangerous one. And she needed to act before it caught on that she knew it was there. She also needed to figure out how long it had been hanging around. Just since she'd gotten drunk? Before then? Maybe since—

Greer grunted a question.

"Keep the girls at Cagney's, at least for the weekend."

Greer looked away from the road, his dark eyes narrowing on her, calculating, examining. Whatever he saw must have given him the answers he sought because after a moment he said, "All right" without asking for further explanation.

Chapter 23

Picked up your girlfriend from jail

She's a fucking mess

You should stop by and see her

AZURE DIDN'T APPRECIATE Greer telling her what to do. But what she appreciated even less was how she found out Rus had been arrested the morning *after*. Rus hadn't called her to bail her out. She hadn't left a message to say she was okay. She hadn't even shot Azure a text to let her know what happened. It was radio silence.

Azure wasn't really pissed about it, although maybe she should have been. Rus's silence hurt more than anything. Because Rus not reaching out, not asking for her help, made the words she'd said the previous night play over in Azure's head on loop.

I didn't want you.

I didn't want you.

I didn't want you.

Azure thought about those words a lot in the hours that spanned between when she stormed out of 157 Mourning Moore and the following morning. And all she could determine from the conversation was that Meiling was right —something was wrong with Rus. The question was, *what*?

Scrubbing at her face, Azure rolled over to glare at the

curtains, which had somehow not been pulled last night. While she didn't have blackout curtains like her brother, Azure had hung a set that would make the morning sun at least bearable by a morning person's standards. Of course, that surmised that she felt like a morning person, which she didn't right at that moment. She didn't usually, if she was being honest. What was that saying? Fake it till you make it? Some bullshit.

The sun had risen and now shone in a cloudless sky, taunting her with its cheerfulness. That bitch.

The only saving grace was that it was Sunday. The singular day of the week that Elwood & Co. wasn't open. And Azure had planned to sleep in, at least a couple hours, before she headed into work. That seemed appropriate after the evening she had, didn't it? When one's girlfriend ripped out their heart and fucking stomped on it, one should be allowed to sleep in for a little bit.

Her phone dinged again, and Azure groaned. Obviously not.

What she found upon turning her phone over and squinting at the notification on the home screen made her groan even louder.

AUNT CARMINE

Emergency Board meeting.

You're going to want to be there.

You've got ten minutes.

Azure had a brief moment to wonder what the fuck they were having an emergency meeting *for* before someone pounded on the front door.

"Goddess grant me the strength." Azure rolled from her bed and hobbled down the stairs. Upon flinging the door open, she found Nesta on the front stoop looking very un-

Nesta-like with a tangled mess of a ponytail—like they'd slept in it—and clothes rumpled, like they pulled them from the laundry. And . . . were they wearing Greer's uniform pants? It was hard to tell with the light coming from behind them, but Azure was reasonably sure they were.

"Oh, thank the Goddess you're still here," Nesta gasped, almost flinging themself at Azure in their rush to grab hold of her and pull her outside.

"Still here?" Azure stumbled after Nesta, her slippered feet catching on the last step before the sidewalk and almost sending her tumbling. But Nesta wasn't slowing down to give her a chance to catch her balance. They were a person on a mission. And their mission appeared to be dragging Azure from her front door across the wet, slush-filled street —soaking her slippers through—to the doorstep of 157 Mourning Moore.

"Yes, I thought you might have left for the meeting already." They lifted their fist to bang on the door. Strange that it didn't open immediately. Stranger still that Azure couldn't hear any sounds coming from inside. The energy about the place was . . . *wrong*. Something off about it settled over her nerves like itchy wool.

"The meeting." Was Azure not fully awake yet, or was Nesta not making any fucking sense? Goddess, she was tired. So very tired. Drama did that to her. She didn't have the energy reserves, wasn't equipped, to deal with other people's bullshit. Especially this early in the morning.

"The emergency board meeting," Nesta said over another hard bang on the door.

"How did you know about that?" Goddess, all this shit had to hit the fan at once, didn't it? And on her day off too. Azure couldn't win, could she?

"Everyone knows about it." Nesta huffed an irritated

breath, and another series of knocks followed, each more frantic than the last.

Azure hadn't thought much about the emergency meeting. The board did that sometimes. It was annoying, sure, but it was usually nothing serious. Except—except Rus had been *arrested* early Saturday morning. That was more than enough time for the rumor mill of Moondale to work its grotesque magic and have that news get back to the board. More than enough time for them to second guess her introductory period. Fuck.

"Icarus! I know you're here! Blue is parked out front! Open this fucking door!" Nesta slammed their fist against it, the window in the door shuddering with the force. They reached for the handle and jiggled it. Nothing. The door refused to budge for them.

"Let me," Azure said, shouldering Nesta out of the way. She wasn't sure why she thought 157 Mourning Moore would open for her. She wasn't its master. Her name wasn't on the deed. And she'd never lived there. It didn't matter that she'd woven her magic into the wards and into the protection surrounding the Yule tree. The house would not yield to her, she was certain. Especially when its master seemed to want to keep everyone out.

Yet, as soon as Azure took the knob, it gave under her hand and she pushed through into the dark foyer.

Taking a breath in through her mouth, Azure tasted how stale the air was on her tongue. It shouldn't have been. It hadn't even been a full forty-eight hours yet since the girls left with Fernando to stay at Cagney's. Meiling had been sending her regular updates since their talk at the shop. But the air here tasted—smelled—like the house had been locked up for decades, centuries.

"Icarus!" Nesta shouted again, starting for the front steps. Azure grabbed their arm and pulled them to a stop.

"I'll get her. You go get the car started so we can leave as soon as she's ready." The words came from an instinct Azure couldn't explain. Nesta hadn't said why they were banging her door down early in the morning, just that it was about the meeting. Hadn't said why they were at 157 Mourning Moore, but Azure could make an educated guess. Rus needed to be at the meeting to defend herself, and no one had been able to get a hold of her. She'd probably let her phone die. She did that sometimes.

Nesta looked Azure over for a split second, as if making up their mind about something—maybe judging if Azure was dressed appropriately for a meeting. She wasn't, but they didn't have time to worry about that, and honestly, Azure didn't care. If the board was going to try to pull some shady shit by having an emergency meeting without providing adequate notice to everyone involved, then Azure was going to show up in her bunny slippers. Nesta didn't seem to disagree as they stepped down from the stairs and beelined for their car parked on the curb.

Finding Rus was easy. All Azure did was climb the stairs to the attic and push the door open. Rus sat there, slumped over her desk, as if she'd fallen asleep in the middle of working. When she didn't stir at the sound of the door creaking farther open, Azure assumed she had.

"Rus," she called softly, hoping not to scare her.

No answer. How long had Rus been asleep? How long had she gone without any rest before passing out? There was no way to tell, even for those who lived at 157 Mourning Moore. Rus was an expert at hiding her weaknesses.

Taking a deep breath, Azure paced across the attic room, her slippers scuffing on the floor, and took Rus's shoulder. Something zinged up along her nerves—a warning, likely from whatever had latched on to Rus. Azure thought maybe she could needle it out then. Pull it to the forefront so she could deal with it directly. But she heard Nesta beep their horn from the street and knew there wasn't time for that. She'd have to deal with it after. Giving Rus a gentle shake, Azure pulled her into the waking world.

"What the fuck?" Rus asked, groggy, wiping the corner of her mouth where drool had gathered.

"The board is calling an emergency meeting." Azure glanced down at what was on Rus's desk. It was some type of array. Something complex, intricate. Something that would take a lot of power. But before she could decipher what it might be for, Rus covered it with a blank sheet from the stack off to the side.

"When?" Rus stretched out her neck, the vertebrae popping loudly. Goddess, she really needed to see a chiropractor, or a doctor. Something. Azure added it to the mental list of things she'd have to deal with once the board was satiated that Rus wasn't going to fly off the handle and bring an undead army into Moondale.

"Right now." Azure went to the wardrobe to pull out two hoodies. One for Rus to throw on over her mussed T-shirt, and one for herself to hide the flannel button-up pajama top she'd worn to bed the night before. Any other time, she might have lingered over the smell of the fabric near her nose. Petrichor. Smoke. The hint of patchouli oil. The smell of Rus lingering from her shampoo and body wash. But there wasn't time for that today.

"*Right now* right now?" Rus's voice was muffled by the fabric of the hoodie, and when her head popped out of the top, her unbrushed hair looked even more unkempt. There was nothing for it. They didn't have time for her to run a comb through it.

"Right now right now," Azure confirmed. The muscles in her arm twitched, itching to offer Rus her hand to guide her down the steps, but she didn't. *I didn't want you* lingered in the back of her mind. "Nesta is waiting with the car."

Rus didn't ask any more questions, and soon they both scuttled down the steps toward the basket where the shoes were kept. After some digging, Rus unearthed an extra pair of sneakers for Azure from the bottom. Warmth settled into Azure's veins, but another honk of the horn from Nesta meant she didn't get the chance to properly thank Rus before they loaded into the car and were on their way.

The room was still cold from the heat being left off overnight, and a shout sounded when Azure arrived with her little party. Everyone appeared to be in varying states of presentability. *At least I'm not the only one in my pajamas.*

Everyone seemed unkempt except Brant Ironwood. He sat at the center of the tables of elders in a neatly pressed dress shirt, his Burberry coat and scarf hung across the back of the chair, as if he were unbothered by the chill that lingered in the air. The expression on his face resembled the cat that caught the canary, and Azure wanted nothing more than to smack it away.

Out of the corner of her eye, Azure saw Phyre shifting from foot to foot, guilt lining her downturned mouth. That answered the question of how the board found out. Azure would get to the bottom of that later. She was sure it wasn't anything half as nefarious as it seemed. Not if Phyre was involved. She'd been Rus's sister in all but name for many years; they grew up in the same orphanage. There was no way she would have intentionally deceived Rus and brought this about. Shaking herself, Azure turned back to the elders seated at the table and frowned.

Nixie Virnan was notably absent. That couldn't be a coincidence. Brant was playing dirty.

"Well?" Brant called from the front of the room, his eyes locking on Rus where she'd entered behind Azure, and suddenly Azure felt every inch that Rus stood above her. There was no shielding the other woman, even if she was thinner than Azure, from the combined attention of the entire room as they swiveled to look at her over Azure's head. "What do you have to say for yourself, Ashthorne?"

"About what?" Rus called back, her voice over-loud, over-confident in the now nearly silent room. She stuffed her hands into her pockets, her shoulders hunching backward in something that might have been seen as arrogance if Azure didn't know her better. But Azure *did* know her better. This was Rus's fighting stance. The one she took the moment before she went into battle. "You're going to have to be more specific, Ironwood."

"The police report says"—Brant lifted a piece of paper from the table, making a big show of pulling his reading glasses down from on top of his head so he could see clearly —"that you broke into the mayor of Ironport's residence and tried to summon a demon."

Azure's body seized up. A demon. Rus had tried to summon a demon? *Why?!* But as she watched Rus from the corner of her eye, the other woman didn't bristle at the accusation. Instead, she seemed to sink further into the slouch of nonchalance. Something was wrong about *that* too. About how unbothered she was.

"If I tried to summon a demon, there would *be* a demon," Rus said, all bravado, and Azure let out an exasperated sigh.

"Rus—"

"But there isn't, is there?" Rus continued, ignoring the warning in Azure's tone. "Produce this demon I supposedly conjured, then we'll talk."

Brant's eyes narrowed further. He looked irritated, and Azure could understand why. Rus was being purposefully insolent instead of contrite as she maybe should have been.

She should have been groveling, asking them to reconsider whatever decision they were going to pass down. Begging them to think again. But Azure knew better than that, didn't she? Rus didn't cower. She didn't beg. Instead, she lifted her head and took whatever was coming her way on the chin.

"And the accusations that you broke into—"

"No charges were pressed against me." Rus shrugged and started toward the front tables, her steps slow and casual. Azure followed, dragged along on the tide of Rus's self-assuredness. Goddess, she really was gone on Rus, wasn't she? "And even if there had been"—Rus licked her lips, pulling a hand from her pocket to examine her nails—"that is outside the Moondale Board of Magic's jurisdiction."

"We are well within our rights to punish those who break the—"

"To those who break the covenant." Rus's voice was soft, deadly. "But as there is no proof that I did, in fact, summon a demon, those other allegations are outside the purview of the covenant. Are they not, Sheriff Greer?"

Greer stood from his chair when called upon. "She's right. There's no recourse for this kind of thing."

If Brant were younger, he might have harrumphed at being checked during this latest bid to prove Rus was unfit to be a coven head. Granted, he wasn't *wrong*. At the current moment, she wasn't exactly acting capable of it. But that was an easy enough fix, once Azure figured out what the fuck was wrong with her.

"It's still not a good look for a coven head to be arrested in a neighboring town." Brant's grip tightened, crinkling the papers. "Consider this a warning, Ashthorne. *All* your actions affect whether you will be given the right to start a coven in Moondale."

"I very much appreciate your concern, Elder Ironwood." Rus swept into a mock bow. "I will take such warnings under advisement. Is there anything else we need to address at this meeting?"

"No, the agenda was simply to discuss the Coven of the Forgotten," Aunt Carmine said, her tone enough to tell Azure she wasn't pleased with this "emergency" meeting.

"Then might we disband? It's Sunday, and rather early." Rus lifted from her bow to shoot the room a winning smile. "I'm sure you all have better things to do today."

The general consensus, as Azure heard it from the muttering around them, was that yes, they all had better places to be. Everyone stood and headed for the door. Rus turned to fire a wink Azure's way, then she disappeared into the crowd and from sight before Azure could catch her and demand answers.

A demon. A summoning. The fucking Ironport mayor's house?!

When she turned to Nesta for support, they shrugged and turned to follow the others out. No help. No one in this town was any fucking help. Aunt Carmine was at her side a moment later, tilting her head toward the offices at the back of the building, and Azure followed her.

Once the door shut behind them, Aunt Carmine drooped. "She needs to be more careful."

"I'm aware." But Azure wasn't sure how she could make Rus do anything, least of all be more careful. Aunt Carmine knew this.

"Ironwood isn't going to let this go. He's going to keep digging. If Rus has anything else in her background, any other record of crimes, he'll find it and use it against her." Aunt Carmine raked her fingers through her messy salt-and-pepper hair, catching in the tangles. Dark circles ringed her eyes, and Azure was forced to consider how many of the people she loved lost sleep over this matter. "This was a warning shot across the broom handle. He'll be back to deliver a killing blow next."

"There's nothing else to find."

"You can say that with confidence?"

She couldn't. But she'd make damn sure it was the truth. Even if she wound up altering records herself.

Azure nodded.

Aunt Carmine seemed to read her intentions in what Azure didn't say and sighed accordingly, her shoulders sagging, but she didn't call Azure on it, gratefully. Instead, she asked, "And this is what you really want, my child?"

It was, but Azure wasn't sure how to put it into words. Wasn't sure how to show the desire and the drive that simmered under her skin to see this thing to fruition. Not just for Rus. Not just for the girls. But for herself. To leave something behind. To prove her life had some meaning. To —

"What if I said I wanted to go back to school?" Azure asked, the words seeming to come from nowhere and everywhere all at once. "To get my doctorate? To maybe become a professor?"

The change of topic didn't even make Aunt Carmine blink. Her face was stoic, unreadable, when she said, "I'd want to know what took you so long."

"The shop —" Azure floundered. She would have known how to respond to outright rejection. But this . . . this was just confusing. "The Elwoods have always —"

"And I'm sure we always will." Aunt Carmine shrugged, turning to head for her desk. She dropped into the chair behind it and bent over to pull something from the drawer at the bottom. "But it doesn't have to be you, Azure. It *never* had to be you. I wouldn't ask you to sacrifice what you wanted for some made-up legacy."

Was that what it was? A made-up legacy? Had Azure spent her entire life aspiring to something none of them even believed in anymore? What a waste. What a *waste*!

"Here. Next time you see Icarus, have her fill these out." Aunt Carmine held out a manilla folder, thick with paper. Duplicates of the forms that were ruined on Friday when Azure and Rus fought.

Azure took them, numb, dazed, by the realization that Aunt Carmine, the head of her family, had never expected Azure to fill the role she'd always stuffed herself into. What other things had Aunt Carmine never expected of her? The elder seat? Was that not going to be forced on her either? Could she give that up? Give up her coven, even? Without her aunt disowning her? Why had she thought Aunt Carmine would hate her for that?

"And if you want to apply to Moondale U's PhD program, the applications are online. I'm sure many of your previous professors would be happy to provide references, but if you'd like me to ask around, I can." So casual. Like this conversation wasn't completely changing Azure's worldview. "As for the shop, I'll reach out to the extended family. Sunila, I think, was talking about taking a gap year. She could fill in while we look for someone else."

"Don't—" Azure blurted, and Aunt Carmine looked up, her lips pursed. "Don't do it just yet. Let me think about it."

"Of course. There is a lot to consider." Aunt Carmine nodded, smiling a little at her. A knowing look around her eyes suggested maybe Aunt Carmine was saying more than the words leaving her mouth. "You have a lot of choices to make. Just let me know before the solstice, will you? So I have time to find your replacement."

"I will. Thank you."

Azure practically sprinted from the room.

Chapter 24

CHOICES.

Aunt Carmine had said *choices*. Plural. Like maybe she knew Azure was thinking of leaving Jade Waters to devote her full attention to the Coven of the Forgotten. Which honestly hadn't been a thing she was seriously considering until that exact moment. Until she realized how close she and Rus were to losing everything. How Aunt Carmine wanted her to be happy, no matter what that happiness looked like. How much freedom it would give her to follow her passions, to find her own path, without having to worry what the rest of Jade Waters would think of her. Suddenly everything else seemed trivial compared to thinking over what lay before her.

The remainder of the day was mindless. She returned home to get ready to go into the shop, then spent time going through stocking and inventory, her thoughts elsewhere.

What would it mean for her if she left Jade Waters? Would she be cut out of all family rituals in the future?

She definitely couldn't become the Jade Waters elder, that she was sure of. But she'd never really wanted to be. The question was, if not her, then who? Violet had been right in saying it had always been someone from their bloodline who held the seat.

Did it have to be?

No. Probably not. Nothing had to be the way Violet had

always told her it had to be. Nothing had to be the way she'd always thought it did.

There were so many options once she set aside the limited perspective Violet had painted her world in. It could be anyone with the Elwood name. Anyone who'd grown up in their traditions. Indigo would make an excellent candidate once he'd matured a little and settled down. And if he didn't want it, there were always their cousins. Sunila maybe, or one of her many sisters, although they hadn't been a part of the Moondale Elwoods for at least a generation. Azure didn't think that would matter. Moondale wouldn't care, so long as she had an Elwood in the seat. Blood, for all it was used regularly in their rituals, was largely meaningless in terms of lineage to magic. Blood was blood was blood. It didn't matter who it came from.

And if that were the case, why did Azure have to be tied to that responsibility? Yes, it's what her father would have wanted for her, for Violet, for the coven. But her father wasn't here. And even before he died, he hadn't been here. He'd left Moondale and his home branch of Jade Waters behind in favor of greener pastures in Boston. Azure couldn't blame him for that; he wanted to be at the forefront of his field to help as many people as he could. Being a doctor worked better in a big city when it came to helping as many as possible.

Plus, from what she'd heard after returning, her mother hadn't wanted to stay in Moondale. Azure and Violet's mother hadn't been a Moondale witch; she'd just gone to Moondale U and met their father. The small-town life wasn't for her, and their father had followed her.

Maybe following the person they loved was a hereditary thing for the Elwoods. Violet gave up her dreams of a family, of traveling the world and healing everyone she could, for the woman she married. Although that wasn't really love, was it? And here Azure was, readying to give up everything she'd always thought would be hers for Rus.

The difference was that Rus wasn't asking her to, and nothing Azure gave up was anything she particularly *wanted* to begin with.

Well, that's it, isn't it? Azure laughed to herself, shaking her head. It'd been so simple all along, hadn't it? Goddess, she was so fucking stupid sometimes. Thickheaded, Aunt Maureen had always said, and she was right. If Azure had stopped and really thought about this before—ignored everything Violet said and her own preconceived notion of duty—she'd have had her answer *weeks* ago.

She needed to tell her siblings first thing, before she made the announcement to anyone else. Get ahead of it lest Violet try to cause a scene at the next board meeting.

Pulling her phone from under the counter, she sent out a quick text to the Elwood Sibling Group Chat.

AZURE

Emergency Sibling Bonding Night.

VIOLET

Will have to cancel date night.

INDIGO

Then cancel it!

Az never calls emergency nights!

It must be important!

VIOLET

I'm aware of that. No need to yell.

INDIGO

Exclaiming is not the same thing as yelling

VIOLET

Of course.

INDIGO

Who's cooking?

I will provide dinner. I was thinking Indian?

INDIGO

works for me!

Tikka Masala

extra spicy

VIOLET

Really? Extra spicy? You complained last time you burned your lips.

INDIGO

And loved every min of it

Violet? Order?

VIOLET

Curry. Medium. Time?

I should be done inventory around five? That work?

INDIGO

Sure, let's eat at old lady times for my two old ladies

VIOLET

Might be a little late. Last patient at 4:30. But I'll bring the wine as an apology?

INDIGO

Not the boxed stuff!

VIOLET

You won't be drinking it. You're underage!

INDIGO

You're no fuuuuuun

VIOLET

I don't claim to be.

Got to go, my next apt just walked in. See you tonight.

AZURE SET HER PHONE DOWN ON THE COUNTER AND returned her attention to her work. She had a lot to do if she was going to make a five o'clock dinner with her siblings, including ordering food and buying a couple better bottles of wine than Violet was likely to bring. She had horrible taste. Alternating between buying the most expensive or the cheapest bottle on the shelf depending on her mood. Neither of which was a good option. And Azure thought they might need the wine for what she was going to tell them. Well . . . Violet would. Indigo would probably be happy for her.

Another notification lit up her phone, and Azure's eyes were drawn to the screen and Indigo's words. He'd texted her privately, away from the group chat.

INDIGO

Where's the fire?

She thought to tell him. It would be nice to have someone on her side walking in. But that would piss off Violet more when things finally came out. So instead of telling her brother what was going on, she said:

You'll see tonight. Get back to your schoolwork.

UGH

Boring

And that was the last she heard from her brother on the matter. Her next order of business was to hunt down Phyre at the forge and figure out what the fuck she'd been thinking telling Brant about Rus's arrest.

A quick glance at Azure's watch told her it was about lunch time anyway, so she turned the sign at the door to "Be right back" and headed down Main Street. Ironwood's forge was attached to a storefront with big bay windows full of glass cases, each sporting dozens of intricate pieces of jewelry designed by the Ironwood clan.

It wasn't their only business, of course, and certainly not the one that made the most money. But it kept them afloat between induction rituals when their services were required for the forging of a witchling's athame.

Without glancing in the window, Azure ducked down the small alley in between Ironwood Jewelers and the bakery next door. The cobblestones were slick, but she managed to make it around back without busting her ass. At the back of the shop, a garage had been converted into the Ironwood forge with a big open door, and the music of clanking tools drifted out into the cool late-autumn air.

Brenton was alone there, his light brown thickly muscled arms moving to the rhythm of the fall of his hammer as he worked. He didn't notice her at first, so focused on what he was doing, but when he did, he stilled, a frown tugging at his mouth, his squared jaw clenching. He dipped the piece he was working on in water, steam filling the air, and Azure stepped in out of the cold.

"If you're here to yell at my sister, you can fuck right off," Brenton said, his back to her, shoulders stiff.

"I just want to understand what she was thinking, telling Brant about Rus." Azure stuffed her hands deep into her pockets and forced herself not to bite the words out.

Anger wouldn't get her anywhere, not with Brenton. He'd close up. Plus, he'd probably bitch to Violet, and she didn't need that drama on top of everything else.

"She didn't know Uncle Brant was here." His shoulders fell a little, and he spun to face her, arms crossed over his chest as he leaned back against the tub of water against the wall. "He came by to 'check in.' Was hanging around outside, eavesdropping like the little creep he is."

"Check in on what? He's never worked a day in his life at the forge." She knew that because Brenton had gotten drunk at Violet and Taryn's wedding and gone off about that and a bunch of other shit. She couldn't remember half of it—she'd been pretty blitzed too—but she remembered that complaint because it had made Nesta do a spit take.

"Fuck if I know." Brenton grunted then let out a breath, his hand raking along his hair where it was tied back in a tight ponytail, plastered to his head. "Look, Phyre's real sorry. She didn't mean to. And she knows it almost fucked up Rus's chances. She's—she's been messed up about it all day. That's why she's not here. She almost set her fucking hair on fire earlier. I had to send her home."

Azure nodded, relaxing a little. She knew what it was like to have someone in your family who couldn't be trusted. Knew how it could make a person feel . . . wrong. After all, that's how she felt about Taryn. And it was probably worse with Phyre since Brant was the only reason she'd been adopted into the Ironwood family at all. "All right. Tell her she's forgiven. But we need to be more careful from now on."

"O'course." Brenton lifted his chin a little. "And let us know if there is anything we can do to help y'all, anything at all. You've got my number?"

"I do."

"Good." He pulled a rag out of his pocket to rub sweat from his neck, and turned back to his project, effectively dismissing Azure. But as she spun on her heel to head back to her own shop he called, "And don't let that bastard win, yeah? I know he's blood and all, but I'm getting a little sick of his high and mighty bullshit."

"I'll do my level best."

By the time the table was set, Azure just waiting for her siblings to arrive, her stomach was in knots. By the end of this Sibling Bonding Night, at least one of her siblings may no longer be speaking to her. And while sometimes Violet made her want to scream — sometimes, she thought maybe it'd be better they weren't on speaking terms — the truth was that Violet was her big sister, and Azure needed her. Maybe not how she once had, when she'd been freshly orphaned and moving to a strange town to live with aunts she hardly remembered from the handful of times they'd met. But the degree to which she needed Violet didn't really matter when Violet may very well cut her out entirely after this.

Still, she would have to face the possibility with her chin held high. If Violet wanted to act that way, wanted to punish Azure for making the choice most likely to make her happy, then so be it. There was nothing Azure could do to stop her, and she wasn't going to let a little pissiness from her sister put her off the idea. Violet would have to get the fuck over it.

"She's here," Indigo said, skidding down the stairs in an oversized crocheted sweater that looked like it was made from scraps and his own ingenuity. He had a long hook and some yarn hanging out of one pocket, likely thinking that if this turned boring, he could work on his latest project. Azure envied him that—the ability to check out and focus on counting stitches. She'd never gotten the trick of it, even when he'd tried to teach her. Her hands didn't move that way. But Indigo, who seemed to flit from thing to thing, could be single-mindedly focused when it came to any kind of soft craft. Hand him a needle and thread, or a crochet hook and some yarn, and watch magic happen in real time. Like making something from nothing.

Coming over to lean on the kitchen counter where Azure was uncorking the wine and pouring two generous glasses, he peered up at her through his bangs. "Is it that bad?"

"It's not great," she confessed. She thought maybe he had an inkling of what was coming, but he didn't say as much, just nodded and picked up her glass to take a healthy sip.

"For my delicate nerves," Indigo teased with a wink. "You should have some too. It's medicinal. Fortify yourself." The doorbell rang, and he slid the glass closer to her, giving her a pointed look. "I'll get the door."

Azure took his advice and gulped down half the glass in the time it took for Violet to take off her coat and shoes and give Indigo a hug. She refilled it before her sister could see what she'd done, and no doubt judge her, then took both glasses to the table.

"So, what's the emergency?" Violet asked, her lips tilted down. Indigo just *had* to go and point out that Azure never called emergency Sibling Bonding Nights, didn't he? If he hadn't, maybe Violet wouldn't have remembered that when emergency nights were called, it was always Violet or Indigo who initiated them. The rarity of Azure doing it made the air that much heavier between them.

"Let's eat first," Azure said and sat before her plate. She didn't know how she'd manage to choke down any food with how her stomach was churning, but dinner smelled delicious. For a long moment Violet stood behind her chair, her eyes fixed on Azure as if trying to ferret out what she was up to, trying to force her to talk. It had worked many a time in the past, but it wouldn't work now. Azure leaned forward and pointedly filled her plate.

Indigo flopped down beside her, Goddess bless him, and followed suit, leaving Violet no choice but to do the same.

What followed was the most awkward half hour Azure had ever experienced in the presence of her siblings. The knowledge that Azure had news for them, had called them all together to tell them something, sat heavy in the air around them. Three times, Indigo tried to start a conversation about school, about a project he was working on, about how the shop was doing as Yule drew closer. And all three times he'd been met with minimal responses. Azure almost felt bad for him, but there was nothing she could do.

When it finally got to be too much for even her, Azure said, "I'm leaving the coven."

Indigo coughed, although she'd made sure to wait until no one had anything in their mouths to speak. Banging on his chest, he asked, "Say what now?" at the same time Violet hissed, "*Excuse me?*"

"I have decided"—Azure sat up straighter, folding her hands neatly in her lap—"that effective Monday, I will be leaving Jade Waters and officially starting the process of joining the Coven of the Forgotten."

"You cannot be serious." Violet's face had gone pinched, her hands shaking where they rested on either side of her plate. She was furious. She had every right to be. But her fury wasn't going to change Azure's mind, and she knew, now more than ever, that she had made the right choice.

This wasn't just what she needed, but also what Rus and the girls needed, what Jade Waters needed. Her loyalties would forever be split so long as she tried to tie herself to both Jade Waters and the Forgotten. Neither would benefit from that. She had to let one go. This was the best thing for everyone involved.

"I am serious. I have already filled out the paperwork. It will go to the Board of Magic tomorrow, making my resignation complete." Azure thought that saying this out loud would make it harder, would make it worse, but it didn't. She felt lighter than she had in weeks, perhaps ever in her life. Free of the mantle of responsibility, and the expectation she realized now she'd placed largely on herself. And for what? It had never brought her any happiness. Never made her feel any more loved or valued by her family, her people. And it had cost her, in the end.

"And what will you do then?" Violet asked as if she didn't already know the answer, as if Azure hadn't already said as much, but she seemed to want to repeat it. As if by her saying the words, Azure would realize how foolish this decision was. She would not. "Tie yourself to the sinking ship that is Icarus Ashthorne? Give up your coven? Your family? Your prospects? And what if Moondale doesn't accept you back once you've left Jade Waters? What if you're cast adrift forever? It's been decades since a witch left their coven not for marriage."

"What prospects?" Indigo pressed, giving voice to the exact thing Azure had been thinking herself. He'd been quiet for much of this conversation, but when Azure looked to him out of the corner of her eye, she saw that he was on her side. They were a united front against their sister. And the support warmed her to the core. Yes, this was right. The people who really mattered, the ones who cared about her happiness, wouldn't begrudge her this. Violet would have to come around to it. "If you mean the elder seat"—Indigo sat up taller in his chair, his eyes narrowing on their sister, readying for a fight—"Az doesn't want it. She never has."

"Don't be selfish, Azure." Violet homed in on her, ignoring Indigo and his puffed-up chest. But that didn't matter because his support gave Azure the courage she needed. Enough was enough. Violet needed to let this go.

"You're the one being selfish!" Indigo snarled, but he settled when Azure patted his arm lightly.

"Yes, I am being selfish," Azure agreed. There was no point in pretending she wasn't. "I'm giving up the elder seat. It'll have to go to another Elwood. I'm also going back to school, to get my doctorate in spellcraft, which means someone else will have to take over the store. But"—she inhaled deeply and forced Violet to look her in the eye, to see the truth in the words that followed—"I hope you'll understand when I say this is what *I* want. I'm doing this because it'll make *me* happy. It's not for Rus. It's not for the girls. It's not for anyone else, it's just for me. Entirely selfish, yes, but how often have I put my own needs on the back burner for others? How much of my own life would you have me give up for a dream that isn't my own?"

"I—You know that's not—" Violet stuttered, floundered, her jaw working over words she didn't quite know how to verbalize. Not yet, at least. She would be able to at some point, but by then it would be done. Azure would have left Jade Waters, and tied herself, her magic, and her blood to the Forgotten.

"I'm going for a walk," Azure said after a weighted silence, pushing from her chair. "When next we speak, Violet, I hope you'll be more understanding."

She squeezed her sister's shoulder as she passed on the way to the door but didn't wait for any further response before she was out in the chill December air. It smelled like snow. Real snow this time. Not just flakes, and flurries, and rain. Snow that might cover Moondale in a blanket of fresh white, washing it clean if just for a few hours before the cars muddied it with their grime.

It was going to be a beautiful night.

Chapter 25

YOU ALWAYS HURT *the ones you love.*

Rus recognized the voice now.

The one that had been lingering at the back of her mind for weeks. She didn't know how she missed it before. How she hadn't realized. No, she *did* know how. She'd been busy, distracted, and it knew her, body and soul. Knew all her insecurities. All her worst thoughts. How to mimic them and use them.

How? Because once upon a time, it—*she* rather—had said she loved Rus.

Her name was Kaytee Williams, and she'd been everything Azure Elwood was not. Loud. Forward. Bold. She didn't stifle herself for anyone else. She had shone like a beacon, her light bright enough that Rus had seen it from across a crowded room. And Rus, fresh after losing Az, her home, her life, her potential for stability, had been swept up in the whirlwind of Kaytee Williams. Just young enough, and stupid enough, to think that what she really needed was the exact opposite of Az.

That was Kaytee in every way, Rus found out eventually, and almost never for the better.

Kaytee never hit Rus, but she'd cut her down in a million little ways. Making her feel useless. Stupid. Immature.

Death by a thousand cuts.

"I can't believe you thought that was a good idea.

Weren't you paying attention?" Kaytee would say, every word a blow. "Fuck's sake, Rus, how careless can you be?"

"And you really believe that?" Kaytee had snorted once when Rus told Kaytee how she believed the dead deserved their respect. They shouldn't be used for gain. Not the way Kaytee thought they ought to be. "They're spirits, Rus. They don't have any rights."

Kaytee was a necromancer too, and Rus felt seen in a way she never had with Az—or anyone else, for that matter. Here was someone who understood her and her craft. Here was someone she could debate the ins and outs of the world of the dead with, where most people wouldn't even talk about it.

"They're just energy."

"They don't have feelings."

"Don't be stupid, you aren't saving anyone."

"What kind of soft-hearted, simple-minded bullshit is that?"

"You're useless as a necromancer if you can't see it."

"Why would anyone want to work with you?"

"Why would anyone trust you?"

"Why would anyone love you?"

The words piled up over the months. One on top of the other, weighing Rus down, down, down, until she felt like they'd bury her.

The necromancer, Icarus Ashthorne, buried alive. Wouldn't that be funny?

And Rus?

Well. Rus just took it.

Because she didn't want to be alone. Because she hadn't been alone since she was a child. Because the world was big and scary when you were a witch without a coven. And worst of all, because at some point she started to believe maybe Kaytee was right. Started to see the cracks and the ugliness in herself that Kaytee said were there. Began to wonder why Az had loved her at all. *If* she even had.

It wasn't until after—after the accident with the undead fox, after Kaytee's death—that Rus realized exactly what Kaytee had been doing to her. Grooming her. Building her into the perfect little necromancer she could use, and abuse, and manipulate to suit her best.

The fox. That should have tipped Rus off. Goddess, she'd been so stupid.

Kaytee had gotten it into her head to stuff a malicious spirit into the body of a fox. Foxes were malleable, she reasoned, already gray as far as good and evil went. Putting a malicious spirit in it should have been easy. Rus told her it wouldn't work, that she wasn't strong enough, practiced enough, to overcome the fox's original spirit. That she should start smaller, if that's what she wanted to do. With mice, move up from there. But Kaytee wouldn't hear it. Wanted something with claws and a bit of bite to send after someone who'd wronged her. Rus never got an answer on what that meant, or who it had been.

The fox fought back. The spirit lashed out. And in the end, there was hardly anything of Kaytee Williams left to bury.

"I see you figured out how to possess a fox," Rus said, addressing the spirit clinging to her for the first time since she'd realized it was there.

Oh that? That was easy. I'm much stronger than I was before.

"Soul eater," Rus muttered to herself, a chill running up her spine.

Bingo! Kaytee crowed. *But not for long. Your body is limiting, but it has its uses. What did you do to yourself, by the by?*

"Not strong enough to summon a demon." Rus snorted. "That's none of your business."

Oh, it very much is my business, since I'll be taking over here shortly. I ought to know its history.

"Over my dead body." Rus's fists clenched at her sides, and she wasn't sure if she was doing that or if it was Kaytee. There had been so many instances over the last few days that now she was second guessing. Had she been the one to say those horrible things to Az? Or had it been Kaytee, drawing on Rus's memories to target Az with the most hurtful words possible?

Precisely. Kaytee cackled.

"Not fucking likely." The ingredients were already there —everything she'd need to exorcise the spirit clinging to her magic, leeching off it, growing fat and ravenous. She just needed to get her hands to stop shaking long enough to draw the circle.

Why not? What have you got that's worth living for? Face it, Rus, there's nothing here for you. Just let me have the body. I promise I'll take care of it.

"I have my girls," Rus said, grinding ingredients into the mortar, her grip flagging the longer it took. Was Kaytee gaining control, or was she growing tired? She couldn't tell. Black spots danced before her eyes, and she resisted the urge to lift a hand and rub at them. "I have my friends. I have . . ."

Az? Kaytee snorted. *You don't have Az. You never did.*

"I did." She did. Didn't she? Before she left, she had Az. Had everything that Az could ever give another person. Her heart. Her soul. Her body. Her . . . not her magic. Rus had never had Az's magic. Because that belonged to Jade Waters and the Elwoods. Not that she wanted it. She didn't have a right to ask that much from Az. And she never *would* have asked for it. She wasn't like Kaytee. She didn't take what wasn't freely given. "I do."

Keep telling yourself that, sweetheart. But the truth is, you didn't. She always belonged to her coven. And in the end, had you not left, she would have chosen them. Or don't you remember what happened the night you left?

Rus did. She remembered it like it was yesterday. Could summon up the musty scent of rain, damp earth, and a house closed up for too long without coven rituals.

Kaytee forced that memory on her now, giving Rus no choice but to relive it.

"We need to break up," Rus said, her voice quiet but firm. She had made up her mind about this, and she wouldn't be talked out of it. Nothing Az could do or say would stop what was coming.

"What are you talking about? We're not breaking up." There was a stubborn tilt to Azure's chin, and it took everything in Rus not to reach for it, to pull her into a kiss. So she didn't look at her. She stared off over her shoulder to keep her resolve.

Rus bit down hard on the inside of her cheek, drawing blood, the pain the only way to keep her focused on what she was doing, what she must do. Whether Az agreed with it or not, this was for the best. "Yes. We are."

Az didn't say anything to that. She just stood there, water dripping from her clothes, and watched Rus tear both their worlds apart. Ruin everything they'd built together. Lightning crashed outside, reminding Rus she was short on time. The bus would leave in the morning, and this had to be done before then. She couldn't leave Az waiting. She had to say it before she left.

"I'm not what you need right now." Rus hardened her resolve with those words, knew them to be true as much as the ones that followed. "I don't think I ever was."

Az said something, but the words got lost somewhere on the way to Rus's ears. They were a warble of upset, of unshed tears. Rus had caused those tears. She watched them blossom and take over Az's eyes. She had made her love cry. Goddess, she really was the worst. A step forward on Az's part was a step back on Rus's. She hated the distance between them. It was killing her.

Whatever. Once she was gone, it wouldn't matter what happened to her. Az would be free. The Board of Magic would be happy. Moondale would be safe from her, from her necromancy.

"You need someone . . . better."

That's still true, isn't it, Rus? Kaytee asked when Rus returned to the present. There was an athame in her hands, but she didn't remember picking it up. Fuck. Kaytee *was* gaining control. Rus couldn't have that. *She still deserves someone better than you.*

"Even if that's true." Which it was. Rus knew it in every fiber of her being. Az was too good for her, always had been. Rus was Goddess blessed every day Az decided to spend in her company, and Rus would never once take that for granted. Not again. "I still have my girls."

As if they wouldn't be better off without you. Kaytee scoffed.

"They wouldn't," Rus insisted. She had to keep Kaytee talking, keep her from tucking Rus away again inside a memory where she didn't have control over her limbs. She squatted on shaky legs to pace in a small circle, sketching it into the floor with chalk. "What are you doing to me?"

You said it yourself, Rus. I'm a soul eater. What do you think I'm doing to you?

"So you aren't just trying to drive me out of my own body by making me fucking miserable." Rus licked her teeth. They tasted like blood. She coughed into the back of one wrist and wet splattered the skin. It was red.

Please, sweetheart. I'm arrogant, not stupid.

Rus grunted. The floor spun under her, but the circle was closed. Now she just had to draw in the characters and fuel it with magic. Would she have enough? She would call someone, but she didn't think she wanted anyone to know about this, to see this. Kaytee was . . . she was a shameful secret. A relationship Rus wanted to forget. Not even Fernando knew about her. Only Meiling and Aihuan's parents had known, and only because they'd been there to pick up the pieces after Kaytee died.

How long had it been?

For a stronger witch, a witch in peak health, a few weeks might not have made a difference. But for Rus, it would. She had to know. A week or two might be the difference between life and death for her.

"How long?" she croaked, her throat dry and tight. "How long have you been hanging around? Leeching off me."

Kaytee laughed, the sound manic, dark, echoing off the inside of Rus's head and making her dizzy.

She was going to pass out soon. She needed to complete the ritual before she did. Before Kaytee could finish what she'd started. Maybe if she could bind herself and Kaytee to the circle, that would be enough.

Long enough to see that everyone around you would be better off without you. Your girls. Your friends. Azure Elwood. This town. They'd all be better without Icarus Ashthorne around them.

Maybe she was right. Maybe they would all be better, happier, without Rus.

Do you remember the pixie?

Fuck. That was almost three months ago.

Rus was going to die.

But if she was going, she was taking Kaytee fucking Williams with her. She slammed her palm, still coated in the blood she coughed up, down onto the edge of the circle.

Her last reserves of power sealed herself and the soul eater in.

Together. In the middle of her attic.

Chapter 26

HER PHONE RINGING was such a foreign thing that Azure jumped when the first bright sounds of some K-pop song rent the air, cutting through the silence of her walk. She'd chosen it forever ago and couldn't remember the artist or half the lyrics by this point. But even that strangeness was nothing compared to the name on the screen.

Evander Greer.

Greer didn't call.

It wasn't just that Azure didn't receive calls—because she didn't—but Greer in particular never once called. Hardly even texted before that morning when he texted to tell her Rus had been arrested. She didn't even know how he'd gotten her number; she certainly hadn't given it to him. Not even when their match was announced. But there he was, his name lighting up her home screen.

Fuck.

Something was wrong. *Really* wrong.

Dread pooled in Azure's stomach as she hit the little green button and lifted the phone to her ear.

Greer didn't wait for her to say hello or even acknowledge she hadn't accidentally picked it up. He started talking as soon as the line connected. "There was a spike at 157."

"What kind of spike?" But Azure had already turned and started back toward 157 Mourning Moore. She didn't need to know what he was talking about to know she needed to be there. Right now. There was only one person Greer would be call her about.

"Massive influx of negative energy." Greer sounded like he was out of breath, like he'd been running. Which made no sense because he always had his phone on him; there was no reason for him to rush to it. Unless he was already on his way to 157 too.

"Where are the girls?" Where was Rus? She didn't ask that because she knew. She knew where Rus was. Only one person in Moondale could or would cause a spike in negative energy large enough to make Greer sound like that. Only one person knew how to conjure and use it. The question was whether she'd be able to harness it safely. And what was it for? Azure's feet stuttered on the sidewalk, scuffing over an uneven patch of pavement.

"Safe. We were all at Nesta's when my phone started losing its fucking mind. That thing Rus created is pretty damn effective. I'd almost be impressed if it weren't, you know, Rus." He was still impressed. His tone said begrudgingly so. Which would have been funny in any other instance, but Azure couldn't find the humor in it now. Couldn't seem to think past the rush to get to Rus, to protect her from whatever moronic thing she'd decided to do this time.

"Does it give us any details?" She could see the house now. It was dark. Not even the string lights outside remained lit, and that was more worrying than anything Greer said so far. Was Rus drawing on the power? Was the house doing it to shield her? Was something else going on?

"Don't go in till I get there. I'm on my way." Greer's truck engine grumbled in the background. He had to know that wasn't going to stop Azure from throwing herself headfirst into danger to protect Rus. "Seriously, Az, don't.

We don't know what she's gotten herself into. And I can't risk —"

"You didn't answer my question." Where was Darcy? Had Rus sent him away? Was he inside with her? Had he flown off to get help? Why hadn't he come after her to tell her something was going on? Was he hurt?

Greer grunted, annoyed, but answered anyway. "No details. Rus hasn't configured it for that yet. It just shows the spikes and where they're located on the Moondale map."

"I need you to call my aunts. They'll know what to do." They'd also probably be pissed that Azure decided to go in after Rus without backup. But in the end, they'd understand her decision because they'd do the same for each other, wouldn't they?

Reaching for the gate to 157 Mourning Moore, she gritted her jaw against the zap of power that jolted her fingertips. "I'm probably about to lose you."

"You aren't going in there, are you?" Panic seeped into Greer's voice, fear making it shake.

If he was at Nesta's, he was at least five minutes away from 157 Mourning Moore. It didn't seem far when she thought about it that way, but every minute counted when it came to this. Every second ticking away could put Rus one step closer to death. Azure couldn't take that chance.

"Don't you dare go in there, Azure." The command was forced. He had to know it wouldn't work.

Azure pushed the gate open and was hit with the sucking emptiness of whatever negative forces Rus had called to herself to do her magic. It didn't feel like spirits — not like Azure had always known them. It was something else. Something darker. Colder. A gaping void, a black hole, that would swallow her and Moondale together and still be hungry after the fact.

"Azure Elwood! Don't you fucking *dare!*"

But she'd already put the phone in her pocket. She left it connected, just in case, and Azure could hear Greer's voice crackling as he raged at her. It wouldn't be long before she lost the connection or her battery drained. Whichever came first. It didn't matter—Greer wouldn't be able to hear what came next.

One step. Two. Like walking through the ocean. The darkness pushed at her, trying to keep her in place on all sides, the pavement beneath her feet seeming to give every time her toes pushed off. But Azure wasn't going to be stopped by a little thing like pressure. Not if Rus was in trouble.

Azure had never experienced negative energy to this extent before. In all the years she'd known Rus, Rus had never played with forces this heavy, this dark. Not even when Aihuan had been in danger.

It seemed like forever ago. Them saving Aihuan. Azure convincing Rus to start the Coven of the Forgotten. Their talk about Rus building a home for herself. Rus had started to. It would take time, but she was trying, putting down roots, and that's all Azure cared about.

The door to 157 Mourning Moore didn't open when she approached like it normally might have. Had Rus told the house to keep her out? Or was the house protecting Rus? Azure didn't know, but she prepared for the magical backlash that could come from either instance as she reached for the knob.

It didn't turn. Didn't give even a little, as it might have if it were locked.

"You need to let me in," Azure told 157 Mourning Moore, tightening her grip on the knob. She didn't want to force it—that might make the magic react against her—and she didn't have time for any potential injuries that would come from it. What if the house didn't let her in? What if she was kept out until it was too late? What if there was nothing left of Rus by the time she reached her?

"Please," she begged. "*Please* let me in so I can help her."

The air shifted, warmed by whatever magic 157 Mourning Moore possessed, and the door creaked open. Not far. Just enough for Azure to force it the rest of the way with her shoulder.

She was panting by the time she got it open enough to slip through. Inside was completely dark, devoid of any light, even from the windows. Like when Indigo drew his blackout curtains. She felt her way across the foyer to the steps. Once there, it was a slow crawl up to the second floor, following the pull of the magic as it drew her in.

Her toe caught on the last step, and she smacked her palms too hard against the wood floor. Not that Azure had been going for stealth; she was sure Rus—or whatever caused this—already knew she'd entered the house. It probably knew the second she stepped onto the property. Still, her hands stung with the force.

Progress became slower once she reached the second floor. For all the times she'd been to Rus's house, even her room, Azure hadn't memorized the house layout, and the second floor wasn't a straight shot like the first floor was from the front door to the steps. So Azure shuffled blindly about the space until she made it to the stairs that led up to the attic.

The pressure seemed to increase when she got halfway up the steps, pushing on her from all sides as if it could compress her into a marble, or a diamond. She had to crawl up the stairs, every movement a struggle until she could finally look over the top one into Rus's attic room.

Here, there was enough light to see by, and it burned at Azure's retinas. But it wasn't the light after so long in the darkness that brought tears to her eyes. No. It was the sight of Rus standing in the middle of her own room, blood dripping onto the floor, splattering across the boards toward Azure. She held her athame, stained red. Cuts ran up and down her arms—superficial injuries if it were just one or two, but they added up quickly. And Rus had started on her legs.

Azure froze for one beat, two—almost too long—then she flew across the floor to Rus, only stopping when she noticed the containment circle on the floor. "Rus! Rus, you have to stop. You have to *stop*!"

"She won't let me out. Little bitch won't let me out," a voice that was not Rus's crawled out of her throat. It laughed, harsh, rasping, cold. "I keep hurting her, and she won't let me out. Fucking idiot. Why won't you let me out?!"

"I'm not letting you hurt them," Rus snarled back, her voice hard, determined. Her knuckles turned white around the handle of her athame, hand shaking as she fought with whatever was inside of her, tried to keep it inside the containment circle with her.

The containment circle. Azure had to get in there with her. That was the only way to stop that thing from hurting Rus even more. The blood had blotted out several of the characters, making it hard for her to tell what kind of magic Rus used to hold this thing inside. She'd have to do some guesswork. A gamble that might get them both killed, but she was willing to take it if it meant she didn't have to sit there and watch Rus hurt herself anymore.

"Foolishly noble! You were always so stupid, Icarus." The thing snarled, using Rus's throat, making every word sound a little like Rus. Her hand shook as she raised the dagger again. "They don't *care* about you."

"That's not the point!"

The dagger swung down toward Rus's leg, and Azure had just enough time to remember something. Something important.

"You were always the best at talisman work, Az. Have you ever thought of combining it with some of the more basic arrays?" Rus *smiled bright and brilliant, her excitement over new magic infectious. "Like if you reworked this into a containment circle. Whew. That could hold almost anything in."*

Azure vaguely remembered the talisman Rus had been talking about, but it didn't matter. Her magic knew what to do. Dipping her finger in some of the blood that coated the floor—she forced herself not to think about how it had gone cold, how that meant Rus had been at this too long, too long —she scrawled the characters for *bright* and *blue* along one edge of the circle, opening a doorway only she could slip through.

If she'd thought the pressure outside the circle was intense, it was nothing compared to what was inside it. As it forced Azure to her knees, she couldn't imagine how Rus was still standing. Her jeans gathered more blood as she crawled to Rus's side.

She didn't know how she managed—maybe because Rus was fighting it the whole time—but she snatched at the wrist holding the athame, stopping it before it could plunge into Rus's thigh. It clattered to the ground, and Rus's eyes focused finally, *finally*, on Azure.

"Oh. It's you." A growl rumbled up through Rus's chest, that thing inside of her turning gray eyes on Azure that she'd never once in her life seen so cold and cutting. Its tongue poked out, licking at the point of one of Rus's canines as it chuckled darkly. "I thought I told you to stay away from the crow witch."

"Rus." Azure wrapped her arms around Rus's middle, holding her fast so the thing inside of her couldn't thrash free, couldn't reach for the knife again, or some other means to hurt Rus. "Tell me what to do," Azure begged, her eyes burning with tears, and she pressed her face into Rus's stomach, clinging to her like a child. "Tell me what to do to help you fight this thing."

It laughed. A hand carded through Azure's hair, gentle at first, like maybe it was Rus, then it tightened into a fist. It yanked her head back so her neck screamed with pain, straining. "Oh, little hedge witch, do you even know what I am?"

"I don't fucking *care*," Azure spat. It didn't matter *what* it was. Azure would do whatever it took to get it the fuck out of Rus.

"Feisty little thing, isn't she? I can see why she likes you." It leaned down, pressing Rus's face close enough to Azure's that she could taste the tang of sulfur and petrichor on Rus's breath. "Are you the one she left for? The one she ran away to free?"

The words didn't make sense, didn't add up, until they did. Rus left *for* her. Thinking it would help her, *free* her. But from what? From a perceived obligation? From the choice of Rus or Greer. There had never been a choice between them—it was always Rus. Always would be.

"You need to get out of here, Az," Rus gasped, the hold on Azure's hair loosening, fingers brushing at her stinging scalp as if in apology. "It's a soul eater. And I don't—I don't know how much longer I can keep it in here with me."

"You have to exorcise it," Azure pleaded. She didn't know how Rus would manage that, but she had to try.

"From the inside?" Rus laughed, the sound mirthless, hollow.

"I'll help you." She pushed every bit of magic rolling through her body into Rus.

Chapter 27

WARMTH FLOODED RUS, making every cell in her body energized with the boost from Az's magic. It was a different kind of magic, but her body knew what to do with it, how to use it. It helped that this wasn't the first time they'd done this; when they'd been young and stupid, they'd thought sharing magic like this was sexy.

Now, it flooded Rus with memories, drawing to the surface all the things Kaytee tried to bury as she slowly poisoned Rus's mind.

The girls sitting at the table, laughing, happy as they shoveled pizza into their mouths a few nights ago. The paperwork Az had brought with her securely out of the way of greasy fingers. There was barely enough space for all five of them. Fernando had suggested maybe he could eat his dinner on the couch, but then 157 Mourning Moore produced a fifth chair, and they'd all squeezed in.

Rus looked over at Az, her stomach flip-flopping in a way that almost put her off her food as Az leaned over to help Aihuan cut up her pizza into little Aihuan-sized pieces.

"So, Lizzie wants to meet the girls," Az said as if she were continuing some thought she'd had. She did that sometimes — started speaking as if they were already halfway through a conversation. Rus hadn't noticed it as much when they were kids, but she did now. What it must be like in Az's mind, constantly going. What else did she keep tucked away up there? If only Rus were a telepath instead of a medium, then she could find out.

"Who's Lizzie?" Meiling asked around a too-big bite of crust.

A bit of sauce sat beside her mouth, and although Rus knew she should say something, she didn't want to. It was so rare she got to see Meiling as a child these days. Every morning she seemed to get a bit older, a bit closer to the young witch who may very well change their entire world. Aihuan was the same. And Rus wanted to hold on to their youth as long as she could, to protect them from the bad.

Kaytee sneered. *But you couldn't protect them, could you?*

The memory shifted, but they stayed in the kitchen.

Rus leaned over the sink, muttering to herself as she cleaned the dishes, her movements harsh, stuttering. She looked up at the window to see the girls watching her over her shoulder. Aihuan's chubby cheeks were puffed out, her brows drawn together as she tried to figure out what was going on. But Meiling . . . Meiling looked terrified. Her face pinched, her lips pursed, jaw ticking as it worked over something she wanted to say.

"Are you okay, Auntie Rus?" Aihuan asked, the words too soft and suddenly too close.

Rus whipped around, jumping at the nearness, and found the little girl beside her, pulling on the edge of her hoodie. How had she gotten there? Aihuan's bright brown eyes flicked from Rus's face to her soapy hands, and she frowned. "Auntie Rus?"

Looking down at her hand, Rus found the knife she'd used to cut Aihuan's fruit shaking in her grasp. As if it wanted to turn its point on her. As if it had a mind of its own. "I'm okay, little monster," Rus said, forcing herself to put the knife down, lifting every finger from the handle one at a time. It clattered into the bottom of the sink, and Rus took a forceful step back. "What's up, Huaner? Did you need something?"

Kaytee's smugness rolled through Rus. *See? You almost hurt her.*

I didn't! I wouldn't! That was you! I'm a good mom!

Squeezing her eyes shut, Rus shifted the memory herself, pulling up the soft rumbling reverberations of a

Kate Bush song and following the trail of it to another memory.

Necromancer's was less busy than normal, the rainy weather driving people into their homes where they could make their own coffee and curl up under a blanket. All Rus could think about was how she wished she was at home with her girls. Wished she didn't have to work when it was so gross outside. Even helping Meiling with homework would be better than working through a rainy Wednesday, and that was saying something. And her knees ached, but that was usual for bad weather these days.

The bell over the door rang, and Rus looked up to see Carmine Elwood wiping her feet on the front rug. They hadn't spoken much since the conversation about Aihuan, which suited Rus fine. The less anyone talked about Aihuan's condition as reanimated, the better. She didn't need the board finding out. That would put an end to everything she was trying to do.

"Icarus," Carmine said as she approached the counter, "a word?"

Rus wanted to say no, probably more than she'd ever wanted to in her life, but she didn't. Instead, she followed Carmine to the table where the girls usually sat. Both of them were at school now, filling their little brains with everything they'd need to be good witches. Things Rus probably never could have taught them.

"What's this about?" Rus asked, tiredness making her body sag further into the booth seat. She hoped Carmine didn't see it for insolence as she might have once upon a time. Not when Rus wasn't trying to be disrespectful.

Carmine didn't answer right away, her eyes focused on the tabletop, fingers brushing over the scrawling line of one of Aihuan's doodles. Maybe Rus should start covering the table with brown paper so Aihuan didn't completely destroy the finish. No. If Aihuan wanted to deface private property, let her. It might be the only time she could get away with it without getting in trouble.

"Aihuan likes to doodle," Rus said, by way of explanation. "Sometimes she misses the paper."

"I see. You know, I have a spell that could—"

"No need." Rus shook her head, her gaze focusing on a neat little bunny in one corner. Meiling had probably drawn it; it was too advanced to be Aihuan's. "This place is theirs as much as mine and Nando's. They should be allowed to leave their mark on it however they choose."

When she looked up from the little rabbit, Carmine was staring at her with an expression she couldn't read, like perhaps she'd never seen Rus before. Hilarious, considering Carmine had been a part of Rus's life for as long as Az had. "I don't think I've told you this before," Carmine said, the words slow, as if she were sorting them out as they left her, "but you're a good mom, Icarus."

The dark closed in again, but Carmine's voice echoed, the warmth from those words glowing bright, an ember Rus could feed, could stoke into an inferno that would drive off the cold of Kaytee. It wasn't enough, not yet.

Rus looked up from her hands into the black landscape that surrounded her, and found Az there, staring back at her. A pale blue dress flowed in a nonexistent breeze around her, her brown skin warm and soft looking. Long plum-colored hair followed the fluttering of her dress. Her brown eyes were almost black in the dim lighting. She was a shining beacon in the dark that made Rus want to reach for her. To pull her in close again. But something held her back, a vice-like grip around her wrist, and when Rus looked at her hands again she saw the curving, pale fingers of someone else.

"What does that woman know?" Kaytee whispered into Rus's ear, giving her a tug around the waist as if to pull her back into the dark. "You're not—"

"Help is coming," Az said, her calm, clear voice bouncing off the emptiness around them, cutting through Kaytee's ramblings. Then she was right in front of Rus, her hand on Rus's other wrist, the touch warm and soothing. It wasn't a band of iron threatening to tear her away from everything she loved like Kaytee's, but a soft pressure, guiding.

"And there's something else." Az smiled and leaned in to kiss Rus, her lips the same gentle, steady, warm pressure as her hand, and Rus was falling, falling, falling, into a haze of memories.

No. Not memories. These things hadn't happened yet. These things might never happen. Wishes. Hopes. Dreams. Were they Az's? Were they her own? Rus couldn't tell. But they buffeted her, loosening Kaytee's grip on her soul.

Rus and Az dancing in the kitchen of 157 Mourning Moore, a sink full of dishes forgotten behind them. A laugh left Rus as she leaned forward to press her forehead to Az's. Amusement danced in Az's eyes. Aihuan squealed, clapping along to the song, trying to get them to move faster to the music. But they kept lazing in a circle, too wrapped up to notice the way the tempo had changed.

The room shifted, and they were in Rus's bedroom in the attic.

The lights down low. The windows open to let in the sounds of crickets and cicadas, the smell of bay water turned mucky from a hot summer's day. But the sheets beneath her skin were cool, and as Az curled in closer, her hand slipping down over Rus's belly to brush between her thighs, she forgot about the humidity outside. Too wrapped up in the heat spreading through her from her stomach.

"Az," Rus rasped, the name leaving her more like a prayer than a word.

"I've got you," Az murmured against her skin, rolling so she hovered above Rus in the bed, her mouth nipping along her collarbone, then down, down, down.

The room shifted again, and they were in front of the Yule tree, presents stacked so high beneath it, there almost wasn't room.

Az had settled nervously beside it on a pillow, Aihuan in her lap.

Aihuan's chubby little hands held a box with a bow that barely fit on it, her fingers picking at the ribbons.

"Can I open this one?" she asked, looking up at Az, her eyes bright, and Rus's heart could break from watching them. They were so good together. Az was so kind, and gentle, and sweet with her girls. The kind of mother they needed.

"You'll have to ask your Auntie Rus." Az lifted her head to shoot Rus a wink over top of Aihuan's head, and Rus's heart leapt into her throat. Goddess. She was lost on Az, wasn't she?

The scene shifted again. This time they stood in a clearing deep in the woods of Moondale, and it took Rus a second to recognize the place. She'd been only a handful of times when she was a child. At the center of the clearing, a large stone protruded from the rocky ground of the mountains surrounding Moondale.

The Heart of Moondale.

The place the founders had tied their magic to in the beginning. It connected to a vein of ore that ran through the whole town, linked to the lei lines, providing safety and magic to every corner of Moondale. The place where she'd go and tie her blood to the land if her coven was approved.

"Why did you bring me to the Heart of Moondale?" Rus asked, tilting her head at Az standing before her. She looked exactly the same as she had in that dark room, only there was a jut of determination to her chin now. A decision made.

"I think you know why."

Maybe she did, but Rus needed Az to say it. Needed to hear the words, even if this was a dream, an apparition, a wish. She needed to know for sure.

"I would have given up everything for you," Az said, instead of answering the question. For some reason, it didn't feel like she was talking about the past, but the present. She paced around the edge of the clearing, lifting her hand to press into the carvings on the trees as

she went. The moon cycles, put there to protect the clearing and the stone that stood as the Heart of Moondale.

Rus's throat had gone dry, sandpaper scraping against it as she tried to swallow with a click. Az wasn't looking at her anymore, but her attention never seemed to waver, the warmth and light of her magic lingering on Rus's skin. A balm. A reminder. It kept Kaytee at bay, but for how long?

"I would never ask for that." To give up her coven? Her place of honor among the Moondale community? Everything she'd ever known? Rus could never ask that of her, would never. She understood too well what it was to not belong to anyone or anything, and she wished that pain on no one.

Az stopped walking but was before Rus in a blink, her hand held in front of her like she wanted to reach for Rus, but she didn't. Something held her back. An uncertainty shifting in her eyes. Rus hated herself for putting that there. For making Az feel like there was any reason to doubt herself and her feelings. A deep inhale, exhale, and Az held her hand out to Rus, palm up.

"What if I offered it just the same?"

Chapter 28

AZURE WAITED, *her breath trapped in her throat, fingers twitching, palm out. Rus could reject her. Could decide she didn't want all Azure offered. And Azure probably wouldn't even be angry about it. It was a lot, after all. The pressure of knowing that Azure left her coven for Rus—what a weight that would be. But Azure hoped Rus realized she wouldn't have to bear it alone. Never alone.*

Her only regret? That she hadn't had the courage to do this before. Maybe if she had, there wouldn't be a soul eater banging its essence against the barrier Azure had built for them. They were safe there, in the Heart of Moondale, but Azure didn't know for how long. She needed an answer. Soon. Still, she waited, didn't rush. Rus would come to her decision in her own time.

"Is this real?" Rus asked, her gray eyes flicking from Azure's outstretched hand to Azure's face, then back.

Azure nearly laughed at the question but somehow swallowed it down. She didn't want Rus to think she wasn't taking this seriously, or that this was some cruel joke from the soul eater. After she'd regained control, she said, "As real as anything else."

"That doesn't answer my question." Rus's cheeks puffed out in agitation, making her look like an irritated chipmunk.

Cute.

"I'd love to debate the quantifiable realness of a shared consciousness and the metaphysical plain I've created to keep that thing away, but we're running out of time here, Rus." Sweat trickled down her spine, cold, making her shiver. The magic was already flagging. Azure wondered if the soul eater was feasting on it, and if

so, how much more of a problem it would be once it was done. What would be left of them if Rus didn't make a choice? "It's getting stronger. I don't know how long I can keep it out of here."

As her gray eyes sharpened, Rus's mouth fell open a little in awe. "You created this place."

"Yes." Azure let out a long slow breath, willing herself to have more patience. She could hold out a bit longer. She could hold out forever if she had to—at least, that's what she told herself. Although it probably wasn't true. The creature slammed itself against the barrier again, and Azure felt it like a bruise blossoming across her ribs. That would be sore later.

Rus chewed on the inside of her cheek for a moment, looked down at Azure's hand then up to her eyes again. She laughed, the sound all disbelief and awe. She grabbed Azure's hand, her fingers clammy and stiff from how close the soul eater was to dragging her through the veil.

Well. Fuck that thing if it thought it was taking Rus from Azure now.

Azure tightened her hold on Rus and pulled.

The attic was frigid by the time they surfaced again, their breaths puffing out around them. They might be in some real danger of frostbite if they didn't deal with the soul eater soon.

Speaking of the soul eater, its darkness lingered at the edge of the circle, sucking in all the light around it. But at least it wasn't inside Rus anymore, leeching from her essence. Azure counted that as a win.

"We're going to have a talk about how you wound up with a soul eater inside you," Azure panted, pulling Rus in closer, not letting go of her hand.

"Later, dear." Rus shook her head, but she looked brighter than she had when Azure first crawled her way up to the attic, even with the blood and magic loss. Something had returned to her. She was more Rus than she'd been in the weeks before this, and that settled Azure more than she'd known she needed. "Now that we've gotten it detached, what's your big plan?"

Azure wanted to roll her eyes at the lightness in Rus's tone. They were facing down a deadly soul eater who had been feasting on a living magical soul for months. A creature that had almost driven Rus to kill herself, or worse, and her reaction was to be glib. But would Rus be Rus if she weren't being glib in the face of danger? Azure raised a brow. "My plan? This is your field of expertise."

"An exorcism of this size . . ." Rus said, her eyes focused on the creature as it slammed against the barrier created by the containment circle. It wouldn't get out, even if the magic had been weakened by their exhaustion. The containment circle would hold long after they were dead. Azure wasn't sure how she knew that, but she did. "It's going to take a little more than two witches. It's going to take a coven."

"Good thing I called the aunts." Azure's head tilted to the side at the sound of footsteps on the stairs. Just in time. The Goddess was really looking out for them, wasn't she?

"They aren't *coven*." Rus huffed, her head tilting back so she could look at the door to the attic over Azure's shoulder. "We need a coven."

"Then we'll have to do the ritual here," Aunt Carmine said, pushing into the room, her breaths coming in hard pants.

"I want you all to know I'm too old for this shit," Aunt Maureen added, shouldering Aunt Carmine out of the way. They were both pale from their trek through the house, and Aunt Maureen held a basket of supplies. Their salvation was at hand.

"What ritual?" Rus asked, her nose scrunching up. The little color left in her face drained away, her freckles becoming even more starkly contrasted against her skin. "Az, no. We can't do a coven binding ritual right now."

"If not now, then when?" Azure pulled Rus into herself and jerked them out of the way of the soul eater hurling itself at them. Aunt Maureen and Aunt Carmine set up the candles, and Azure breathed a little easier. Aunt Carmine would understand what needed to be done when she heard, and Azure was grateful no one else had tagged along. While the magic of the other Elwoods would make this easier, Azure didn't want them to witness this. Didn't want Violet to voice her opinion—not now, not when things were so close.

"What if Moondale doesn't accept our offering?" Rus shifted on her feet. Moondale's rejection was a very real possibility, but Azure wasn't worried. If Moondale was going to reject Rus, why give her a house like 157 Mourning Moore? If Moondale was going to reject Rus, why give her a shop right across the street from Elwood's? If this wasn't Moondale's plan all along, why keep throwing them together as she seemed intent on doing? "She could reject us."

"I don't think she will," Azure assured but said nothing else to explain it, even as Rus's eyes darted around her face uncertainly.

Rus didn't seem to have an answer. "You're impossible. Do you know that?"

"I do." Or at least, she knew Rus seemed to think so.

A wall of magic flared up in front of them, Rus protecting them from another attack, even though it seemed to weaken her further. Her eyelids hung low now, her body sagging against Azure, her nose bleeding lightly. They were running out of time.

"A coven of two?" Rus asked, her head bobbing as if it took everything she had to keep her chin lifted. Azure wasn't faring much better. The amount of energy it'd taken to help Rus throw the soul eater from her body was immense, even with the Elwood bloodline and Moondale giving her a boost. It likely didn't help that she'd already made her choice to leave Jade Waters, already begun the process mentally. She needed to tie herself to another coven, or her claim on Moondale's magic would be renounced completely.

"Moondale doesn't care about the numbers." Azure shrugged and turned to see how the aunts were faring. They'd finished setting up the candles and had pulled a bit of ore from the basket. A chip broken off from the Heart of Moondale. It wasn't the same as visiting the heart itself, but it would do in a pinch until they could make the journey into the mountains and complete the ritual themselves. "All she cares about is whether your heart is in it."

"Needy bitch," Rus muttered, but she didn't argue further.

"This is going to hurt," Aunt Carmine warned. She'd moved up to the edge of the circle, a bit of parchment in her hands. Azure didn't need to see it to know it was the Jade Waters member list. Magic hummed through it, making it glow, and Azure knew if she looked, she'd see her name written neatly side by side with Violet's and Indigo's.

"Just do it." Azure clenched her jaw. She didn't know what it would feel like to have her name removed from that coven list, but there were stories—horror stories, really. Of how the pain could be so intense, it could drive a witch off her broomstick. How some witches had killed themselves after being removed from their coven lists. The emptiness that could consume a witch. The way it could set them adrift.

"Az." Rus's fingers squeezed around hers, a comforting weight. The shield magic she'd used to separate them from the soul eater was fading fast, eaten up by the creature that seemed to grow in size every second they dawdled. They didn't have time to waste.

"I won't be unmoored for long," Azure said, and she wasn't sure who she was trying to convince more—herself, or her aunts. They looked at her with such sadness, it made her eyes burn.

Aunt Carmine moved first, nodding and lighting a flame on the tip of her finger before pressing it to the line where Azure Elwood's name sat between her siblings'.

The heat started under Azure's skin, burning brighter for how cold it was in the room, like standing too close to a fireplace after having been out in the snow all day, numb and prickling. Then it grew, and Azure *screamed*.

A quick glance showed that her skin wasn't bubbling, blistering, sloughing off, but it felt like it was. It felt like her whole being was aflame. Her knees buckled from the pain, and she and Rus lowered to the floor. Rus pressed cool fingertips to Azure's face to chase away the worst of it. She didn't know how long it lasted—how long she relied on Rus to protect her, trusting the woman she loved to look after them both when she couldn't—but eventually it eased off. And Azure was left panting, her body trembling all over.

"We don't have to tie her now," Rus said, her voice a warble in Azure's ears. Goddess, she needed to get a hold of herself. They didn't have time for her to fuck around being incapacitated.

"Do it," Azure pushed the words through a throat raw from screaming. "Tie us both to the land, so we can get rid of this fucking thing."

Rus opened her mouth, likely to tell Azure they should wait until she was more recovered, until she felt more like herself, but Azure wasn't having it. The soul eater slammed into Rus's shield again, and the floor shook beneath them. It wouldn't be long. Maybe thirty seconds? A minute? And it would be on them, ready to suck them dry so it could escape the containment circle. They needed Moondale's magic *now*.

"Even if we do this," Aunt Maureen warned, her voice a whisper, "it doesn't guarantee Moondale will grant you her blessing. It's not uncommon for a land to reject someone after they've left a coven."

She was right, it wasn't uncommon. In fact, Azure would wager it was more common for a town to reject someone trying to change covens outside of marriage than accept them. Land could be fickle that way; it wanted what it wanted. But Azure knew without a doubt that this was what Moondale wanted from her and Rus, had *always* wanted. Moondale had done everything in her power to make sure they would wind up together again. Had called Rus home when she thought Rus was ready. Had given Rus a house across the street from Azure. Had given her a shop across from Elwood's. It was too much coincidence for it not to be a positive sign.

So Azure lifted her head from where she'd been panting into Rus's shoulder and said, "It'll work. Trust me."

Biting her tongue, Aunt Maureen huffed a breath, but Aunt Carmine already had everything ready. She held the athame out to Azure through the barrier. With her gaze locked onto the soul eater, Azure took it and pricked her finger with the point before doing the same to Rus's.

"Only a drop," Aunt Carmine said. Aunt Maureen took the dagger back, and Aunt Carmine held out the piece of ore.

"Are you really sure you want to do this?" Rus asked, her fingers tight on Azure's wrist to keep her from reaching for the ore. Azure lifted a brow, and Rus seemed to take the gesture for what it was because she huffed a laugh. "Right.

Of course. When has Azure Elwood ever done something without being sure?"

The answer was far more often than Rus would think, but that was something they could discuss when they didn't have a soul eater trapped in a containment circle with them.

"Together," Azure said, lacing her fingers with Rus's again, but keeping their pointer fingers held out.

Rus nodded, and they both pressed the beads of blood on their fingertips into the stone.

Blinding white light flared from the stone, washing out everything in the room for a moment too long. When it faded, Azure's ears rang and she was dizzy as if she'd stood up too fast. But magic hummed in her veins again, refilling all the empty spaces left behind after her name had been removed.

Rus didn't waste any time. She let go of Azure's hand—but didn't move far—to turn her attention to the soul eater now pressing itself so close to the edge of the containment circle, it looked like it had smashed itself into one smokey line of essence.

"Kaytee Williams," Rus said, her voice echoing with the voices of every spirit she'd ever summoned. The wind picked up, lifting Rus's hair from her shoulders. Her hands glowed more brightly than Azure thought she'd ever seen them before.

Whatever boost Moondale had given her magic was . . . *a lot*. And damn it if Azure didn't want to help Rus feel out all that she was capable of now. To feel the raw power that simmered under Rus's skin and see how far she could push herself. She'd had eleven corpses guarding 157 Mourning Moore a few months back; Azure wondered how many Rus could control now that Moondale had gifted Rus her blessing. Azure shook herself.

"I hereby banish you," Rus continued. Her words

boomed now with finality. "To the farthest reaches of the After. To the places no soul willingly treads. May you spend a million years lost in the mire of that place and never return to the land of the living."

There was a pop—a bottle of sparkling wine gone flat, but still carbonated enough for the difference in pressure to make a sound—and the soul eater disappeared, taking the darkness with it. Light, sound, life flooded the room again, and Azure gasped at the first full breath she'd taken in what felt like days.

"Well," Rus said, her voice faint, "that was easy."

Her body swayed, and Azure caught her just before she hit the floor. Lowering them both slowly to the wood, Azure bent forward to press her forehead against Rus's own clammy one. Her gray eyes were open but blinking slowly.

"That was a bit harsh, don't you think?" Aunt Carmine asked, her tone that of a disapproving schoolteacher.

"No." Azure fixed her aunt with a glare. The tension stretched between them for a moment then—

Rus laughed, bright and hoarse, and drew them all out of it. When Azure looked down at where Rus's head rested in her lap, Rus was smiling so wide her eyes were crescents. She was so beautiful, even pale and spattered in blood, that Azure thought not for the first time of the engagement ring still in her jewelry box back home.

Chapter 29

BRANT IRONWOOD LOOKED like he was about to have an aneurysm, and honestly, Rus couldn't be happier. Not because Brant Ironwood had a bulging blood vessel that may very well kill him—although that *would* have its perks—but because for the first time in what felt like years, she wasn't alone.

Az stood so close, they might as well have been holding hands. They weren't. But Rus could feel the heat of Az's skin against her own, a comfort and a balm all in one. Soothing. She heard Meiling shift in her seat behind them. The girls had come with them tonight, stayed up well past their bedtime, so they could see the outcome of what would become their coven. Rus prayed to the Goddess that she and Az didn't fail them.

"I still vote nay," Brant said, his goatee quivering. He looked entirely pleased with himself that somehow he'd convinced the other board members of his plan. His plan being that the vote had to be *unanimous*, without a single nay, for Rus and Az's coven to go through. It was stupid as fuck—Carmine had even said so, in so many words. At this point, it was more than obvious he was only doing this to hold things up, likely in the hopes that Rus would call it quits. Joke was on him. Rus was obstinate to a fault and would continue to haunt him until she got what she wanted or she was exiled from Moondale—whichever came first.

"Any particular reason why?" Az's jaw ticked with her

irritation. Rus wondered how long it would take before Az flew across the room and throttled Brant with his overly expensive scarf. Was that shit Burberry? How could a government official in Moondale *afford* Burberry? Something didn't add up. Rus shook herself.

"She brought a soul eater into Moondale!"

A gasp rippled through to the back of the meeting hall, and Rus wondered how many of them had already known and were just doing it for dramatic effect. She resisted the urge to roll her eyes, but that didn't stop the magic that flittered up around her fingers at the mere hint of her irritation. It was almost too easy to call upon it now, like it sat just under the surface of her skin, where before she'd had to dig deeper for it. Was Moondale giving Rus an extra boost because she sensed Rus was lacking? Or had Rus not been at full strength in so long, she didn't know what it felt like? She'd have to run some experiments to find out.

"Rus didn't *bring* a soul eater into Moondale." Az had shifted forward, her weight rolling onto her toes. Her magic rippled between them, brushing Rus's skin like a cool breeze, smelling of salt water and sand. Rus rubbed her knuckles against the back of Az's hand, and that seemed to calm her, her stance settling back.

"Az is right. If anything, the soul eater is your fault." Rus shrugged, stuffing her hands into her pockets, her shoulders settling into a slouch of nonchalance. She wasn't going to let Brant see how riled he got her; Az did enough of that for the both of them.

"*My* fault?" Brant sputtered. The other members of the board had gone oddly still. They knew exactly what she meant. They weren't stupid, and their memories weren't *that* short.

"Yes. That soul eater latched on to me when I slipped through the veil to find Aihuan a few weeks back. Which, if you'll recall, I wouldn't have had to do if the board helped me protect my daughter to begin with." The words left her in a slow drawl, and Rus relaxed further into her slouch. She knew exactly what she was doing, how disrespectful she looked, and at this point she didn't give a fuck. The board had dragged its heels about helping protect Aihuan, and she'd been kidnapped, so Rus did what she had to. Whatever consequences came from that were entirely their fault, not hers. "But I digress."

Brant sputtered, his hands flapping against the table, banging a little as if that would bring order to the room now full of whispers and sneers. Good. If Brant wanted to drag her through the mud, he wasn't going to do it without getting some dirt on his nice suit. And Rus did love an audience.

"You're right," Carmine said, her quiet voice slicing through the commotion in a way Brant's never could. "We failed your witchlings, and for that we will be forever sorry."

"Agreed." Cliantha met Rus's gaze with what Rus could only assume was meant to be remorse, but it didn't quite reach her eyes. False platitudes in the name of getting what she wanted. Fuck, Rus hated politicians. "But that being said, there was another matter to our agreement, was there not?"

Ah. So *that* was it then. They couldn't block her petition, so they may as well get everything they could out of her, right? The urge to roll her eyes returned, and a headache started behind her eyes at the resistance. Az reached over and brushed the back of her hand against Rus's. Warmth shimmered up Rus's arm to lift the hairs in its wake, and Rus sighed.

"Yes, the Ghost Tracer." Rus turned her head to find Greer where he sat in the row behind the girls. When he met her gaze, she nodded. "I completed a prototype last week. Sheriff Greer has been testing it. Sheriff Greer?"

He had already shuffled to the end of his aisle and made his way to the front to stand on the other side of Az. Rus noted that Greer had dressed in his uniform, likely to seem more official since he was *testifying*, and she wondered how much she'd have to thank him for this. Would Cagney let her go back to being mean to him anytime soon after such a huge favor? *Likely not, knowing my luck. Fuck.*

"The Ghost Tracer, for all its name is stupid," Greer said, and grunted when Az trod on his foot, shooting her a glare, "is surprisingly effective. We would not have known about the soul eater if not for the radar's ability to notify a user of energy spikes. Once it's refined, I think it'll be a great boon to our community and to magical law enforcement." He deflated when he was done, as if he'd practiced the speech and it was a relief to get the words out.

"We're already working together on some improvements," Rus piped up. "The hope is that by the end of next year, it'll function at a level where it can predict potential differences in energy fluctuations. Kind of how your weather app might. My thinking is that this could be used for planning rituals and festivals as well as keeping an eye on problem areas that might draw malevolent spirits."

"And when do you expect to be at a stage where this can be used by Moondale citizens? By the centennial maybe? That's this coming fall," Nixie pressed, leaning forward on the table. She had a gleam in her eye Rus didn't think she cared for, but she could understand why. A tool like this would be infinitely useful for more than just their community. All the folk could use something like this. Rus just needed to get it ready to go wide.

"Fall? Definitely." Rus shrugged, licking her lips. "Barring any more unforeseen circumstances."

"Of course. Of course." Nixie nodded her understanding.

"I can set every member of the board up with the beta run before we leave, if you'd like." Maybe that would push them over the edge on her application. "You know, provided the Coven of the Forgotten is accepted."

More muttering broke out behind her, but she tuned them out, instead focusing on the board members. These people would decide the future of her little family, her little coven, not the masses. She needed to look for any tells. Az shifted beside her, and Rus leaned in to press her shoulder into Az's, warmth spreading all along her side where they touched.

"Keep in mind," Carmine said, once more cutting through the chatter, "Moondale herself has already accepted Icarus and Azure as a coven. Any decision we make that goes against her may have unforeseen consequences."

That seemed to seal it, and Rus was so grateful for Carmine that she could have kissed her. Well, maybe not. That'd have been super weird.

Brant's eyes narrowed on Rus, and she could practically hear the accusations. That she'd tricked them. That she forced them into this. That in binding herself to Moondale with Az, they'd undermined the board, gone behind their backs. Whatever. Let him think what he wanted. So long as she got her coven, she didn't care.

Nixie's lips pursed like she wanted to say something, but instead she looked at the witches to her right. They would have the final say if they were to go against the original mandate of needing the vote to be unanimous. Thankfully, Rus knew she already had one of the three covens on her side. Of course, she also knew she had one who would rather see her skinned alive than allow her to stay in

Moondale. Cliantha Greer would be the tie breaker. Rus hoped the Ghost Tracer would do its job.

Az reached between them, threading their fingers together and stilling the fidgeting Rus hadn't realized she started. A long slow exhale released the tension in her shoulders, and she turned to smile at Az gratefully. Az looked back, her gaze steady, and they lingered there for their own small eternity. Rus wished she could live in these moments. Wished they would swallow her and Az and hide them away from the real world. But all too soon, the real world came rushing back in.

"The Moondale Board of Magic approves Icarus Ashthorne and Azure Elwood's petition to start their own coven within its borders," Cliantha Greer said at last, her voice sharp and clear, and the last of Rus's worries left her. "In spite of Elder Ironwood's misgivings."

Goddess above and below, they'd done it! They'd convinced the board! She still wasn't even sure how.

"This will be probationary," Cliantha continued, and Rus just managed to not tune her out for the joy buzzing through her brain, "as you currently only have three adult members. We expect you to have five by next year, am I understood?"

"Yes, ma'am," Rus said at the same time Az asked, "What does probationary mean?" Because Az was always looking out, trying to sort how things would affect them. Rus was so lucky to have her.

"It means that the Coven of the Forgotten will for all intents and purposes function as an official Moondale coven, but until it has proven viable, it will not have a voice on the Board of Magic." Cliantha cleared her throat under the cutting glare Az sent her way. "This can be renegotiated at a later date, once the coven's roster has grown."

Az stiffened further beside Rus. Rus knew she was on

the verge of arguing semantics, of asking more questions, but Rus didn't have the energy for that. So she leaned in and whispered in Az's ear, "Take the win."

Az grunted a reply but didn't press further.

"Thank you, Elder Greer," Rus said with a bow, tugging Az back to their seats where the girls waited with a billion questions.

"If that will be all," Carmine called the room to order again, "I call this Board of Magic meeting to a close." She clapped once, and the room fell into chaos.

Rus got caught up in all of it. Everyone wanted to talk to her, tell her how they believed in her, how they thought her coven was a great idea. Funny how when it looked like you were on the right side of things, people were more than happy to lend their support. But when the board had been against her necromancy years ago, everyone was happy enough to condemn her.

She looked over at Az, standing next to her on the steps to the Board of Magic, still holding her hand, and decided it didn't matter if they wanted to condemn her or put her on a pedestal. She had her coven, her family, and that's all she needed.

Az noticed her staring, and when she looked over at Rus, she smiled, sending Rus's stomach into a flurry of butterflies. Az yanked Rus in close by their linked hands and pressed their lips together.

Right there.

On the steps of the Board of Magic.

For all of Moondale to see.

Yeah. This was the perfect start to the Coven of the Forgotten.

Chapter 30

MUCH TOO SOON, Rus was carried away on the sea of well-wishers, her gray eyes bright, cheeks flush with victory. Much too soon, Azure had to let her go. Not for long, mind you. Azure wouldn't let Rus go ever again for long. But at least for the moment. So said the key to 157 Mourning Moore that Rus pressed into her hand just before she departed. An invitation. A promise.

And that's when she saw Brant from the corner of her eye. He was off in the shadows, watching the celebration much the same way Azure did when she went to a party out of obligation rather than because she wanted to. With the crowd of people congratulating Rus moving toward the parking lot, carrying Rus away on a sea of bodies in the cold dark December night, he moved up to Azure's side.

"You're going to regret this," he said out of the side of his mouth. Likely to keep from being overheard.

Azure cut her eyes to him, focusing her attention on this new problem. "No," she said, lifting her chin. "I don't think I will."

But that didn't mean she didn't believe he was a threat. Didn't mean she didn't see what he was insinuating. She knew. She was bold and confident, never stupid. Azure would have to keep an eye on him and his.

Brant scoffed and shuffled off again, walking through the grass to avoid the hoard of people surrounding Rus and her girls. Azure met Rus's eyes over Nesta's and Cagney's heads, a little smile passing between them, knowing.

"I'll see you at home," Rus mouthed, her brows pinched as she looked at something just over Azure's shoulder. Azure turned and found Nixie standing on the steps to the Board of Magic building, waiting. When Azure returned her gaze to Rus, she winked.

She waited until Rus and the girls were out of sight, loaded into Blue on their way back to 157 Mourning Moore, before turning to face Nixie Virnan. It had been only a couple of weeks since she made the deal with the elder of the Ladies of Nimue, and she had almost been able to forget about the favor she owed.

Nixie tilted her head, and Azure followed her back inside the board building—where someone had already magicked the place clean and shut off the lights—then through to the offices at the back. Holding up one knobby finger, Nixie pressed her hand into the door of her office, blue light shimmering outward from her palm and into the wood, cutting off all sound from the outside world. Once that was done, she turned her attention back to Azure.

"You owe me a favor, Azure Elwood," Nixie reminded, her tone gentle as she moved to lean against her desk instead of the cane she regularly walked with.

"I do." No sense in denying it. Azure's debt sat like an itch under her skin, always one false move from turning into hives. "But our deal was that you'd ensure the Coven of the Forgotten became an official coven of Moondale. It is, as of now, not."

"It is."

"No. It is in a probationary period." Azure crossed her arms and leaned back against the wall next to the door. She didn't like playing this game; she knew it was dangerous. Nixie held all the cards, and if Azure gambled wrong on this, she'd not only royally fuck herself, but Rus, the girls, and Fernando as well. Still, she needed assurances. "Until it has five adult members."

"There will be two more." Nixie shrugged, seemingly unbothered by Azure's pushback. Which was good. It meant Nixie wasn't going to ask her to do something harmful. Hopefully. "Don't ask me how I know. I just know."

"All right." She wanted to ask. Of course she did. Precognition wasn't terribly common, even among folk. And as far as she knew, Aihuan was the only precognitive folk in Moondale. But there were other ways to see the future. Other avenues to find answers. They weren't as reliable, but she supposed maybe they were a little more so if someone had been alive as long as Nixie and made a study of them. "So what is it you want from me then?"

"Something is rotting in Moondale. Something festering and rank," Nixie said, which didn't really answer the question. But Azure was willing to wait it out. "I'm sure you've noticed it. Seen the signs of corruption among the board."

No. She hadn't. Except . . . Except a Burberry scarf. A new car. The way Brant pushed his weight around without any kind of pushback from the rest of the board. There would have been other signs, things she had probably missed. She didn't spend enough time with the board to notice everything, but . . .

"You want me to spy for you," Azure murmured, her eyes lifting from where she'd been staring thoughtfully down at her boots. "But the Coven of the Forgotten won't have a seat on the board. Not until we're out of the probationary period."

"Not officially, no," Nixie allowed, tapping her fingers lightly against the handle of her cane. "But they'll want you to come in and report on what's happening with the coven. For your part, it would be wise if you or Rus insinuated yourself into those conversations. And then there is the discussion about the centennial. It would behoove you and Rus to have your coven settled before then."

"Can I do that without an elder seat?"

"Has that stopped you thus far?" Nixie fired back, a smile playing at the corner of her lips. And she was correct, it hadn't stopped Azure. Not from showing up to every closed- or open-door meeting in the last two months. Not from petitioning directly with clan elders. Not from digging through board records. She'd been doing all the things that an elder should do, without even having a coven to serve. "Besides, we'll need all hands on deck preparing for the centennial. The plan is to bring in young members of the community who show promise, and begin training them for positions as elders. Or at least, that's my thought process. What the others are thinking, only time will tell."

"When it comes time for us to have an official seat—"

"It'll be up to you and Rus to decide. But in the interim, your wife has plenty on her plate already, and as I understand it, you will be going back to school full time. I realize that getting a doctorate will take a substantial amount of your time and focus, but without a store to run, there should be enough left over to help me with this."

It sounded reasonable when she said it that way. It *was* reasonable, and correct, in fact. Because Azure did need to be in the room when the board discussed the fate of her coven. What better way to ensure that than to make it clear she was readying them for a seat on the board.

"It's not like I have much choice anyway," Azure grunted, but she wasn't half as annoyed as she sounded.

Nixie hummed, her eyes bright. "You start work the first of the year."

Chapter 31

THERE HAD BEEN some talk among the board about waiting until the weather was warmer, the frost thawed, and winter had broken its hold on Moondale. But Rus wouldn't hear of it. She knew having the induction ritual in the middle of winter—just before the winter solstice—would make for a smaller crowd of watchers. Knew it would mean half the board would probably fuck off, leaving the ceremony parts to the covens exclusively—probably just Carmine, really. But she was fine with that. They didn't need a packed house to receive Moondale's blessing officially.

In fact, it might be better if they didn't have a packed house. Fernando was nervous as fuck. He'd been fidgeting all through dinner, pushing food around his plate, not making eye contact. Rus would rather spare him if she could.

She wished she could be in the room with him, helping him get ready for this, but there was something nice about being holed up in her attic bedroom with Az. Both of them facing different directions as they shimmied into their floor-length black gowns.

Black. White was traditional for induction rituals. It signified purity. It signified innocence. It was for witchlings just graduating, just starting out. For folk who hadn't seen the world yet, who were untainted, untraumatized but what lay beyond Moondale's wards. But none of those things applied to them. So Rus had decided on black.

Black velvet, in particular.

It felt right. She'd started this journey in a velvet dress, and she'd continue it in a velvet dress.

"We'll need to find Fernando a familiar and get him an athame. I'm not sure where we'll find a familiar at this time of year. They usually hibernate during the winter. At least, until they have a witch, of course." Rus tugged at the edges of the plunging V-neck on her dress and sent up a prayer to Hecate that it wouldn't slip open any further so everyone could see her boobs. Because that's exactly what she needed. The flowing three-quarter-length sleeves tickled her forearms as she moved. She was going to freeze her ass off up there.

"I already took care of it."

"Of finding him a familiar? How?"

Az made a soft noise of disagreement. "Of getting him an athame. I've already set up an appointment for him this weekend with Brenton. He just needs to choose his ore."

"Az," Rus murmured, her breath catching in her throat. "You didn't have to do that. I could have handled it."

"He's coven," Az said, like that was explanation enough. Maybe it was when she said the word *coven* like the word *family*.

Rus's heart clenched in her chest, her fingers fidgeting with her hair, which did nothing at all to change how it looked. She couldn't seem to sit still, and now that her dress was on, there wasn't much else to do.

"I'm unsure about this dress." The floorboards groaned under Az as she presumably twisted and turned in front of the mirror to get a better look at herself in the dress Rus had chosen for her.

"Oh come on, Az. Embrace your inner Morticia." Rus

still hadn't turned around yet. She was almost afraid to. Afraid she'd see Az in that dress, the slinky velvet clinging to her curves, the high neckline with the embroidery accentuating her jaw, the trailing train, and not be able to let Az walk out of that room. They'd have to cancel the entire ceremony because Rus couldn't keep it in her pants. Or she'd do something equally embarrassing like asking Az to marry her.

"Does that make you Gomez?"

"Oh, absolutely." Rus spun to fix Az with a wide grin, fully intending to play into the role of Gomez, the words "I would die for you. I would kill for you" on the tip of her tongue. She promptly choked on them. What came out instead was a strangled sound.

Az smiled, her dark red painted lips spreading, and crinkling her eyes, making her look that much more beautiful. Amusement danced in her dark eyes, light and teasing. "We should get going. We wouldn't want to be late to our own induction ritual."

Then she turned, the trail of crushed black velvet crawling along behind her as she made her way to the door, not once bothering to look back and make sure Rus was following.

"Wait. Az. You can't just walk out of here like that. You can't just swan off!"

Az didn't stop, her footsteps making the stairs creak on the way to the second level.

"Rude! So rude to your poor girlfriend!" But Rus followed behind her, careful not to step on her train, her eyes fixed on the sway of Az's hips.

SHE SHOULD HAVE WORN A COAT. IT WOULD HAVE RUINED the whole aesthetic, but she definitely should have worn a coat. But hey, at least Brant Ironwood wasn't in attendance! Rus would take the cold any day over having to listen to that windbag.

"If we're going to get started, the girls have to go stand with the others," Carmine said. She stood off to one side of the large stone that sat at the center of the clearing. The ritual required at least one elder from the board, but Carmine and Nixie Virnan had both made the trip up the mountain. It was more than Rus had expected. So was the fact that Maureen, Indigo, Greer, Cagney, Phyre, Brenton, and Nesta had joined them too. There was no sign of Violet, but that wasn't exactly surprising.

"Why can't we help too?" Aihuan asked. Her arms were tight around Rus's neck, the wool of her coat making Rus's skin itch. Meiling stood beside Fernando on the other side of Az, her jaw set.

"Because it's not your turn yet, little monster."

"But . . . I want to be a part of your coven." Aihuan's lip trembled, her fingers fisting in the hair at the base of Rus's skull and yanking a little.

"I know, sweetheart, but—"

"Who says you're not a part of our coven?" Az asked, breaking Aihuan from her pout. "Just because you haven't had your induction ceremony yet doesn't mean you aren't one of us. You will always be one of us." She looked across the way to where Meiling's arms were curled around her middle. "Both of you."

Fernando nodded, and Rus murmured her agreement when the girls looked to her, warmth curling in her belly. Leave it to Az to diffuse a tantrum before it even got started.

"Why don't you go stand with Auntie Cags?" Rus

murmured, setting Aihuan on her feet when Meiling came around to collect her. "We'll just be a few minutes."

Aihuan huffed but let Meiling lead her over to where the other adults stood next to the tree with a waning moon carved into it. Close enough to watch, but far enough not to confuse the Heart of Moondale.

Nixie cleared her throat, moving closer to the pale gray stone. It gleamed in the moonlight, just like the white gowns Nixie and Carmine had donned. They, it seemed, had decided to go the traditional route.

A ceremonial dagger, encrusted with polished gems, glinted as Carmine passed it to Az, who sliced her palm then held it out to Fernando. When he was done, Az reached for Rus's hand, taking it in her own, her blood still dripping softly down onto the stone, which stood at about knee level.

Az met her eyes—offering her a little smile that Rus returned even if it felt like it shook—then nodded. A returned nod, and Az dipped her head to slice into Rus's palm, to let Rus's blood join Azure Elwood's and Fernando Perez's on the red-stained Heart of Moondale.

"Let us begin," Nixie said, and the humming started.

glossary

While not required, this glossary is intended to offer further context to the world of Moondale.

pronunciation guide

- **Aihuan:** Aye-hoo-wahn
- **Meiling:** May-lee-ng
- **Jiejie:** Gee-ay-gee-ay

terms guide

Witch Terms

- **Athame:** A ceremonial blade used in ritual magic.
- **Aura:** An emanation surrounding the body of a living creature , regarded as an essential part of the individual.
- **Covenless:** A witch who does not belong to a formal coven.

- **Familiars:** A living creature (traditionally a cat) attending and obeying a witch.
- **Folk:** A word used to reference any person of magical lineage.
- **Moonmother:** A witch assigned by a child's parents to take responsibility for the child in the event the parents are unable.
- **Poppet:** A small figure or doll used in sorcery or witchcraft.
- **Possession:** The act of having one's body inhabited by a spirit.
- **Reanimated:** A being that has been brought back to life through magical means.
- **Soul Eater:** A spirit that has consumed another spirit as a means to gain power.
- **Spellcraft:** The act of creating new or using existing spells.
- **Talismans:** An item, or paper, inscribed with magical characters or runes to perform a specific spell.
- **Wards**: A magical barrier set using either spellwork, talismans, or runes to protect a specific place.

Chinese Terms Guide

- **Jiejie:** A familiar way to refer to an older sister or older female friend, used by someone substantially younger.
- **Niang:** Mama
- **Baba:** Papa
- **A-:** Familiar diminunitive
- **-Er:** A word for "child", added to a name to express affection.

board of magic files

Circle of Jade Waters
WITCHES
best known for scholarly pursuits

Elder: Carmine Elwood

Members:

- Carmine Elwood
- Maureen Beecher
- Violet Elwood
- Taryn Elwood
- ~~Azure Elwood~~
- Indigo Elwood
- Sunila Elwood

Circle of the Silver Flame
WITCHES
best known for weapons & wand makers

Elder: Brant Ironwood

Members:

- Brant Ironwood
- Brenton Ironwood
- Phyre Ironwood

<u>**Circle of the Crimson Tide**</u>
WITCHES
best known for security & ward work

Elder: Cliantha Greer

Members:

- Cliantha Greer
- Evander Greer

<u>**Clan of Crescentia**</u>
FAIRIES - Cupids
best known for their skills in matchmaking

Elder: Enfys Snowthorn

Members:

- Nesta Holyore
- Dillan Holyore

<u>**Grove of Elderwood**</u>
DRUIDS
best known for their agricultural skills

Elder: Gilroy Herne

Members:

- Gilroy Herne
- Cagney Cashel

<u>**Chesapeake Pack**</u>
WEREWOLVES
best known for their efforts forest preservation

Elder:

Members:

<u>**Circle of the Emerald Forge**</u>
WISH GRANTERS
best known for preservation of the Moondale lei lines

Elder: Dhiren

Members:

<u>**Ladies of Nimue**</u>
WATER FOLK
best known for their efforts in bay preservation

Elder: Nixie Virnan

Members:

<u>**Clan of the Unseen Moon**</u>
UNSEELIE FAE
best known for

Elder: Yaereene

Members:

<u>**Sisters of the Meadow**</u>
SEELIE FAE
best known for

Elder:

Members:

<u>**Coven of the Forgotten**</u>
WITCHES
best known for their advancements in magical technology

Elder:

Members:

- Icarus Ashthorne
- Azure Elwood
- Fernando Perez

about lou wilham

Born and raised in a small town near the Chesapeake Bay, Lou Wilham grew up on a steady diet of fiction, arts and crafts, and Old Bay. After years of absorbing everything, there was to absorb of fiction, fantasy, and sci-fi she's left with a serious writing/drawing habit that just won't quit. These days, she spends much of her time writing, drawing, and chasing a very short Basset Hound named Sherlock.

When not, daydreaming up new characters to write and draw she can be found crocheting, making cute bookmarks, and binge-watching whatever happens to catch her eye.

Learn more about Lou and her future projects on her website: http://louinprogress.com/ or join her mailing list at: http://subscribepage.com/mailermailer

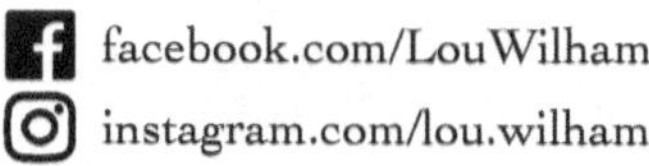

facebook.com/LouWilham

instagram.com/lou.wilham

also by lou wilham

The Witches of Moondale
    The Hex Next Door
    The Ghost of Hexes Past
    Home is Where the Hex Is
    A Hex To Remember

The Hunters of Ironport
    Overkill
    Fresh Kill
    Kill Your Darlings

The Fae of Eventide
    An Offer Fae Can't Refuse

Sanctuary of the Lost
    Of Loyalties and Wreckage
    Of Love and Ruin
    Of Hope & Blight
    Of Blight & Ruin

Completed Series
The Heir to Moondust
The Tales of the Sea Trilogy
Villainous Heroics
The Clockwork Chronicles
The Curse Collection
Benvolio & Mercutio Turn Back Time

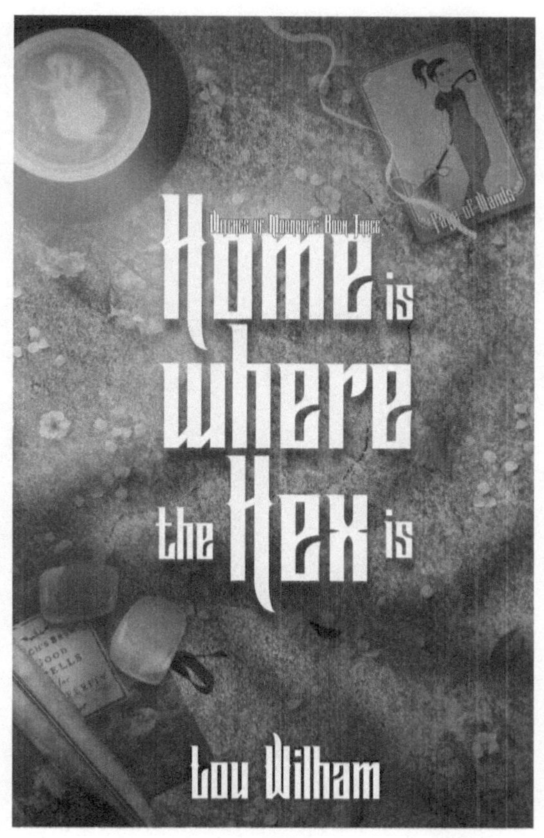

Sneak Peek!

continue reading for a sneak peek of Witches of Moondale book #3: Home is Where the Hex is

Please note: This is an unedited sneak peek.

Order your copy!

Chapter 1

RUS JERKED AWAKE.

Her left foot was *freezing* where it hung over the edge of the bed, the blanket not covering it. She must have kicked the covers off in the middle of the night. But that wasn't what woke her.

Something was holding on to her, the grip cold, insubstantial, but tight around her ankle.

Something not alive.

A spirit.

When reaching across the bed for Az turned up cool, empty sheets, Rus shimmied closer to the nightstand, careful not to dislodge the shade's grip as she bent her head over the edge of the bed to peek down beneath it. The face peering back at her was young, with wide eyes staring unblinking and glassy. Likely a little older than Aihuan when they died, but not by much.

"Hel—" Rus croaked, stopped, cleared her throat, and tried again. "Hello there, little one. Would you mind letting go of my foot?"

They looked at her for a moment, head tilted, then released her ankle with a muffled "Sorry."

"It's all right." Rus shot them a smile and slid from the bed to kneel on the floor next to it. "Why don't you come out here, and we'll have a chat?"

They frowned, their upturned nose crinkling in thought. "Why?"

"I just want to know why you're here." Rus scooted back to give them room as they slid out from underneath the bed, joints popping and jerking in a way that was not at all human. Objectively terrifying, if Rus didn't know that spirits tended to forget how living things moved. "Can you tell me your name?"

"Isabel."

"That's a nice name." Where had Aihuan found this one? The school? The graveyard? The coffee shop? They needed to have a discussion—*again*—about bringing spirits home. Thankfully this one wasn't some nastier being masquerading as a child, but it was only a matter of time before Aihuan came across one of those. It was a miracle she hadn't thus far. "Do you know what happened to you, Isabel?"

"I was sick." Isabel shrugged, not meeting Rus's eyes.

They looked around her attic bedroom instead. Taking in the pile of clothes in the corner that Az was consistently on her about, the mess that was her workspace, and the wilting plant Az was trying to revive on the windowsill. Az hadn't moved in, but she'd made herself at home there just the same. Mixed her dirty laundry in with Rus's. Piled her books on one nightstand. Added one of Indigo's crocheted blankets to the end of the bed. It made the space homier. And Rus had hardly noticed until that very moment, seeing it through someone else's eyes, that it had happened, so subtle was Az's infiltration into her personal space. *Infiltration* maybe wasn't the right word, but Rus digressed.

"I waited."

"You waited for what?"

"For my mama to come," Isabel said, meeting Rus's gaze finally. "But she never did. And then I laid down."

Tears lodged in Rus's throat, making it hard to find her voice again, but find it she did. Because someone needed to help Isabel move on. To see their mama again. "How long have you been stuck here?"

Isabel shrugged again.

Rus didn't know why she'd bothered asking. Time moved differently for spirits. But it was a point of pride to gather as much information as she reasonably could before she helped a spirit move on. To document it at least for herself so she could find patterns in the kinds of spirits that stayed and the ones that didn't. So far not much had come of the data, but one day, maybe it would.

"Huaner said you could help me find my mama. That's why she brought me."

Of course she did. It would be annoying if it weren't so painfully sweet. Aihuan believed her auntie Rus could help every spirit and didn't see any reason why she shouldn't. It wasn't like it hurt Rus to do it—she just didn't want Aihuan bringing every stray shade into the safety of their home, thereby making all Rus's carefully constructed wards virtually useless.

"You can, can't you?"

"I'll do my best." Already Rus's magic flittered around her fingers like mist, glowing and green, reaching out to answer its witch's call. But even if she didn't say it, she knew that Isabel's mama might already be gone. She may have reincarnated, hoping to find her child again somehow. Rus couldn't leave Isabel to languish though. They needed to be given the opportunity to find peace, whatever that looked like for them. And they couldn't do that on this plane.

"What do I need to do?" Isabel asked, their voice small as they shrank back into themselves, away from Rus's extended hand and the magic that had settled into the scars on her bare arm.

"Just take my hand, and the magic will do the rest."

"Will it hurt?"

"No. It won't hurt at all." She didn't know that, not for certain. But many a spirit had returned from the After to aid her when she needed it, and not one of them had ever complained. Add that to the fact that they never screamed when she sent them over. She'd have to ask next time a spirit visited her to help out. It'd be good to have an answer once and for all. Then she'd have something to tell the spirits who asked. She hoped they felt warm when they crossed. Safe. Loved.

Isabel stared at Rus's hand for a long moment, their fingers twitching where they rested against their thigh, warring with their indecision. Unsure. Rus couldn't blame them for that. She didn't have any answers about the After. She didn't know what it was like there. She didn't know how it felt to get there. She didn't know how spirits adjusted. Nothing. All she knew was that's where the dead belonged, not on the plane of the living where they would either fade or slowly lose their grip on themselves and what was real, making them destructive.

"This is what Huaner meant when she said I could help you," Rus pressed. She didn't know what time it was, but she could hear Fernando and the kids downstairs eating breakfast. She needed to get down there and help get the girls ready for school or she'd never hear the end of it.

When Isabel didn't move, Rus let out a soft sigh. "Would you like to say goodbye to Huaner first?"

Isabel nodded, the bob of their head making their hair fall into their face. They looked like that scary little girl from *The Ring* like that.

"I'll go get her. But then we need to get you moving along, all right?"

Another nod and Rus stood, her knees creaking as she went. The back stairs groaned to announce her presence in the kitchen as she came into view of the round table where her little family sat. Well. Most of her little family. Az was in class already. "Huaner?"

"Hmm?" Aihuan asked, raising her head from where she'd been shoveling waffles into her mouth.

"Can you come upstairs with me for a minute?" Rus was careful not to let on that there was a spirit in the house. Meiling was still afraid of them and had grown comfortable in the knowledge that they couldn't cross the threshold of 157 Mourning Moore unless invited in.

Aihuan looked at Rus for a moment, then her eyes widened and she nodded, wiggling down from her chair. When they made it to the landing on the second floor, she looked up at Rus and asked, "Are you mad?"

"I'm not mad." Rus's shoulders drooped on a deep exhale. It was hard to be mad at Aihuan when she was technically doing the right thing, and when she looked adorable doing it. Big brown eyes, and curly hair wild around her face. She probably hadn't brushed it. Another task to add to Rus's ever lengthening list for the morning. "But I do recall asking you to please not bring them into the house. Remember?"

"But it was cold out last night." Aihuan's bottom lip poked out, her eyes going even bigger somehow. Goddess above and below, Rus was a fucking sap for the puppy eyes, and everyone seemed to know it. "And Issy is afraid of the bugs."

"Huaner, we agreed they could wait on the back porch, but not in the house." Rus let her tone dip into something more authoritative. This was a rule, firm and set in stone. She could not budge on this. Lest Aihuan bring something dangerous into their home on accident. "Understood?"

"Yes, Auntie Rus." Aihuan huffed.

"That's my little monster." Rus smiled and pushed the

door open to her bedroom where Isabel waited. The spirit lit up when they saw Aihuan, their face forming a bright smile the likes of which Rus had never seen on a ghost before, and they moved forward to hug Aihuan tightly.

"You're going then?" Aihuan asked, but she sounded happy about it. No sadness or regret tainted her voice. No hint that she'd miss her new friend. "Auntie Rus is going to help you cross over?"

"She is. I just . . ." Isabel looked at Rus for a moment then ducked their head shyly. "I wanted to say goodbye."

"This isn't goodbye," Aihuan said with a smile full of wisdom far beyond her years. Rus wondered where the fuck she'd learned that. Az probably. Elwoods were like that, chock-full of wisdom and bursting at the seams with their goodness. Az especially. "It's just see you later."

"How much later?"

"Who knows! But if you want to come back and visit, you just have to call out to Auntie Rus." Aihuan turned to look up at Rus, her expression earnest. "Right, Auntie Rus?"

"Right." Rus nodded, offering what she hoped was a confident smile. "Just call for Icarus Ashthorne, and you can come back to visit."

"But even if not"—Aihuan shrugged—"I'll see you again someday."

And wow, okay, Aihuan being that all right talking about her own future death was weird. Rus needed to cut this short before these two sent her into an existential crisis. She didn't have time in her schedule for one of those today.

"All righty, let's get this show on the road. You've got school." Rus swiped at her face, hoping neither child would notice how the corners of her eyes burned with tears. But if the looks on their faces were anything to go by, they had. She reached out her hand, her bright green magic reaching with her, and took hold of Isabel's shoulder.

There was a moment where Isabel looked up at her and smiled, then the spirit was gone. Sent to the After, to hopefully be with their mother. Maybe she'd been right, maybe it didn't hurt them after all. Quiet settled around Rus and Aihuan, and they both breathed a little deeper before Aihuan looked up at Rus and asked, "Can I have some chocolate chips on my waffles?"

"Uncle Nando said no, didn't he?" Rus laughed softly, brushing her fingers through Aihuan's hair and getting caught in the tangles.

"Yes." Aihuan huffed.

"I'll make you a deal. You let me brush your hair, and you can have exactly ten mini chocolate chips on your waffles. How's that sound?"

"Mm!" Aihuan dipped her head in agreement, and they headed back to the kitchen where Fernando and Meiling waited.

"Az was gone early this morning," Rus said, hoping to head off any conversation about what had just happened upstairs as she made her way to the pantry to grab Aihuan her chocolate chips. When Fernando raised an eyebrow in question as she dumped exactly ten onto Aihuan's plate, Rus shook her head.

That seemed to be enough of an answer for him, but the little white mouse on his shoulder—his familiar, Calida, or Cal for short—moved onto her back paws, pressing her tiny face in toward his ear to murmur to him. When she was done, Fernando smiled and nodded before returning his attention to Rus. "I thought you said Az wasn't moving in?"

"She's not. She just spent the night last night." Heat crawled up Rus's neck at the mention of Az spending the night. It wasn't like they had *done* anything. Not yet, anyway. There was time. And still lots to talk about and sort out between them. But she hadn't thought *that* was where the conversation would head when she'd brought it up. In retrospect, maybe she should have. Still, it was a good way to head off the discussion about the spirit who'd been hiding under her bed when she woke up.

If only it didn't make Rus so unsettled. An emotion she couldn't source. Yet.

"Last night. And the night before that."

"And the night before that," Meiling added unhelpfully.

"And the night before that!" Aihuan agreed, shoving a big bite of waffle into her mouth.

"Are you three going to get to a point anytime soon?" Rus groused. She'd poured herself a cup of coffee, unable to force down the smile that came from seeing Az's mint-green mug on the drying rack next to the sink. Damn it.

"Why don't you just ask her to move in already? Make it official," Fernando pressed, hiding his coy smile behind a mug that looked more milk than coffee. He was being a jerk and he knew it, bringing this up in front of the girls. Thankfully, they didn't seem to mind one way or the other. They liked having Az around, but they weren't going to try forcing her hand.

"It's a process." Rus turned to look out the window, the dreary late spring mist creating a fog through which she could only just see the house next door. The last owners had moved out a couple weeks ago. Nesta—one of Rus's friends and the one who'd sold her their current home, 157 Mourning Moore—was the realtor on the sign, but they'd asked Rus to take a look at it before they really put their effort into selling it. They needed to know if the last owners left anything behind, like unsettled spirits. She'd have to check on that this afternoon, after the rush at Necromancer's had calmed down. It would be easy money, as far as Rus could tell. She almost felt guilty accepting the commission. But Aihuan was growing like a cemetery weed, and she and Meiling would need summer clothes soon. "I don't want to rush things."

Not rushing things had been entirely her idea, not Az's, because Rus knew they couldn't go back to how things were, and she wasn't sure how they'd work now. Or if they'd work at all. Maybe they wouldn't. Maybe once all the drama and the danger died down, Az would see what a fuckup Rus still was and leave her like she should have all those years ago.

Either way, Rus couldn't risk it with the girls involved.

Meiling snorted loud enough that it sounded like it might have hurt. When Rus turned to look at her, she was smiling, sarcastic and cutting. Fucking teenagers, man. "You'll be married by next year."

Oh. Oh, Rus hadn't thought about it but . . . but she did *want* that. Shit, how had her thirteen-year-old known she'd wanted that, and Rus hadn't known it herself?

"Next year? I'm calling November," Fernando joined in. "We've got a pool running."

"Oh, a Samhain wedding!" Meiling brightened. "Auntie Rus, a Samhain wedding!"

"What pool?" Aihuan, who was the only one *not* a traitor in this fucking house, asked. "Can we go swimming in it?"

"It's not that kind of pool, Huaner." Meiling rolled her eyes. "It means they're betting."

"You know telling me about the pool kind of skews the results, doesn't it?" Rus sneered at Fernando, who held up a hand and rocked it back and forth. She scoffed, clicking her tongue, and pushed it from her mind. Because giving it too much thought, looking at it too closely, would only intensify the ache in her chest. The reminder that maybe that was a thing she wanted. A thing she *shouldn't* want. A thing she shouldn't *let* herself want. She wasn't right for Az. Never would be. It—

"It doesn't matter," Rus sniped, her sour thoughts turning her tone to something less playful. "A'ling, the bus is here!"

Meiling grunted, dropped her dishes in the sink, and headed for the door. "Bye, Huaner!"

"Bye, jiejie!" Aihuan stuffed another bite into her mouth that was more chocolate chip than waffle, and the door creaked open to let Meiling run down the walk for the bus.

"And you, little monster, agreed to let me brush your hair, remember?"

"Fiiiiiine."

"What about me?" Fernando asked, his eyes dancing with good humor. Little shit.

"I'm not talking to you until I've finished my coffee." Rus held her mug up as if she were cheers-ing Fernando and took a big gulp from it. "Till then, nothing out of you."

Fernando raised his hands in surrender, but the grin on his face said this conversation was far from over. Because nothing about returning to Moondale was ever going to be easy.

acknowledgments

I always start these things but thanking the reader, and this one is no different. I want to thank you—whether you're a returning reader or Lou is new to you—for picking up my little indie published book, supporting my dream, and following along with Rus and Az on their journey. Without readers, I can't do what I do, so I greatly appreciate the support.

If you loved every moment of Rus and Az's story (as I hope you did) please leave a review, follow me on social media, or give me a shout out. I love hearing from you guys, it's really the best part of writing.

Next I'd like to thank my family who supports me in this weird journey I'm on to become an established author. They show up to my signings, they listen to my rants about my characters, they look at my covers and tell me when they're complete shit (I design my covers FYI), and they're the best people to have in my corner, no joke.

Then there is the small hoard of beta readers I had look at this bugger to tell me if any of it actually made sense, and if I'm as funny as I think I am (turns out I am). Thanks Tanya, Meg, Val, and Steph! You guys provided so much helpful feedback you don't even know.

And of course my editor, Brenna. Who I have only worked with one on small project before, but who gave this story all of her love, just as I did.

And last but certainly not least, thank you to my small writing support group. Tiss, Elle, and Jasmine—without you there would be no Lou.

more books you'll love

If you enjoyed this story, please consider leaving a review.

Then check out more books from Midnight Tide Publishing!

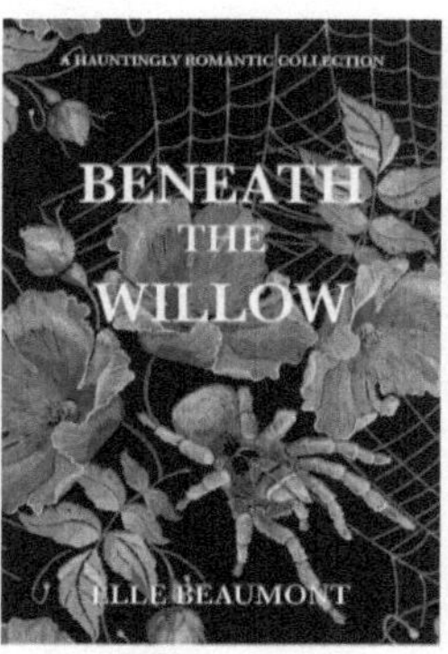

Beneath the Willow by Elle Beaumont

LOVE DESERVES A SECOND CHANCE.

Something lurks deep within the mysterious inn, and when a paranormal expert arrives, so does an unexpected visitor.

A woman pores over letters she discovered in an old bookstore, and every time she reads them, she can feel the presence of the man who wrote them, making her uncertain of her sanity.

A spirit plagues the owner of an inn, but when a paranormal investigator arrives, he requires the aid of the anomaly, or the owner risks losing everything.

After a tragic loss, a man leaves his old life behind. Beginning a new adventure should be easy, but when a friendly ghost appears, he realizes nothing ever is. But with memories of his past haunting him, will he ever be truly ready?

BENEATH THE WILLOW IS A ROMANTIC COLLECTION OF GHOST stories that will haunt you long after reading. From newfound love to rekindled flames, and even healing after loss, these contents are dark, beautiful, and tragic, surely inspiring heart-pounding moments and tears.

Available Now

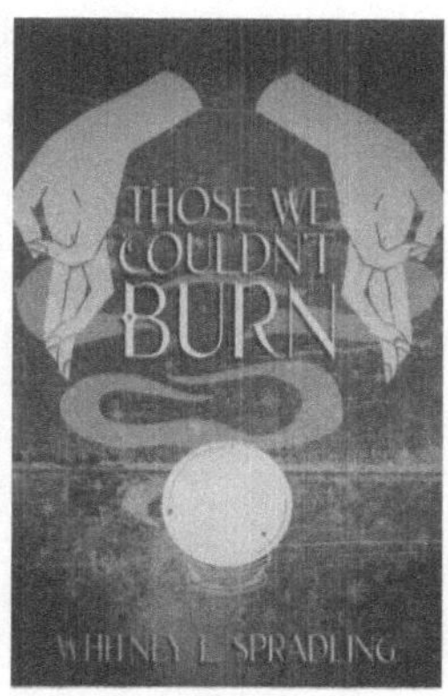

Those We Couldn't Burn by Whitney L. Spradling

WORLDS COLLIDE when an ancient vision brings a witch and witch hunter together.

Prince Tyberius Berkshire, witch hunter extraordinaire, has been set with an impossible task—discover the truth of an ancient vision to keep his family on the throne. His world crashes down around him, when an intricate piece of the vision's puzzle falls into place in the form of a purple-haired witch.

Neave Paker has spent the past ten years quietly taking revenge against the witch hunters. Until the prince of the hunters captures her. Taken to the palace, she's given the choice to either work for the enemy or burn at the stake.

Together, they set out to discover the truth. But difficulties lie ahead as they fight attraction and animosity. When they uncover more than they bargained for, the unlikely duo must determine what is more important to them: their beliefs or their hearts.

Available Now

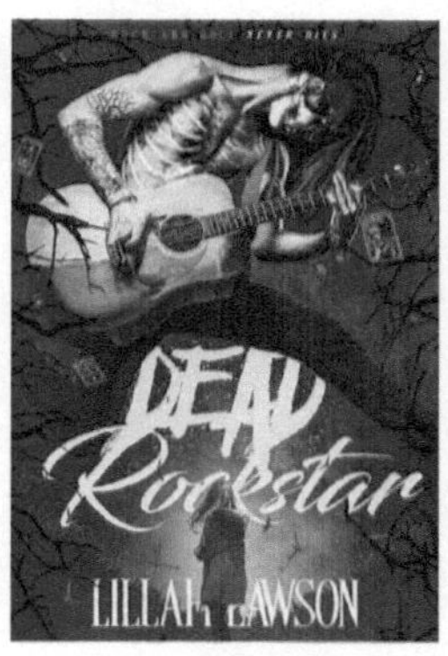

Dead Rockstar by Lillah Lawson

Stormy Spooner is at her wits' end. Careening towards bitter after a nasty divorce, she sometimes wonders what her life is becoming.

After unearthing a cryptic set of lines from a dusty album cover, Stormy tries the impossible: to resurrect Phillip Deville, enigmatic former frontman of the Bloomer Demons. Stormy's love for her favorite dead rockstar knows no bounds...but it was all supposed to be a joke.

When she answers a knock on her door the next day and finds herself face to face with the dark-haired rock god of her every teenage fantasy, her entire world is turned upside down.

Turns out, she's awakened more than just Philip, and Stormy will have to do battle against a cast of strange characters to keep herself and her new undead boyfriend safe.

Available May 15, 2024